Thank you for buying *Lighter Than Air*. I hope
you enjoy reading my story.
In buying this book directly from me you will
have an 'author signed' copy, but more
importantly, every book sold will increase my
charitable donation to
THE SPECIAL TRUSTEES OF
MOORFIELDS EYE HOSPITAL.
Check my website at www.susan-pope.co.uk
for details of my on-going donations to them.

If you enjoy the book, I would ask you to be my
ambassadors and to perhaps do one or more of
the following to help increase sales:

- Buy extra copies as Christmas or birthday
  presents.
- Tell everyone you know about the book and
  show it to them.
- Pop in to all bookshops and ask them if they
  have *Lighter Than Air* by Susan Pope, on
  the shelf to buy. (They may not yet, but if
  sufficient people request it, they will put it
  on sale).
- Also, request to borrow the book from your
  local library, (even if you have a copy).
- Last but not least, would all you internet
  users please post a short review on the
  guestbook page of my website.

Thank you and happy reading

Susan Pope

Susan Pope was born in Gillingham, Kent in 1944. As Susan Taylor, she originally trained as a secretary and also in classical and ballroom dancing, which she later taught.

The desire to write took hold during the angst, teenage years but was buried under living other dreams. Dance teacher, professional photographer and various administrative roles filled the years. Children Diane and Michael followed. Susan still works part-time and cares for husband Mark, who is blind.

Over the last few years she has attempted to find her niche, her voice as a writer. Susan hopes with the publication of *Lighter Than Air,* her first full-length novel, she has begun to achieve this dream. She also hopes through book sales, to make an ongoing charitable donation to Moorfield's Eye Hospital, towards their research into genetically inherited eye conditions.

www.susan-pope.co.uk

Lighter Than Air

Susan Pope

Lighter Than Air

To Ann & Arthur

Enjoy.

Susan Pope.

4/11/2008.

Vanguard Press

VANGUARD PAPERBACK

© Copyright 2008
Susan Pope

A CIP catalogue record for this title is
available from the British Library.

ISBN 978 184386 461 5

Vanguard Press is an imprint of
Pegasus Elliot MacKenzie Publishers Ltd.
www.pegasuspublishers.com

First Published in 2008
Vanguard Press
Sheraton House Castle Park
Cambridge England

Printed & Bound in Great Britain

"In a Zeppelin you do not just fly but travel in every sense of the word in the most wonderful way you can imagine."

Hugo Eckener

Dr Hugo Eckener was the head of Luftschiffbau Zeppelin GmbH, the company originally responsible for the construction of the *LZ 129, Hindenburg.*

ACKNOWLEDGEMENTS OF SOURCES

My grateful thanks are extended to:

The late John Duggan, master Airship Historian, and his partner Gisela Woodward, whose help and support was immeasurable. Much of the technical detail, relating to the *Hindenburg* airship, was researched from John's book 'LZ129 Hindenburg – The Complete Story', published by Zeppelin Study Group (2002).

Hybrid Air Vehicles, (formally Advanced Technologies Group), for information on the design and technical complexities of modern hybrid airships, giving acknowledgement in particular to their innovative 'aircushion landing system'. Thanks also to Gordon Taylor, Marketing Director of Hybrid Air Vehicles, for his time and encouragement.

Brenda Bailey of the Quaker Friends Movement. Her publication entitled, 'A Quaker Couple in Nazi Germany' and her lecture paper on 'The Integrity of German Friends during the Twelve Years of Nazi Rule', were both inspirational in creating the role of Quaker Friends in this book.

Chris Sawyer of Authors' Aid who appraised my first draft. Her critical analysis helped me define my characters' motives and improve the flow of the story.

RAF News, the official newspaper of the Royal Air Force, for the use of their name and for access to back copies for information on the Kosovo crisis of 1998-9 and the situation in Iraq during the same period.

Wing Commander, Melvyn Pound, RAF Regiment, for his input on the deployment of missiles from Tornado jet aircraft and on RAF disciplinary procedures.

Google and Yahoo search engines, for websites visited too numerous to mention.

Friends and family for their help and encouragement, especially to my daughter Diane and my son Michael for never doubting I could achieve my aim to write *'Lighter Than Air'*. Your love, support and loyalty were more inspirational than you will ever know.

Susan Pope

PROLOGUE

JONNO'S DREAM

Romney Marsh, Kent. March 1980

He was still half asleep. In this hypnotic state, when the window to his subconscious remained open, he dreamed. To the eight-year-old boy, the gigantic vessel in which he floated was a vast space ship for intergalactic travel. He was on a wonderful journey when inexplicably the ship was instantly engulfed in flames. The beautiful dream disintegrated as he was plunged into a dark void.

He awoke with a sense of loss he could not comprehend, then, terror subsiding, lowered the sheet gripped tightly over his head. The horrible images had evaporated but the pungent, acrid smell had not. He flicked on the lamp, and saw tiny curls of smoke creep under the door. Now his purpose was clear. This time he must rescue everyone and redeem himself; heroes did not have bad dreams.

Jonno did not panic. He scooped up his treasured divers watch and as he put it on, the lamp flickered and went out. He reached for his torch, and then remembered the game from the previous night. It had been his searchlight; the moths and mosquitoes were the enemy aircraft. He had downed ten fighters and two bombers before the batteries died.

Without the torch, he would have to follow the blueprint in his mind. He dropped to his knees and opened the bedroom door a crack. The landing was very smoky, acidic fumes took his breath away, burning his throat and stinging his eyes. He turned his head back towards his room and took a deep breath. He shut his eyes tight and then dived onto the landing, crawling to the opposite door.

His head pulsated with the drum of fear. This was not a dream, not a game. The fire was real, his life threatened. Not just his life, but those of his mother and father, his brother and sister, and the beautiful old farmhouse in which they lived – all depended on what he did now. The terror of his dream resurfaced but so did his resolve. He pushed open the door to his parents' bedroom, squeezed through the gap and then shut it tight behind him.

The room was bathed in moonlight; his mother, Kathryn was alone in the bed, still sleeping. She stirred, her long dark hair cascading over the pillow. He wanted to wake her gently, but his light touch involuntarily gripped her, transmitting his fear like an electric shock. She sat up, wide awake. He could see his own frightened face in the moonlight, reflected in the dressing table mirror. He pulled at his mother's hand and she reached out to take him in her arms as she always did when the bad dreams came.

"No!" he protested. Tears streamed down his face. "It's come, the fire's come!"

But she had smelt the fumes and was already moving. As the doe scents the lioness, protecting her young and flight became one simultaneous action. She crouched down, pulling him to the floor. He was shaking uncontrollably, his eyes full of fear.

She gripped his shoulders firmly. "Where's the fire, Jonno? Is it in your room?"

"No, Mummy," he croaked, "down the stairs!" His voice wailed with rising terror. "Where's Daddy?" He felt his mother stiffen as she held him close.

"He's not home yet, he's not!" she whispered, her face pressed to his, wet with tears.

Now the fumes were coming round the door, making them cough and fight for breath. They moved to the window, breathing the clear night air. But Jonno knew they would not escape that way, leaving the other children behind. His mother's eyes were wide and staring as she struggled to speak.

"We must stay together. Are you ready?" He nodded, grasping her hand.

They kept close to the floor and opened the door. Thick black smoke billowed into the room, initially knocking them back. They had to reach the other children's bedrooms at the opposite end of the landing, away from the stairwell. She gripped his hand tightly as they crawled along blindly to his sister's door. The smoke thinned, its path diverted into the two, now empty, bedrooms. As Kathryn pushed the door open, Jonno broke from her grasp and ran to the bed.

He pulled back the covers shouting, "Wake up, Sarah!"

His mother did not wait for Sarah to wake, lifting her ten-year-old daughter bodily from the bed. She was no lightweight, but Jonno saw his mother empowered with a strength he did not know she possessed.

"Hold on to me, Jonno," she commanded. "Keep moving!"

It was impossible to crawl now and they staggered into the passage. The smoke billowed thick again. Sarah awoke and they all began to choke and cough, their eyes streaming. Jonno took the lead pulling his mother by her nightgown. He tried to breath but there was no air, only foul, putrid smoke which hurt his chest and stung his eyes. He fumbled for the door handle and pummelled with his little fists. The door burst open and they fell inside. He kicked it shut with his foot. They lay on the floor coughing and wheezing but there was no time to rest. Paul stared at them in a daze. He was big for a twelve-year-old, already a half grown man.

"Open the window!" gasped Kathryn. They were overcome from breathing the smoke and fumes but as Paul lifted the big sash window, Jonno knew what they must do next. His constant dreams of fire had prompted their father, David, to drill the children thoroughly in fire safety and evacuation from the house.

It was well after midnight when, driven by fear, one by one they dropped from the upper window. The heat was intense, scorching bare feet as they ran across the kitchen roof and jumped to safety. They had followed David's instructions exactly; his foresight had saved their lives.

As they breathed fresh air at last, the initial relief was immediately overshadowed by an even greater terror. David's car, used every night as a minicab to earn extra money, was parked inside the gate. He had returned home before the fire started.

Jonno was first to react and ran to the nearest window. "Daddy, where's my Daddy!" he screamed in blind panic. Sarah took up his cry. The window was blackened, illuminated by a faint orange glow deep inside the house. They ran from window to window, door to door, their screams and cries for their father were pitiful, but unheeded.

Kathryn ran after them like a mother bird, flailing her arms, vainly attempting to catch and comfort her offspring. Then she watched in horror as Paul emerged from the shed, wielding his father's wood-axe.

"Stop, Paul! No!" she screamed as he stumbled towards the house. She pursued him and grabbed his shoulder, spinning him round as he began to swing the axe towards a window. "No!" she yelled, "you would die in there!" Kathryn threw her full weight against him to counter the momentum of his swing. They fell to the ground in a heap of arms and legs, the axe narrowly missing Kathryn's head. Paul struggled to his feet, standing over her, the axe still in his hands.

She shouted again, her voice rasping harshly, "Get your bike! Go to Mac's garage!" She was gulping for breath, her voice a strangled croak. "Raise the alarm… get the fire brigade!"

He stared at her, seething with anger, seemingly blinded by the need to follow his own course of action.

"Go!" she screamed as she scrambled to her feet.

Paul's eyes burned with deep resentment. Then he threw down the axe and ran back to the shed to obey his mother's orders.

Jonno and Sarah had clung together, witnessing this frightening scene. Jonno had only ever known love. The fire had turned the people he loved into monsters and he felt an overwhelming sense of guilt. This was his fire, the fire from his dream; it was all his fault. Paul was gone a long time and when at last the fire engines were heard approaching from the road, it was already too late.

Kathryn and the two younger children had watched, helpless and in fascinated horror, as the fire had taken hold of the old farmhouse. Brilliant orange and yellow flames had flickered at the windows; a leaping, writhing, flamenco dance; a crescendo of fury culminating in the sound of bursting glass like the cracking of a thousand castanets.

As each window in turn had given way to the heat, the fire within had become the furnace without. The flames had leapt up to the eaves like a pack of hungry wolves, consuming walls, roof, and everything they owned and loved to total destruction.

Their faces had burned from the intense heat though they shivered in their night clothes. Clouds of hot ash had scorched their hair and skin and the dreadful smell of burning had flared in their nostrils, searing eyes and throats, but still they had not turned away. On his return, Paul had stayed with the firemen, trying to help put out the flames, but there was nothing left to save.

When at last the dawn leaked across the sky, like spilt water diluting the darkness and washing away the stars, the harsh cold daylight revealed the blackened charred remains of their home. Then came the dreadful confirmation from the fire officer. David had been inside the house and had perished in the fire.

CHAPTER ONE

THE HOMECOMING

Marham, Norfolk. June 1999

It was more by a quirk of fate than from any preordained plan that this particular homecoming took place at RAF Marham in Norfolk.

Groups of expectant families watched the Tri-Star touch down on the runway and taxi to a halt at the start of a beautiful English summer's day. The returning RAF personnel looked tired but cheerful as they filed from the aircraft in their combat fatigues.

Tornado Navigator, Johnathon Amis, paid scant attention to the Station Commander's words of welcome. At six foot two, he had an advantage and, blinking against the morning sun, his dark eyes scanned the crowd for familiar faces as he descended from the aircraft. After ten weeks on operational duties in the Balkans' war zone he felt drained but elated. The words of his commanding officer, back in Corsica, were still fresh in his mind. 'You are to be included in the operational honours list to receive the Distinguished Flying Cross.' Emerging as he was from a very bloody war, he felt able to hold his head high and rejoin the human race for the next two weeks at least.

As he stepped onto the tarmac, the two groups converged. It was then he caught sight of his sister as she waved to him from within the throng of people. She stood out from the crowd, wearing a bright red polka-dot dress, her long blonde hair flying with the breeze.

"Jonno!" she called. "Over here, Jonno!" He waved back, making his way towards her and his mother, Kathryn.

Sarah hugged him. "It's so good to see you!" she said. "Did you come under attack? Was it bad?" Her rapid-fire questions continued. "Did you see the refugees? It's been all over the news for weeks. We were so worried!"

"Hey, slow down, drama queen." He laughed at her exuberance, returning the hug, "You don't change, do you? Look, I'm all in one piece."

Kathryn stepped forward to prise him from his sister's embrace. "How about a kiss for your Mum?" she said, locking him in her own arms. During all his seven years in the RAF, Kathryn and Sarah had never missed a homecoming.

The whirl and click of the motor drive on a photographer's camera alerted him to the presence of the media. A male photographer, accompanied by a female reporter, approached them. Their security badges announced they were from RAF News.

"One for the paper, sir?" the photographer asked.

"Why not?" Jonno replied, putting his arms round Kathryn and Sarah. The newsman's camera caught the image reflecting another safe arrival home.

"Can I take your names for the caption?" asked the girl.

Jonno had become aware of her as the cameraman approached them. He looked, and then looked again. There was something quite arresting about her. She was startlingly attractive yet in an unassuming way. In height, she was around five-foot-six, but with an elegant poise. Definitely worth that second look. Her formal black dress was short and sleeveless, in striking contrast to the soft creamy skin tones of her perfectly proportioned limbs. Dark glasses obscured her eyes, making her seem mysterious.

"Your names?" she repeated.

He was embarrassed to realise he had been staring at her. "Oh, yes, sorry," he stammered, losing his natural calm. "Er... Flight Lieutenant Johnathon Amis... and this is my mother, Kathryn, and sister, Sarah." He watched as she scribbled symbols on her pad, dumbly fascinated by her long fingers. His eyes were drawn to her graceful neck, high cheek bones and deep auburn hair, swept up in a pleat.

"That's Johnathon, with an 'o'," said Sarah. "He's Jonno to us." Sarah's intervention caused him to recover his power of speech.

"She's been saying that all my life," he said, trying to hide his embarrassment. "My sister is my spokesperson."

"Lucky you," the girl quipped back, and they all laughed.

Anxious as he was to leave the base, he suddenly felt he couldn't just walk away and needed to know more about her.

"What's your name?" he asked, trying to keep his thoughts in order.

She seemed to hesitate, but then she lifted her hand up to her face, removed the dark glasses and said, "Lisa, Lisa Hartnell."

He found himself looking into eyes so unusual they took his breath away. Deep pools of almost emerald green, flecked with gold. Beautiful eyes that sparkled in the morning sunlight, and yet they seemed strangely familiar. He began to trawl through his memory. There had been a lot of girls, but who did he know with eyes like hers? Someone from his past reminded him of this lovely girl.

Her photographer colleague had moved on, busy capturing other family groups on film. "Come on, Lisa," he shouted. "More names over here!"

"Right there, Martin!" she called out. Then she turned back to Jonno. "Can I ask you something, Flight Lieutenant?" Her eyes looked straight into his.

"You want my autograph?" he joked. Their mutual gaze seemed locked on an invisible thread.

"Maybe." She laughed nervously and looked away. "Martin and I are conducting in-depth interviews for stories on the Balkan crisis. Would you like to take part?"

"Which part can I take?" he joked again, striving to remain calm.

She smiled, calmly ignoring the playful overtones in his comment. "Can you come back to the base tomorrow, around eleven?"

Now that his leave had officially started, returning to the base could not have been further from his mind, but he already knew he would, just to see her again.

"I should be delighted," he said. "I'll have to clear it with my CO first, but thank you for asking me."

She extended her hand and he shook it. "No, thank you,"

Her hand was soft and warm to his touch.

"I'll look forward to it," was all he could think to say. Their eyes met once more. The photographer was calling for her again. Jonno watched the colour in her cheeks rise to a soft pink blush.

Her voice came to him in a whisper. "Can I have my hand back, please?"

He jumped. "I'm sorry," he said, releasing his hold. "Goodbye, Lisa." He had not intended to be forward or to embarrass her and she hurried away to join her colleague, not looking back.

He watched her disappear into the crowd and hoped he had not offended her. Then Sarah and Kathryn locked arms with him, steering him away. His sister was chattering on about their plans for his leave, but he wasn't really listening. He was still thinking about Lisa. In those few moments he had been captivated by her. But he had also experienced a curious sense of déjà vu.

At last the family left the base, piling into Kathryn's old Volvo estate amid her shopping and Jonno's kitbags. The drive home was a short one. Greengate Lodge was only three miles away on the other side of Marham village. It had been Jonno's home since he was eight years old, but it would always be Granddad Max's house.

As they drove through the familiar country lanes, he thought about that first arrival. Their grandparents had opened not only their home but their hearts, helping the shattered little family rebuild their lives. They had stayed and he smiled to himself, remembering how his grandfather had taught him to laugh again and keep a sense of humour. Granddad's TLC had worked on him and Sarah. Paul was also close to his grandfather, but over the years he had distanced himself from the rest of the family.

As his mother drove through the village, Jonno shook off thoughts of the past. "I have something special to tell you," he said. Then he paused, suddenly embarrassed by what he was about to say. "They're going to give me an award."

"You're joking!" exclaimed Sarah. "A real award! Which one? What for?"

"Oh, it's nothing much, only a DFC." His face burst into a wide grin as his sister predictably squealed again with excitement. She almost leapt over from the back seat towards him with a kiss and a hug.

"Oh, how wonderful!" said Kathryn, trying to keep her eyes on the road. "Tell us what happened." She was brimming over with pride.

"Yes, what did you do?" asked Sarah.

His mind slid back to the horrors of that day. No, he couldn't talk about it now, not in detail. "I'll tell you all about it later," he said. "It's still a bit hush hush." He shrugged it off. It could wait until the official announcement and report.

His mother turned the car into the driveway of Greengate Lodge. They entered the open double gates and the Volvo crunched onto the gravel driveway. She parked in front of the house and as they unloaded the car, Jonno looked for the familiar figure of his grandfather. He was normally always at the door to welcome him.

"Where's Max?" he asked. The 'granddad' had been dropped many years ago.

"Probably asleep," said Kathryn. "He's not been too well recently." He frowned. "Only his blood pressure and a cold," she added, "nothing to worry about."

Max had always been so active, and alert they had never thought of him as old, but since Grandma Sadie had passed away two years ago, their grandfather had seemed to age quickly. Jonno was impatient as Sarah unlocked the front door.

"He will be eighty-five next week. He is beginning to slow down," she said, but Jonno had already entered the house ahead of her, anxious to find his grandfather. Max had enjoyed a long career in the RAF until his retirement at Marham. He had influenced both Jonno and Paul to aim for flying careers.

Jonno found him dozing on the bench in the rear garden. The air was heavy with the scent of summer roses, planted by Sadie in this corner. It was Max's favourite spot. In spite of the warm day, he wore his tweed sports jacket and a straw panama hat. His eyes were closed, but as Jonno approached he opened them and a broad smile filled his wrinkled face.

"Off to the cricket are we, Max?" Jonno clasped the old man's hands. They felt very cold.

"Chance would be a fine thing, lad. I could still knock 'em for six." His voice was thin, like a tuneless reed pipe.

Jonno sat down next to him. "Mum says you've not been too well. Have you got a cold?"

"Cold be damned," he replied, a little more strongly. "Bloody doctor's tablets make me feel like a corpse!"

Sarah had joined them in the garden. "They're to keep your blood pressure down," she said, kneeling on the grass beside them.

Max winked at Sarah. "Down, but not out, eh sweetie?" He turned to his grandson. "Anyway, young Jonno, how are you? Still showing those Yanks how it's done?"

Jonno smiled wryly. "Something like that, Max. It's a pretty nasty situation out there and we've made a bit of a mess of Belgrade."

"That's war, son, same as in my time." Max warmed to the subject. "We've been following it all on the telly. It's amazing! The photography and how much detail they show. I take my hat off to you young chaps. Your machines are a hundred times faster than our old kites."

Jonno nodded, acknowledging the old man's enduring enthusiasm for combat flight. "I have something good to tell you, Max. I hope you will be pleased."

His grandfather looked up at him.

"They're going to give me a DFC in the honours for Operation Allied Force."

The old man gasped with obvious delight and shook his grandson's hand warmly. "Congratulations, son, I'm so glad I've lived to see the day." His head nodded approvingly. "You must tell me all about it later. You know I'm very proud of you, you and your brother."

Jonno was swiftly reminded that he wasn't the only family member involved in the current Kosovo crisis. "Have you heard from Paul?" he asked, knowing that Max was the one person his brother would contact.

"Ask your sister, we haven't heard for weeks." Max's speech had slowed down. He suddenly seemed exhausted and Jonno was not sure if this was natural tiredness or sadness over Paul's lack of contact. He looked to Sarah for confirmation; she shook her head. Jonno was not surprised. Sometimes he wondered if his brother cared at all about the family.

"I'm sure we'll hear something soon," he said, patting Max on the knee. "I'm home for two weeks; perhaps we can have a day out together. We can go to the cricket if you like."

"That would be grand, son." Max's voice dropped back to a whisper, his eyes closed once more.

"I'll leave you to enjoy the sunshine," he said, standing up. He walked away, acutely aware of how frail Max had become. A little stab of fear reminded him that peace, as well as war, could rob him of loved ones.

He paused on re-entering the large kitchen which had always been the hub of family life at Greengate, and allowed the scene to wash over him, enveloping him with its familiar sense of security. His mother was there, preparing a salad for lunch. He went over to her. Silver streaks showed through her dark curls and he was suddenly aware how careworn she looked.

"It's great to be home, Mum," he said. "You look tired. What's worrying you?"

She continued with her chopping. "I worry about all of you. That's what mothers do." She turned to face him. "Especially you."

"Why me especially?" He was surprised. "You know I have a charmed life."

Kathryn dropped her gaze and turned back to the kitchen counter. "There's no such thing," she said. There was a sad finality in her voice. The ghosts of the past were never far away.

Jonno was sorry, although he had intended the words light-heartedly. But it was true that the family had always considered him to be psychic. The fire nightmares, which had plagued his early years, had later been interpreted as a warning of the house fire which took his father's life. Jonno had been hailed a hero for saving the rest of the family. Sometime during his early teens, the nightmares had ceased and he had forgotten all about them. Although even now, he sometimes experienced a sixth sense, even a prior knowledge of events.

Sarah came in from the garden and went to the fridge. "Cold beer?" she asked him.

"Love one," he replied, and taking the can from her hand, he moved to the big oak table on the other side of the room. He sat down on the long wicker settle under the window. From there, he could see Max still dozing on the garden bench.

Sarah followed his gaze. "We're so glad you'll be here for Max's birthday," she said. "You know we've planned a surprise party."

"Yes, wonderful!" said Jonno. "Who's coming?"

"Most of his pals from the bowls and cricket clubs, and lots of people from the base, and…" Sarah looked out of the window again and lowered her voice. "I've managed to track down three of his old flying buddies through the Veterans' Association. Altogether we'll have about thirty guests and Mum has booked the club lounge at the base."

"That's fantastic!" Jonno was pleased he would be part of his grandfather's special day. "Have you arranged a fly past?" he asked, baiting her along.

"I thought you would have arranged that for us – Flight Lieutenant," she said with mock indignation poking him in the ribs. They started to wrestle, laughing and scrapping, just as they always had.

Kathryn called out to them. "If you two don't pack it in there'll be no lunch!" She was laughing too, her pensive mood lifted.

It was a family joke and a constant source of amazement to friends that Kathryn's three children were all so different. Paul was a redhead with dark freckles and the image of his father, David. But unlike his father, Paul was a loner. Two years younger, Sarah was blonde like her grandfather had been in his youth. Not only did she have his good looks but also his sense of humour.

Jonno also had his grandfather's sunny disposition but in looks, he was dark, like Kathryn. Deep olive skin and jet black hair was their genetic inheritance from Kathryn's mother. Sadie had met Max when he was stationed near Woomera, in the Australian outback in the fifties. She had been quarter Aboriginal and was only seventeen when they fell in love. Max had eventually brought her back to England as his wife.

Kathryn raised her voice. "Sarah, you haven't told Jonno your own news."

"What news?" His curiosity was aroused.

"I'm starting a new job in London, beginning of August." She was out of breath from their tussle.

"London!" He was surprised and released his arm-lock on her.

"Yes," she said, smoothing back her dishevelled hair. "It means I'll have to find somewhere to live within commuting distance, that's the only snag."

"Nonsense!" said Kathryn, bringing the finished salad bowl over to the table. "You can't stay buried in Marham all your life. It's far too good an opportunity."

"What's the job? Loo polisher at Buck House?" he teased.

Sarah lunged at him, feigning an ear cuff. She picked up an envelope from the dresser, took out the contents and began reading importantly. "Position of Legal Secretary to our United Kingdom sector in the City of London – Reporting directly to the senior partners – Responsible for translation of Contracts and other documents, from French and German to English and vice versa – Bla-de-bla…" She gabbled on breathlessly. "Here's the punch line brother, the starting salary is twenty-six thousand pounds a year!"

"Wow!" said Jonno. "How good is that?"

Sarah laughed at him. "For a mere legal secretary-bird, yes, it's very good."

"So all those years of swotting and exams finally paid off," he said, patting her on the back. He was thrilled for her. "How do you feel about moving away?" He was very aware that Sarah had always been happy to live at home.

"I'll have to find a bed-sit somewhere, I suppose." She went over to Kathryn. Her enthusiasm seemed to wane. "I'll come home for weekends. They say London dies at the weekend." He sensed this statement seemed to satisfy mother and daughter.

He left them together and went out into the garden. It was a rare, premonitory moment. Sarah's new life would be good for her and in time she would be happy, of this he felt quite sure.

He also felt very sure and confident of his own future. Combat conditions had brought out the best in him. He was deeply affected by the atrocities he had witnessed, but his award was a great honour, and he hoped it would lead to promotion within the Service he loved. At this moment he thought, his life couldn't get much better. Then Lisa came back into his mind. The memory of her perfume, mingled with the scent of roses, prompting second thoughts.

CHAPTER TWO

LISA

"What is it like? When you actually come under anti-aircraft fire, what are your thoughts and feelings?"

Lisa's voice was vibrant, and as Jonno sat facing her over a small table in the Officers' Mess, she was even more stunning than he'd remembered from the previous day. He closed his eyes to block out her image and recall the sorties in the Balkans.

"It's mesmerizing. The light and colour is fantastic, like a huge firework display coming up from the ground and bursting all around." It was still so vivid in his mind's eye. "You have to keep reminding yourself that you're actually under fire from hostiles."

She looked up from her notebook. "My sources tell me congratulations are in order for you, Flight Lieutenant. DFC?" Her head was slightly inclined, eyebrows raised quizzically.

Jonno's face registered his surprise. He had arrived at the station early and waited patiently while she interviewed other crew members. Today she wore a cream dress. It was fitted and low cut, accentuating her figure. Her auburn hair fell loose to her shoulders, like a curtain of burnished gold. He had been watching her intently, imprinting every feature, every gesture in his mind, storing the images away to bring out and cherish later.

"You're quick off the mark," he said with a nervous smile. "That was still classified until this morning." Her eyes had an almost transparent clearness; limpid pools. If he slipped he felt he could drown, fathoms deep.

"So are you allowed to tell me about it?" She moved her head to the opposite angle, waiting for an answer.

"After an exclusive, are we?" he bantered, acutely aware of his own nervousness. Her eyes were so captivating, so familiar. He lowered his gaze and immediately found himself admiring the perfect curves of her body as she moved. He forced himself to look away. He wanted to win her respect and make a good impression, not to embarrass her.

"I have clearance to talk about what happened that day, but you'll have to wait for the official announcement on the award," he cautioned. "There are others and we mustn't upstage them."

She gave a little laugh, illuminating her face. "That's okay," she said. She looked straight into his eyes, her pen poised over the notebook, waiting.

He was finding it difficult to concentrate and he wanted to make a joke to break the tension. What he was about to say however, was no joking matter. He took a deep breath and began with the events which had led to him and his pilot officer to each be recommended for the DFC.

"My pilot, Squadron Leader Pete Meredith and I, were leading a four-ship formation in the first of a wave of attacks against pre-identified targets." She began writing in her notebook, using the shorthand symbols he had noticed the previous day.

Her questions continued. "How long did the missions last?"

Listening to her voice his pulse quickened. He felt his hands tremble and he rested his elbows on the table, his fingers pressed together in front of his mouth, as though he were praying.

"From RAF Bruggen in West Germany, each one took around seven hours. We were striking at military installations and infrastructure targets, all under cover of darkness. We also had to refuel in midair from the VC10 tankers three times during every mission."

"So what happened on this particular mission?" she asked.

Jonno closed his eyes and remembered. Telling Lisa what happened was almost as nerve-racking as the actual events.

"We had successfully completed our attack on an ammo dump and I was trying to locate a tanker to refuel and turn for home. We were flying near the Albanian border. The dawn was breaking when we saw a group of refugees moving along the road, fleeing from Kosovo. There were about thirty of them, mainly women, children and old people.

"We saw three aircraft on our radar, moving towards the group and identified them as Serb fighters, MIGS in tight formation about five miles off. The column of refugees was an easy target for the Russian built fighter planes to attack with cluster bombs or even with machine guns."

"And how did you respond to that situation?" Lisa's face was alive with interest.

"Pete and I made a crew decision to break from our flight plan and give chase. I also guided two Puma helicopters to the area to stand by for casualties while we gave cover." He recalled their split-second decisions on that day. "The lead MIG was coming in low over the road. We fired off our air-to-air missile and dispatched him only half a mile from the civilians. The other two MIGS broke away and disappeared, but we continued our patrol until the 'copters escorted the group safely over the border." He recalled the elation he had felt at having saved so many civilians from certain death. He had seen the evidence of other groups which had not been so lucky.

"What about your fuel?" she asked. This question reminded him of the final hurdle crossed that day.

"By then we were critically short," he said. "After a few hairy minutes, I located a VC10 tanker on the other side of the border. We were at last able to refuel to make the return journey to Bruggen, but it was a close call."

All this time Lisa had continued writing in her notebook. "Two more heroes make the long journey home." She smiled up at him. "That will be my header for the feature."

He laughed. "Sounds a bit pretentious; we were only doing our job."

"And a fantastic job too," she replied, still writing in her notebook.

Now she had her story he sensed the interview might be coming to an end. She had hardly left his thoughts since yesterday. If she were to hurry away he feared he might never see her again. He wanted to know everything about her.

"Do you live locally, Lisa?" he asked.

She seemed surprised by his question and stopped writing to answer him. "Oh no, I come from Stratford-on-Avon."

"Ah, the Bard's country," he said, hoping to show he had some literary awareness.

"Yes, but I'm staying locally with Martin."

Jonno tensed and looked away; he should have guessed she wouldn't be alone.

He rubbed his fingertips together, visibly displaying his unease.

The corners of her mouth rose in a smile like a crescent moon as she continued speaking. "Martin – and Julie, his wife, but it's only temporary."

Jonno sighed, hoping his relief was not too apparent. He wanted to ask her so many things, but she cut him short.

"I only have a couple more questions, Flight Lieutenant. Can I finish the interview?"

"I'm sorry Lisa, please continue." He was acutely aware his time was running out.

"Tell me about the Squadron's move from Bruggen."

"The move to Solenzara, the French base in Corsica, was to cut flying times in half. We were ready to start operations from there by first of June, but within a week the bombing campaign was halted. You know the rest."

"Yes," she said. "Peace keeping troops are in and the bombers are out."

"Down, but not out," he corrected. "We'll remain on standby for the present."

"But they let you have home leave?"

"Bruggen is my Squadron's home base," he said. "But a lot of us don't have family out there. My UK leave was cancelled back in February, along with the rest of the crews who flew in yesterday. Including time in the Gulf before Kosovo, I haven't been home for nine months."

"Do you miss home and your family?"

"Always, very much," said Jonno.

She looked straight at him. "Is there anyone special you miss?"

He held his gaze to hers and thought how much he would like her to be that special person. His hands were clasped together tightly on the table, the knuckles white with tension. "Is this part of the interview, Miss Hartnell?" His formality belied the very personal tone their conversation had taken.

"Answer the question, please," she said very quietly. Her professional manner continued, but she had stopped scribbling in her notebook.

"If you mean, do I have a romantic association with anyone, well, that depends." He tried to appear detached but she was still looking at him. He babbled on, "I've met someone recently. I'd very much like to ask them out."

"Why don't you?" she asked. Then she looked away. "She can only say, 'No'."

"I'm hoping she'll say, 'Yes'. What do you think I should do?"

"Just ask her," she said. He sensed a slight impatience in her voice, or was it disappointment? She stood up closing her notebook. "Thank you for your time, Flight Lieutenant." The formality continued. "You've been very forthcoming, and of course the article will not mention any names." She started to turn away and he knew it was now or never.

"Lisa?" His voice had an urgent tone. She turned back to face him. "Lisa, would you have dinner with me tonight?"

For a moment she looked taken aback, and he thought she would refuse. Then a shy smile spread across her face and her eyes seemed to brim over with merriment. The sense of panic he had felt rising within him ebbed away.

"I would love to," she said at last. "Besides, you must have known, she couldn't say no, could she?"

Jonno borrowed the Volvo and collected Lisa from Martin's home in nearby Kings Lynn. She looked fabulous, in a long silk dress of mint green which clung to her figure. Her shining auburn hair fell around her slender shoulders. When she walked, it looked as if she was floating; like a Greek goddess, ageless, timeless. That thought opened the conversation.

"I hope you like Greek cuisine," he said as they drove out of town.

"I think so," she replied. "I like mousaka, so I guess I do. Where are we going?"

"Have you heard of the Constantia Cottage restaurant?"

"Oh, yes I have, but I've never been there. Fabulous Greek food and live Greek music, by all accounts." She seemed happy with his choice. "But it's near Cromer on the coast, isn't it?"

"Our booking's not until nine o'clock, so I thought we'd do something else first." He glanced away from the road to gauge her reaction. "Any preferences?"

"It's such a lovely evening, a walk in the fresh air would be wonderful," she suggested. "I've been stuck in the office all day."

"Excellent," he said, "I know the very place and it's sort of on the way, if you don't mind going the long way round to Cromer." She laughed again and he realised Lisa was as nervous as he.

He drove on to Norwich and parked the car near the old Cathedral. The pavement bars had opened their doors and set their tables and chairs outside. Music and the bubbling sound of conversation and laughter rose and fell as they walked towards Bishops Bridge.

The pathway led down beside the river. Oak, birch and ash trees towered overhead, and banks of green willow stretched their fronds into the flowing water, transforming the view into a perfect rural landscape, far removed from the nearby old town setting.

They stopped, absorbing the serenity of the scene. Damsel flies in their patriotic reds and blues danced their mating ritual, conjoined in pairs, kissing the white flowering watercress which grew in abundance at the margins of the river. Ducks quacked and dabbled and moorhens darted in and out of the reed beds. He watched Lisa's expressive face as she took delight in their surroundings.

"It's beautiful here," she said. "So peaceful, don't you think?"

As the evening sun caught the golden lights in her hair and the soft green of her dress rippled in the breeze, she seemed to blend into nature's colour scheme: fragile and transient as if she wasn't really there. He caught his breath and his emotions stirred with an odd mix of fear and joy.

He looked back at the river. "Yes, it's great to be home and it's great to be here." He wanted to add, 'with you', but he didn't want to reveal his growing feelings for her. They were too new and precious to risk. As they walked on again she linked her arm through his and he took her hand.

"So what do you do when you're not flying, Johnathon?"

"Jonno," he corrected, "please call me Jonno."

Her face lit up. "I thought that was your family name," she said. "For nearest and dearest only."

"It is," he said amused. "So, what would you like to call me?"

"Jonno," she said, with a coy smile. "Yes, that's fine by me."

He caught her gaze and felt the delicious sense of raised emotion that comes with new love.

Reluctant as he was to mar the moment, he was desperate for an answer to the question uppermost in his mind. "Lisa, please don't take this the wrong way, but I keep thinking we must have met before."

She stopped walking, surprised and apparently perplexed by his question. "Oh no, I don't think so. Why do you ask?"

"I know it sounds really crass and I can't fix a time or a place." He sighed, trying to make his meaning clear. "It's more a feeling that I know you. I sensed it the moment we met."

"But that was only yesterday." She did not seem to share his intuition.

"I think it was before that." He dropped his voice to a whisper. "A long time ago."

"No, I'm sure you are mistaken." Her smile was replaced by a puzzled expression. "I think I would have remembered if we'd met before. Perhaps I remind you of someone else?" Her eyes were wide open. The deep green pupils dilated in the soft evening light, making them appear sad. "Another girl, perhaps?"

"Oh no!" He answered quickly, anxious to dispel the sombre mood he had created. "It wasn't anyone else, definitely not." There had been other girlfriends but no one remotely like Lisa.

He began to feel he had blundered, so he steered the conversation round. "Perhaps it's just that I feel at ease with you, as if I'd known you for a long time." They continued to walk arm-in-arm, hand-in-hand. To his relief her smile returned, lighting up her exquisite features.

"So now, tell me what else you like to do?" she asked as they walked on again.

"Oh, cricket, rugby, all sports. Almost obligatory in Service life and of course, it keeps the fitness up to scratch. What about you?"

"I like horse riding. It's been my passion since I was twelve years old."

"My sister Sarah rides," he said. "Mum owns a cottage up the coast. When we were kids, they used to ride along the beach and bring the ponies right up to the kitchen window."

"How lovely! And did you ride with them?"

"No. Paul and I used to go fishing with Max."

"Paul?"

"Paul is my elder brother. He's a pilot now, flying Harrier jets. His squadron's in Kosovo, but he doesn't keep in touch with the family much."

"And who's Max?"

"Max is our grandfather. We came to live with Max and Grandma Sadie when I was eight." They had reached an old wooden bench and sat down facing the river, so close their bodies touched.

She didn't ask anything, but when he looked into her eyes the questions were there. Before he realised, he was telling Lisa all the family history. Even the painful parts he never normally spoke about. He wasn't seeking sympathy; he never did that with girls. It was a strange feeling, that he wanted Lisa to understand him, to know him as a person. As the details emerged she seemed to draw closer and her hand gripped his a little tighter.

"It must have been very difficult for all of you," she said, thoughtfully.

He nodded in reply and they turned towards each other. He caught the scent of her perfume once more and the desire to kiss her was overwhelming. He lifted his hand to her face and smoothed back a stray strand of hair from her cheek.

"There," he said, "that's twice I've made you look sad."

The corners of her mouth rose again and her eyes brightened.

"That's enough about me," he said. "Tell me about you and your family." Jonno was perplexed to see the sad expression return.

"My childhood was rather lonely. I am an only child and my parents are rather aloof. I used to think I must have been adopted, but I wasn't." She smiled at him again. "Probably why I like horses; they're big, wild and aggressive and their love is enduring."

"Did you have your own horse?"

She shrugged with a dismissive humph. "Not allowed. When I had to be at home I lost myself in music. I used to play the piano."

He sensed Lisa also wanted him to understand her background. Losing one parent was terrible but not being really loved or understood by two parents was probably worse.

"Do you still see them?" he asked gently.

"Not more than I have to. But I love being a journalist and it takes me all over the country, so life's okay." Her mouth formed a smile, but her eyes remained sad.

"Do you ever go abroad for RAF News?" He wanted to steer away from emotionally crippling topics.

"I get to cover stations and events in the UK. I probably would go abroad if I stayed with them, but I'm moving on soon."

Jonno felt his hand grip her shoulder more firmly. "Moving where?" he asked. Even though he would be returning to Germany at the end of his leave, he must not lose contact with Lisa now.

She placed her hand over his in a reassuring gesture. "I'm ninety-nine percent certain of a job with the 'Sunday Voice'," she answered. "It's a golden opportunity and I'm hoping to work on features. The paper has moved from Fleet Street to brand new premises in the Docklands. Everything is 'state of the art', but I'd have to live in the City."

"Well, that's very strange," he said.

"Why? What is?" she asked.

"Sarah is also moving to London to start a new job."

"Oh, that's good," she said. "Maybe we have the same birth sign. When's her birthday?"

"Sarah's birthday?" he hesitated. "…May twenty-seventh."

"She's Gemini, so it's not that." She seemed disappointed.

"When's yours?" he asked.

"I'm Virgo, September twentieth."

Jonno shook his head, almost disbelieving.

She squeezed his hand. "Tell me?" She was laughing at his puzzled expression.

He could no longer suppress his feelings and cupping her lovely face in his hands, he kissed her gently on the lips. "That's my birthday too," he whispered, and he took her in his arms. This time she kissed him back, gently at first, and then with a passion which matched his own. He felt a deep longing within him at last being fulfilled.

At that precise moment in the warmth of their embrace, with the evening sun casting a glow across the water its rays touching their skin, he felt a cold chill run right through him. As if a dark shadow had crossed the sun.

CHAPTER THREE

FLYING HIGH

Daylight was already filtering through the bedroom curtains when Jonno finally closed his eyes and slept.

He had lain awake for hours, thinking about Lisa and the strange emotions she had stirred in him during their wonderful evening together. She was, without doubt, the most beautiful girl he had ever met, but it was more than a mere physical attraction, she was different, very special. Yet there was something else which eluded him, like a picture slightly out of focus.

By the end of the evening, they had enjoyed a superb meal at the Greek restaurant on the north coast and talked endlessly, getting to know each other more intimately. After enduring the hardened world of war, he had been relieved to find his romantic side was still intact and that this particular girl could stimulate his finer feelings. As he eventually fell asleep, he could still not shake off the constant conviction that he already knew her from somewhere else. Some hours later, he re-awoke with a start and a sharp intake of breath. For a brief moment he experienced the same feeling he'd had the night before by the river; a cold, empty, hollow feeling that had no logical connection.

Lisa evoked so many emotions, he felt sure he was falling in love. Like a rush of adrenaline, the feelings were all euphoric, all except this one. Cold and empty did not fit with warm and happy. He pondered for a moment on one of Grandma Sadie's sayings from Aboriginal folklore: 'Bad feelings contain a message – open your mind and listen.' The déjà vu experience was threatening to eclipse the joy surrounding this new friendship.

He breathed out again and relaxed. This was all getting out of hand. Perhaps his experiences of war in the former Yugoslavia were making him jumpy and a bit hair-trigger. A lot of the guys suffered from post-war syndrome. Well, he reasoned, if he was a war hero, he was not going to be a victim. He looked at his watch. It was eight-thirty a.m. The sun streamed in through his window and it was far too good a day to waste on sleep or imagined losses.

Today was catch-up day; correspondence and a few phone calls to old friends. Kathryn had a long list of 'man' tasks, little jobs Max could no longer manage. Jonno took pride in using the tools Max had used to teach him carpentry skills and the like. Any feelings of nostalgia that threatened to undermine his good humour were consciously pushed away.

He took Kathryn and Max to the Marham Village Cricket Club for lunch. There was a match on today and he left his grandfather to watch the game while he caught up with old friends in the bar. He was pleased to see that Ian Walters, the current club chairman, was still making overtures to his mother. He knew she liked Ian, but Kathryn had never allowed things to progress beyond the occasional dinner date; Jonno wished she would. All day long he felt he was just killing time. He had another date with Lisa that evening. The feel-good factor reasserted itself.

The sea front at Cromer was bustling with summer visitors and the theatre on the pier was brightly lit. But it was Lisa who brightened up the scene for him. In white denim jeans and jacket and a soft pale blue top worn next to her skin, she seemed to shine.

They watched the lights flash around the words, 'Seaside Special' on the overhead hoarding. "I've always wanted to see that show," she said. "It used to be on the telly every Saturday night during the summer when I was a kid."

He laughed. "I remember it too. It was Sarah's favourite. You two have a lot in common." He smiled to himself, thinking that Lisa might look like a sophisticated lady, but she was just a kid at heart. That pleased him and he wanted to please her. He led her over to the box office. "Any seats left for tonight's show?" he asked at the counter.

"Only the dearest in the front stalls," said the attendant. "Fifteen pounds each, but the show starts in ten minutes."

"Two please," said Jonno, "in the middle."

Lisa's face registered her surprise and delight. "We'll go dutch," she said, as they ran down the pier to the theatre at its head.

"We will not!" he answered emphatically, and then he laughed. "You can buy the ice-creams."

When they emerged from the theatre two hours later, it was dark and the evening entertainment on the promenade was in full swing. A noisy funfair nearby dominated the scene. He saw her eyes light up; the kid was back. So he led her through the entrance. Coloured lights flashed and barkers shouted for their custom as they walked between the rides and stalls. They stopped at the rifle range and Jonno watched with amusement as Lisa took aim and missed every target.

"The ducks are quite safe from you," he said, scoffing at her efforts. He lifted a rifle to his shoulder and potted every one. He'd won medals for shooting and knew he was showing off, but it was worth it to see the look on her face as he bagged a soft toy white rabbit and gave it to her.

She cuddled it. "I hope the rabbits are safe from you," she said, frowning and shielding the toy inside her jacket.

"This one is," he said, pulling her close and kissing her gently on the lips. They moved on around the fair, drawn by the music and bright lights towards the carousel. They stood watching the horses plunging and rising until they came to a halt. He lifted her up the step and onto a black horse.

"And you!" she said, as he stepped back down to the ground.

"No!" he shouted. "I want to see your face as you go round." She struck up a pose like a glamour model and they laughed like silly teenagers.

Traditional fairground organ music played as the carousel began to turn. Jonno walked and then ran to keep her in view. She waved to him until he at last gave up the chase, quite out of breath. She came round again, still waving to him. The carousel began to turn faster and the flying horses angled out. He stood watching every turn, waiting to catch a glimpse of her as she flew round. She didn't wave now, gripping the twisted stay with both hands. He smiled, thinking of the 'G' force stress when he was in his Tornado.

The speeding horses became a blur. Lights and colours streamed together in a spinning kaleidoscope. He could no longer see her clearly and the hypnotic music seemed to wail and warp out of tune, underscored by the deep throb of the diesel generators. Now he couldn't see her at all and the feeling of disquiet and panic crept over him once more.

His conscious-self was nagging that there must be a problem with the ride and that he should raise the alarm! But he was rooted to the spot, unable to move, confused by his impotence. The ride began to slow down. His eyes refocused on the individual horses once again; brown, white and then the black, with its white clad rider. The pieces of the picture clicked back into their rightful places and he was left wondering what the hell was going on in his head.

Later they sat on the beach in the dark, munching hot chips. She made him laugh and the joy of being with her returned. He really wanted the relationship to continue but, he wondered, did she?

"I've only got these two weeks on leave, but can I see you again?" he asked tentatively.

"I'd love to," she answered. "But I have to be in Yorkshire tomorrow for two days, covering open days up there. Sunday, I have another assignment. Monday's my day off though."

Jonno felt deflated. Monday seemed a lifetime away. He had wanted to ask her to Max's party at the station on Sunday, but now he couldn't. "Monday then?"

"Okay, ring me Monday around nine o'clock," she said. "We can spend the day together if you like."

"I'd like, very much," he said and they shared a greasy, salty kiss. Now he would have to wait three whole days, but he was happy to know she did at least want to see him again.

The Hurricane Club was a favourite venue for private functions at RAF Marham. His grandfather's birthday celebration was a Sunday lunch party and Jonno had arrived early to play host to the many invited guests.

Sarah's veterans were now holding full stage with their endless stories of daring, sometimes mad exploits as young pilots. Jonno warmed to their boyish humour, the three old aviators keeping the guests amused while Jonno and Sarah kept everyone's glasses full. No one had noticed Kathryn slip into the room with Max and quietly manoeuvre round to the side of the group.

One of the veterans, known as 'Buck Taylor', was recalling an incident when Max and one of the other pilots, called Ginger, damaged their spitfires.

"When the Commander-in-Chief saw the damage," Buck told the guests, "he said to Max: 'What the bloody hell happened here?!'" Another voice suddenly boomed across the room.

"Damaged sustained during a dog-fight, Sir!" Everyone turned in surprise. It was Max, sprightly and alert. He was greeted by a clamour of cheers and applause. The man known as Ginger went over to him and gripped his hand.

He turned to face the assembled audience and said, "What Max omitted to tell the C-in-C, was that the dog-fight was between us two and there wasn't a Jerry in sight!" Gales of laughter rocked the room and Jonno watched with affectionate pride as Max seemed to come alive. His eyes were bright and his frailty fell away.

There were so many people from across the years that had made the effort to come and celebrate with them. The thought had just occurred to Jonno that he should have arranged press coverage.

Suddenly, there was Lisa, standing in the doorway talking to Kathryn. He stopped dead in his tracks, momentarily confused, and then he hurried across the room to greet her.

"How did you...?" he began. She was smiling as he strode up to her and squeezed her hand.

"Surprise!" she said, laughing at his puzzled expression. "I told you I had an assignment today."

"I asked Lisa to come," said Kathryn, by way of further explanation. "It's no good expecting a man to organise anything," she continued, addressing her remarks to Lisa. "I hope you'll stay and join the party."

"Why, thank you, Kathryn, I'd love to," she replied warmly.

Jonno was still too taken aback to react as Kathryn whisked Lisa over to where Max was seated, surrounded by his old buddies. Lisa proved just as adept with a camera as Martin had been, taking photographs of Max with his RAF pals. She spent some time interviewing all the veterans. Jonno watched her intently, little believing she was again in his presence, so close to him in this unexpected encounter. He was suddenly aware that his sister was standing next to him.

"Shut your mouth and stop staring," she whispered. "You look like a goldfish." They both began to laugh, but she had reminded him not to be so intense. As his eyes sought Lisa again, she looked up and smiled. She had finished her interviews, so he went over to her.

"Well, they certainly deserve more than six column inches in the News," she said. "Between them they have over a hundred and fifty year's service with the RAF."

"I couldn't agree more," he said, putting his arm round her and steering her towards the bar, where they joined Sarah.

"Which edition will your story be in, Lisa?" Sarah asked her.

"Next week, I hope. This is one of my last assignments for RAF News."

"So soon?" said Jonno, taken by surprise.

"Yes, I've had my job offer from 'The Voice'," she said, looking pleased. "They want me to start as soon as possible."

"Well done you!" said Jonno, by way of congratulations. He fell to thinking about the future.

"I'll probably move to London after you've gone back to Germany." Her face searched his, as though waiting for a reaction.

In answer to her unspoken question he said, "The whole Squadron should be moving back to the UK soon, provided this war is over."

Sarah cut across them. "Did Jonno tell you that I'm starting a new job in London?"

"He certainly did," Lisa answered, turning her attention to Sarah. "I'm hoping to go down soon to look for somewhere to live. Would you like to come with me? We could look together."

"That sounds a wonderful idea." The relief in Sarah's voice was obvious. Jonno was pleased twice over. His sister would have a friend to help her adjust to life in London and Lisa would have another contact within his family.

"Let's drink to that, shall we?" he said. They raised their glasses till they touched. As they sipped their drinks, Jonno found himself once again looking into Lisa's eyes, oblivious of his surroundings. A flickering memory began to form in his head, but he was roused from his reverie by a commotion near the door. Laughter and loud voices echoed in the hallway outside and the half-formed picture in his mind faded away. He looked up and saw his mother entering the room with his brother, Paul.

Kathryn was obviously overjoyed that her eldest son was not only home and safe, but in time for his grandfather's birthday celebration. She was taking him over to the table where Max and the veterans were seated, and she called to Sarah and Jonno, beckoning them to join her.

His sister hurried over but Jonno did not move. His emotions were always mixed where his brother was concerned. He had taken too many knocks from Paul to be sure of his ground. From a family viewpoint he was pleased Paul had come, and under his hesitance was the half-forgotten feeling of brotherly love. But this was tempered by the knowledge that it would not be reciprocated. Also, for some strange reason, he did not want to introduce Paul to Lisa, as if he did not want to expose her to anything or anyone who might possibly represent a danger. It was a ridiculous notion, which he knew he should suppress, but as he realised Sarah was steering Paul in their direction, he wished the meeting could have been avoided.

Paul was in uniform and looked immaculate. When he addressed Jonno his eyes were riveted on Lisa. "Sarah says this delightful young lady is your latest conquest."

To Jonno, the words seemed deliberately chosen to put him in a bad light.

Paul was still staring at Lisa. "I'm sure she'd love to meet your elder brother." He seemed to be waiting for a formal introduction. Jonno sensed Lisa's embarrassment. He also realised that Paul was already quite the worse for drink, apparently consumed before coming to the party.

He put his arm around Lisa in a protective gesture and tried to suppress his annoyance at Paul's cavalier arrogance. "Lisa, meet my brother, Paul."

Paul's smile was more a leer as he shook Lisa's hand. "Group Captain Paul Amis," he said, emphasising his rank. "Charmed to meet you, Miss Lisa? ..." He left the question of her surname floating in midair. Her hand was still firmly grasped in his.

"Lisa Hartnell," she said softly and, Jonno thought, reluctantly.

Paul raised her hand to his lips and kissed it, simultaneously clicking his heels together.

Jonno felt Lisa's body stiffen as though she were repelled by Paul's mock chivalry. But for Jonno, the act was even more appalling. The feeling of déjà vu gripped him once more. Had he been watching a scene from a long forgotten movie it could not have been more real. This had happened before, and he knew instinctively that Paul was going to make trouble, for him and for Lisa.

The remaining days of Jonno's leave slipped by far too quickly as he sought every opportunity to spend time with Lisa. Like the fuse on a time bomb, the days glowed and sparkled, then burned down towards when they would inevitably have to part. Paul's unexpected appearance at the party and his interest in Lisa had, however, served as a warning. Jonno realised that his feelings for her were so strong he could not risk losing her to another man, certainly not his own brother.

He found himself almost in awe of her very presence: her mannerisms, her walk, her voice. She was like a long forgotten melody remembered, yet slightly out of tune, the notes not quite in the right order. He just could not identify why he though he had known her previously. The way she would suddenly turn her head to face him, setting her long auburn hair dancing on her shoulders. How she would stretch and flex her long fingers, as though they sought a better task than scribbling in a notebook. Was this what falling in love was all about? He had never experienced such intense emotions before and he needed to know if she had the same feelings about him. Time was running out, so was opportunity.

When Kathryn first brought the family to live at Marham, she had used the fire insurance money to buy a cottage on the coast. Now it was mainly used as a holiday let and Jonno had arranged to use it for the last three days of his final week's leave. When he asked Lisa if she would go with him, she seemed unsure about going away together so soon. The problem with Service life was that he did not have the luxury of time for a proper courtship.

"It could be another six months before I see you again," he told her. That prospect seemed to be the decider and so she booked her remaining leave with the newspaper.

The old Volvo estate was pressed into service once more as they set off for the short trip to Norfolk's north coast. The property was aptly called 'Seal Cottage', for colonies of common and blue seals could often be seen basking on the sand banks which appeared at low tide. Millions of water birds also visited the area and the view from the windows was an ever-changing panorama of wildlife on the move.

When they pulled up next to the cottage, big blue skies and miles of golden sand beckoned to them. They left the car and headed towards the deserted beach. They walked and then ran across the dunes, tumbling over and laughing with the sheer joy of being alone together. The sun was high in the sky and the sea breeze cooled the heat of their bodies, ruffling their hair and clothes. They lay down between the dunes, locked in each other's arms, the coarse sand rubbing their exposed skin. They sought each other's mouths, tasting the sweetness of their kisses through the salt on their lips.

The hot sun beat down on them and Jonno knelt up, pulling his shirt over his head. His muscles rippled and his skin glistened with sweat as he looked up and down the deserted beach.

"There isn't another soul for miles," he said, looking down at her. They peeled off their hot jeans and felt the cooling breeze on their skin. Slowly and delicately she released the tiny pearl buttons on her silk blouse. The fine soft material caught the breeze revealing her perfect, rounded figure. Their bodies touched with a tingle of static electricity.

"Let me love you, Lisa," he murmured softly in her ear. She didn't say anything but the consent was in her kiss. Their desire, their need and their passion for each other were overwhelming.

He felt the full roundness of her beautiful breasts in his hands and the hard sweetness of her nipples in his mouth. She moaned softly as he lay over her. Gently at first, he lifted her body towards him and she gripped him very tightly, arching her back to receive him. As he thrust deep inside her, they both gasped from the thrill of that first penetration.

Their love was like a ballet, rhythmic movement without words: a pas de deux, a joining of hearts and minds as well as bodies. Gasping for breath, their bodies wet with perspiration, they reached the moment of climax, thrilling each other simultaneously and crying out with the joy of the moment, wanting it to last forever. They lay together in the sand, listening to the ebb and flow of the waves on the shoreline and the coarse cry of the gulls overhead, drinking in the afterglow of their love-making.

Later that night at Seal Cottage, they sat by the bedroom window in the twilight and looked out across the water. As darkness fell, the tops of the waves reflected silver in the moonlight and they listened once more to the sound of the sea through the open window. Jonno felt sure of her at last, she had given herself to him unconditionally and it was wonderful. Then he thought about the imminent end to his leave. As he kissed her soft, full lips he felt as if he had been asleep all his life and now he was awake and alive.

"I love you, Lisa," he said. "I feel as though I have always loved you, since the beginning of time."

Her eyes were moist, like morning dew on deep green leaves. She stroked his face with her fingers. He wanted her and the want was overwhelming. They moved to the bed and she put her arms around his neck, her eyes willing him to love her again.

"I love you too, Jonno," she said. She had matched his words of love with her own, yet she clung to him as though she were afraid. "Tell me this is not just a holiday romance."

He spoke gently. "I have been looking for you all my life. We can be together forever, if you want it as much as I do."

She pressed her body close to his. "I do! Oh yes, I do," she whispered, twisting her long legs around his hips, moulding herself to him as he entered her once more.

For a single moment he wondered how he had existed before she came into his life, and how unbearable the hurt would be if he were to lose her. He pushed the thought away; this time there would not be any ghosts from the past, nor dark shadows to eclipse his euphoria. Their words of love had bound them together far stronger than the act of love alone, but the reality was he knew that very soon they would have to part as their lives took them in opposite directions.

CHAPTER FOUR

LIGHTNING STRIKE

The Arabian Gulf, September 1999

There had been what the RAF term 'an incident'. Looking back, Jonno concluded it was the lightning strike which had begun the catastrophic chain of events.

The whole affair might have been dealt with at the sortie debriefing. The incident could have been talked through, analysed as a 'one-off' error, and consigned to history and experience. That might have been the case but for two additional elements. Firstly, though not at war, they had been on a mission in hostile territory. Secondly, Jonno's childhood nightmares had returned, with a vengeance.

Eight weeks after leaving the UK at the end of his leave, he was back in the Middle East, patrolling the Iraqi no-fly zones. This provided the perfect environment for him and all the Tornado crews to use their training and skills to the maximum. It was what they all wanted to do. Conditions at Prince Sultan, their Saudi air base, were spartan. The desert area more resembled a large Bedouin camp than an RAF base, space that was shared with the much larger United States Air Force allied contingent.

They slept two to a tent and in the main, flight bonding continued on the ground. It had with Jonno and his pilot, a genial Welshman, affectionately known as 'Merry'. Squadron Leader Pete Meredith was his senior by six years and was an experienced pilot. He had taken part in the first Gulf War in 1991 and they had crewed together now for nearly a year: in the Gulf, the Balkans and now back in the Gulf. Merry had become the elder brother Jonno wished Paul had been, his mentor and friend.

The dreams had begun again soon after arriving at the desert camp. At first, all the recently deployed personnel had difficulty readjusting to the hot and sandy conditions. Everyone was wrestling with their own inner feelings, and one man's bad dreams tended to go unnoticed. In combat conditions they had to react as an extension to the multimillion-pound machines they flew. Fear, and the adrenaline it created, needed to be channelled and used as fuel to power the brain for split second decision making; the theory was that the 'fear factor' could keep you alive.

Their arrival at the camp was followed by several days of feverish activity as they shook down and prepared to start intensive night sorties. It was around the middle of the night and, for the first time since returning to the desert, Jonno had fallen into a deep sleep. He was drifting, just as he had as a child, in the wonderful, vast space ship. He was aware of returning to the cavernous craft after a long absence, enjoying the feeling of being in familiar territory. Then the dream was overtaken by the nightmare. Fear gripped every part of him as the flames filled the ship. He knew how it would end and he tried to escape back to reality. He shouted and screamed to get out of the flaming inferno, to stay alive. As he shouted and flailed his arms about, he was roughly shaken awake by Merry.

"Steady on!" he yelled, putting a controlling arm around Jonno as he writhed and shook uncontrollably, sweating profusely. "You'll wake the whole bloody camp. Sounds like the hounds of hell are after you."

Jonno couldn't answer him; the images were still too vivid. He fumbled for the light switch; he needed light to re-orientate and get a grip.

"Bad dream, eh?" said Merry.

"Nightmare," Jonno replied, barely able to speak.

"Want to talk about it?" asked Merry.

"No!" said Jonno a little too quickly then added, "No thanks Merry, sorry I woke you. You go back to sleep." Merry grunted and returned thankfully to his bed.

After a while, Jonno switched off the light and lay in the darkness, still not believing how very real the nightmare had been. Hard as he tried to suppress them, the horrible images remained, overwhelming his conscious mind. He lay listening to the hum of the diesel powered generators. The sound of diesel engines had featured in the dream. It was nonsense of course, for they had been running all the time he was asleep.

Other details from the dream resurfaced and the shadowy figures of his travelling companions swam before him. As a child, they had been strangers to him, now they seemed more familiar, people he felt he knew. One was bad, an evil enemy. The other was good, a loving companion, but they had all suffered the same terrible fate. Then he experienced a forgotten emotion, first felt long ago in the aftermath of his childhood dream, the acute sense of loss which at the time he had not understood.

Now he did, for he had experienced the same emotion during his recent UK leave. He recalled the night of his first date with Lisa. Their exquisite kiss on the banks of the river as the sun set, followed by the sudden intrusion of bad vibes which had turned him cold and then the incident at the fair when Lisa seemed to disappear from the carousel. It was the same bad feeling: love displaced by utter emptiness. The subconscious mourning of a lost lover for a lover lost.

When Jonno had first left the UK for Germany, he and Lisa had texted and talked several times a day on their mobile phones. Since he had returned to the Gulf, phone calls had become difficult and her responses to his calls had fallen off. In a letter he had received from Sarah, she had told him that Paul's squadron had been posted back to the UK and that he had become a frequent visitor to the London flat which Sarah and Lisa now shared. Jonno had a deep unease about Paul's intentions towards Lisa. He prayed she had not had a change of heart regarding his brother.

Preparations for the night flights to start took up most of the next day. At twenty-three hundred hours Merry and Jonno were at last strapped into their seats and ready for take off. It began as a straightforward night sortie: four Tornados, on a two thousand nautical mile, round trip from Prince Sultan. Theirs was the number two aircraft.

These flights were predictable, but never quite routine. As they approached the Iraqi border, Jonno's eyes scanned the instrument lights, the skies, and the ground in one sweep. He repeated this over and over, checking the status of the weapon system for the possible threat from Iraqi aircraft and missiles. Constant vigilance without let up as they sped on their Gulf mission at five hundred miles an hour, only fifty feet from the ground.

Not long after crossing the border they were buzzed by a lone MIG fighter, as used by the Iraqi Air Force. It was in violation of the UN resolutions which excluded them from the designated air space. Like angry wasps to the head, they were more a nuisance than a threat. The Tornados' role was to warn them off and chase them away; engaging in hostilities would be a last resort.

The number two Tornado was detailed and undertook the chase warily, for the MIGs could lead the allied aircraft in a dance right up to the edges of the zones, towards the Iraqi triple-A gun emplacements or mobile missile launchers on the ground. These posed the greatest danger: always on the move, always with questionable cargo. Would they be the expected SAMS or SCUDS of predictable range, or something else? The constant talk of Saddam's secret weapons of mass destruction kept the Tornado crews on double alert. The MIG disappeared from the radar screen but Jonno was alert to the possibility the pilot could have called on reinforcements.

They rejoined the formation and were now almost halfway into the mission. The wing of four had split in half and they were flying in parallel track with the number one craft – two nautical miles' lateral split. Jonno continued in scanning mode. The high level of concentration in the cramped confines of the cockpit was always exhausting.

Every crew had their own routine for keeping each other on top alert. Talking via the intercom; carrying out instrument checks and visual reconnaissance, interspersed with chat and banter. Merry was prone to burst into song as his way of breaking the tension. He did so now, 'Men of Harlech' filling the cockpit with his deep Welsh baritone voice.

Jonno was in sombre mood. He had not recovered from the trauma of his nightmare; it was weighing heavily on his mind. Also, he had again been unable to contact Lisa during the day and missed her terribly. His training normally ensured all personal thoughts were put aside during flights but tonight he was finding it difficult to concentrate.

The sky was coal black, peppered with bright stars. There was no moon to give soft light or cast shadows. He knew the desert landscape was mainly flat, broken by dunes and the occasional rocky outcrop, but tonight it was a black hole, a total void. Any threat from below would not easily be seen with the naked eye. Their reliance was placed in the radar-warning receiver to alert them to trouble.

It came suddenly, and in a totally unexpected form. A brilliant flash of white fork lightning lit up the sky. From high in the heavens it angled down to earth, momentarily illuminating the entire landscape. In the immediate aftermath of the intense lightning strike, wearing his night vision goggles, Jonno had seen the tell tale glow of two missiles, probably at launch, many miles away. They would now be streaking towards their Tornado at twice the speed of sound. As a blind, newborn animal will seek its mother from her body heat, so within seconds, the missiles' infra red seeker-heads would lock on to their exhaust heat, find and destroy them. Instinctively, he checked the radar screen but there was nothing.

He yelled a warning to Merry over the intercom. "Missiles at four o'clock! Radar alarm not responding! Change course, get the hell out of here! Now! Now!"

As the years of training kicked in, Jonno started to operate the onboard defensive aids, his hands moving automatically around the cockpit, hitting a succession of switches.

"There's nothing on my screen!" boomed Merry's voice over the intercom, "you'd better be bloody right!"

Merry took the aircraft up in a steep, almost vertical climb. At a pre-designated altitude he released their ALARM missile. Together with Jonno's flack and foils, they might still confuse or destroy the Iraqi weapons. Merry pulled the aircraft hard left under full throttle. They both almost blacked out under the G force stress as the Tornado veered steeply away from the imminent threat. Computers were not infallible; survival was always of the quickest. Jonno heard Merry's voice alerting the number one craft to the threat from the missiles. They too changed course and banked away in the opposite direction, swearing abuse at Merry and Jonno. As the two aircraft streaked away from each other only ten seconds had elapsed since the lightening strike.

Now clear of the danger zone, Merry yelled angrily. "What the hell was that all about?" His voice crackled over the intercom.

"I saw the missiles tracking directly towards us, the computer didn't respond but I saw them!" Jonno's voice was shrill and stressed.

"Yes," answered Merry, "and I took evasive action, even though the attack alarm didn't sound, but I didn't see them and neither did the computer!"

Jonno didn't answer him. The glow from the speeding missiles had appeared real enough and he had taken the correct defensive action. His eyes had barely moved from the spectre of burning lights. Two ghostly images had travelled vertically across his line of vision as if burning along an invisible rope. As Merry had changed the Tornado's course, the rope had angled directly towards him and the two images had moved into parallax, fusing together, growing in intensity. So intense was the light, he could almost feel the heat as they burned towards him. Jonno's eyes had darted back to the radar screen, not believing its refusal to acknowledge so real a threat. Then, just as suddenly, the sky was once more in darkness. The light, the fire, the threat, had gone – vanished, as if it had never existed. Now he was desperately trying to debrief himself. The whole scenario was wrong; something was definitely missing from the equation.

Merry's voice came over the intercom once more, curt and clipped, his friendly Welsh intonation gone. "ALARM missile detonating now!" he said as he destroyed their multimillion-pound weapon over the desert.

Then his anger boiled over, "What the bloody hell's the matter with you?"

There was no reply.

"Flight Lieutenant!" he repeated shouting.

The answer came back over the intercom. "I did see them." Jonno's words sounded flat, spoken without conviction. Doubt had begun to gnaw at his conscience.

Merry gave a sigh of exasperation and fell silent. They were still airborne and in hostile territory and had to return safely. He had already brought the Tornado back to their projected course and speed to link up with the number one. They still needed to rendezvous with the flying tanker, refuel and return to base. The questions would have to wait. Unfortunately for Jonno, Pete Meredith would not be the only one seeking answers.

After the post flight debriefing, all four crew were instructed to get some rest. There would be further questions later before an incident panel.

On reaching their canvas quarters, Merry sounded apologetic but not sympathetic. "Sorry," he said, "I couldn't cover you on that one. If I hadn't used our ALARM missile against your mythical SAMS we might have got away with it. As it is..." He let his voice trail away, his face told the rest. Jonno was in deep trouble and Merry could not afford to be a part of it.

They turned in. Merry donned ear plugs to shut out the day's activity from the camp and was soon fast asleep. Jonno was left with his own thoughts, but sleep did not come. He checked his watch, it was nearly noon. He desperately wanted to talk to Lisa. He needed to hear her voice, to draw comfort from her reassurance, her words of love. But he couldn't tell her he had messed up and was in trouble, for he could not believe it himself. By tonight he would probably know his fate, for it was in the hands of the inquiry panel.

He sent her a text message on his mobile phone. 'Need to talk urgent. Please ring back next two hours. I love you J x.' He would have to wait for her reply.

The bed felt rough with the ever-encroaching desert sand and sleep still evaded him. He stared at the canvas roof, listening once more to the generators. He pondered on the fragility of happiness, how fate could creep up and wipe it out unexpectedly. His high flying career – now in the balance; the idyllic childhood that was swept away in one dreadful night; and now his love for the most wonderful woman he had ever known. Was that also in jeopardy?

CHAPTER FIVE

LONDON CALLING

London, England, September 1999

Lisa had been in the middle of her own briefing when her mobile phone, vibrating in her pocket, alerted her to the text message. Her concentration did not waiver as she continued her feverish note-taking, but she was itching to read the text.

In July, Lisa had joined the popular national newspaper, the 'Sunday Voice'. For her it was a 'dream come true'. Like Jonno, she was on a constant high, her adrenaline flowing from the heady world of journalism.

But she was also in love and not for the first time. She had imagined herself in love on several occasions since her sixteenth year, but this time it was very different. Not only was she convinced that in Jonno she had met her soul mate and the man she could be happy with for life, she was totally confident his feelings for her were just as strong. There was only one problem, for the foreseeable future they would be apart for ninety percent of the time. That was something with which Lisa was finding it difficult to deal.

When Jonno left the UK at the end of his leave, she had struck up a firm friendship with his sister Sarah. They went horse riding together on the Norfolk beaches and enjoyed nights out in local pubs and clubs. When they had checked out the accommodation available in London, it had become clear their best option was to share a flat.

In August she and Sarah had moved into their new London home, a swish, fourth floor apartment in the Docklands. 'The Quays' were a part of the heady rush to reinvent the old East End docks, London's smart new commercial and residential centre. It directly overlooked South Dock Marina with Canary Wharf beyond, the back drop to a stunning view of the Thames.

The view, and the luxury of two bedrooms, did not come cheap, but when they had first seen the apartment both girls had sensed a feeling of peace and tranquillity. 'Head in the clouds' was their verdict and it had become an oasis from their very demanding work places. Living with Sarah had also helped Lisa feel closer to Jonno.

"Never forget, this is a Newspaper, with a capital 'N'!" boomed the voice of Biddy Jackson, the Features Editor. She was a big lady with an even bigger voice and she liked to indulge in inspirational talk for her team. The team consisted of Assistant Features Editor, Caroline Trump, who was today out on assignment, Lisa, whose only title so far was, 'the new girl' and Neal Armitage, a junior reporter so young he still sported a cheeky schoolboy grin.

Biddy continued speaking, her voice rising over the noise of the running presses as she led them on a daily tour through the print machine shop rolling out the next edition.

"If I asked you to write a story about camel dung, I would expect your article to come from a completely fresh angle, to excite reader interest and sell millions of copies!"

She thrust her work folder at Neal and diverted from their route to speak with the machine minder; her huge form rolled like a giant jelly across the print room floor. Bonding with the work force was all part of Biddy's persona and she wanted the team to learn from her example. Lisa took the opportunity to slip her mobile phone out of her pocket and read the text from Jonno.

'Need to talk urgent. Please ring back next two hours. I love you J x.' She bit her lip. The call was timed nine-forty a.m. Gulf time was about two hours advanced in the summer, so it was around noon there now. She began to worry; the message sounded important. She pushed the phone back inside her pocket, wondering how soon she could slip outside the building to make the call.

Biddy swept past her, resuming the parade back to her office. Lisa was becoming used to her boss's eccentricities and she fell in behind, ready to catch Biddy's pearls of wisdom and, more importantly, the day's instructions.

Back in her office, Biddy hoisted her enormous frame into an extra large sized chair behind an equally large desk. It brimmed over with accumulated paper work. Empty coffee cups and over full ashtrays vied for space with filing baskets, folders and loose papers, all with Biddy's scrawled, handwritten comments and instructions.

"Lisa darling, please sort this lot into some sort of order," she said, waving a hand over the offending mess. She moved away to give Lisa full rein over the desk. Still in awe of her new boss, Lisa began on the task.

Biddy perched awkwardly on another chair. "Now you two, what do you know about alternative health therapies?" For a moment, neither of them answered, uncertain what was expected. "Come on; give me some headlines! Neal?"

He pulled a face. "Umm ... Keep fit with an acupuncture kit?"

"What, do it yourself?" Biddy quizzed. Neal shrugged his shoulders, he didn't have an answer.

"Find out boy, that's how you learn." She turned to Lisa. "Headline?"

Lisa thought quickly. "Lame ducks learn to swim?" It wasn't exactly an off-the-cuff answer; health was an area in which she was keen to specialise.

Biddy's mouth dropped open in surprise. "Meaning what exactly?"

"Hydrotherapy treatment for arthritis sufferers?" She phrased it as a question seeking approval.

"That," said Biddy, "is better, but you can't call them 'lame ducks'. Not now, with PC breathing down our necks. But good, it shows you're thinking along the right lines."

She started pacing up and down, or rather rolling round and round, a sure sign her thought processes were in full flow.

61

"I'm going to assign you to work with Caroline, she's our health writer." She continued. "We're going to run a series on the benefits of alternative therapies alongside conventional treatments. She's a good writer and you'll learn a lot from her. What do you think?"

Lisa could barely contain her delight. "When can I start?"

Biddy smiled and lit another cigarette from the one she was smoking.

"Caroline will be back tomorrow, but as you're so enthusiastic, we'll have a dummy run with your lame duck." She chuckled at the pun. "You never know, we might even use it."

Lisa's mind was racing ahead. "I'll contact the Arthritis Research Council and check out hydrotherapy pools."

"That's it, girl, you know what to do. Now, I want to see a draft, with your ideas and contacts by tomorrow. We'll see how it looks."

"What about your desk, Biddy?" Lisa was still balancing piles of unsorted paperwork.

Biddy laughed. "Neal can tidy up while he puts his brain in gear. If he can't manage that he'll be on his bike without a puncture outfit!" She roared with laughter at her own joke.

Lisa made a hasty exit to save Neal's embarrassment. She knew she was being tested and was determined to succeed. She hurried off to her desk in the general office and checked her mobile again; Jonno's deadline was nearly up. She left the building and gravitated towards the river. She wanted a good signal for her mobile to try to reach him in the Gulf.

'It has not been possible to connect you.' She tried again and heard the same frustrating message. This was always happening since Jonno moved to the Middle East. Communication between them had become sporadic, to say the least.

Lisa composed a text message. 'Sorry no signal will try later. Love you too L x.' She called in at the sandwich bar and took her lunch back to the office. Alarm bells were ringing in her head. But, she reasoned, it was pointless to worry about Jonno until she could talk to him. She immersed herself in her writing project. She had nets to surf and phone calls to make. Meticulous research had to come first and then she could write a feature, in Biddy's terms, 'to excite reader interest'.

It was four-thirty when she left the office again, retracing her route back to the river. This time the ring tone on the international network came through. She felt a tingle of excitement waiting to hear his voice. For a heart-stopping moment there was no reply. Two precious weeks, that was all the time they'd had together, but they had pledged their lives to each other. Now that seemed a world away.

"Lisa?"

"Jonno, at last! Did you get my text? What's up? Are you okay?"

She heard him laugh. "Hold your horses. Questions, questions."

"But you said it was urgent. What was?"

"It was then; I just wanted to hear your voice before I attended a flight inquiry."

Lisa knew enough about the RAF to realise the implications of his statement. "Inquiry into what? What's happened?" It began to sound as if Jonno was in trouble.

"It's nothing really, just a sortie that went awry. I think we had a technical problem, but the panel don't agree. Navigator error; I've been grounded, temporarily."

Lisa felt numb. "Grounded! They can't do that to you, you're a war hero!" She heard him give a half-laugh.

"I'm afraid they can and have. Lisa, please don't get upset, I can't say any more. No one was hurt and no aircraft lost. It's really a bit of a storm in a teacup. I'm flying back to Germany tomorrow for some tests."

"What sort of tests? Are you ill?"

"Oh, the usual," he said evasively. "I'll be back out here in a few days, you really mustn't worry. One more thing, you can tell Sarah, but neither of you must say a word to Mum or Paul, promise me."

"Of course I promise, but you must tell me everything, I want to help you."

"I'll give you more details when I get to Germany, but it's nothing to get steamed up about. Now tell me what you've been doing. How's the job going?"

"Okay. I'm working on a story. My first lone feature, if they use it."

"They'll use it. What's it about?"

"Oh, health issues and such, it's not very exciting."

"Yes, but it's your first feature, so it is exciting. I wish you luck. Now tell me you love me."

"You don't have to ask me that, you know I do."

Then he said, "Have you seen Paul? I hear he's back in the UK."

Lisa was taken by surprise; she hadn't intended to say anything, for she knew how he felt about his brother. "Yes, he's been to the flat," she said cautiously. "But he comes to see Sarah. I'm afraid your brother doesn't impress me."

"If that's true you'll be the exception to the rule. Paul has a way with women; they usually fall at his feet." He sounded as though he had expected her to fall for his brother.

"Well, this woman is already in love with one RAF officer and she's not about to change her mind." Her tone was emphatic. "I love you, Jonno and don't you forget it." She couldn't tell him of her mounting dislike for Paul, for she did not want to be responsible for enlarging the rift in his family.

He responded saying, "I love you, Lisa, and I will always love you."

He was normally cheerful and confident, always joking but now his voice sounded hollow and empty, as if he was keeping something from her. She suddenly felt afraid and overwhelmed by a desperate need to be with him.

"Perhaps I could fly out to see you in Germany, maybe for our birthdays. Would that be possible?"

"Darling, that would be fantastic!" His spirits seemed to brighten, but then doubt crept into his voice again. "As to whether it's possible, I'll find out when I get to Bruggen."

"Let me know as soon as you can, I love you and miss you so much."

"I love you too, Lisa, for eternity." The line went dead.

Now it was her turn to feel empty inside. She could not imagine what could have occurred for him to be officially grounded. She would have to go back to the office, but she had lost the drive to complete the work on her 'lame duck' story. Her thoughts for the moment revolved around a blue bird whose wings had been clipped.

It was nearly seven-thirty when Lisa put her key in the door to the apartment. She kicked off her shoes and padded across the lounge carpet to the window. The panorama always lifted her spirits: a bird's eye view of the busy metropolis, putting things into perspective.

Hearing noises from the kitchen, she called out. "Is that you, Sarah?" She was partly absorbed, watching a dinghy make its way across the marina and continued addressing her flat mate. "Guess what? Jonno is being sent back to Germany." She turned away from the window and went towards the kitchen. "I don't know what happened but he's been grounded..." The words died on her lips and she stood frozen with shock in the doorway. It wasn't Sarah in the kitchen – it was Paul.

He stood up from the fridge, closing the door.

She stared at him, open mouthed, aghast at what she had unwittingly told him.

"Well, I never," he said, with a smug, supercilious look on his face. "What has my little brother been up to now?"

Mounting anger loosened her tongue. "What are you doing here, Paul? Hiding in the kitchen?"

"I wasn't hiding!" He laughed at her obvious discomfort. "I was getting myself a drink." He rattled ice cubes in the tumbler he held and then covered them with foaming coke. He offered her the glass but she ignored the gesture, turning away. "So," Paul pursued her into the lounge. "What's the young scallywag done now?"

"It's not for me to say, I wasn't supposed to tell you. But perhaps you can tell me why you're always running Jonno down?" She was almost shaking with controlled rage. "He's not a 'scallywag' and he's not 'been up' to anything!" Lisa was determined to defend Jonno's reputation.

"Why is he grounded then?" Paul seemed equally determined to do him down.

Lisa felt really angry. "I don't know why, but I do know he needs our love and support right now, not condemnation. Where's yours, brother?"

Paul threw his head back and laughed. "My dear girl, we are talking about the Royal Air Force, not the nanny state. If he's cocked-up, they'll throw the book at him."

Lisa wanted to wipe the sarcastic grin off his face. "Bugger the RAF Paul, I'm talking family. You're his brother, for God's sake."

The grin disappeared, to be replaced by an icy look of pure hate. "And you, Miss Hartnell, know bugger all about this family." He turned his back on her and moved to the window.

Lisa was still angry, with him, and with herself for breaking Jonno's confidence. She wasn't going to be drawn into any further argument or give Paul anymore information, but she wished Sarah had warned her of his visit.

Just then, Sarah emerged from her bedroom, oblivious to what had transpired between Paul and Lisa. She had showered and changed from her business clothes into casual wear.

"Hello, Lisa, you're late home. Paul wants to take us down to Chelsea on the river boat. Do say you'll come," she said.

The thought of spending an entire evening with Paul filled Lisa with dread.

"Oh, no thanks," she said, trying to sound casual. "I'm much too tired to go out tonight."

Sarah looked disappointed. "We'll wait for you to change. Please come, you'll love it."

Lisa hated to trample on Sarah's innocent enthusiasm, for she loved her like a sister, but her dislike for Paul was stronger, heightened by tonight's episode.

"I'm going to have a long soak in the bath and an early night," she said breezily, picking up her shoes and bag. "Thanks all the same." She touched Sarah on the shoulder as she passed her, saying, "You go and enjoy."

She went quickly into her bedroom and closed the door, unable to stand being in the same room with Paul any longer. She would have to explain to Sarah about Jonno's predicament later. No doubt now, she would hear about it from Paul first.

CHAPTER SIX

JOURNALISTIC LICENCE

Caroline Trump oozed enthusiasm. Lisa could well understand her rising to be Assistant Features Editor. Rising was just a figurative expression, for Caroline was barely five feet tall. They had both arrived early for the busy day ahead and had met up for morning coffee in the office Caroline shared with Biddy Jackson.

Caroline's dark curly hair moved constantly around her expressive face as she scanned Lisa's draft notes. "This is spot on!" she said. Her deep rasping voice always came as a surprise from someone so petite. "I'm not sure I agree with Biddy about PC in this instance." She peered over the top of tiny gold-rimmed specs, chuckling at Lisa's serious face. "Yes, 'Lame Ducks take to the Water' might still prove to be a good title."

Lisa began to relax, knowing she could be on the way to having her first feature in print.

Caroline looked up again. "This hydro pool in Surrey you found on the internet looks really good. Of course it's not NHS, but I'm sure you'll get most of the background you need from them. When are you going?"

"Day after next," explained Lisa. "They have a physiotherapist to help the arthritis patients."

"Excellent!" said Caroline. "Try to interview several patients at different stages of therapy." She paused. "It would be nice to find a positive outcome. Then perhaps we could do a follow up later as to why more facilities are not available through the NHS. What do you think?"

"That's exactly what I had in mind to do." Lisa was pleased at Caroline's reaction; her confidence needed a boost. With Jonno away and the future uncertain, her life currently revolved around her career.

"Well, I'm going to give you your head on this one. I feel sure you will handle it just right."

Lisa couldn't help feeling encouraged by Caroline's obvious enthusiasm.

"In the meantime, I want you to come with me tomorrow to do some more investigative journalism."

"Where to?" said Lisa, wondering when she was going to catch her breath. There was certainly no time to put her feet up in this job.

"We're going to a hypnotherapy workshop. It's a sort of open session where interested parties get a taster of the range of services on offer." Caroline made it sound like a cheese and wine party.

Lisa frowned. "Aren't they a bit theatrical?" she asked. "Mind control and doing silly things on command?"

"You mean like those awful shows on telly?" Caroline passed a glossy brochure to Lisa. "Not according to the blurb, at this Clinic. Read it yourself."

Lisa quickly scanned the pages: 'Doctor Tony Reeve – spent many years as a practising doctor of psychiatry in American hospitals and psychiatric units, where he worked in teaching hospitals training psychiatrists to use hypnosis as a therapy. He is a qualified medical doctor and psychoanalyst and has used hypnotherapy for many years as an aid to healing the mind and body. Dr Reeve came to England five years ago to teach. He opened this clinic and stayed.'

Something in her quick appraisal struck a cord with Lisa. "Can I keep this to read, Caroline? It sounds impressive. Did you say we are going tomorrow?"

"Yes, so we'll soon find out how impressive. The address is near Wembley Arena. We're due at two o'clock, so we'll leave at one and if there's time we'll have lunch on the firm. Is that okay with you?"

"Absolutely fine," said Lisa, "but can I ask a favour?"

"Ask away," said Caroline, busy filling in the squares on her wall planner.

Lisa knew if she didn't ask now it would be too late. "Can I have next Monday and Tuesday off?"

"Ouch!" said Caroline, and then she laughed. "Days off in this game are rare as hens' teeth! There's always the next deadline to be met. Hols have to be booked months in advance and being off sick is a hanging offence!"

Lisa was crestfallen, she hadn't anticipated a problem.

"Is there a particular reason?" Caroline asked.

She hadn't wanted to give a full explanation or invite more questions. "My boyfriend's going to be in Germany for a while. Our birthdays are on the same day, the twentieth. I'd like to go over and see him."

"Ah!" said Caroline. "Is this your RAF officer? I thought he was in the Gulf."

"He is … was," Lisa hesitated. "He's back at Bruggen for a while; it's the squadron's home base." She hoped that was enough to satisfy Caroline's curiosity.

"Oh, well," said Caroline, "provided you've completed a full draft on the Duck story and given me your input on our hypnotist, I think we can let you fly off for a double birthday celebration. Your boyfriend is a very lucky man."

"Thanks, Caroline," she said in her quiet, calm voice. "But I'm the lucky one, he's quite a boyfriend."

Lisa had arranged to meet Sarah for lunch at the Waterside Tavern. It was very busy but they managed to find a table outside overlooking the river. She had carefully thought out how she would broach the issue of Paul's visits to the flat, but Sarah spoke first, stealing her initiative.

"Paul was so disappointed you didn't come with us last night, you missed a treat."

"I doubt he was, Sarah," Lisa retorted, slightly losing her cool. "Besides I didn't want to listen to his endless gibes at Jonno. I think he delights in winding me up." Sarah looked dismayed, which made Lisa feel uncomfortable.

"Oh no! I'm sure you're wrong about Paul," said Sarah, "I know he comes over as sarcastic, especially over Jonno, but it's just brotherly rivalry, he doesn't really mean it."

"You mean he doesn't mean to be mean?" Lisa knew she sounded sarcastic now and hated herself for it. They had never had a cross word since moving in together, now they were set to argue over Paul. Lisa attempted to swallow her anger along with the words she had prepared. Instead she said, "Did Paul tell you what's happened to Jonno?"

"That he's gone back to Germany?" said Sarah.

"And?"

"And what?" said Sarah, looking anxious.

Lisa sighed; Sarah obviously didn't have the full story. So she told Sarah about her telephone conversation with Jonno. Sarah was mortified.

"Oh, no! Poor Jonno, what on earth could have happened?" She looked as if she was going to cry.

"Please, don't worry," said Lisa, rummaging in her bag for a tissue, "I'm flying out to Germany at the weekend. It's our birthdays on Monday, so I'm hoping we can be together."

Sarah looked up with a weak smile. "I hadn't forgotten, that will be super." Then the anxious look returned. "Suppose you can't see him?"

"He's not under arrest," Lisa said quickly, and then she paused, "I think they think he may be ill."

"Psychic yes, but surely not ill?" Sarah was now visibly agitated.

"What do you mean, psychic?" said Lisa.

Sarah then told her about Jonno's childhood dreams and psychic episodes. Lisa already knew about the dreadful night when their father died, but Sarah explained how Jonno's dream had apparently alerted him to the fire and how he had saved the rest of the family.

Sarah continued. "Do you think he could be suffering from combat fatigue?"

"That's the most obvious cause." Lisa wanted to reassure both Sarah and herself. "He's been in the Service for seven years, with an unblemished record and now he's up for a DFC. I can't believe this is more than a minor blip."

"I hope you're right. I don't think Mum could handle another crisis and it would finish Max, I'm sure."

"You're not to tell them," Lisa said emphatically. "Jonno stressed that to me. It's why I was so annoyed I let it slip to Paul, he wasn't supposed to know. Please tell him to keep his mouth shut, Sarah."

"I will, but I wish Paul and you could be good friends," said Sarah.

"It's up to him," said Lisa, shrugging her shoulders. "He should learn to love his brother again, like he did when you were children."

Sarah sighed, "That was a long time ago, before Dad died." She looked at Lisa with sad eyes, "We can't turn the clock back, can we?"

"No, we can't do that," Lisa answered, "but we can and must move on."

The black London cab nosed its way through the usual lunchtime traffic towards Wembley. Lisa and Caroline were already running late and the promised lunch was now being consumed in the taxi, courtesy of two instant lunch packs. Lisa was re-reading the brochure for Dr Reeve's clinic.

"They go to great lengths to stress the therapeutic benefits," she commented to Caroline, as she struggled to open a yogurt pot.

"That's because hypnotists have always had a bad press," said Caroline. "It's our legacy from the Victorians: witch doctors, voodoo, hypnotists, all tarred with the same brush."

"So, to include it in our alter-health series, we have to prove the case for using hypnotherapy as an alternative medical tool?" Lisa was asking the question.

"Or not, as the case may be," Caroline answered, absentmindedly offering Lisa a cigarette even through Lisa didn't smoke. "We go, as always," continued Caroline, lighting up, "with an open mind. Observe, assess, report, leaving the reader to draw their own conclusions. We are not judge and jury, rather prosecution and defence, both sides equal."

"Or not," laughed Lisa, "as the fancy takes you." She opened a window to allow the cigarette smoke to escape.

Caroline quipped back. "It depends if I fancy this Dr Tony Reeve guy. If he's a sexy hunk, he'll get a good press from me. That's the beauty of being small. You tall gals look into their eyes, I take their inside leg measurements."

Lisa was still laughing when the taxi pulled into the curb and they hurried over to the entrance for the clinic. The drab, grey facade of the building was in stark contrast to the warm, welcoming atmosphere inside. Soft lighting, pastel walls and thick plain carpeting radiated an aura of calm to the surroundings.

Caroline gave the smartly dressed receptionist a hasty apology for their late arrival, but the smiling young lady seemed unperturbed. She told them Dr Reeve had waited to begin the session because he knew they were on their way. After clipping ID badges to their jackets, she ushered them through to an equally tranquil room where the presentation was about to begin.

The chairs were arranged in a semi circle. Only two were vacant, one to the side and one in the centre. Caroline moved to the side seat, leaving only the centre chair available for Lisa. Dr Reeve raised a hand to acknowledge their arrival but he did not speak, allowing them to sit down and compose themselves. Tony Reeve was seated in an executive chair, his hands on the upholstered arms. Its swivel mechanism allowed him to move to any angle to directly face any one person in the audience seating.

As he began to speak, his strong, steady voice immediately commanded Lisa's attention. She felt a shiver travel up her spine and wondered what was she about to experience?

CHAPTER SEVEN

THE HYPNOTIST

"When man received his early wake-up call, it was from the birds and animals. Millions of years ago, mankind evolved in the heart of nature. He lived in the rhythm of the world around him and was much more aware of being a part of the universe than we are today, in spite of our greater knowledge and technological advancement.

"We have only to observe the few remaining aboriginal cultures left on earth to verify this: the Native American Indian; the African bush man; the Australian aboriginal."

Lisa settled more comfortably into her seat and relaxed. The morning had been hectic, trying to complete work before she and Caroline left the office. Tony Reeve's voice, with its warm, American accent, rippled over her like smooth chocolate, compelling her to listen.

"Modern man has gained much in material wealth and advancement, but he has also lost many things. Primitive man could find food in a barren landscape, divine water in a dried up river bed, heal without the use of modern medicines and communicate without words through mental telepathy. He knew, without the benefit of scientific analysis that his mind worked on two levels, the conscious and the subconscious."

Tony Reeve's eyes moved from one person to the next around the circle of listeners as he spoke. He wore a dark blue suit, white shirt and was immaculately groomed. Lisa gauged he was in his late forties, with steel grey hair and piercing blue eyes. His monologue continued.

"The subconscious drives our instincts, the secret mechanisms of the body and mind that keep us safe, that ensure our survival, as individuals and as a species. Primitive man was aware of all these things for he was able to enter the subconscious mind through a form of self-hypnosis. For all hypnosis is self-hypnosis. No one can make you say or do anything whilst under its influence against your will.

"I teach self-hypnosis. Once you have learned the principles and experienced the benefits, a little practice will enable most of you to enter a state of deep relaxation, and then you can access the subconscious levels of your mind. The level where everything you ever did, ever saw, ever heard is stored. The complete story of your life, from your birth right up to today is there. A micro-film of memories waiting to be rerun… waiting to be recalled."

Lisa had a note pad and pen in her hand as always, but she realised she had not made a single mark on the page. She was so intrigued by Tony Reeve's words that she knew she would remember everything he had said.

"And what, you may say, is the purpose of recalling any of these memories except as a curiosity, a peep show? The answer is that sometimes, locked in our past, is the key to our present problems. Negative childhood imprints, effects of past failures, self-doubt, fears and phobias. Any of these may be rooted in our past. Finding and exploring the original influence can help us to overcome present traumas which are blocking our lives, your lives, hindering your efforts to reach your full potential to live a full and happy life.

"We can't change history. But can we rewrite it?" He paused, his eyes moving across his audience once more. "Through hypnosis we can change a subconscious memory of a past event and give a different interpretation. We can remove guilt, fear, a bad habit, a deep sorrow, even a physical pain. Yes, we can rewrite the effects of history, if it serves a good purpose."

Lisa looked across the room to Caroline, trying to gauge her reaction, but Caroline's eyes were riveted on Tony Reeve. She wondered if it was his words or the man himself that was holding her colleague's rapt attention. Lisa did not think she would be convinced until she saw Tony's theory in action. She suddenly became aware that he was looking directly at her.

"At this point in the proceedings, I would like to give you a little demonstration, so that you can better understand the power of hypnosis." He was smiling at Lisa, a friendly, open smile. She remembered his words earlier about mental telepathy.

He continued unperturbed. "Is there a smoker in the room who would like to give up?" he asked, addressing everyone. Lisa could not believe her eyes as Caroline raised her hand.

"Ah," Tony said, standing up. "One of our visiting journalists, come and sit over here."

Caroline almost rushed to the centre seat vacated by Tony Reeve. She looked so small and vulnerable; Lisa could not believe her feisty colleague would willingly submit herself to be a human guinea pig. Surely not just in the cause of journalism?

It was as if Tony had once again picked up her thoughts. "Tell me," he said to Caroline, as his eyes scanned her name-badge. "Why do you want to do this?"

"I genuinely would like to give up smoking." As she spoke, she looked up at Tony with a wide-eyed innocence.

"When did you make this decision, Caroline?" he asked.

She looked at her watch. "About thirty seconds ago," she replied with theatrical timing and was rewarded by a wave of laughter which rippled round the room.

Tony warmed to Caroline's humour but was not diverted from his purpose. He smiled and said, "You have to be committed, I can't make you do something unless you really want to."

Caroline was aware she had everyone's attention. "First of January two thousand, smoking will be banned in all our offices. If I don't give up by then I'll probably get the sack. So I need all the help I can get."

Tony smiled and nodded his head as the room buzzed with comments about smoking policies at work. Lisa felt Caroline posed quite a challenge to Dr Reeve, but he didn't say any more and let a natural silence fall on the room. He turned her chair side on to face a blank wall, and dimmed the lights to a single, soft, pale illumination. His attention then was fully on Caroline.

First he asked her to concentrate on her breathing, filling her lungs and expelling her breath, counting the seconds in and out for each deep breath. Then he encouraged her to visualise each part of her body in turn, relaxing her muscles, draining away tension, taking her into the hypnotic state. Caroline's eyes were closed but Lisa could not tell if she was in a trance or not. Tony continued speaking in his rich textured voice.

"You are entering a long, dark tunnel. This is your life tunnel and represents the time you have already lived. We are going back down the tunnel. We are looking for a set of memories. We must keep going back until we find them. We are looking for the very first time you smoked a cigarette, your first puff; the first bitter taste." Caroline's head started to roll from side to side; it looked quite alarming. "Where are you, Caroline?" he asked.

"At the fair on the heath, it's come for the Easter holidays." Caroline's voice sounded different. She spoke naturally, but her voice had lost its gritty edge.

"Where is this?" Tony asked her.

"Near where I live, Blackheath," she responded.

"Are you alone?"

"No, Eddy is with me and Red, Sal and her brother Don. I like him a lot."

"Who are these people?"

"My friends from school."

"How old are you Caroline?"

"I'm fifteen, we all are except Don. He's seventeen. I think he likes me."

"Are you smoking now?"

"Yes, it's my first smoke; Don gave them to us."

"What does it taste like?"

"I think it's yuk! But I mustn't let the others know."

"Why not? If you don't like the taste you should say so. It's not very grown up to pretend you like something you don't, is it?"

"Maybe..." Caroline was hesitating.

"Throw it away and tell Don you don't want to smoke it, you don't like the taste." He paused, as if allowing this instruction to merge with the memory. "Now let's leave your friends at the fair and come back to the present."

The next part of Tony Reeve's therapy was equally intriguing. He took Caroline through a series of visualisation techniques, gradually changing the way she thought about smoking and used it as a prop every day. He sought out when she needed to smoke and substituted a different reward for not smoking. During this part of the session Caroline did not seem to be so deeply hypnotised, but she was receptive to Tony's various suggestions. Changes in diet or the timing of her day; little treats she could afford with the money she would save; the pleasure of breathing clean air, smelling fresh and not coughing, especially in the mornings. Finally, he asked her to visualise taking a packet of cigarettes out of her bag, breaking each one into pieces and throwing them away. After a few moments he told Caroline she could wake up and start her new life as a non-smoker.

Lisa waited to see how Caroline would react. She could not believe it would be that easy.

"I need a drink." That was all Caroline said when they eventually left the Wembley Clinic around six o'clock. Lisa was beginning to think the whole experience had been too much for her normally talkative colleague. For her part, Lisa felt she had been party to something quite profound. But she had only been a witness, the experience had been Caroline's.

As the whole reason for the visit had been as journalists, Lisa was anxious to record the event and wanted to question Caroline for her reactions. She waited until they were comfortably seated inside a local wine bar and Caroline had downed the best part of a glass of white wine. She had remained silent, as though she was still in a daze.

Lisa couldn't wait any longer and started firing questions. "What did it feel like? Was it like sleep? What did you see?"

Caroline put up her hand, palm out saying, "Stop! Slow down." She drained the rest of her drink and eventually found the right words to convey her thoughts. "That has to be the weirdest thing I have ever experienced."

"Do you mean unpleasant?" asked Lisa.

"Oh no, not a bit." Caroline became her animated self again. "No, it was fantastic, amazing!" She waved her hands about to express her meaning. "I went right back to when I was fifteen, I remembered every detail. I was having a night out with friends."

"Yes," said Lisa, recalling what she knew from the session. "You fancied a boy called Don and he gave you your first cigarette."

"But that's the funny thing about it," said Caroline. "Until now I had forgotten every one of those kids. This morning I couldn't even have remembered any of their names, let alone the occasion it happened. I can't get over it." She was apparently still savouring the memory from her youth. "Don, Don Ellis – that was his name. How could I have forgotten him?"

Caroline fell silent again staring off into the distance. Then Lisa watched her rummage in her bag for her packet of cigarettes. She waited, curious to know if long ingrained habits could change instantly. She looked on, open mouthed, as her colleague crushed the remaining cigarettes into the ashtray.

Caroline looked at her with a self-satisfied grin and announced, "I don't smoke."

Lisa didn't know which of them was more surprised.

CHAPTER EIGHT

GROUNDED

Bruggen, West Germany, September 1999

When Jonno found himself back in Germany, sans squadron, he felt isolated – very much a cog without a wheel. In fact he had the feeling he wasn't even a cog. The planned closure of RAF Bruggen had been put on hold. Current NATO commitments had stayed its execution, but with most of the squadrons based there currently away, the place already seemed only half alive.

He had been allocated a room in the medical block. It was spartan and impersonal, but he didn't have a choice. By the end of the second day he was awaiting his test results. They had taken blood and urine samples, presumably to test for drugs. There had also been aptitude tests and sessions on flight simulators. Of these he was confident his reactions and answers had been one hundred percent. Tomorrow he was due to see the shrink. On this score he was much more apprehensive.

He had spoken to Lisa on his arrival as promised. Even over the phone he could hear the anxiety in her voice.

"I'm absolutely fine," he had reassured her. "There's nothing wrong and I'll soon be back with the squadron."

"Can I come and see you? I've got four days clear from Saturday," she'd pleaded.

His heart had leapt at the prospect, but it wasn't that simple. "I'll let you know tomorrow. I should have the 'all clear' then." Much as he wanted to see her, he was beginning to think it was not such a good idea.

When they had met at Marham in June he had been full of confidence and elated by her attentions. Now he felt like a prisoner and a failure. Desperate as he was to keep her trust and love, he couldn't allow her to see him like this, even if it meant cancelling her visit.

That evening he hit rock bottom. He was not a heavy drinker like Paul, but he was now on his third glass of Napoleon brandy purchased from the NAFFI shop. He was aware there was something very odd about his current plight. His actions had been out of character: completely at odds with his training and his own self-imposed standards of discipline. He realised he would have to dig deep into those reserves if he was to climb out of the hole he had dug for himself. He tried to concentrate on working out a strategy to ensure he would survive with his career intact, but the brandy had slowed down his metabolism and eventually he fell into a fitful sleep.

He was drifting again in the wonderful spacecraft. It was a glorious feeling; any vestige of depression was lifted. He was on the fabulous voyage with his companion. He had a deep emotional connection with her and could almost feel her warm, loving presence, but he could not see her face.

Then the antagonist was there: intruding, hostile, apparently forcing a wedge between himself and his lover. He experienced anger and fear in equal proportions. Like the three sides of a triangle, they moved physically. Love – hate – fear, love – hate – fear, yet they remained the same distance from each other. They moved again, but the puzzle remained unsolved.

The evil man's face was hidden by a dark shadow; the female lover's was obscured by a bright light. His emotions were in utter turmoil. The bright light grew in intensity, glowing. Then horror gripped his very soul as an apparent act of spontaneous combustion triggered an explosion of brilliant light and heat, flashing across the whole spectrum of his vision. He was consumed by a raging fire, swallowed alive by his own terror. He awoke, sweating, shouting and shaking, his head still full of the nightmare images.

He went to the bathroom and scooped cold water over his head and face. As he emerged from the towel, the mirror reflected the image of a stranger. He ran his fingers through his hair, recognising this habitual nervous habit. He scrutinised his reflection. The eyes were almost black, accentuated by dark circles from his recent sleepless nights. He wanted to peel back the layers which had formed covering his own identity; to find the real Jonno Amis again.

The following day he arrived ten minutes late for his appointment with the psychologist. He had been summoning every vestige of positive thought he could muster. He had to tough it out today and get the 'all clear'.

The doctor's name was Smith. He was around forty, thin and balding. He wore small rimless spectacles and spoke in a quiet, detached voice. They had completed the routine part of the interview. Now Smith was homing in on the specifics.

"In your own words, Flight Lieutenant, I want you to explain to me exactly what happen during the sortie."

Jonno knew Smith had read the official report, including his own version of events, but he went through the whole scenario again. Somehow he felt less convinced about his contention that the radar signal must have been faulty. But the images were burned so deeply in his mind he could still not believe they had been wholly a figment of his imagination.

Smith listened in silence, reading Jonno's file. Then he changed the direction of his questions. "Tell me about your background, your home life."

Jonno recounted growing up at Greengate, his grandfather's influence on him and his brother to join the RAF, and he outlined his exemplary record to date in the Service. He was justly proud of all that he had achieved and his desire to remove this stain from his record must have been obvious.

Again, Dr Smith listened in silence. Then he asked, "Tell me about the night of the house fire, the night your father died."

Jonno was taken aback by the question and the fact that this information was in the file. It was the one part of his life he never discussed, yet he was well aware why Smith had raised the subject. He evaded the question with one of his own. "You surely don't think there is a connection?"

When Smith replied, Jonno knew he was right. "Anxieties are sometimes buried very deep; they don't always lie on the surface."

Jonno could feel his temper rising and fought to control it before speaking again. "My record speaks for itself. My mind is sanitised against such influences."

Smith was not to be diverted so easily from his purpose. "So you don't want to tell me about that part of your life?"

Jonno gave a deep sigh. "Dr Smith, I have spent years erasing the memory of that night from my mind. It was necessary for me to move forward and be what I am today. Isn't that how you guys tell us to deal with our problems?"

He ran his fingers through his hair, his frustration growing. "I need to put the lid on this and get back in the air and get on with my career."

Smith smiled; a condescending smile. "Of course you do, but we must be absolutely sure it's safe for you to do so. Now, it's clear to me, talking to you, that you are suffering from stress and anxiety."

Jonno interrupted him. "That's only because I've been grounded. I was fine up till then."

Smith ignored him. "I'm putting you on a course of drugs which you must take as prescribed." He looked pointedly at Jonno over his spectacles. "I will see you again next week when we should have the results of all the tests."

"What do I do in the meantime?" Jonno was smarting with indignation.

"Officially, you are on sick leave. Take a few days off the base, it will do you good. But don't fly anywhere and don't leave Germany." He proffered his hand, which Jonno shook reluctantly.

Walking back to his quarters, his thoughts were a confusion of anger, frustration and misery. The only good thing was he and Lisa could spend their birthdays together as they had hoped. All he wanted to do now was talk to her and confirm the arrangements. She was the one bright spot in all this mess and he couldn't wait to hold her in his arms again; the RAF could go to hell.

It was Saturday morning and Dusseldorf Airport's arrivals lounge was teeming with life. Weekend commuters and tourists bustled about their business and reunited bodies clung to each other. When Lisa's flight arrival clicked on to the display screen, Jonno stationed himself opposite the flight passengers' exit. He wanted to see her from the first possible moment. As the minutes ticked by he became anxious, wondering if she had changed her mind about coming.

A party of noisy Japanese tourists pushed through the doors with two trolleys and children scattering around like apples spilling from a bag. Trailing in their wake was Lisa, momentarily caught in the confusion. She looked fabulous, in a dark green trouser suit. As his eyes focused on her familiar outline for a moment he was rooted to the spot. Then he ducked under the barrier, hurrying towards her. As they came together, her arms full of hand luggage, he hugged her tightly and kissed her full on the mouth. He took her bags and she smiled up at him. He could tell from her expression, she had not changed her mind.

Once outside, he hailed a taxi and showed the driver an address on a piece of paper. The driver gave him a 'thumbs up' sign and they climbed into the back of the cab. Oblivious to their slow progress through the congested airport road system, they embraced and kissed again. A long, slow, deep kiss, reaffirming their love. They touched one another, revelling in the joy of seeing, hearing, smelling one another and being together again.

When she eventually caught her breath, she asked him, "Where are we going?"

He smiled. "That's a surprise, I hope you'll approve."

She whispered back, "I don't care where we go as long as we are together."

As he gazed once more into her exquisite eyes, they filled with a look of concern. "Tell me why you're here, back in Germany?" she said softly.

Her words brought him up with a jolt. "I will, later – promise," he said, stroking her cheek. "Please be patient. Let's settle into our accommodation first. I know you are going to love it." He put on his best cheery smile and she seemed to let it pass.

Jonno had spent the last two days making the arrangements for her visit. She had to leave again on Tuesday evening and he couldn't bear to think about that now. He had planned their itinerary to fill every moment of the next few days and he had much more important things to discuss with Lisa than this current blip in his fortunes.

The Mercedes taxi sped away from the terminal and out on to the autobahn, travelling south. They passed the signs for Köln and Bonn and then took a country route, following the Rhine River. The driver turned into what appeared to be a private estate, surrounded by dense woodland.

He asked her to close her eyes and when the car stopped he opened the door, taking her by the hand, "Come, my lady," he said laughing. "Your castle awaits you."

They stepped out of the taxi and she opened her eyes and gasped in surprise. They were indeed outside a beautiful German castle. A huge manor house built in the Gothic style with turret towers. A moat surrounded the entire building; the access road to the main entrance passed over an old stone bridge.

"Are we staying?" Lisa asked, as Jonno paid off the driver and collected her bags from the boot.

"Of course, m'lady, where else would you stay but in a castle?" He grinned, savouring her pleasure and enjoying the return of his own good humour. He pointed to a signboard painted in German gothic lettering: "Castle Hotel of the Rhine," he interpreted.

Lisa sighed. "How wonderful, I'm going to sleep in a real castle!"

He laughed, shepherding her towards the entrance. "Who said anything about sleep?"

They did sleep eventually, much later that night, in the intricately carved, wooden four poster bed which dominated their room, between hand-embroidered cotton sheets and surrounded by drapes of red and gold brocade. A blissful sleep preceded by the exquisite act of making love. Rediscovering, and discovering more about the joy of their sexual union.

During the afternoon, they had wandered though the castle grounds, following pathways through the rhododendron groves right up to the forest edge. Further on, the landscape dropped down towards the river. As they viewed the vast open countryside that formed the Rhine valley, he pulled her close to him.

"I'm so glad you are here, my darling. I love you so much." They kissed, deep and long. A silence fell between them.

"Do you want to talk now?" she asked in an undemanding way. She seemed almost to have created a right time for explanations.

He wanted to get this over and not let it dominate her visit. More importantly, he did not want it to change her opinion of him. And so he gave her a brief outline of the events which had resulted in his grounding and return to Bruggen.

"As I told you, I think the whole issue has been blown up out of all proportion," he said.

Lisa had listened in silence, holding his hand as he spoke. "I can't believe they did this to you over one isolated incident," she said, frowning.

"That's part of the trouble, and I also feel betrayed. After the initial reports, my pilot, good old Merry, was quizzed again." Jonno sounded bitter. "There's a second report where he told them I'd had repeated nightmares and shown lack of concentration on a number of occasions since we'd been back in the Gulf."

"That can't be true, surely?"

He shrugged his shoulders, he was finding this very difficult, "The dreams perhaps, once or twice, but lack of concentration when flying?" He shook his head almost in denial. "Well, if I didn't give a hundred percent, I certainly wasn't aware of it."

She lent forward and kissed him, "You must try not to worry, darling," she soothed. "You'll soon be back in the air."

He smiled and kissed her again. He wanted to drop this discussion now and change the subject. As they turned back towards the castle, he began telling her his plans for their weekend. "Tomorrow we are going on a boat trip. We have to go to a place called Konigswinter to pick up the boat at three o'clock."

"Where does the boat go?" asked Lisa. She seemed delighted with the arrangements he had made.

"Not telling you!" He laughed. "It's another surprise, so you'll just have to wait and see."

That evening they dined in the castle's banqueting hall, dedicated to the ancient Knight's Order, surrounded by suits of armour. The old stone walls were heavy with paintings, coats of arms and the weapons and trophies of war. Some of the hotel guests, who appeared to be regular visitors, were dressed in medieval costumes, adding to the atmosphere of the evening.

They talked, catching up on the weeks since they parted. Lisa was obviously very happy in her new job and with life in London living with Sarah. She showed him her two draft stories for the paper. He praised her writing and her style and was intrigued by her article on hypnosis and the effect it had apparently had on Lisa's colleague, Caroline.

"Has she really managed to stay off the weed?" he asked as he poured more wine into their glasses.

"So far, yes. Poor old Biddy Jackson is now under pressure to quit too." Lisa chuckled, "Yesterday, she kept goading Caroline to have one whenever she lit up, so Caroline challenged her to visit Tony Reeve."

"And will she?" he asked.

"I don't know," she said, looking thoughtful. "Submitting to that sort of therapy is a very personal decision. That's the slant I've used for my article. What do you think?"

Jonno was thoughtful. "Yes, I know exactly what you mean. Still it's got to be better than drug therapy."

She gave him a questioning look.

His thoughts had returned to his own situation. "The first thing they did when I arrived was test me for drugs, which I never touch. Now dear Dr Smith, the psychologist I saw this week, wants to pump me full of them." He shook his head, disbelieving that he could be in this position. "If I get hooked on his antidepressants and valium I'll never fly again."

"What are you going to do?" she asked.

"I already have," he said, his face beginning to break into a broad grin.

"Have what?" she said puzzled.

"Flushed them down the toilet!" he said, laughing out loud.

She laughed too, and he stood up, pulling her to her feet. Many clocks around the castle struck ten as they climbed the staircase up to their room.

CHAPTER NINE

CASTLES IN THE AIR

Lisa awoke to shafts of light streaming in through the window. Sunbeams illuminated the rich furnishings and polished wood surfaces. She pinched herself; it was not a dream. Jonno stirred and she listened to the sound of his breathing as he continued to sleep.

Their frank discussion over his grounding had revealed a different side to his character; his vulnerability, his Achilles' heel. Yet now she felt she loved him more. It was easy to fall in love with a hero – knowing his weaknesses and helping him gave purpose and meaning to their relationship. Something else was intruding into her thoughts; Jonno had described his nightmares to her. Sarah had spoken of similar childhood dreams relating to a fire. Now these were apparently plaguing him once more.

She reached out and touched his cheek. She had never felt love and desire so strongly for anyone else. The emotions were overwhelming and she knew she would do everything in her power to help him overcome his present difficulties.

He opened his eyes, his expression a mixture of joy and relief. Reaching out, he traced his fingers around her face. "You are real," he laughed, stretching his arms.

Lisa sighed, thinking how much alike their thoughts were. "No dreams?" she asked tentatively.

"Sweet dreams – of you, but no nightmares, thank God, and how are you this perfect morning, m'lady?"

"I feel wonderful!" she said, rolling over into his outstretched arms.

He enveloped her, and nuzzling her neck, he whispered, "I love you so much, my Lady Lisa."

"And I love you, Sir Jonno," she said, smiling with pleasure at his touch. "Tell me again what we're doing today."

He looked at his watch on the bedside table. "The taxi is booked for two o'clock. Before that we'll have lunch here at the hotel. I'm afraid we've missed breakfast, which leaves us a couple of hours to kill. What shall we do?"

He caressed her breasts under her silk negligee and she responded by tickling him under his arms. He grabbed at her hands and they rolled over together in a breathless rough and tumble. They loved again, teasing and playful at first, but then with an energy and passion which took their love to a deeper, higher level.

Later, after they had showered and dressed ready to leave the room, a quiet contentment fell between them. Lisa wore a brown and gold casual suit and Jonno was in a dark blazer and beige chinos.

They stood close to one another and he took hold of both her hands, looking very serious.

"What is it? What's the matter?" she said, perplexed by his manner.

"I was going to wait until tomorrow, on our birthdays," he said, putting his hand into his pocket. "It's this," he pulled out and opened a small box, his hand was shaking. In the box was an exquisite diamond ring. He stood very close to her and he went down on one knee.

Looking up, he said, "Will you marry me, Lady Lisa?"

She gasped with surprise. "Jonno!"

He took the ring from the box and held her left hand. "I must have an answer or I will die," he said, trying to keep his features serious.

She laughed with joy and amusement. "Of course, my Lord, I will marry you, for better or for worse." Jonno stood up and slipped the ring over her ring finger. It fitted perfectly; a high bridge, platinum setting with three large square-cut diamonds in a simple band of white gold.

"I hope it will always be for better," he said, kissing her hand.

She looked at the ring, hardly daring to breathe. "It's beautiful," she whispered. "The fit, it's perfect."

"Confession time; I had to enlist Sarah's help with your ring size." He smiled apologetically. "But I didn't say anything about getting engaged, I promise no one else knows."

Lisa was incredulous. It had not occurred to her that he would ask her to marry him; he was full of surprises. She was so happy. Everything now felt right, like a lost key turning in its own lock at last, opening the door on their future life together.

As night fell, the parade of little river boats took on a carnival atmosphere. Jonno and Lisa's boat was at the head, behind were dozens more. Each was trimmed with a display of white lights from stem to stern. They sat close together, arms entwined and looked out from the open promenade deck. The seemingly endless line of boats navigated up the Rhine in the darkness, like a long string of stars fallen from the sky shining across the water.

During the afternoon cruise they had enjoyed spectacular views of the many castle fortresses and palaces, some just ruins, along both banks of the Rhine. High up on the rolling hills, they dominated the skyline, sentinels to the warlike history of the region. They had travelled south on the boat from Konigswinter to Oberwesel, where a wine festival was in full swing. Young girls in national dress invited them to taste the many different wines, local cheeses and other food items, specialities to that part of the valley. They had wandered through the town, watching displays of traditional German music and dancing. As dusk set in, they'd rejoined the boat for the trip back north.

Tonight it was the finale for all the festivals held throughout the summer. Even Jonno did not know quite what to expect, but for Lisa the whole event was a complete surprise, another of Jonno's magic tricks. As each fortress came into view, it was illuminated against the night sky by red fire flickering around the ancient structures. Up on their high ramparts they were silhouetted against the skyline; castles, apparently in the air. Music was being relayed from the river banks. The dramatic German compositions of Wagner, Beethoven and Mendelssohn filled the night air.

As they cruised slowly by, fireworks shot up into the sky from below the castles. Huge rockets showered brilliant cascades of coloured stars filling the night sky – red, blue, yellow, green and white. With every conceivable colour and pattern they illuminated the whole Rhine valley with a kaleidoscope of fire magic. The entire display was mirrored in the dark surface of the water, right up to the sides of the little river boats.

"Isn't it fantastic?" Lisa shouted to Jonno over the noise. He grinned and hugged her to him as they reacted with delight at each new eruption of sound and colour. As the boats moved on up the river, passing between the various castle spectacles, the little houses along the river banks displayed flickering candles in their windows: a chain of lights joining the towns and linking the festivals.

The river boats finally returned to Konigswinter around midnight. They disembarked on the quayside and were jostled along with the excited crowd to view more entertainment; bands played and people danced everywhere. They moved on up the town towards the castle Drachenfels. They could see the jagged ruins of the high towers, which was all that remained of the once proud castle.

Lisa held on tightly to Jonno's hand. As they climbed up the hill, she stumbled on the old cobbled road and he grasped her more firmly.

"Look out for the dragon!" he said menacingly.

"What dragon?" She raised her voice above the growing strains of Wagner's 'Ride of the Valkyrie'.

"Siegfried's!" he shouted back. "He killed it then bathed in the blood."

Lisa grimaced, screwing up her face. "Ugh! Disgusting."

Jonno laughed. "It's a legend; I read it in the guide book. But truth is stranger than fiction, so watch out!"

At that moment the hillside erupted. More fireworks lit the sky right over their heads. The ruined towers were illuminated from behind with red Bengal fire. They had reached the highest point possible. A huge bonfire had been set alight and red flares soared high up around the ruins, ignited in the conflagration. The crowd surged towards the bonfire and they were pulled haplessly along.

Lisa became aware of another source of activity behind them. The sound of live drumming was following the crowd, people changed direction to see what was happening and the crowd jostled in confusion. She was pushed and shoved with the weight of bodies and lost her grip on Jonno's hand. The crowd pulled them apart and forced them in opposite directions. He was lost from her view as the enormous head of a dragon appeared in the void. It danced with the thrusting, twisting, staccato moves of a traditional Chinese dance.

To Lisa it seemed incongruous on the dark mountain side; Chinese culture, in this staunch German community. Stranger still that Jonno had warned of its possible intervention. The crowd moved back to allow room for the enormous beast, propelled by human dancers under its canopy, leaping to the drummers' rhythm.

Lisa looked around frantically. She could not see Jonno anymore. His tall physique normally stood out above any crowd, but there was neither sight nor sign of him. Crowded places were not her strong point and without his comforting presence she became alarmed. She darted across the dragon's path in the direction she had last seen him as they were separated.

"Jonno! Jonno!" She tried to shout over the cacophony, but her voice was drowned out. She pushed forward and tried to get away from the crowd pressing round the dragon spectacle. She looked towards the only source of light, the huge bonfire, and moved in that direction. Then she caught a glimpse of him again; a tall, dark shape, silhouetted against the glare of the fire.

Relief turned to horror as he appeared to be walking directly towards the flames. She stumbled and yelled, fighting her way towards him. She reached him at last, dangerously close to the fire, its flames leaping thirty feet and more up into the air.

Grasping his arm, she shouted, "Thank goodness! I was afraid I'd lost you." He did not respond. She shook his arm. "What's the matter?"

He was staring into the flames, his face contorted with fear and terror. His arms were stiff and he was shaking. Lisa realised he was displaying the classic symptoms of shock. Her initial dismay was quickly overtaken as her first-aid training kicked in. Putting her arms around him, she physically dragged him away from the source of his trauma. She looked around frantically for somewhere to sit him down; there were too many people but none to help.

She managed to propel him towards a grass bank. "Sit here, sit down!"

He slumped on the grass. Then she tried to break into his trance by rubbing his hands and arms.

She slapped his face and shouted at him. "Jonno! Jonno!"

He gradually came round, as if waking from a dream. His eyes eventually focused on her face.

"Oh, my darling! You're here, you're still here!"

"Of course I'm here, it was you who disappeared," she shouted in desperation.

"But you were lost in the fire." He choked on the words. "I saw you in the flames!" He was totally disoriented and traumatised. As he held her tight, he pressed his face to hers, wet with tears.

"It's all right, I'm here, nothing happened. We were just separated." She soothed him like a lost child. "It must have been a trick of the light, it wasn't real."

They clung together on the dark hillside, tears now of joy and relief. Lisa was just beginning to realise the true extent of Jonno's problem, yet she had pledged him her love and knew she would always be there for him. For better or for worse, that's what she had promised when he put the ring on her finger.

The RAF doctor might not be able to reach the core of Jonno's anxieties, but she knew another doctor who just might have a solution.

CHAPTER TEN

DOWN TO EARTH

London, England, September 1999

Just before midnight on Tuesday evening, Lisa passed through the flight passengers' exit into the arrivals hall at Gatwick. Sarah waved frantically to her from the other side of the barrier. Lisa had only been gone four days but they hugged like long-lost sisters.

"It's so late, you shouldn't have come," Lisa scolded. "I could have got a cab."

"No! Don't be silly," Sarah said dismissively. "Besides, I couldn't wait to see your ring. Show me, show me!" Lisa laughed at her childish impatience. She had sent Sarah a text message about the engagement. They had wanted her to be the first to know.

During the flight home Lisa had reflected on her visit to Germany. Being with Jonno again had crystallised her feelings; she loved him so much. Just thinking about him invoked a giddy adrenaline rush, yet after the traumatic incident at Castle Drachenfels their relationship had undergone a subtle change. From being purely ecstatic lovers, she had realised her strong, six foot hero was not a superman; he was vulnerable and currently in need of a lot of tender loving care. She felt a growing sense of responsibility for him, an almost maternal instinct to protect him.

Tonight Sarah was driving her Peugeot 206 which she had used to go home at the weekend.

"How are Max and Kathryn?" Lisa asked.

"Mum seems tired, and Max is not too well again. The doc says it's just a general slowing down, in other words – old age."

"He's such a lovely man," said Lisa reflectively. "Jonno is a lot like him."

"How is my little brother?" Sarah asked her.

"He's fine really." Lisa wanted to play down any suggestion that Jonno was ill. "He's annoyed at the fuss over this incident that grounded him, but hopeful he'll be back flying very soon." Lisa changed the subject quickly. "We stayed in a real castle run as a hotel, it was fabulous!" She spent the rest of the journey recalling her visit, but she said nothing of the incident at Drachenfels' Castle.

"Where's Paul now?" she asked.

"He's back with the squadron in Bedfordshire," Sarah replied. "But he could turn up again any time."

Lisa wanted to justify her feelings about Paul. "This is hard for me to say because he's your brother, but the way he talks about Jonno, always running him down, it's a sort of character assassination and it really gets to me."

Sarah gave a little laugh. "You're an only child, Lisa, so I suppose you would see it that way. I grew up with those two trying to outwit each other and I understand them. Jonno can be just as bad, it's a brother thing."

Lisa could tell she wasn't getting through to Sarah. "Yes, but he seemed almost delighted to learn his brother was grounded. I don't call that brotherly rivalry. Frankly, he's the one that has got a problem."

Sarah didn't answer her immediately. She drove the last few yards into their parking space, switched off the engine and sat looking out over the marina. Then she turned to Lisa.

"There is nothing wrong with either of my brothers. They just went through a terrible experience in their childhood. We all did and I'm afraid it's left its mark. I have spent all my growing years since I was ten trying to hold this family together."

Lisa was shocked to realise Sarah was near to tears and she reached out for her hand.

Sarah continued, her voice full up with emotion. "You're the best friend I've ever had, and it'll be fab if you become my sister-in-law. But you have to realise, the family and all its history come with the package. Don't tear it apart and only take the bits you like."

Lisa coloured up with shame. Sarah was right. If she was going to marry Jonno, she would have to try to understand the relationship between the brothers. She leaned across the seat and kissed Sarah on the cheek. "I'm so sorry if I sounded selfish. I'll try and help you keep order between them."

As they took the lift up to their apartment Sarah looked relieved and Lisa was thankful to have avoided an awkward moment. Yet in spite of her promise to Sarah she still felt a nagging doubt over Paul's true motives towards Jonno and now, towards herself.

Lisa's return to work the following day was like entering a throbbing beehive. The general office was filling up with workers, each intent on playing their part in the great design of producing the 'Sunday Voice'. Phones rang, voices were raised as laughter and shouts filled the night's void. In Biddy's office, she and Caroline had commenced their early morning meeting and were in heated debate. Neil was plying them with hot coffee in an effort to lower the temperature.

"Hi, sweetie, how was Germany?" said Caroline, breaking off from her conversation with Biddy as Lisa entered.

"Fabulous!" Lisa replied, flopping into the vacant chair by the big desk. "Travel certainly broadens the mind."

"We'll have a chat about it later," said Biddy. "Meantime, Lady C and I can't agree on the running order for the alter-health features. The dead line for number one is looming."

"How many are there?" Lisa asked.

"Four ready now, including your 'Ducks'. Congratulations by the way, good piece." Biddy sipped her coffee and beamed a smile at Lisa. "See, here's the proof." Lisa reached across the desk.

Caroline grabbed at her hand and gave a whoop. "What's this?"

Lisa coloured up with a weak smile. "My engagement ring."

Both women fell on her with kisses and words of congratulations, examining the ring, the features temporarily forgotten. Embarrassed by the fuss, Lisa steered them back to the work agenda. She looked at the proof for her story. With the pictures, it filled a full page and her photograph and name were at the top; she was thrilled.

"Looks good, eh?" Biddy chuckled. "You'll go on to do hundreds more, but you'll never forget this one."

"Run it first, if it's ready," said Lisa. "It'll give us more time to finish the others."

"I agree with that," chipped in Caroline.

"Okay," said Biddy and she lit up a cigarette.

Caroline pointedly moved away from her. "Roll on Millennium," she commented dryly.

Biddy looked at Lisa and shook her head. "Thus speaks the ex-smoker and ex-friend, soon to be ex-assistant features editor!"

"That," said Caroline, ignoring Biddy's sarcasm and addressing her remarks to Lisa, "brings us back to the argument. I don't want to run the article on Tony Reeve until Biddy's undergone the treatment."

"And I don't want to be hypnotised!" Biddy raised her voice and then puffed furiously on her cigarette.

Lisa smiled at their intolerance towards each other. "Look, guys," she said, "Tony's therapies cover a lot more than just quitting smoking. How about we run everything else we've got; meanwhile we re-evaluate Tony's work and do a mini series just on hypnosis, to give it better coverage." Caroline and Biddy looked at each other.

"Why didn't you think of that?" said Biddy.

"'Cause you were too busy yelling," answered Caroline. She turned to Lisa. "More visits to Tony Reeve, I'm all for that. He's a hunk!"

Lisa laughed. It was difficult to keep her two senior colleagues on track, but she was actually following an agenda of her own. "I'd like to see how he deals with other phobias. His work covers so much, we can't just highlight smoking."

"I heartily agree!" said Biddy. "I may visit your hunk after all, but not to stop smoking."

Caroline winked at Lisa. "Okay, boss, we get the picture," she said, looking happy with the outcome. "I'll get on the phone and fix a date with Tony." She laughed seductively.

Lisa retreated to her desk outside, musing that half an hour with those two was more exhausting than a whole day's work.

"This is delicious!" said Lisa, tucking into the tuna salad Sarah had prepared for their supper. "It was so hectic today I didn't even stop for lunch."

"I know exactly what you mean," said Sarah. "We're really busy at the moment with new contracts. Translating legal documents is a nightmare, especially the German briefs."

"I can imagine," said Lisa, putting her knife and fork together. "Makes my job seem easy. Will you excuse me; I have to phone Jonno now."

"Give him my love," said Sarah as Lisa retreated into her room.

"I will. Leave the dishes, I'll do them later, my contribution," she said, closing the door. She lay on her bed and called up Jonno's mobile number. The ring tone went on for a long time before he answered.

"Hello." His voice sounded flat and lifeless.

"Jonno, darling, what's up? You sound terrible."

"Oh, Lisa, I've been longing to talk to you. I miss you and I'm so fed up." He didn't need to tell her, she could hear it in his voice.

"Oh darling, I miss you too. Isn't there anyone else you can talk to?"

"Only Smith and he's the problem. I wish now they'd banged me up. At least then I would have known there would be an end and a return to normality. It's as though I'm in solitary with no release date. Oh, and Smith is a bastard."

"What's he said now?" Lisa felt afraid for Jonno, he seemed so despondent.

"He won't sign me off to return to duty, not even desk duty! I'd do anything; the inactivity is killing me."

"You must talk to someone else, not a medic. Who's in charge?"

"I'd have to approach the Station Commander to get over Smith."

"Well, do it." Lisa didn't know how else to advise him. "Just say you need to have some duties, or boredom will really send you crackers."

"I'll think about it, work something out. Anyway, my darling fiancée, how are you? God, do I miss you."

"And I miss you, like crazy. But work is hectic as always. Make sure you get the paper on Sunday, my story will probably be run."

"I thought ducks waddled," he said wryly.

Lisa laughed, as much with relief that he still had his sense of humour, as at the joke. "They do, and you must keep smiling. I love you, Jonno, you mustn't lose hope."

"You're wonderful, Miss Hartnell. If you were here now I'd make love to you all night long."

"Dearest Jonno, our day will come and our nights too."

"I'll definitely talk to someone tomorrow."

Lisa could hear the change in his voice.

"You've kicked me out of the hole I was slipping into."

"You do that, darling. Don't let Smith grind you down; that's not his job."

"My precious Lisa, I feel so much better for talking to you. Take care and remember I love you."

"How could I forget," she answered softly. "Sarah sends her love and I'll speak to you tomorrow night. Love you lots, bye."

"Bye, darling." He was gone.

Lisa lay on the bed, happy and sad together. Already the path of their relationship had moved in an entirely different direction and her love for Jonno was being tested in a way she could never have anticipated, but it was unshakeable. She didn't care if he ended up sweeping the streets, she would never stop loving him.

CHAPTER ELEVEN

THE MEETING

Marham, Norfolk, November 1999

This time, when the transport plane hit the runway and came to a halt, there was no welcome party. It was a routine RAF flight from Bruggen to Marham, but for Flight Lieutenant Jonno Amis it was the best homecoming ever. The last few weeks had driven him into a private hell as Doctor Smith had continued his treatment of counselling and drugs. The former was ineffective, for Smith had failed to gain Jonno's confidence from the outset, and the latter had all found their way into the German sewers.

During this time, the night traumas had intensified. They were more frightening than anything he had ever experienced, even flying in combat conditions. Worse still, the blurred image of the half-forgotten loving companion, had attained sharp focus as Lisa. She had now become, quite literally, the girl of his dreams. Yet he wished desperately it was not so, for whenever he closed his eyes hell's fires now awaited both of them. He knew he had to stay in control and constantly repeated his childhood mantra – heroes did not have bad dreams.

Jonno's lucky break had come when Smith himself had been unexpectedly recalled to the UK. The Bruggen station commander had then decided a sick Tornado navigator was one burden too many. Jonno found himself on the way back to Marham for reassessment, with a view to resuming non-flying duties. If he passed muster on that, after some retraining, he could be back in the air. But for the present, it was enough to be going home and best of all, to be near to Lisa. Yes, in spite of the circumstances, this was the best homecoming ever.

His hopes of being fast tracked back to his squadron were dampened the following day when he reported to Marham's Medical Officer. The administrative process was not to be hurried for the benefit of one displaced navigator. He was to report the following week for more tests; meanwhile he could live off base at home. To his immense frustration the sick leave status would, for the present, continue.

Kathryn was pleased to have her youngest son home, even though she was concerned for his well-being. All she knew was that he was suffering from mental fatigue after his prolonged spells of duty under combat conditions. That was not uncommon among servicemen, whatever the colour of their uniform or the badge they wore. Jonno resigned himself to more waiting while the RAF deliberated over his future.

Lisa was being kept too busy by the paper to travel up to Norfolk, so Jonno had taken his own VW Golf out of mothballs and driven down to London. It was Friday evening and he was waiting outside the new dockland offices of 'The Voice'. He walked up and down in nervous anticipation, his sheepskin jacket warding off the cold east wind blowing from the river. The Indian summer had quickly turned to autumn.

It seemed an eternity had passed since the wonderful weekend when they became engaged, soured by the incident at Castle Drachenfels. The last thing he had wanted was for Lisa to view him as a 'lame duck' or to feel sorry for him. He was determined to be upbeat and give her hope for a wonderful future together.

He watched her emerge from the building, clutching an arm full of folders. She waved with her free hand and immediately his mood was uplifted. They ran to each other and he wrapped her in his arms, hugging her to him tightly. The relief, knowing she still loved him, was overwhelming. They laughed, they kissed and both tried to talk at once.

"You first," he said, relieving her of the burden of files, as they began walking the short distance to The Quays.

"It's wonderful to have you back. How long will you be here? Has the sick leave ended?" They stopped and he kissed her again.

"You journalists are all the same, nothing but questions. If this is an exclusive I want a big fat fee, otherwise I'm saying nothing!"

She grinned mischievously. "Well, I can't offer a fee but I can offer to share my bed tonight. Would that get me an exclusive?"

He gave a long, low whistle. "That, Miss Hartnell, will get you almost anything you want, but I hope your offer is also exclusive." They had reached the apartment block and left the chill wind behind.

Lisa did not answer until they were in the lift. She looked up into his eyes and whispered, "You are my only love; there will never be anyone else." They were still locked in a deep kiss when the doors opened on the fourth floor.

This was his first visit to the apartment and his brief tour of inspection ended when they reached Lisa's bedroom. Their pent up emotions released in a frantic scramble, ripping off their clothes and giving way to a hot passion of frenzied love making which was over in minutes.

"I'm sorry," he said, "That wasn't very considerate of me."

"Don't be sorry, it was wonderful!" She kissed his naked chest. "Instant orgasm isn't just for men you know."

He curled round her back, cupping her breasts in his hands, caressing her nipples and nuzzling her neck.

"I've missed you so much," he said softly.

"And I've missed you too, my darling, but tonight we are dining on the firm with Biddy and Caroline." She pushed her way out of the bed, dragging him half way across the edge of the mattress. "You shower first," she said wrapping herself in a blue fluffy towel robe and tossing him a bath sheet. "I'll fix some coffee." Reluctantly he concurred.

The coffee was hot and strong. They sipped it as they dressed to go out.

"I hope you're following the features every Sunday," she asked him, throwing a large cashmere sweater on over her bra. He held her close to him again, pushing the sweater back up and kissing her cleavage. She pushed him away gently and drank some more coffee.

"Of course," he answered. "I've read every one. Yours are just as good as Caroline's; you make a good team. Are you going to specialise in health? You write like an expert."

"Oh, no," she said, "but I'm glad you think so. We are going to start a new series just on Dr Reeve in the New Year. It was put back because he's been out of the country." Lisa stood in the lounge to finish applying her makeup. Jonno watched from behind, viewing her reflection in the long mirror.

"This is the hypnotist you told me about," said Jonno; "fascinating."

"It's all kosher, he really does cure people." She looked at Jonno via their reflections, as though to gauge his reaction. "I've wanted to ask you for sometime if you think he might be able to help you."

He was taken aback, not by the suggestion but from the realisation that Lisa thought he still needed help. He chose his words carefully, anxious to dispel any notions she might have that he was anything but a whole and normal person.

"He would have been a lot more interesting to talk to than dear Dr Smith, but I don't need any more doctors. I've come home for retraining. I'll soon be flying again."

They were ready to leave the apartment and headed for the lift. "Well, you can talk to him tonight; he's coming to dinner with us."

They were carried down to ground level and went out into the cold once more. He began to wonder if tonight's meeting had been stage-managed. As he drove them to the restaurant, he questioned Lisa more closely.

A meal out on Biddy's expense account was apparently Lisa's reward for her work on the alternative health series and the

107

publication of three of her own features. She also told him it was Biddy who had insisted Jonno should join them for the evening and that inviting Tony had been Caroline's idea.

"But I do think it's a good opportunity for you to meet Tony," said Lisa. "I know you will find him as interesting as I do."

Jonno reversed into a parking space and prepared to leave the car. "I'm getting the impression you think I should talk to him about my situation," he said, a little tight-lipped.

"Well, I certainly think you should consider it." Lisa squeezed his hand tightly. "Once you've met him I'm sure you'll feel the same." They crossed the road and Jonno thought hard about the impending meeting. He decided to keep a low profile during the evening's proceedings. Besides, when it came to cross-examinations, he was no match for three female journalists.

The restaurant, known as 'Chelsea Ram', was on the edge of London's Chelsea district. It was already busy when they arrived a little before nine o'clock. They found Lisa's senior colleagues in the bar, enjoying pre-dinner cocktails. She couldn't help feeling quite smug as she introduced her fiancé to them. She could tell from their appreciative looks they more than approved of her tall, dark handsome hero.

"Delighted to meet you both and thank you for inviting me," Jonno said to them. "Lisa has told me so much about you." Jonno could charm the ladies just by being himself and Lisa was glad she had not told them the real reason he was back in the UK.

"Tony not arrived yet?" she asked Caroline, whilst doing a balancing act with her cocktail glass, top heavy with assorted fruits, bells and whistles.

Caroline shook her head without taking her eyes off the entrance. "Oh, boy, am I looking forward to seeing him again." She sighed, licking the sugar coating round the top of her glass seductively.

Biddy looked despairingly to Lisa and Jonno. "She was worse than this when we did a series on celebrity footballers; she's man mad!"

Caroline scowled. "Oh, shut up, you're only jealous." Lisa laughed at their juvenile banter.

"This is a very nice restaurant," said Jonno, looking round and apparently trying to ignore the girl talk. "I hope the food is as good."

"It is," said Biddy. "We use it a lot for business dining. Lady C and I like it because we can smoke here." Biddy had emphasised her last words, apparently waiting for a reaction from Caroline.

A look of regret passed over Caroline's features and then she smiled. "That no longer interests me." Her eyes were still riveted on the entrance. "Here he is!" she called out. Then she hurried over to guide Tony in their direction.

"Good evening, everyone," said Tony. "I hope I haven't kept you waiting." Lisa was again struck by his smooth, velvet voice. He still carried the air of a professional doctor, in dark suit, pastel shirt and silk tie. In his quiet courteous manner, he shook everyone by the hand. When Lisa introduced him to Jonno, she hoped that he could sense the relaxing atmosphere which seemed to follow this extraordinary man around. It was important to her that Jonno judged Tony as a health professional and not as some quirky theatrical freak.

They moved into the dining area and began studying their menus. Tony sat next to Jonno, immediately engaging him in casual conversation about his role in the RAF. She listened apprehensively, but it was evident that Jonno seemed at ease with Tony's unruffled manner. When everyone had placed their orders, Tony tasted and chose two different wines. He seemed a connoisseur, so they were happy for him to indulge them with his choice, particularly when he insisted the wine waiter should give him the separate bill.

"Now, ladies," he addressed them collectively, "tell me about your proposed features for your paper."

Biddy looked to Caroline, "This is your baby, fire away."

"Well, Tony," Caroline began. "I personally was so impressed by our session at your clinic, we have decided we would like to cover more aspects of your work; the whole range of your therapies. What do you think?" The conversation paused while the waitress served their starters. "By the way, I haven't had one cigarette since our visit." She looked pointedly at Biddy. "What's more amazing is I haven't wanted one!"

"I'm pleased for you." Tony smiled at her. "Seeing is believing, isn't that right, Lisa?" She was startled, and reminded how she had thought he could read her mind.

"It is," she answered, amazed at his perception.

He pushed his starter round the plate, eating very little. "My subjects come to me as patients, some I see one to one; others agree to take part in open sessions, like the one you attended. I have to gain their consent before inviting journalists. How many visits would you want?"

"Two, maybe three," suggested Caroline. "It would depend how many aspects of your work we eventually cover."

"I'm very protective of my reputation," Tony turned his head from one to another as he spoke, ensuring he had everyone's attention. "I have never wanted to exploit the entertainment value of hypnotism, that's not my objective, but I fear it may be yours."

"Oh, no, Tony," Caroline interjected. "That's not our intention. This particular series aims to highlight alternative health therapies which cover a very wide spectrum. We want to give our readers enough information to show that they can and do work, with case studies where possible." The waitress returned to clear the table and then their main courses were served. Tony poured the chosen wines.

Biddy opened the folder she had brought. "Have a look at this, Tony." She handed him the draft article on smoke cessation, which was mainly Lisa's work, as Caroline had been the subject.

Lisa felt proud and embarrassed together. She was developing a high regard for Tony's professionalism and hoped he would approve of her interpretation of his work.

He studied it carefully. "This is excellent, Lisa, well done. If you show all my work like this, I will be happy."

She was pleased at his reaction, and said, "Your brochure details so many different aspects to your work. Holistic Hypnotherapy, Neuro Linguistic Programming, Time Line Therapy, Past Life Regression; it all sounds very technical. We would like to give readers a simple picture and show them what the therapies can achieve for ordinary people. Like you said in your address to us, people with blocks stopping them living ordinary lives." She glanced towards Jonno; he certainly seemed to be following the conversation. She could only hope he was making the connection with his own problems.

Tony paused from attacking the roe deer steak which he and Jonno had both selected from the menu. "You could write a book; in fact I have, several."

"Can we borrow them?" asked Caroline. "Background information would be very useful."

"I'd be delighted to let you have copies." Tony seemed flattered. "You should be able to attend a suitable session soon, possibly next week."

"That's perfect," said Caroline, beaming a smile at him. "But what I am dying to know more about is past life regression. Since my experience under hypnosis with you, I'm fascinated by the whole concept."

Tony put his knife and fork together and sipped his wine thoughtfully.

"Unfortunately, journalists always home in on this one. I suppose it's because there is still a mystery surrounding its credibility. It smacks of the staged theatricals surrounding hypnotism."

"And you don't agree," said Caroline, hanging on his every word. "As a professional doctor, how would you justify its use?"

"Caroline, you experienced regression. The difference was, it was within your own life time, you know it was a true event. If you read my book, 'Back to Life', you will understand the therapy used is the same. The difficulty comes with accepting a 'past life' as genuine."

Most of the other diners had left the restaurant and a hush had fallen on the room. Lisa had been listening intently to Tony's explanation. "And is it genuine? Do people really experience past lives?" she asked. Another sidelong glance at Jonno reassured her he was also deeply engrossed in Tony's explanations.

"It's not that simple to answer your question." Tony looked at all of them in turn. "As a doctor, I have to keep my eye on the ball, not the field of play. The ball is the patient's problem: phobias, panic attacks, night traumas, eating disorders, myriad problems brought to my clinic. I have to attempt to find their source; that is my objective." He paused again, sipping his wine. His audience remained silent, waiting.

"On occasions through hypnotherapy, subjects have apparently regressed to a point before their birth in this life time, giving details and descriptions of apparent past lives. During hypnosis, this is not uncommon. Some patients seem to regress to past lives as easily as they do to past events in their present life. Providing I can reach the seat of their traumas and help them overcome them, I do not think proving the reality is important.

"Who am I to question what is true or what is fantasy? My job is to heal. If others wish to concern themselves with proof, let them do so. I only know what I have witnessed many times: that the therapeutic benefits in releasing subjects from mental scars and traumatic influences are the same whether the root cause is in this life, or an apparent past life. But I also know that some subjects have regressed and given us information which could not have come from any other source, except from talking to the dead."

CHAPTER TWELVE

PHANTOM

When Lisa awoke the following morning, she was alone in the bed. Through the open door she could see Jonno by the lounge window, looking out over the marina.

"Enjoying the view?" she called out sleepily. He looked up quickly as if startled from deep thought. He smiled at her and walked back into the bedroom.

"Not as good as the view in here," he said, lying down beside her. He smoothed back her hair and traced his fingers round her face. She felt his gentle kiss on her lips and the warmth of his body pressing close to her. Desire smouldered between them and in that moment making love was all that mattered.

Later, over a breakfast of tea and toast, Lisa's thoughts returned to the events of the previous evening. When they had left the restaurant, they'd given Tony a lift back to Wembley. He wanted to give Lisa copies of some of his published books, and inevitably, he had invited them in for coffee.

The social visit had been partly contrived by Lisa. She had hoped Jonno would talk to Tony about his problems. But he had let the opportunity pass, apparently still confident that he didn't need any help. She was still hoping he might change his mind.

"What did you think of Tony Reeve? You didn't say much last night."

He grinned. "I decided to keep my thoughts to myself. You girls were well into your specialist interview techniques, especially Caroline." He laughed now. "She's a real comedian, and I gather she's a bit hooked on your Dr Reeve."

Lisa winced at the memory of Caroline's efforts to flirt with Tony during dinner. "Yes, but what did you think of his theories and the whole concept of hypnotic regression?"

"You mean, why didn't I ask him to help me?" His tone indicated they should settle this question for once and for all.

Lisa sighed. "Well, yes I suppose I do."

Jonno's face clouded over, thoughtful and serious. "If you want the truth, yes, I think he probably could find the source of my nightmares. But I'm not sure it would help and I'm not sure if I want him to."

Lisa opened her mouth to utter a protest but he gently placed one finger over her lips, silencing her.

"I know when my problems began and it happened in this life – not a past life." He hesitated, shaking his head and the reference was obvious. He didn't say any more and then his smiling face clicked back on.

She didn't want to let it go. "I do understand, darling, but we could explain this to Tony. He is such an experienced doctor, maybe he could still help you to overcome the nightmares."

"I think we should wait and see." He stood up and faced her. "I feel much better being back in England, especially when I'm with you. Perhaps you are my best therapy."

Lisa knew she was losing the argument. "But we can't be together all the time, not at the moment." She stood up, close to him and they wrapped their arms around each other.

"Unfortunately, no," he said, kissing her forehead. "So like I said, let's wait and see. I'm sure I'll be okay now, so you mustn't worry." He squeezed her tightly and grinned. "Now, tell me what delights have you planned for me today."

"Oh, gosh, yes! I almost forgot. We've tickets to see 'Phantom of the Opera' tonight," she told him, brightening up.

"Hey, how did you manage that?"

"Goes with the job," she said. "Biddy acquires all sorts of perks from celebs hoping for free PR. When she knew you were coming to town, she gave them to me."

He laughed. "Well, I think your boss is a very nice lady."

"I need to go shopping," she said. "I can't go to the theatre – I haven't a thing to wear."

"Don't wear anything then," he joked. "You'll cause a sensation in the West End."

"Yes, and get arrested!" Lisa replied, laughing with him.

"Come on then, we haven't a moment to lose. If we're going shopping I expect it will take all day!"

Half an hour later they were outside the apartment and Jonno hailed a taxi.

"Where are we going?" she asked as they bundled in the back.

"Knightsbridge," Jonno said to the cab driver, answering her question. They stopped outside the world famous Harrods department store and he led Lisa inside. This was the Jonno she knew and loved – full of surprises, charm and humour. He whisked her straight to the jewellery room.

"I want to buy you a pair of earrings, something to wear to the theatre tonight, your choice."

After much deliberation, Lisa eventually chose a pair of white gold droplets, studded with square cut diamonds from Tiffany. They matched her engagement ring.

"Thank you so much," she said, a little overwhelmed. It wasn't so much the value of the gift, but Jonno's desire to please and surprise which constantly delighted her.

When Lisa emerged from her room that evening ready for the theatre trip, she was wearing a simple black dress and white jacket which they had also bought during their shopping trip. The new earrings stood out against her long auburn hair.

"You look wonderful, Lady Lisa," he said, making a low bow.

"Why, thank you, Sir Jonno," she joshed back and they laughed at their own little joke before taking the lift down to the ground floor and the waiting cab.

The black cab dropped them outside Her Majesty's Theatre in the Haymarket, where 'Phantom' had been playing to packed houses since 1986.

"I have actually seen the show twice before," Lisa confided. "But it is my favourite musical."

"Well, this is a first for me," said Jonno as they entered the foyer.

"First time to 'Phantom?'" she asked.

"First time to see any musical," he confessed.

Lisa looked aghast.

"But I'm sure I'll love it!" he added quickly.

Neither of them was disappointed. When they emerged into the crowded London night several hours later, Jonno had to agree that the whole theatre experience had been thoroughly enjoyable.

"Fancy a curry?" he asked her. "I'm famished."

"Oh, yes, good idea," she answered, realising they had not eaten since lunch time.

They walked with the crowds up to Piccadilly and then on into Soho, where they found an Indian restaurant which was to their particular liking. It was a little after midnight when they at last returned to the apartment at South Dock Marina.

Alone at last, fine clothes and jewellery were soon discarded. As Lisa surrendered to Jonno's love making, she felt utterly complete, as though she were renewing every vow of love made to him since the beginning.

"I want to love you all night long," he declared, as they lay naked and entwined on the bed.

She wanted that too. Fate had brought them together again and she didn't want to waste a minute of the time they could be together. "Wonderful," she whispered. They kissed and loved again. But eventually they both fell into a deep, relaxed sleep.

Lisa felt as if she had barely closed her eyes when suddenly she was very much wide awake as the room was filled with a dreadful noise. Momentarily she was paralysed with fear. She realised the bloodcurdling sound was coming from Jonno, as though he were choking or drowning. She leapt out of the bed and switched on the light. He seemed delirious, thrashing out his arms and sweating, the dreadful noise still coming from his throat.

"Jonno! What's wrong? Wake up!" she shouted. She was frantic, thinking he was ill with fever or food poisoning. Then it dawned that he was having a nightmare. She had not witnessed this before, only the incident at Drachenfels. She started to panic and thought if she didn't wake him he could die.

She fought to keep a grip on her emotions and rushed to the kitchen, filling a jug with cold water. Back in the bedroom, she splashed the water on his face, but the writhing and groaning continued. In total panic she threw the entire contents of the jug over him and screamed out. "Wake up, Jonno! Wake up!"

The cold water caused him to jerk and spasm. Then the noise stopped, everything stopped and he lay quite still, he didn't even seem to be breathing. Fear and panic took complete hold of Lisa; she had never felt so desperate. She slapped his face and shook him bodily, shouting out his name over and over, not knowing if he was dead or alive, asleep or unconscious. Tears streamed down her face and she grabbed her mobile phone to dial 999.

Suddenly he shuddered and his eyes opened wide. He sat up gasping for breath, like a drowning man. Lisa dropped the phone and threw herself at him, wrapping him in her arms. "Oh, my God, you're all right, you're alive, I thought you were dead!" she sobbed and clung to him.

He couldn't speak, still gasping for breath and dazed. He was in a trauma of his own and seemed unable to comprehend what had happened.

She fetched him more water and he drained the glass. As Lisa calmed down, she began to refocus on Jonno's state of mind. "Was it another nightmare, tell me?"

He nodded in reply, his face contorted, still apparently in shock that it had happened again.

"I thought you were having a heart attack or a seizure." Her anxiety reasserted itself. "I honestly thought you had stopped breathing!"

He just lay there, staring into space.

She was helpless with despair. "Speak to me, darling. Please say something!"

The extent of her anxiety seemed to register with him as last. "I'm sorry, I'm so sorry, please forgive me."

"I don't want you to be sorry! It's not your fault – but it is your problem – our problem if you like, and we've got to stop it happening!" She tried to assemble her thoughts.

He forestalled her. "I will see Tony Reeve, I promise you." His voice was flat, he was defeated and exhausted. He leaned back on the pillows and pulled Lisa tight against his chest. She waited until he fell once again into a natural sleep before extricating herself from his arms.

She did not sleep. The happy interlude had been shattered and the true extent of Jonno's psychosis had brought her down to earth with a resounding bump. It was as if he was two different people; as if some dark force was controlling certain aspects of his personality, like the Phantom, she thought. When it materialised, his mind seemed to be taken over by irrational thoughts and images, in a place where she could not reach him. She wanted the nightmare to end. Not just his nightmare, but the one she also now had to endure. The only good thing was that Jonno had agreed to consult Tony Reeve. But she would have to act quickly, before he could change his mind.

Jonno did not change his mind, although it might have been easy for him to be sceptical, perhaps even cynical, about Tony's hypnotic regression theories. Service life, particularly his war service, had moulded him into a fighting machine full of positive action and devoid of fanciful notions. Yet at the same time he recalled that when faced with death, his own or others as he had been in Kosovo, it was spiritual emotions which emerged to dominate life and death situations. Hardened, battle-weary soldiers had recorded such experiences, and others would listen and understand without doubt or derision.

It was another ten days before he was able to see Dr Reeve at his clinic for an assessment and the year had rolled over into December. The nightmares continued unabated and he could no longer pretend these strange happenings were within his control. There were dark places in his mind which terrified him and drew him relentlessly back into the nightmare, over and over again. Something had to happen to break the cycle of self-destruction. This seemed to be the only course open to him and now he was impatient to begin.

Tony had rescheduled his appointments to accommodate Jonno's need to see him at the weekend. The RAF was not being told and during the week Jonno had to be at Marham. He felt a twinge of apprehension as he approached the premises in Wembley with Lisa on the Sunday afternoon.

"Do you want me to stay with you?" she asked him.

"Yes, I'd like that," Jonno answered, as they rang the doorbell. "For once in my life I need all the support I can get, especially yours."

Tony opened the door. His staff did not work Sundays, but he lived 'over the shop' as he put it.

"Come in, come in." He greeted them warmly. "Coffee's on." He ushered them into the comfortable reception lounge. "Make yourselves at home and relax." He poured the coffee from a steaming percolator.

Returning to the clinic, this time as a willing patient, Jonno began to experience the calming atmosphere which Lisa had tried to describe to him. It surrounded Tony himself and was reinforced by the design and décor of his premises.

Tony spent the next hour questioning him in detail on everything significant that had ever happened to him. About the terrible tragedy of the fire which killed his father and his relationships within his family; his experiences in the RAF and even his love life. Tony used a cassette tape machine to record all these details. He even asked Jonno how he had felt emotionally at the time.

Jonno joked with him. "I'd better have a copy of that for when I write my memoirs."

Tony smiled. "As a navigator you will appreciate I need a map with grid points and references to find my way through the labyrinth of your mind." He continued. "At the moment all the evidence points to the night of your father's death as being the most probable source of your traumas. X marks that spot on your map."

Jonno nodded in agreement. "This is the reason for my reluctance to undergo hypnotherapy. I have spent my whole life suppressing the emotions attached to that night and I don't want to relive them."

"But that could be a false trail. We could find ourselves in a completely different place." Tony steered him in another direction. "You also said the dreams began before that night."

"That's what Sarah told me," interjected Lisa. "She said they started long before the fire, when you were just a tiny child."

"That's why after that night," said Jonno, "everyone concluded I was psychic."

"And what about your conclusions," said Tony. "Do you believe you are psychic?"

Jonno seemed to ponder on this, his eyes scanning the framed landscape watercolours which hung on the opposite wall, before answering. "Yes, I believe I am, although I have never tried to cultivate it, more the opposite. I experienced intuitive feelings as a child, although I didn't know then that was what they were. But since the nightmares began again, those feelings have also returned."

Tony was completely absorbed in Jonno's explanation. "In what way?" he asked.

Jonno shrugged his shoulders, clearly having difficulty with his answers. "I have odd feelings and intuitions – unbidden thoughts. The sort of thing that triggered the disastrous incident in the Gulf when I saw the glow of two missiles; I can still see it now in my head. But according to the evidence and other witnesses, they were never there."

Jonno rubbed his eyes, as if that might make them go away. He saw a look pass between Lisa and Tony: a confiding look from which he was excluded. He was beginning to re-experience the despair which had gripped him after the incident. "I seriously, seriously need your help."

Tony stretched out his hand to Jonno. "And you shall have it, young man." Tony poured more coffee into Jonno's cup. "All I can tell you is that under the hypnosis, even if you do relive your worst nightmare, eventually this will lead to a healing process. If it helps to clear away the blocks stopping you moving forward, it will also help you to grieve over something which has been suppressed. You have to be prepared for that."

Lisa slipped her hand into his. "Are you?" she asked him.

Jonno's eyes were downcast and he didn't answer her. He looked to Tony again. "Will I be cured?"

Tony smiled. "Not today you won't. It's not quite like stopping smoking although the principle is the same. It may take several sessions to get to the root of the problem. But I have never yet failed to give a patient a positive outcome."

Johno turned his eyes back to Lisa. He so wanted to make her his own; to marry her and share a wonderful life together, but at this moment his life was a mess and still falling apart.

"Yes," he said. "I guess I am ready, but it has to be now. If I were to walk away my courage would probably desert me."

"Of course," said Tony reassuringly. "We can start straight away, Jonno, just a short session for you to understand the process. But there is no hurry," he added in his smooth American drawl. "We have all the time in the world."

CHAPTER THIRTEEN

WHO IS KARL?

They moved into Tony's consulting room and Jonno was asked to lie down on the couch. Lisa sat on one side behind his head, Tony on the other, in front of him. Tony demonstrated some deep breathing and relaxation exercises which Jonno would have to practise every day. They were an essential precursor to successful hypnotherapy. After a while, Jonno mastered their rhythm and found he was gradually becoming less tense and more focused.

There was no swinging pendulum, only Tony's carefully modulated voice talking him through his breathing pattern. He began to feel a little more comfortable, sleepy even, as he entered a deeper state of relaxation.

Tony's voice droned on. "I want you to imagine you are walking down a long, dark corridor. We are looking for a particular place. We are searching for your earliest memories, when your troubles all began."

Jonno was drifting, surely asleep, but he could still hear the deep monotonous voice. He was in the long, tunnel-like passage. At first it was dark, then he saw a light. The light grew brighter, it was daylight...

He reached out and touched a wooden surface. It felt rough with tool marks, dust and oil.

The voice asked, "Where are you?"

The scene was clear, strange yet familiar. He heard himself answer, "I am in a workshop."

"What kind of workshop?"

He looked around, whitewashed walls, high windows, more benches. "I work here," he said.

"What are you doing?" asked the voice.

123

He looked down on the bench. "I am assembling a piece of machinery."

"Do you know what it is?"

He recognised his work. "It's an engine, a combustion engine for a car."

The voice prompted him again, "Where is this?"

Jonno hesitated. "A car factory, we make cars."

"Who are you?"

"My name is Karl…" He hesitated again. "Karl Stock…? Karl Stocker…? I don't remember my other name."

The voice was persistent, "Do you know where this is? What town or city?"

There was a pause, and then Jonno spoke again. "Stuttgart, I live and work in Stuttgart."

"In Germany?" the voice seemed surprised.

"Yes, I am German."

"When is this? Do you know the date?" The questions kept coming.

"Nineteen thirty something… I'm not sure."

"Do you have a family, Karl?"

His answers were becoming more assured. "My mother… and my father, he works here also."

"What is this place where you both work?"

"I can't remember, but we make cars and trucks… Times are difficult, things are changing." Jonno shifted and seemed uneasy.

"Why are things changing? What is wrong?"

"There is a dark shadow over our lives. I feel… I feel afraid."

Jonno seemed visibly anxious. Tony did not ask any more questions but allowed him to rest, still deeply hypnotised.

Daimler-Benz Engineering, Stuttgart, Germany, August 1933

Karl looked up at the clock on the machine shop wall. Yes, thank God, he had completed all the jobs on his work schedule and within the new times allowed. He wiped the sweat from his face with the sleeve of his overall. His foreman, Otto, loomed over him. He was clutching his clipboard and looking more harassed than usual.

"You're finished, yes?" he snapped.

"Yes, I've finished, but I don't know how long we can keep up this pace."

"As long as we have to, young Stockhausen; the trade union no longer has a say. Not only do we have to work harder, from next week our pay will be cut."

Karl shook his head. "What more do they want, blood?"

Otto glanced around to ensure he was not overheard. "That too, if necessary, my young friend. We all have to pay for the Führer's rearmament programme, to rebuild the glorious Fatherland."

As if on cue the loud speakers, recently installed on the machine shop wall, burst into a military anthem. Everyone stopped work and stood to attention, their right arms outstretched in the ridiculous Nazi salute. Otto and Karl did likewise. As the anthem finished they all shouted, "Heil Hitler!" then immediately resumed their tasks to make up for the time lost.

As Karl took up his tools again, a big cloak of misery settled on his shoulders. 'What should he do? What could he do?'

The voice interrupted his thoughts. "I want you to remember how you found Karl. When you want to return to this lifetime I will say, 'Go back and find Karl,' and you will be here again." There was a pause and then the voice spoke again. "Now you are coming back to the present. On the count of three, you will wake. One, two, three, wake up, Jonno."

He opened his eyes. The machine shop had gone. He was back in the clinic with Tony and Lisa.

"How do you feel?" Tony asked.

"Incredible!" Jonno's face was registering disbelief. "It wasn't at all what I expected."

125

"What did you expect?" Tony asked.

"I truly expected to go back to the night my father died, the night of the fire, but it was completely different." Jonno shook his head in dismay, totally overawed by his experience. "It was so strange, so unexpected."

"Well, maybe your problems did begin elsewhere, perhaps in a previous life. You spoke of feeling afraid. Do you know why?" Tony's questions were dragging the images into Jonno's conscious mind, reinforcing the memory.

He considered Tony's question carefully. He was finding it difficult to believe he had just undergone a past life experience. "Umm, Germany… in the nineteen thirties: not a good place or time to be," he said. "Could I just be projecting a bad time in history that I already knew about?"

"Yes, you could," Tony agreed. "But would you have chosen to tell it from this particular view point? It seems disconnected from Nazi Germany – a car plant in Stuttgart?"

Jonno nodded in agreement. "This person, this Karl, I felt his fear. It was to do with a personal problem, with his family or someone else, but I don't know who or what. I would like to have known more."

"Maybe you will, in time," said Lisa.

"Well," said Tony, standing up. "We'll need to monitor any improvements you experience as the therapy progresses; that's if you want to continue."

Jonno caught hold of Lisa's hand. As their hands touched she looked into his eyes. "It has to be your decision," she said, smiling at him.

Jonno didn't really need encouragement; his curiosity had been keenly aroused. "What happens next?" he asked Tony.

"Today has only scratched the surface," said Tony. "I expect we will have to dig a lot deeper to find the true source of your troubles or produce any visible change in your traumas. But it will happen, Jonno, of that I have no doubt."

If Jonno's apparent past life was raising more questions than answers, his present life was posing more immediate problems.

On Monday morning the six o'clock alarm dragged him back to reality. He quickly silenced the clock and gently kissed a sleepy Lisa before rolling out of the bed. As he washed and shaved, Jonno realised they had slept soundly all night. He quickly scanned his mind for any vestige of dreams, but there were none. That, he thought, was at least a step in the right direction.

Thirty minutes later he left the apartment for the drive to Marham. He was due at the base today to report to the Chief Medical Officer, Dr Johnson. Jonno hoped he would at least be returned to desk duties. Resuming his flying career would have to wait. He clung to the hope that as they had not said 'no', they might eventually say 'yes'.

Driving gave him the time and opportunity to contemplate the previous day's revelations, if that was what they were. Who was Karl? Was he a real person or a figment of his imagination, dragged up out of a long forgotten book or film? If he had been 'regressed' to when his troubles first began, why had he not experienced the night of the fire when his father died? What he had experienced made no sense whatsoever. Pre-war Germany did not figure in his present life or connect with his present troubles. He was intrigued, but certainly not convinced, that he had even had a past life, let alone as this character Karl. Yet the emotions he had felt during the hypnosis, the fear, was almost palpable.

Just before Tony brought him out of his trance something else had occurred. He tried hard to picture the scene again. He had a vague impression of someone else being there, a conversation. Something happened, but it had gone back into his subconscious mind. He was more curious than alarmed. Would he experience the same time and place in any subsequent session with Tony Reeve? Would he find Karl again?

Dr Johnson was, it seemed, a doctor of the old military school. He was twice the man Smith had been, in size, stature and humour. However, even he did not recommend a return to a fighter jet navigation seat, just yet.

Jonno played down all the symptoms which suggested any type of mental breakdown had occurred. And he emphasised his desire to return to flying duties with his squadron as soon as possible.

"I'm sure that will be the eventual outcome, Flight Lieutenant," said Johnson. "But unfortunately you will have to go before the Medical review board before that can happen. I have to show we have given you a thorough overhaul." He laughed, "Put you back in working order, so to speak."

"Work of any sort would be good," said Jonno. "I can't stand all this hanging around doing nothing."

"You can return to light duties. I'm sure they can find you something to do in the admin office. I'll have a word with the Station CO, Chris Bailey. There's a project coming up in January and it could be just the ticket for an intelligent chap like you." Johnson seemed pleased with himself. "We can't have you moping about, can we?"

"So, what do you want me to do now?" asked Jonno, wanting a definite answer.

"Ring me tomorrow at ten o'clock," he said, writing in his diary. "I will have a plan for you to follow by then. Meanwhile drop all that medication stuff they gave you at Bruggen." He was already writing up his notes. "Goodbye, Flight Lieutenant."

Jonno beat a hasty retreat from the Medical block and breathed a big sigh of relief. He was out of Smith's clutches; he had begun treatment with Tony Reeve and Johnson seemed a bit of a 'pushover'. Now all he had to do was convince Marham Station Commander, Chris Bailey, that he was the right man for his project – whatever that might turn out to be.

"So what's the project?" said Lisa. It was the following weekend and Jonno had returned to London. They had met up in Hyde Park and were now weaving a path through the joggers and horse riders.

"I won't know until I get my marching orders," he replied. "But I think it's more a routine admin task. It has to be better than sitting around Bailey's office making tea and running messages, which is what I have been doing all week." The day was grey and a light drizzle began to blow in their faces.

"Still, even that is better than nothing," said Lisa. She was very aware that Jonno felt humiliated by his loss of flying status within the service. They diverted out of the park to cross the busy road.

"Anyway, all I know is that it's off-base and will take a week." He pulled Lisa close to him as they jay-walked through the speeding traffic in Park Lane. "So I can't tell you what it's about, my little journalist." They continued walking up to Marble Arch and turned into Oxford Street. They had intended to start on their Christmas shopping. As far as the eye could see there was a huge tide of humanity filling the pavements, all with the same intention. They diverted off the main road and found a bar which was not too crowded.

"Have you been sleeping better this week?" Lisa asked him once they were seated with their drinks.

He sighed, shaking his head. "It would be easy for me to say all the nightmares and dreams have stopped. That is what I said to Dr Johnson. But I won't lie to Tony and I can't lie to you. They are still dogging my nights and even during the day I can suddenly find myself reliving the nightmare scenarios. At times, it's bloody awful." He looked into Lisa's eyes apparently seeking some sort of reassurance.

"We'll just have to wait and see what happens," she said. "Tony hasn't really started yet." Her words did not seem to have the desired effect.

"I know there's no instant cure for me," he said. "The worry is even with Tony's help, there may not be a cure at all."

129

At noon the following day, they arrived once more at the Wembley clinic. Jonno explained his precarious position at Marham to Tony as they sipped coffee in the reception room.

"If the RAF doctor knew the full extent of my nightmares and hallucinations, I know I would never fly again."

"You do realise that I can't promise they will stop; your case is very complex. Regression therapy is not an overnight cure." Tony's piercing blue eyes looked from one to the other.

"We understand that," said Lisa, "but you are our only hope." She was holding Jonno's hand as though the problem was theirs, equally.

Tony smiled at their anguished faces. "In view of what is at stake, I will give your case a high priority. But first, we have to banish all this tension. You need to be completely relaxed, both of you."

He suggested they went out to lunch at a nearby restaurant. "Good food and a glass of wine is the best way I know to relax," he said, as he ushered them into the dining room. "Besides, I'm starving." The meal was excellent, and they were all glad of the opportunity to converse and unwind.

When they returned to the clinic two hours later, Jonno felt really mellow, and under Tony's expert guidance he again found himself entering the strange but compelling hypnotic trance. Once more he was drifting on the journey into his own subconscious mind.

He heard the echoing words. "Go back and find Karl." He felt hot from sudden exertion and wished he had not sprinted so hard.

CHAPTER FOURTEEN

PERFECT LOVE

Stuttgart, Germany. August 1933

Karl had been running for a full five minutes. He was young and fit but his heart hammered faster than the fall of his feet on the pavement and his breath came in short rasps. He slowed to walking pace, taking great gulps of air. Without stopping, he turned full circle to look back down Charlottenstrasse, the way he had come. Was he being followed? Members of the Sturmabtelung, the SA paramilitarie, were easy to spot in their brown shirts, but there were other informers everywhere, anonymous, invisible. It wasn't hard running which had reduced him to a physical wreck, it was panic induced by fear.

There had been an undercurrent of growing fear for months. It was an emotion he had refused to recognise. For to give it form, to acknowledge it, would have allowed it to become real. Now it had risen up like an evil genie, so powerful a force he could no longer pretend it did not exist.

The Nazi Party had appeared to be the answer to everyone's prayers, promising to sweep away the old class ridden politics and clamp down on the far left communists. But since Hitler had been appointed Chancellor of the coalition government, he had systematically dismantled the fragile democracy by declaring all other political parties illegal or forcing them to dissolve. Every aspect of their lives – the trade unions, the Christian Churches, youth groups, music societies, even his mother's sewing circle – all were now controlled by the new government, and used to coerce the population with Nazi propaganda. Assured that for the moment at least he was not being followed, Karl continued his journey.

Until recently he had always enjoyed the hour long, leisurely walk across the sprawling city of Stuttgart from his home in the southeast suburbs to visit his fiancée, Elizabeth and her family. They lived in one of the new fashionable houses at Weissenhof in the northwest district. Elizabeth's father, Joseph, was a lawyer and her mother Wilma, a lecturer at the University. They were an intellectual family, whereas Karl's own background was working class. Like their daughter, Elizabeth, the Ekharts were warm, kind, generous and loving. Yet in the current wave of anti-Semitic violence and harassment led by the Nazi military wing, Elizabeth and her family were totally at risk – for they were Jews.

As Karl passed by the small and graceful Schillerplatz, the city's old-world square, the historic buildings seemed to press in on him. He cowered, as he saw a vision of the ancient walls crumbling and falling. Rivers of blood oozed from the broken masonry and spread across the street, washing round his feet. He shook his head and forced himself to focus on his surroundings. Everything was normal; he was letting his imagination run wild as usual.

The argument with his father the previous night had been terrible. His mother's pleadings still rang in his ears. He had always been a good and dutiful son and followed his father's wishes but this time Karl knew he could not obey him. Karl's apprenticeship with the Daimler-Benz engineering company had been granted through his father's good name. Manfred Stockhausen had been with the company since its inception at the turn of the century

When Karl had begun his association with Elizabeth two years ago, Manfred and his wife Anna had not opposed the friendship. Elizabeth's parents were highly respected members of the Stuttgart community, involved in local music festivals and charity work. They were good people, his father had often said as much. Karl and Elizabeth had become engaged in September 1932 and both families had joined together for the celebrations. His parents had embraced Elizabeth as their future daughter-in-law. Everyone's cup had been *overflowing, especially his own. Now his father expected him to break off the engagement and disown the Ekhart family.*

Tonight was a warm evening in late August. The shadows grew ever longer as Karl made his way through the city centre. Shops and businesses were now closed, but pavement cafes and public houses were open for evening trade. In better times the city would have been thronged with revellers. Good company, good beer, singing and dancing in the streets in true Swabian tradition. Now the atmosphere was very different. The few people still out huddled together in small groups, speaking in undertones. Everyone was watching everyone else.

Two SA Storm Troopers emerged from one of the bars. The response from the people outside was immediate: raised arms, and the 'Heil Hitler' greeting. Karl disappeared round the next corner and hoped they had not seen him. He had performed this ridiculous act at work today, and sung the wretched 'Horst Wessel Song'. Even now this was being relayed over the loudspeakers here in the beer gardens! He would have liked to stop and quench his thirst but he pressed on, avoiding eye contact with those he passed, hoping no one knew him; expecting to be denounced at any moment as a 'Jew-lover'.

Elizabeth had become his whole reason to live. He loved her to distraction. She was beautiful – oh yes, to him very beautiful – and she was always so happy. When she laughed, her long dark hair danced on her shoulders, glinting with gold and copper in the sunlight. Hers were such slender, delicate shoulders and her pale, ivory skin, so soft and warm to the touch of his hand. Her perfect lips, always smiling, and when they kissed... he was lifted up, beyond reality to a perfect world where only they existed. But most of all, when he looked into her eyes, he was lost. Fathoms deep, drowning in the depths of his emotion. He would never, could never give her up, whatever his father now demanded.

He had basked in the reflected glory of Elizabeth and thought himself the luckiest man alive. If her beauty was not enough, she was also a very talented pianist, drawing praise and admiration from far and wide. Stuttgart abounded in concert halls and classical music venues. Many local families nurtured budding musicians and singers. Karl played the flute passably well and had entered some of the flourishing local festivals and competitions. But compared to Elizabeth, he was a rank amateur. When she played he would close his eyes and think he was in heaven. Skilfully, her long fingers would weave their magic across the piano keys. Listening to Elizabeth play was always an ethereal experience.

She had been accepted to train at the Berlin Music Academy and fulfil her ambition to become a concert pianist. She was so looking forward to going, even though they would have been apart. That was why they had become engaged. But when Karl had visited her last week, Elizabeth was distraught. She had shown him a letter from the academy. It was curt and short, only Aryan students were being given placements; she no longer qualified.

What had been acceptable in 1932 was unacceptable now. In the space of a few short months, weeks even, the nasty little Austrian corporal was tightening his hold over Germany and its people, persecuting the so called 'enemies of the state'; aliens, gypsies, communists and Jews. How could the Ekhart family be enemies of Germany? Truer patriots could not be found. Joseph had served in the Army during the Great War as Karl's own father had done. Frau Ekhart was a writer and a Professor of European History. Elizabeth was highly regarded in local music circles. The family were lapsed, non-practising Jews. They were as German as his family were. The whole concept of anti-Semitism was barbarous and outdated. Karl had argued long and hard with his father when he had demanded he break off the engagement and his association with the Ekhart family.

Karl had shouted and stormed. "You cannot tell me what I must do. I am twenty-four and I will marry Elizabeth. You cannot stop me!"

134

His mother had wept and pleaded for them to cease shouting. Karl and Manfred had never argued before; she was bewildered and afraid. Manfred had calmed and lowered his voice. "No, my son, I cannot stop you, but I fear the State will."

"What do you mean, Father?" Karl had protested. "We are all Germans. It is not a crime to love a Jewess or to marry one. I cannot agree to end our betrothal, never!"

His father had sat down then, his shoulders hunched, his head in his hands. "Oh, my son, my son, how can I make you understand? I am not against Elizabeth or her family. It is the Jewish race itself which is in peril. If we do not follow the Nazi line, if we oppose them in any way, we also are doomed.

"You saw it for yourself last Saturday when we went to the Rally in Nuremberg: the flag waving and cheering, the singing and chanting, and then the torchlight procession. When Hitler spoke with the mass of SA men in front of him, ten thousand Germans were ready to die for him! I tell you now; Hitler is just waiting for President Hindenburg to die. When that happens, the coalition will be swept away, the National Socialists will take absolute power and we shall find out what a dictatorship really means. Then God help the Jews and the communists. In fact, God help us all."

Karl had put his arm around his father's shoulders. "We must rise up and oppose him. We cannot let him do this, Father!"

"No, no! Oh, no my son," Manfred had said, despairingly. "That would be futile and very dangerous. You can call me a hypocrite, but we have to appear to support them and keep our true beliefs hidden. We are fortunate here in Stuttgart. You and I have good jobs and are not likely to lose them. Now the rearmament process has begun, new contracts are received everyday. We must keep our heads down and look after our own interests if we are to survive."

Karl understood his father's perspective, but he was young and idealistic and he was in love with a Jewess. There had to be another way for him to make sense of this terrible situation.

"But Father, you have seen what is happening in the workshops. Seven Jewish workers were sacked today. Good men for no reason! The trade union is banned and in its place these Nazi puppets run the show with their endless stream of propaganda and anthems over the loud speakers. They worship Hitler like a god and demand we all do the same. Is there nothing we can do to stop this madness?"

"There is nothing." Manfred had raised his hands in an empty gesture, saying, "If we speak out against them, we will be sent to the concentration camps or killed."

Karl knew in his heart that his father was right. Manfred was a good man and a good Christian. He was a patriot and could see through the Nazi propaganda to its real objectives and those of its fanatical leader. Outright opposition would be suicide. Many had already tried and paid the price.

At work today Karl had been summoned to the Manager's office to be told that he had been selected to work with a new development team on a project for the Zeppelin Corporation. They wanted diesel engines for the new airship, and had put the contract out to tender. It would be a sister ship to the 'Graf Zeppelin' and fly the world. It was very important work and the company were well placed to win the contract. To be on the team, Karl would have to be cleared by the Nazi run Trustee Council. That would be impossible unless he did as his father said and ended the engagement to his beloved Elizabeth.

By the time he had crossed the northwest corner of the city and climbed the hill to Weissenhof to reach Elizabeth's house, Karl's heart was heavy. He looked back down the hill. From here he could see right across the city. Beautiful Stuttgart, the only home he had ever known. How could these vile people invade his perfect world and take away his happiness? He was being torn apart, for he wanted to follow his father's wishes to keep himself and his family safe, but now he also had a duty to stay by Elizabeth's side, *regardless of the consequences. There surely had to be another way, the Nazis could not hold all the cards.*

He stood on the pavement as the growing dusk enveloped the houses, and lights began to glow from windows and street lamps. The Ekharts' garden was magnificent, with elegant iron gates and ornamental railings at the boundary. A red quarry tile path led up to the big oak front door. Still visible in the twilight were the sunken lawns on either side, their slopes bursting with summer blooms and alpine rockery plants.

Standing in the half light, he listened as Elizabeth began playing the piano. He was transfixed as the haunting melody of Beethoven's Moonlight Sonata reached out to him. The notes cascaded down from the upper balcony window. Rising and falling like a mountain spring, it washed over him, gathering speed, taking on a life of its own. Deepening – widening – until it was like a river. Drowning him emotionally and carrying him away. Tonight, her playing reflected the deep sorrow in his heart. But in his mind, the answer to his dilemma was beginning to form. He must persuade her to leave Germany and then find a way to follow.

The piano fell silent and looking up he saw Elizabeth on the balcony. She waved and called to him. "Where have you been, Karl? We were so worried. You must come in quickly, my love."

Karl glanced up and down the street, checking for watchers, then hurried to the front door where Elizabeth came out to greet him. She was flustered and anxious and taking his hand, led him round the side to the rear garden. "We can talk in the summer house," she whispered. "No one will hear us there."

They hurried to the wooden circular house which was half-hidden by flowering shrubs and bushes in the centre of the garden. They climbed the steps to a little veranda and fell into each other's arms. Both were desperate for the love and reassurance which only the physical presence of the other could give. In that moment Karl knew he could never, ever forsake her; he loved her too much.

137

"Oh, my dear Karl," she began. "You look very serious. Are things so bad? Tell me quickly. We have not been out all week, even Papa. It is not safe."

Karl held her close, breathing in the sweet smell of her hair, her skin. He gently kissed her forehead, her cheeks and then her lips. Tracing his fingers across her face, down her neck, then gripping her shoulders tightly he looked into her beautiful, aquamarine eyes.

She smiled at him, though her face glistened, wet with tears. "My poor Karl, tell me what is happening," she said. He marvelled that she thought only of him.

"It is you who are in peril, my darling," he said, "you and your family. Every day the situation becomes worse. You should all leave Germany as soon as possible. All Jews should do so before it is too late."

Elizabeth shook her head; she was puzzled and confused by Karl's words. "Oh, no, Karl, Papa says he has seen it all before. There have always been times when anti-Jewish feeling runs high. It will die down again. You must not worry so much, we will be all right."

Karl was at a loss to explain what he had witnessed over the last few days. He looked up to where stars were beginning to emit tiny pinpricks of light as the sky turned from blue to deep violet. How he wished they could be up there instead of here on earth, faced with this terrible nightmare. He tried again to persuade her.

"This is not like the other times, you must understand. There are speeches and rallies every day. Hitler is allowing his Storm Troopers to run riot. Jews are being hounded out of their jobs and their homes, beaten, and killed. Others are being arrested and taken to the concentration camps." He pleaded, "You must leave now. It is no longer safe here."

Elizabeth stepped back out of his embrace, clearly alarmed. "Leave Germany and our home. Leave you? How can you say such a thing?" She looked bewildered, and tears began to stream down her face. "It cannot be so bad, it cannot."

Karl wiped her tears with his handkerchief. He wanted to take away the pain she was feeling, for he felt it also. "I don't want you to go. I love you. But I want you to be safe. Wherever you go, I will follow as soon as I can. We will be together then, forever. Please believe me."

Elizabeth began to cry in earnest and they clung together once more, neither able to speak. After a while she looked up and he met her eyes, eyes that would always hold him spellbound.

"You say you love me, Karl."

"I do," he answered tenderly.

"Tell me how much you love me."

"I love you more than life itself. But I want us both to live, to be safe and stay together forever."

Elizabeth's face brightened. "Then we have nothing to fear, my Karl."

"Nothing?" he asked. Elizabeth pressed his hand between her own two hands. He looked down at her engagement ring which he had given her with such pride and hope for their future life together.

"Nothing to fear," she repeated. She spoke in a whisper, yet her voice was strident, excited even, "Perfect love casts out fear. We have perfect love, so whatever happens now you and I will always be together, I am not afraid anymore."

He thought how very brave she was, even though her life was in danger. In her own special way and with her cheerful optimism she had brought calm, joy even, back into their lives. In spite of himself and the fact that their whole world seemed about to be destroyed, a feeling of hope began to seep back into his heart.

Yes, they had perfect love and nothing would ever come between them. He would have to plan and to scheme, but they would escape and be together always.

CHAPTER FIFTEEN

FINDING ELIZABETH

London, England, December 1999

If Jonno had any belief in the theory of the parallel universe, here was the proof. During the hypnosis, the window between his conscious mind and his subconscious mind opened. Under the guidance of his skilled therapist, piece by piece, the details of another person's life flowed into his consciousness. Throughout, he was also aware of his surroundings in the Wembley clinic and the sound of Tony's clear, warm voice.

"Who are you?" the voice began.

"I am Karl Stockhausen." Details were clearer now; he had remembered his second name.

"Hello, Karl. Where are you?"

"I am crossing the city."

"What city?"

"Stuttgart, I am walking to my fiancée's home."

"You are engaged, how wonderful."

"It was wonderful, but now I am very unhappy."

"What is her name?"

"Elizabeth Ekhart, she is the most beautiful and wonderful girl in the world." He spoke with a true depth of feeling. "I will love her for eternity."

"Then why are you sad?" Tony continued to probe every answer for more clues.

"She is a Jewess. My father demands I end our engagement." Now there was pain and anger in his voice.

Tony spoke again, "What will you do?"

"I don't know what to do. I have reached her home now. I can hear Elizabeth playing the piano. Listen, does she not play magnificently?"

Tony could hear nothing, but he answered, "Wonderful! What does Elizabeth do?"

"She was a music student. She was going to Berlin to study, but they have cancelled her place."

"Why?"

"Because she is Jewish." His voice sounded very bitter. "Hitler is evil. I hate him!"

"You are in a very difficult situation, Karl."

"I have to deal with it; I will find a solution, for Elizabeth's sake." Jonno was becoming restless and uneasy.

"You must rest now," said Tony. He stopped the questioning and motioned to Lisa not to speak, but he left his tape recorder running. After a few minutes he woke Jonno from his trance. "One, two, three, wake up Jonno."

When he opened his eyes, he didn't speak but lay on the couch blinking and in deep thought. He turned his head and looked at Lisa. Tony went over to a side table and poured coffee from his ever-hot percolator, and he set the tray on a low table beside them.

Jonno sat up and drank the coffee gratefully. He continued to look at Lisa as though he was seeing her for the first time. "Do you remember when we first met," he said. "I was sure we had met before; that you reminded me of someone else?"

"Yes, I do," she answered.

He lowered his voice and looked away. "It was Elizabeth," he said softly, as if he could not quite believe it himself. "If I am …was, this man Karl, then you must have been the girl Elizabeth."

Lisa looked alarmed and deferred to Tony. "Surely that's not possible – is it?"

Tony spread his hands as if to calm a possible conflict. "Remember," he said, "we are not dealing with what is or is not possible. I have to analyse anything which is causing stress or anxiety emerging from Jonno's subconscious thoughts. I have to help him resolve all these problems and clear his mind." He sat back and sipped his coffee, and then he continued.

"To answer your question, Lisa, group-soul reincarnation has been well documented over centuries. In many Indian religions and others, it is considered quite normal. Souls enter new lives in pairs or as a group. They work out their Karma together, repairing harm and paying back debts from previous lives. They believe souls are eternal and grow towards perfection through reincarnation. Many eminent psychologists have also written about group-soul reincarnation."

"But what about you? Do you believe it?" Lisa said earnestly.

Tony laughed. "I learned to suspend my beliefs a long time ago. None of what I do using hypnosis has any scientific basis, and is therefore, contrary to all my medical training. But I never cease to be amazed by what can emerge under its influence and, used as a therapy, the fact is – it works!

"In Jonno's case, we must accept all the facts that come forward during these sessions. Hopefully, we will follow Karl and Elizabeth's story to its conclusion. Then perhaps Jonno will find a resolution. Closure on a troubled past should give closure to his troubled present."

Jonno had been listening to Tony and Lisa's conversation, but he was still deep in thought.

Tony spoke to him again. "How do you feel about Karl now?"

Jonno sighed deeply. "This time I felt a strong empathy with him, I sensed his emotions. I felt his love for Elizabeth and his pain at their situation."

"And Elizabeth, what was she like?"

Jonno looked at Lisa again. "It's not exactly a physical resemblance. She is small with darker hair, but her eyes, she has Lisa's eyes. I knew instantly she is Lisa."

Tony continued with his questions. "What does Karl look like?"

"I think he is fair, his skin is much lighter than mine. In the workshop he wore a brown coat, an overall. But today he was dressed in good clothes, a suit of dark checked wool and a white shirt."

"Do you remember anything else?" asked Tony.

Jonno closed his eyes and thought hard. "I had been running. When I stopped, I was very hot and short of breath."

"Do you know why you ran?"

Jonno seemed unaware that his recall had slipped into the first person and that Tony had followed his lead.

During the next hour Tony continued to interrogate Jonno intently on everything he could remember. More and more details emerged. So much, it was unthinkable not to accept that this was a true account of events from over sixty years ago. Tony's tape recorder had captured every word and by the time Lisa and Jonno eventually left the clinic, they had been with Tony for most of the day.

Tony was going over to the States for Christmas and the extended Millennium break. Jonno did not know where he would be in January so there was a question mark over when the therapy could continue. But the days flashed past with work and preparations for the holiday. At Marham he had been assigned to helping with preparations for a Millennium party to be held on the airbase.

Two days before Christmas a letter arrived for him at Greengate Lodge. The envelope stood out from the wedge of family Christmas cards. It was the official confirmation of his award. His current situation had no bearing on his past achievement. But because of current commitments in Iraq, details of the award ceremony would not be known until after the New Year. The letter however, did not invoke the sense of pride in him it might once have done. At the moment, this particular hero was feeling anything but brave.

When Christmas Eve dawned, Lisa was still in London finishing her Millennium feature for the paper. Jonno awaited her arrival anxiously but it was evening before she was free and able to drive up to Norfolk. She arrived at Greengate Lodge around eight-thirty to be with him for the extended holiday.

On Christmas morning he was delighted to see her revel in the luxury of his family's traditional Christmas. From the holly boughs in the porch to the fairy on top of the six foot pine tree in the lounge, thanks to Kathryn, every detail was perfect. Even Paul's brief visit had revealed a courteous, bountiful side to his personality; full of charm and presents for all.

"There you are," Lisa commented to Jonno. "Even Paul can be a perfect gentleman on Christmas Day."

Jonno checked his watch and smiled. "That's because it's only twelve-thirty. Give him time and a few jugs at 'The Stag' and then hope he doesn't come back." He didn't, and Jonno couldn't help feeling glad.

Early on Boxing Day morning Lisa and Jonno drove to her family home at Stratford-on-Avon. It was the first time he had been invited to meet her parents and she had warned him that it would not be like Greengate.

Mr and Mrs Hartnell greeted them like visiting strangers. They were charming and overly polite to Jonno. The house was full of Dresden china and wool carpets. Original paintings by little known artists adorned the walls and the cutlery was all monogrammed, polished silver. Jonno was treated to a conducted tour, proudly undertaken by Lisa's mother, Myra.

"Does your Mother collect art, Johnathon?" she asked him after reeling off the pedigree of a fourth original work.

Jonno smiled politely, "My grandfather has two watercolours of the Battle of Britain," he said. "But he, of course, took part in the real thing."

"Oh!" said Myra, "how interesting."

She moved on to give more details of uninteresting pieces of china, apparently unaware of the irony in Jonno's words. He was thankful when Lisa reappeared to rescue him from her mother's clutches.

Sherry was served before dinner and Jonno began to realise this was not laid on for his benefit. Life in this sterile family home was always like this. After dinner, Lisa's school certificates and photographs were brought out in two perfectly assembled leather-bound albums. She squirmed with embarrassment as her mother regaled all her achievements up until she went to work away from home.

"Of course, we were very disappointed Lisa did not go to Oxford. Her father was at Oxford, you know. Tell Johnathon about Oxford, George."

Myra raised her voice to her husband in a commanding manner. Jonno caught Lisa's expression as she rolled her eyes up to the ceiling and sighed.

"Yes, Balliol College, remarkable place Oxford. I rowed you know." It was the first time George had spoken for himself.

Jonno felt desperately sorry for Lisa. Her parents did not seem to appreciate their talented daughter. He felt compelled to speak up for her. "But of course she has an excellent career now. You must be very proud of her."

Myra Hartnell looked bemused. "You mean as a newspaper reporter." she said disparagingly.

"Your daughter, Mrs Hartnell, is a top features writer with a very influential Sunday newspaper. You could say she is one of the country's leading journalists." Lisa dug him in the ribs and he moved out of her reach. He may have overstated Lisa's exact position in the journalistic hierarchy, but Myra's conception of what her daughter did was very much understated.

In spite of the distance, Lisa insisted they drive back to Norfolk that night. Once in the car, he could sense her relief.

"Why do you let them undervalue what you do?" he asked. "I'm very proud of you and so should they be."

"They stopped being proud when I refused to go to Uni. Then when I moved away from home I ceased to exist; their child Lisa was a different person."

Driving in the dark, Jonno could hear the emotional bubble in her voice. He thought about Kathryn. Her relationship with her children was always much more important than what they did.

"Now you know why I don't go home unless I have to," she said, as if closing the door on their visit.

"Well, I hope you and I will be more considerate towards our children when the time comes." This new train of thought seemed to take her by surprise and lift her spirits.

She leaned over and kissed him on the cheek. "When will that be?" she asked coquettishly.

"Whenever you want," he answered, smiling to himself in the dark.

CHAPTER SIXTEEN

MILLENNIUM

An aura of anticipation surrounded the Amis family as they set out for the Millennium party at the airbase. Lisa had been at the heart of the media hype that had whipped the general public up into a frenzy of expectation. As she sat in the back of the Volvo she could not help also feeling a little uneasy about the forthcoming celebrations.

Marham's 'B' hangar had been transformed and she had been relieved to know Jonno had something to do after his weeks of boredom as he had pitched in with the preparations. The main area of the hangar was decked out with flags and bunting, and a Glenn Miller tribute band was already in full swing as they found their way to their reserved table. Outside, a spectacular display of pyrotechnics was to take place at midnight. It was this part of the night's celebrations that was giving rise to Lisa's disquiet. When Jonno's sick leave status had been replaced with 'light duties', he had settled in well. She was anxious to keep him away from the flash points which might trigger another bad experience.

The band had jazzed up the quickstep rhythm and several dance fanatics were already on the floor giving an exhibition of swing and jive. Lisa was enthralled as the men threw the girls over their heads and between their legs, twirling and twisting in circles. More and more couples took to the floor with less energetic versions and when the tempo slowed down, she and Jonno joined in. It was the first time they had danced together and it was wonderful to find how easily they moved to the music, so comfortable together in each other's arms.

"Where did you learn to dance so well?" she asked as he held her close, dancing cheek to cheek.

He laughed, "Life in the RAF is not just learning to fly you know."

Lisa relaxed, happy to be with the man she loved on this special night. The dance band stepped up the tempo once more and Lisa could see Sarah and Max laughing and clapping to the music. She realised that not only did she love Jonno, she loved the whole family; except perhaps Paul, although even he had his good points.

Kathryn was constantly meeting and greeting old friends and being asked to dance by male admirers. A sudden thought came to Lisa. "Why has Kathryn never remarried?" she asked Jonno. "She is a very attractive lady."

"I asked her the same question once," he said as they continued to dance round the floor. "See that chap she's dancing with now." Jonno turned so that Lisa could see his mother and her partner. The man looked like a younger version of Max: tall, greying and immaculately dressed. "That's Ian Walters, his wife died about six years ago. He's asked Mum several times to marry him," Jonno confided.

"Do you think she ever will?" Lisa asked him.

"I, for one, hope she does," he whispered as they danced. "Now Sarah has flown the nest, there's only Max, and then what for Mum?"

Lisa couldn't answer that question but she felt a surge of love and admiration for her future mother-in-law.

The band played on and the evening hummed along in true RAF party style towards the midnight hour. The serious drinkers hugged the bar while the serious dancers hogged the floor. But the majority were happy to enjoy a little of both and watch the other two groups drink and dance to oblivion.

Lisa and Jonno were not really surprised when Paul suddenly put in an appearance, for he was always turning up unexpectedly. Remembering her promise to Sarah, Lisa greeted him warmly as a brother. He briefly paid his respects to all of them and then disappeared again in the direction of the bar.

As midnight approached, the band leader started the count down for the final minute of the century. The family joined hands with those around them, even Max was on his feet. By the time they had counted down to 'ten', the hangar echoed with stamping feet and clapping hands as the last few seconds of 1999 ticked away.

As the first chime of twelve rang out for the year 2000, pandemonium broke loose as the party-goers went wild, drowning out the rest of the chimes. They cheered and screamed. Hooters, horns and whistles blew. People sang and kissed and hugged. Emotions ran like an electric current round the hangar. The family wrapped themselves together in a loving rugby scrum, tears mingling with the laughter. Paul was nowhere to be seen.

The loud retort of a fire cracker signalled the start of the firework display outside and everyone surged towards the entrance as the big doors were opened. It was a damp but mild night for the time of year, but nothing could suppress the charged excitement of the Marham crowd. Lisa clung tightly to Jonno's hand, determined they would stay together.

The display began with bursts of leaping flame and colour. Multicoloured glittering stars flew into the night sky, cascading back down. Each loud eruption and burst of new colour was greeted with more cheers. Lisa thought about the spectacular Rhine fireworks and Jonno's bad reaction. The noise grew deafening as the spectacle became bigger and brighter.

The chatter-chatter of automatic small arms fire, interspersed with the resounding boom of the cannon – the whizzing and cracking of grenades and rifle shots – all perfectly mimicking the sounds of a battle. If Jonno's condition was combat related this could provide the trigger. Even the smell of gunpowder hung in the air and assaulted her nose with its unique acidic odour.

But none of these associations appeared to cause Jonno any distress. She looked up into his face as he pulled her closer to him. He was laughing and perfectly relaxed. The display moved to a large backdrop on scaffolds with cleverly constructed tableaux. A

Spitfire waggled its wings before burning out; an RAF badge all in blue light; then a huge volley of rockets shot up into the sky, releasing showers of coloured stars in overlapping cascades; the thunder claps were deafening. Lisa wrapped her arms around Jonno even tighter. She was so relieved that he was showing no signs of distress; this really was a turning point.

The final display was for the millennium. The number 2000 appeared in changing colours surrounded by a blitz of star fountains and thunder crackers. Another volley of multicoloured rockets with ear splitting bomb blasts signalled the end of the display.

As the crowd dispersed, Jonno helped his grandfather to his feet. Max had thoroughly enjoyed himself, but he was obviously very tired.

"I think I'd like to go home now, would you mind, son?" Jonno was the designated driver for the evening and had not drunk any alcohol.

"Me, too," said Kathryn. "It's been a wonderful evening, but I'm bushed."

"No problem," said Jonno. He kissed Lisa and said, "Stay with Sarah; I'll only be ten minutes."

She wanted to go with him but Sarah was already dragging her back towards the party where loud, thumping disco music had taken over from the dance band. Arm in arm, the two girls hurried back inside. They were cold from standing around and the disco rhythms beckoned them on to the floor. After boogieing along to their favourite dance tracks for sometime, they were soon over-warm, and made their way towards the bar. They joined the crush of bodies queuing to be served.

"Hello, gorgeous." The drunken voice came from behind Lisa. She knew it was Paul even before she turned round. She tried to move away but he caught hold of her arm and she couldn't move.

"How about… a New Year kiss… for your to-be brother-in-law, lovely, luscious Lisa." He slurred the words and his eyes were glassy.

The space around the bar area was very congested and he was breathing alcohol fumes in her face. Her back was against a wall and as Paul pushed himself closer to her, she felt trapped and claustrophobic. She looked round frantically for Sarah, but she had moved down the bar out of sight. Before Lisa had a chance to speak or shout, Paul clamped his hot wet mouth over hers and held both her arms in a vicelike grip. She tried to move her legs to knee him or stamp on his foot, but he pressed his hot clammy body against hers, pinning her to the wall.

Shocked and overwhelmed by his audacity and strength, anger boiled up inside her. She twisted her head violently to escape his lips slobbering over her. Now she could breathe again, she started to struggle and shout, "Get away from me, Paul, you're drunk!" She tried to push him away, using the wall to lever herself out of his grasp.

Suddenly Paul was ripped away from her and spun around. Relief turned to fear as a fist smashed into Paul's face. It was Jonno's fist. His eyes were blazing, his face contorted with anger. A red welt arose across Paul's mouth and blood dripped from a split in his bottom lip.

Horrified, Lisa pushed between them shouting, "No!" to Jonno.

Paul's retaliatory swing caught her in the back and she fell against Jonno. Timely intervention from Sarah defused the brothers' anger as she threw the two glasses of cold water she was carrying in Paul's face.

Lisa was winded, but continued to push Jonno away from the conflict, leaving Sarah to deal with Paul. Lisa didn't stop until she had managed to pull Jonno outside into the cold night air. If it became obvious a fight had broken out, both brothers could spend the rest of the night in the cooler and then face charges. It was a prospect neither could afford.

Lisa's happy New Year had been swept away. She pushed him into the shadows and threw her arms round him as if to hide him from view. Tears of despair rolled down her cheeks. "Why did you do that? He's your brother for God's sake! I could have handled him." Lisa's mind was in turmoil, trying to comprehend the possible ramifications from what had happened.

Jonno held on to her and closed his eyes. He was shaking and his face was full of anguish. "I swear I did not know it was Paul until after I hit him!"

Lisa was taken aback. "Who the devil did you think it was?"

He closed his eyes again, "I saw you grappling with a man in uniform, a stranger. It was a gut reaction to save you. I didn't think!"

Lisa was finding this difficult to take in, but Jonno's face bore the same expression it had on the night in Germany when he swore he saw Lisa in the flames of the bonfire; now it was all happening again. The jagged edge of fear cut into her, tearing at her hopes for a settled future. Perhaps Jonno was right after all and there was no cure for him. She looked at him in disbelief. "Jonno, Paul wasn't in uniform tonight!"

CHAPTER SEVENTEEN

HARD HATS AND HELIUM

Cardington, Bedfordshire, January 2000

It was one week later when Flight Lieutenant Johnathon Amis left Marham Airbase with his project in the bag. The sky was a pallid shade of January grey and the icy north wind held the promise of snow – a reflection of Jonno's mood.

To have been entrusted with an assignment off base was a step in the right direction, but the nature of the job seemed mundane. It was a routine administrative task and had nothing to do with supersonic jets. He was going to Cardington airfield in Bedfordshire. Not to the RAF Station, which was on wind-down to close in a couple of months, his point of contact was with a private company housed in part of the old airship hangars. It rankled with him that he might still be sidelined away from his beloved Tornados. In a phone conversation he had voiced his concerns to Lisa.

"Beggars can't be choosers," she had replied testily, and he had realised she was running out of patience. She was right of course, he was begging, but for his old job back, his chosen career as a Tornado navigator.

When Lisa had gone back to London after the holiday, she had assured him everything was fine, but Jonno knew it was not. His run in with Paul after the Millennium party at Marham airbase had upset Lisa. He cursed his impulsiveness, yet he could still see the dark image of the stranger in uniform forcing his attentions on her. He could even visualise the outline of an officer's peaked cap.

He had promised Lisa and Sarah that he would apologise to Paul, but so far he had been denied the opportunity for his brother had not been back home. Yesterday he'd left a message of regret on Paul's mobile voice mail. Also, at the girls' insistence, Kathryn and Max had been kept in the dark about the whole unfortunate incident. Jonno could think of a lot of places he would rather be going to than his intended destination, for Paul was in Bedfordshire and his base was close by.

Many people were still on holiday and the traffic was light as he drove across country via Kings Lynn and Peterborough, then down the A1 to south of Bedford. Cardington seemed to be in the middle of nowhere. In this huge, flat area of countryside the two giant sheds could be seen for miles, dwarfing everything else in the vicinity. They were old and ugly, like the abandoned relics from a race of giants, but their vast height and enormous length ensured they were constantly in demand by those who, over the years, wanted to relive the dream and perfect the technology of airship travel. Currently, a company called LTA Limited were operating from the number one shed. Jonno had to make contact with their head honcho, Hugh Charlton.

From the brief outline he had been given by the Marham Station Commander, Hugh Charlton had assembled a group of very competent and experienced engineers, who had now evolved a revolutionary airship design. LTA – Lighter Than Air – to give its full title, had approached the Ministry of Defence with a paper outlining potential military applications for their giant cargo airships.

Jonno's brief was to carry out an initial survey of the set up at Cardington. Any private company seeking to do business with the MOD had to jump and squeeze through a lot of hoops. While the top brass at Whitehall deliberated over whether there was any future in the whole concept, the RAF had been charged with assessing the integrity of the company on the ground. Everything had to conform to stringent military requirements. Jonno's report would form only a very small part of the decision making process, but if his ticks were in the wrong boxes they didn't stand a chance.

Entering the airfield, he passed through two checkpoints. Both were manned by armed RAF sentries. Jonno parked the Marham pool car and, braving the cold wind, he walked towards the number one shed. Up close, the towering structures were even more overpowering. One side of the vast door had been rolled open about twelve feet and seemed to be the only entrance. Two men were entering the shed ahead of him. One wore dark overalls, the other was in a distinctive white lab coat; he caught up with them.

"Excuse me!" he called out and they turned around. "I'm looking for Hugh Charlton." The two men exchanged furtive glances, and then the man in overalls walked away.

"See you later, Charlie, good luck," he said over his shoulder. The man in the white coat then spoke. "I'm Hugh Charlton," he said holding out his hand. He was shorter than Jonno, a slightly stocky man of about forty-five with sandy coloured hair and blue-grey eyes. Jonno responded immediately, sensing a warm sincerity in his firm handshake.

"Everyone here calls me Charlie," he added smiling. Now it was Jonno's turn.

"Flight Lieutenant Johnathon Amis," he said. "I think you are expecting me."

Jonno presented his credentials and a copy of the letter telling Hugh Charlton of his visit.

"I certainly am, Flight Lieutenant." He glanced at the letter. "Well, where would you like to begin?"

Jonno's brief case was bulging with the paper work that had to be filled in for the survey. "Perhaps we should put our heads together and work out a schedule for the week," he said, not wishing to appear officious.

"That's fine by me," said Hugh Charlton. "Come inside," and he led the way into the shed.

Jonno looked around him. The all steel structure towered a hundred and fifty feet over his head. The metallic canopy creaked and groaned and the early morning light chinked through rows of high windows facing east. The long sides sloped inward and above this, the top section of the building sat like an arc, holding the eight hundred foot apex roof expanse without central supports. The dim, far end of the shed seemed to disappear into a dark tunnel. There was a lot of activity down one side where people were working in groups of two or three. Any sounds they made seemed absorbed into the vast empty, cathedral like void above them.

Jonno's eyes were drawn to the central space about fifty feet away where two fully inflated airships were hovering just a few feet from the ground. The largest, which he estimated to be about a hundred feet long, was a conventional grey blimp, of the shape Jonno had seen many times, with the gondola for pilot and passengers under the long belly. It was tethered by lines, fore and aft, to two blue tractor units; it drifted to and fro in the draft from the open door.

The second, he took to be a scale model. It was less than half the length of the other craft, but of a completely different design. As they drew nearer he could see the hull was very wide, like two ships moulded together. The outer covering was brilliant white and with fins to the rear and slit windows to the front it seemed alive. When they were level to the airship, Charlie stopped.

"What do you think of our baby 'Sky Lark'?" he asked Jonno.

"Very impressive," Jonno replied. He wanted to ask a lot of questions but felt this was not the right moment, so he said, "I think this week will be extremely interesting Mr Charlton."

"Oh, it will be," said Hugh Charlton, as they continued walking across the vast open space. "But please, call me Charlie."

He led Jonno over to the working area and they eventually sat at a desk by the work benches.

"I do have an office outside in one of the old buildings," said Charlie. "But I spend most of my time in here. We work as a team, so I have to be where the action is."

"How many employees do you have?" Jonno felt this was a good place to start and shuffled through his papers looking for the relevant documents.

"These guys are not all employees as such," said Charlie. "Five of us are shareholders; we own the Company. Then there's my secretary and PA, Alison Lomax and a further fifty employees on the permanent payroll." Flicking through the paperwork Jonno began to realise the enormity of his task.

Charlie seemed to understand his dilemma. "I've a copy of our Company report and balance sheet here," he said, waving an impressive folder in the air. "It will answer a lot of your questions and it details our 'Sky Whale' project."

"Ah, thank you, that's excellent," said Jonno, taking the folder, somewhat relieved.

"Now, I think I'll introduce you to Alison," said Charlie, "She can give you all the background information. Tomorrow you and I can start on the technical stuff," and he led the way back out of the shed.

Alison was probably in her mid thirties, small and neat, wearing a black trouser suit. Her short dark hair fell around her face in perfect symmetry. Merry eyes sparkled as they darted between Jonno's face and the papers on the desk. Her accent told him she was a Scot with the sweet intonation of a Highlander. After Charlie had made the introductions he seemed to hover by the door. In a brief exchange between him and Alison, they were not so much hawk and dove but more like a pair of matched song birds. On the pegs in Alison's office hung a yellow oilskin coat and a hard hat. Jonno felt she would willingly don either in the course of working for Charlie, for there seemed to be a rather special relationship between them.

"Right," said Alison after a brief look through the paper work. "How about we go through each section and answer the straight forward ones? Then we can make notes of the sections needing further information."

"That's fine," said Jonno, "but I will have to go back to the shed, and I need to take some photographs." Alison and Charlie looked at each other as though they had known this would be the case.

"Young man," Charlie said with, Jonno thought, a measure of emotion. "You can ask anything, photograph anything, and you can even fly anything! This MOD contract represents my life's work." He paused and looked despairingly at Jonno.

"Without it," he shrugged his shoulders with an empty hands' gesture, "well, at best we would have to move the project abroad, and at worst, LTA will go under. We can't continue without more funding."

Jonno felt moved by Charlie's little speech but knew he must remain impartial. He glanced up at both of them. "Let's hope I am able to give a good report on the work you are doing," he said trying to sound upbeat. "I'm not here to cause you any problems, quite the reverse."

Charlie laughed, and the tension was broken. "No, of course you're not," he said. "I'll leave you in Alison's capable hands." He went to the door, then he hesitated again.

"Coming to the pub tonight, Allie?"

"Of course," she answered. "Six o'clock, if we're finished here." She turned to Jonno. "Would you care to join us, Flight Lieutenant? We go every night, just for half an hour."

"Thanks for asking," said Jonno. "Maybe another night, I have yet to book into my hotel in Bedford." Jonno would have liked to join them, but knew that at this stage he should keep his distance. Equally, he did not want to offend them, so he added. "But please, you must both call me Jonno, and then we'll all be on first name terms."

The week progressed much better than Jonno could have envisaged, opening his eyes to a world of flight which had largely passed him by during his career. Consequently, his respect for Charlie and his team grew daily.

By day three he began to realise there was a special relationship between everyone at LTA. He had experienced it himself in the RAF during active service – the unique undercurrent of enthusiasm and cooperation which bonded teams involved in a project – one that they all passionately believed would be a success.

Charlie had explained to him that the small profit from the CR15, the conventional blimp already in production, albeit with a small order book, was currently providing the funds to develop their exciting main project, 'Sky Whale'. Jonno had been researching everything he could find about airships, ancient and modern. He absorbed technical details like blotting paper. Being up to date had always given him an edge in his work – that was until now. Now he felt cut off from his own project and his personal data bank was quickly becoming out of date.

'Sky Whale' intrigued him. He had gleaned from LTA's Company Report that two airships were planned for the series. 'Sky Whale' would be over 1,000 feet long and carry 1,000 tons. A smaller version, dubbed 'Sky Dolphin', would be 200 feet long, a mere one fifth the size of its big sister. The 'Sky Lark' was purely a prototype, but at fifty feet long it would no doubt also act as the PR model for the whole series.

This morning the temperature had dropped, but so had the wind. The sky was clear blue and the sun shone brilliantly, transforming Cardington airfield and the surrounding countryside into something more like an English heaven. With the advantage of good light, Jonno was taking his photographs. Firstly of the outside area and then inside shed number one. Charlie watched him, not intrusively, but ready to answer his questions.

Jonno moved to the best angle to photograph the 'Sky Lark' and looked through the viewfinder. "She looks like a child's toy in this huge space," he commented to Charlie.

"She is a toy!" was Charlie's retort. "But she is in the best traditions of project development. Scale models always precede grand inventions, particularly very big ones." He laughed loudly and continued, "The Titanic started life in a tin bath. You should know that!"

Jonno did, and he laughed with Charlie. They both knew only too well the old maxim that there were no icebergs in the tin bath. He had a lot of questions of his own to ask outside the brief of his survey, so he seized the opportunity. "I understand the Germans are working on their own giant airship at the moment. Is this a race?"

"The only race is to obtain funding from various Governments," said Charlie. "There are currently two German companies working on heavy lifting airships. You could also say they are ahead of us in the race. They both have airships the size of 'Sky Dolphin' up and flying, but I'm not worried by them."

"Why not?" Jonno was curious to know why Charlie seemed so confident and what was so special about 'Sky Whale'?

"I'll tell you," said Charlie. "Basically, they are putting new wine in old bottles. They have modern materials, state of the art construction facilities, computer technology and inert helium, everything that should make their projects successful. They are better funded than we are, but they have overlooked one thing." Charlie paused dramatically.

"What is that?" Jonno asked.

"Design!" Charlie pointed to the 'Sky Lark' floating on its mooring ropes. "Their designs use the same technology that we abandoned after the R101 crashed in 1930! The Germans themselves abandoned rigid airships after Hindenburg in 1937. Now they are still stuck in the same old groove of rigid and semi-rigid designs."

"What's wrong with the old designs?" Jonno wanted to hear Charlie's explanation.

"They're totally inflexible!" He obviously held very strong views on the subject. "Looking at the applications for which airships are best suited today, the old designs are seriously compromised." Charlie led the way over to 'Sky Lark'. "We looked at every advantage a modern heavy lifting airship would have over other forms of transport. Very large cargo capacity; cheap running costs; faster than sea transport. Every possible application we could envisage was ruled out using the old designs."

"Why's that?" asked Jonno, leading him on.

"Because they need costly facilities at each end of the journey; hangars, masts, men. Lots of men to assist with landing and take off."

"And 'Sky Whale' doesn't?" Jonno questioned.

"'Sky Whale' doesn't." Charlie's version was a statement. "She doesn't need a shed, she doesn't need a mast. She doesn't even need men on the ground except from the crew she carries. She can land anywhere in the world, any terrain, even on water."

Jonno smiled to himself at Charlie's obvious pride in what had become his life's work. "When can I see it in action?" he asked. Viewing a test flight was part of Jonno's brief for the survey.

"Weather permitting, twelve noon tomorrow. It should be just right for best test conditions. She will be flying remotely, so you can monitor her and us at the same time."

"I'll certainly look forward to that, thanks, Charlie," Jonno called out as they both moved off to continue the day's work and make their separate preparations for the forthcoming test flight.

That night, at the hotel, Jonno had another nightmare. He awoke with a sudden jolt, roused out of the burning wall of death by a terrible scream, probably his own. He lay shaking and sweating in the strange room, trying to get a grip on himself. He listened, wondering if anyone had heard and might come to the room. As the minutes ticked by and no one did, he breathed a sigh of relief and began to think more deeply about what he had just experienced.

This had now been going on for months. The regression therapy had, so far, not had any effect on his night traumas and he was disappointed. What it had done was raise a lot of questions. Now he wanted to find some answers.

The regression had revealed the life of a young German man in nineteen thirty-three. The past life persona had no obvious connection with his life as Jonno Amis. He needed to look for parallels, points of connection. The only one to emerge so far was Lisa. He took himself back into Karl's world and thought about Elizabeth. Was she really Lisa or had his mind jumped to make that connection because Karl was in love with Elizabeth as he was in love with Lisa? Words of wisdom came to him. As if from nowhere he could hear Grandma Sadie with her little gems of Aboriginal folklore. 'The eyes are the window to the soul. Look deep into the eyes to find the one you seek.'

There was something else – a tiny tenuous connection which he had almost overlooked. The boy Karl had been selected to work on a project: diesel engines for a new German airship.

CHAPTER EIGHTEEN

'SKY LARK'

In the darkness of pre-dawn, a blanket of fog had formed over the Cardington airfield, sealing in its secrets like a closed book. When daylight began to penetrate, warm air currents created by the unseen sun metamorphosed the fog into a swirling ground mist.

As Jonno drove onto the airfield he saw the two giant sheds rising out of the gloom in the early morning light. He felt strangely excited at the prospect of witnessing the test flight. Charlie's enthusiasm was contagious and had re-awakened the boy in Jonno.

As he entered number one shed, the team members were already at work. He dispensed two coffees from the vending machine and walked over to join them.

"Ah, breakfast!" said Charlie, taking the cup from Jonno's proffered hand. They sipped the hot but indifferent brew from the paper cups.

"Are we 'on' or 'off'?" asked Jonno, for everything depended on the weather.

"Both, I hope," said Charlie with a wry smile. "The flight is certainly on, but cast-off may be delayed." He emphasised the term 'cast-off'. "Remember, she's a ship, not a plane." He started walking towards the work area. "Come and inspect the flight plan."

Jonno followed him across the hangar space, chuckling at Charlie's contradiction. After more than a hundred years, even the experts could not agree on the correct terminology for airships.

Alison had also been up bright and early and was now attaching pens to a pile of clipboards. Over several other layers of warm clothing she wore the bright yellow oilskin. The rest of the team joined them and Charlie held the pre-test briefing. Everyone had a part to play, for every aspect of the ship was still under development and needed to be evaluated. One detail, if overlooked, could abort the test and jeopardise the project. They could not afford costly errors.

By eleven o'clock the conditions were looking much more favourable and the huge shed doors were rolled back to allow the little 'Sky Lark' and her entourage to leave the giant cocoon which had been her birthplace. Now she was filled with the precious helium gas she was guided, fore and aft, by the two blue tractors. She followed, stirred only by the light breeze, to strain against her captive mooring ropes.

Out in the open she took on a different perspective. Fifty foot long and half as wide, she had been towed to the far end of the airfield, away from the sheds which dwarfed everything. Now she was the giant, rolled along by the little team of Lilliputian soldiers.

By now the sun had burned away the morning mist and the 'Sky Lark's' hull seemed filled with luminous light, glowing white in the brilliant winter sunshine. A haze still surrounded the field, partly obscuring the far hedgerows and distant landmarks. Jonno wasn't used to being a passive observer without an active role; he felt oddly disconnected.

Charlie's voice echoed across the open space. "Data recorders stand by!" His words reverberated via a megaphone. "Ground tests to commence in one minute!"

Jonno shook himself and stamped his feet, forcing his concentration back to the scene before him. He glanced at his clipboard and re-read his notes. 'Ground Test – Aircushion Landing System.' This was the most important part of today's tests. They knew the airship could fly, but holding her to the ground without the aid of men or ropes was the key to their design and development strategy.

As 'Sky Lark's' engines kicked into life, another member of the team took over the megaphone and was barking out instructions. Others were running about and had divided into two groups around the blue tractors. 'Sky Lark's' engines went into high revs and the noise level increased. She had been buffeting about like a toy balloon, now she became rigid. She rose up about two feet, as her hover aircushions extended. Two oblong platforms protruded like a pair of giant snow shoes from the underside of the flat body. The motors revved even higher as air was sucked out from inside the skirts, creating a vacuum between the ground and the ship, gripping her, limpet like, to the earth.

"Cast off!" shouted the megaphone man and the ropes were untied at the tractor ends. The two blue towing machines were then each driven a few yards away from the airship.

A spontaneous cheer went up from the dozen or so people scatted round the prototype, followed by a ripple of applause as she performed her solo party piece. Free at last of the restraining ropes, she gripped the ground with her hover skirts.

Jonno took more photographs. Unbidden thoughts entered his head and he started to think about Lisa, wondering if she was still sore with him. His efforts at damage limitation since the Millennium holiday had not had the desired effect. Their phone conversations this week had all been brief and her words had somehow lost their warm feel; he needed to made amends. Emotionally he was walking a tightrope and his safety net was fragile as gossamer.

"Stand by for lift-off!" came the shout. Everyone scattered to fulfil their given roles. Jonno moved closer to Charlie and his Design Manager, Geoff Hales. They had the remote control panel and the guy with the megaphone. The rigid skirts collapsed as the bow thrusters took control of the airship's nose. Without further assistance from men or ropes, the helium lift was allowed to take 'Sky Lark' upwards about two hundred feet. The fledgling was at last out of the nest and on the wing.

The rear engines were started-up to control the fin mechanisms, and the planned test flight manoeuvres began. The hover skirts had not fully retracted, giving the underside a ragged look. Charlie was cursing about this limiting the speed trial. He and

Geoff were deliberating on the cause and possible remedies. The tests moved on. Forward thrust; reverse thrust; wide circles; tight turns. Every possible combination of these, including the critical 210 degree turn, all executed keeping the ship in perfect trim.

From Jonno's view point, with the naked eye, the airship remained in equilibrium. Through his camera's viewfinder it was even more apparent. His skin pricked with a familiar eerie tension.

"Circle round once more!" The words echoed in his head, repeating like the cry of a carousel barker, over and over; round and round. The airship appeared to make huge circles in the sky. Faster – tighter – faster until it was spinning like a top. Jonno felt giddy and light-headed. The wind whistled in his ears like the noise in a wind tunnel. As the ground rushed towards him he thrust out his hands, dropping the camera. For a second he was stunned and then he was up, up in the sky.

'I knew I would fly again,' he thought, elated by the sensation. But this was different, he wasn't buckled in the seat of a jet, but walking, as though on solid ground; traversing a long promenade with big slanting windows. He looked down on green fields, an enormous lake and a giant hangar. There were buildings, houses, factories. Now the scene was misting over with fog. He couldn't see anything clearly but he heard a voice calling out his name, a woman's voice.

"Jonno, Jonno!" It came from far away whispering on the wind. He opened his eyes, it was Alison, and she was looking down at him. He was lying on the ground.

"What's the matter?" she said, concerned. "Are you ill? Do you need a doctor?"

He turned his head and saw the prototype was back on the ground surrounded by the team. No one else seemed to have noticed him keel over. He scrambled to his feet and retrieved his camera from where it had fallen.

"No, I'm okay," he said to Alison. "I must have tripped over and banged my head." He groaned, rubbing his forehead. "I'm so sorry, what a stupid thing to have happened. I hope I didn't interrupt the test flight?"

"Oh, Lord, no!" said Alison. "Wild horses wouldn't stop them. Are you sure you're all right? You look a bit green."

"Absolutely," he said, anxious to brush the incident aside. "I must have fallen over my feet when I looked through the viewfinder." He laughed. "I think I'll walk back to the shed and check the camera. Thanks, Alison."

With that, Jonno turned away and walked despondently back up the field. He needed to be on his own. For the first time since the incident in the Gulf, he had to face the fact that what he thought he had seen was not real. It was an illusion, just as the missiles had been an illusion. He was certain now of one thing, he must resume the therapy with Tony and the sooner the better.

His work on the survey was complete and he happily took up Alison's invitation to join them for a farewell drink on the Friday night. He liked these people; they still had a purpose, a dream. Maybe some of it had rubbed off on him, like a magic dust.

The old country pub with its low beams and smoke-yellowed ceilings, was already busy with patrons celebrating the end of the official working week. Charlie elbowed his way to the bar while Alison and Geoff took Jonno over to their table.

Alison chuckled as she removed a 'reserved' notice. "Good old Derek," she said, referring to the publican. "He always reserves our table when they're busy." Her Highland accent was like spring water trickling over stones, interspersed with splashes of laughter. They sat down. Geoff Hales had a doctorate in science and physics. Charlie had referred to him as 'the Doc', always prefacing their discussions with the catch phrase, 'What's up, Doc?'

"Work aside," Doc said to Jonno, "have you enjoyed your week with the mad airship men?" He was leaner and taller than Charlie, possibly a little older, but they were otherwise cast in the same mould and had apparently worked together for decades.

167

"Charlie promised me an interesting week and it certainly has been. I just hope you get your funding," Jonno replied.

Charlie rejoined them, carrying their drinks and settled himself between Alison and Jonno. "I suppose you are off now, back to the world of supersonic flight," said Charlie as he passed Jonno his glass.

"Actually no, just to Marham. I was wondering if I could come back here again sometime, unofficially, as a visitor?"

"Of course!" said Charlie. "Though why you'd want to trade a Tornado for an airship is beyond me."

"Hey, Charlie, don't knock it!" chipped in Doc. "Can't you see he's a convert. Welcome to the 'Worshipful Order of Airship Men', young man."

"One other favour," said Jonno as their laughter died down. "When I come, can I bring a friend, a lady friend?"

"Yes again," said Charlie, "but can I ask why you would want to?"

Jonno smiled. "My fiancée is a journalist, a features' writer. I know she would be fascinated by your project. I'm gagged under the Official Secrets Act, but you can talk to her and she might give you some PR. What do you think?"

"Sounds good to me, about a month from now would be good." As Charlie spoke, he looked at Alison and took hold of her hand. Their exchanged smiles were intimate and Jonno felt intrusive.

Doc winked at him. "Love's young dream," he said, rolling his eyes to the ceiling. "Just ignore them."

Jonno nodded his understanding, reminded he would be with Lisa the following day.

Doc continued saying, "Four weeks tomorrow we should take delivery of what will be 'Sky Dolphin One'; the fabric hull that is."

"Oh, fantastic," said Jonno. "Two hundred feet long, isn't it?"

"She is," he affirmed. "Cut and welded by a specialist producer from our own computer-aided design tapes. The manufacture alone is a mammoth task."

"What about the rest of the components?" Jonno asked.

"Everything she needs to fly will be ready," said Charlie, drawn back into the conversation.

"And it's okay if I bring Lisa with me?"

"History in the making," said Charlie dramatically. "Perfect story for a journalist."

"Let me get another round in," said Jonno, rising to his feet. "We must drink to the 'Dolphin'."

"Can't refuse that," said Doc, draining his glass.

Jonno went up to the bar and elbowed his way into a gap, waiting to catch the barman's eye. The polished mahogany bar was horseshoe shaped and a rowdy group of RAF officers were being served on the far side. As the barman moved away from them Jonno had a clear view. Eyes bored into him; it was Paul. Surprised, Jonno raised his hand to acknowledge his brother while his mind raced to work out a strategy; he didn't want a confrontation here.

Paul continued staring at him without any sign of recognition. The barman approached Jonno, blocking his view. Jonno took his drinks and returned to the table. He hoped Paul's failure to acknowledge him meant he would leave him alone.

Jonno sat down with his new friends and raised his glass, "Here's to 'Sky Dolphin', and all who fly in her."

"Sail in her," corrected Charlie, and they raised their glasses, laughing at the same old joke.

"What brings you to Bedford, little brother?" Paul's voice cut across the conversation from behind Jonno. His hopes at avoidance were dashed. As always, Paul had him at a disadvantage. However he answered, he knew Paul would try to make a fool of him.

To avoid the direct question, Jonno said to the others, "This is my brother, Paul."

But Paul was following his own agenda. "I thought you were still grounded and on sick leave." His tone was a charade of mock concern. A stunned silence fell on the group, for Jonno had told them nothing of his current position.

His mind raced ahead in an effort to outwit his brother. "No, Paul, I'm currently seconded to other duties. Official business for the MOD, but it's confidential. That version was my cover story; sorry to disappoint you."

Paul's face betrayed his confusion and disbelief. He was, as usual, a little drunk, and clearly caught off balance. He stared blankly at Jonno, who had stood up to face him, creating a barrier between Paul and the group at the table.

"You're a bloody liar!" Paul blurted out and he turned on his heel, disappearing into the crowd round the bar.

Jonno resumed his seat, "Sorry about that." He felt obliged to offer some explanation. "Unfortunately, my brother and I are not very good friends. He was trying to score points, but I think I won that round, which makes a welcome change."

The three at the table looked amused, acknowledging the subterfuge. It was blatantly obvious Jonno's little sojourn at LTA was not part of a covert operation, but discreetly, when they eventually parted company later that evening, none of them said a word about the incident.

CHAPTER NINETEEN

MARKING TIME

On the following Monday morning, when Jonno arrived in the Administration office lugging all the paperwork from his survey, he looked at the 'Order of the Day' pinned to the notice board. He felt quite flattered to see he had an appointment with the Station Commander at fifteen hundred hours. It read, 'De-brief MOD survey – Flight Lieutenant J. Amis'. He spent the morning checking every sheet of paper, ensuring he had missed nothing. He also put his films into the lab and was promised by the technician that the prints would be ready after lunch.

Since the end of his sick leave, the 'light duties' status had assigned him to the Station Commander's general office. He didn't have a specific job and was, in reality, a glorified office boy. Only the Commander himself, Group Captain Chris Bailey, seemed to appreciate that Flight Lieutenant Amis possessed a keen analytical mind, which was why he had been sent to Cardington. Chris Bailey was also acquainted with the Amis family and he wanted to be instrumental in Jonno's rehabilitation.

Three o'clock came, and after the preliminary salute and handshake, Group Captain Bailey dispensed with formalities, addressing Jonno by his Christian name. He flicked through the survey, spending more time on the summaries. Then he studied the photographs.

He looked up. "Well, Jonno, you appear to have done a first class job here, considering it's not your field. Did you encounter any problems?"

Remembering his blackout during Sky Lark's test flight, Jonno was immediately on his guard. "None whatsoever," he replied, also recalling that Alison was the only witness and he was fairly sure he had convinced her it was just a fall.

Chris Bailey gestured to the paperwork now spread over his desk. "You have apparently covered the MOD's requirements admirably; let's hope they think so. Well done and thank you." There was a pause as Chris swivelled round in his chair, apparently deep in thought. "These tasks don't come along too often. We need to find something else for you to do. Any ideas?"

"How about re-joining the Squadron and getting back in the air?" Jonno knew he was sticking his neck out, but felt it was worth the risk.

"If the decision were mine, you would be," said Chris. "But unfortunately, it's not. That's for the Medical Review Board to decide in due course."

"But when?" said Jonno, rather bitterly. "How long do I have to wait?"

Chris Bailey shrugged his shoulders. "It's not so much a question of time, as procedure. Our Dr Johnson saw you when you first arrived and immediately took you off sick leave. He didn't see what all the fuss was about, and I'm inclined to agree with him. However, the MRB will not consider your case without a report from the Consultant Psychiatrist with the Department of Community Mental Health."

Jonno groaned. "Why can't Dr Johnson make the report?"

"As I said, it's procedure," Chris sounded almost apologetic. "The MOD set the unit up, so we have to refer all cases to them. It's a lodger unit based here at Marham."

"How long?" said Jonno, not liking one bit what he was hearing. "There's a war going on out in Iraq, yet I am still excluded."

"You don't have to tell me," retorted Bailey, a little sharply. Then he moderated his tone. "Dr Johnson put the referral through last week. You should be seen within a month. You must look on this as a temporary setback."

Jonno closed his eyes and sighed resignedly.

"I'm sorry; it's the best we can do." Chris Bailey stood up, indicating the interview was at an end.

Jonno stood also. "Thank you, sir, I do appreciate your help." They shook hands again.

"All part of my job," said Chris. "Your survey on the airship people is excellent. I will ensure you are given full credit for your work, alongside any other reports."

Jonno squared his cap, saluting the senior officer and left the room. Once again his good humour had deserted him. It seemed every time he picked himself up, fate knocked him back. Now he would have to endue a whole month of uncertainty, and then what? His whole life seemed to be on hold; he felt he was just marking time.

The following Saturday morning Lisa was busy at work. She had moved from the sprawling general office in with Biddy and Caroline. Both her senior colleagues were full of praise for the way in which she had become a full member of the features' team and for the quality of her journalism.

"Not more!" she exclaimed, as Neal tipped another pile of letters on her desk.

He gave her one of his adolescent toothy grins, "Your Dr Reeve has unleashed a mini tsunami in the post room: smokers, gamblers, alcoholics – every sort of phobic going – all looking for a magic cure."

"Don't be a sceptic, Neal," said Lisa defensively. "This guy can work some pretty powerful medicine. You must come and watch him sometime."

Neal shrugged his shoulders. "How are we going to answer all these?" He seemed more interested in reducing the workload.

"We're not. Tony Reeve is, via the postbag column. But I need your help this morning."

Neal groaned, looking at the pile of accumulated mail. "I've a footie match to go to at two o'clock."

"Promise we'll be done by twelve," said Lisa, anxious to retain Neal's help and goodwill. They spent the morning sorting the letters and tabling the most frequently asked questions.

"That should be enough for this week," said Lisa. "When I see Tony tomorrow, I hope we'll get some answers."

Neal was fidgeting with his watch. Lisa looked at the clock; it was twelve fifteen.

"Sorry, Neal, off you go – hope you enjoy the match," she said to the empty space left as he made a quick exit through the door.

When Lisa came out of the main entrance, she could see Jonno waiting at the bottom of the flight of stone steps. They had not seen each other for two weeks and he stood watching her descend. As she approached, he held out both his arms. Whatever doubts or differences of opinion may have been hovering over them in recent weeks, they were pushed aside as she was once more enveloped by the huge emotional tide of love which existed between them. She silently hoped that this was the original Jonno returned to her and not the strangely altered version she had come to know of late.

They kissed sensuously and he murmured in her ear. "Have I got you to myself for the rest of the day?" He held her close, wrapping her in his arms.

"All day and all night," she answered softly, and they kissed again, long and deep.

The cold January wind soon drove them to seek sanctuary in the nearest bar offering hot food. The smell of steaming country soup and hot bread assailed their senses and as they ate they planned the weekend.

"Tony can see you tomorrow at two o'clock."

"Marvellous!" said Jonno, sounding relieved.

"I have to be at his clinic at eleven in the morning," said Lisa. "He's going to start giving me answers for our letter column. The features on his work have created a lot of interest."

"If I turn up around twelve-thirty, do you think he would come to lunch with us? I feel I owe him that."

"That's a super idea. I'm sure he'll be up for that." Lisa felt pleased that Jonno seemed enthusiastic about resuming the therapy. When he was in Bedford she'd got the impression he was despondent about his lack of progress.

"Have you spoken to Paul and made your apologies?" She was anxious to keep her promise to Sarah to help mend the rift between the brothers.

"Yes and no," he said. "I saw him, but I'm afraid an apology was not on the agenda."

"What do you mean?"

Jonno told her about the incident in the pub which, it seemed to her, had widened the gap between them.

"You really owe it to the family to knock this one on the head before your estrangement with Paul gets any worse." She was anxious for common sense to prevail. "I feel responsible because it was over me."

"I can only repeat what I said at the time. It was because I thought he was a stranger molesting you that I hit him." Jonno's tone was one of self-righteous indignation. "Besides, he deserved it; his behaviour was outrageous."

Lisa realised the subject was best dropped for the present; tempers had obviously not cooled sufficiently for any reconciliation.

Jonno hadn't said anything else about the week he was away but as if on cue, he began to tell her about the airship project at Cardington.

"You and I have a date to go back in a few weeks' time, when the second airship is ready to begin flight tests. They could certainly do with some good PR, and you would find it fascinating."

"Umm, sounds interesting," Lisa replied. "But I'll have to talk to Biddy first."

"I'll put you in touch with their PA, Alison Lomax. She'll tell you everything you'll need to know."

"Well, I'm very pleased your week at Cardington went so well."

Jonno smiled and squeezed her hand, but he said no more and Lisa wondered if there was something he wasn't telling her.

They spent most of the afternoon shopping and then went to the cinema. Now they were back in the Quays' apartment. They had just finished a Chinese take-away and were sitting in the semi-dark by the high view window. They looked out on the moving spectacle of lights below: cars, boats and people still on the move, regardless of the bitter cold weather.

"So did Bailey come up with a job for you this week?" asked Lisa.

"Yes, with TIW," said Jonno. "Tactical Imagery Intelligence Wing to you."

"That sounds very impressive. What did you do?"

"They do some very important work, but they also have a wet film lab doing straight forward developing and printing. That's where I've been and I'll show you what I did." He stood up, going to his outdoor coat and fishing in the inside pocket. He opened a buff envelope. "I spent most of the week practising my printing skills using the negs from Cardington."

He switched on the brass up-lighter and spread the prints on the table. "I had to sneak this set out," he said. "What do you think of them?"

"What's this strange looking craft called?" She picked up one of the prints.

"That's 'Sky Lark', the prototype."

Lisa examined the images taken in the hangar and during the test flight. "Why are they all dead level except this one? She's tipped sideways."

"It wasn't the airship tipped sideways, it was me; I keeled over." His voice had dropped to an apologetic whisper.

She looked at him, momentarily closing her eyes. "You'd better tell me about it."

They sat down again on the sofa and Lisa listened in silence while he told her about his blackout on the test field and his strange vision of flying over an unfamiliar landscape.

"None of this is easy for me," he said despondently. "I feel humiliated and ashamed of this psychological crisis in my life. Seven years service without a stain on my character and now all this."

Lisa interrupted. "But it's not a stain on your character. Dozens of service men suffer combat fatigue."

Jonno shook his head. "I don't think this was triggered by combat fatigue. There is another reason, to do with me alone."

"But what?" she questioned.

He looked into her eyes. His look was so penetrating it made her shiver. "I don't know yet," he said. "I just hope Tony will find the reason, I'm so glad you persuaded me to see him."

On Sunday Jonno arrived at the clinic at twelve-thirty as agreed and took Lisa and Tony out for lunch. One of the local pubs advertised a range of traditional roast dinners chalked on a board outside. They smelled delicious and didn't break the bank.

He'd had a bad night. He had not dreamed, but he hadn't slept either. In fact he had tried not to, hoping to avoid the trauma of Lisa witnessing him in the throes of another bad nightmare.

During lunch the conversation was all about the newspaper features and the public's response in the letter column. When they returned to the clinic, Tony's attention was fully on Jonno.

"I'm afraid my nightmares and hallucinations are as bad as ever," Jonno explained.

"I'm sorry to hear that," said Tony. "But I did warn you this could happen, Jonno. Don't lose faith in the therapy. We have to find the root cause of your anxiety and that may take some time."

Jonno nodded his head. He knew there was no guarantee he would even have another past life experience, but he was prepared to give the therapy one more chance. As he lay back on the couch

177

he tried to clear his mind of all his jumbled thoughts. He needed to open up the channels that could lead him back into the past. He desperately wanted to go back to the time when he was Karl Stockhausen, when he was in love with the beautiful girl called Elizabeth.

As he heard Tony's voice say the phrase, "Go back and find Karl," the temperature in the room seemed to drop. He suddenly felt very cold.

CHAPTER TWENTY

SILVER NIGHT

Stuttgart, Germany, December 1935

It was after midnight and the temperature had dropped below freezing. The paths and roads glinted white and silver as ice formed on the wet surfaces, making them treacherous underfoot. White hoarfrost covered the bushes in the gardens adjacent to the pathway. They stood out like rows of white flowers in the moonlight. Ice had crept up the windows of nearby houses, forming white patterned curtains, obscuring the view for anyone inside. Karl was thankful for that, the less visible they were the better. This was a journey he wished they did not have to make.

They had left the safety of Stuttgart's Quaker Meeting House and kept close to the shadows, stopping and listening before moving on to the next pool of darkness. The city streets were deserted. Few people dared venture out after dark, let alone at this hour of the night. If Elizabeth were discovered, she would be held as an alien, for her passport had been seized, her citizenship removed. Karl too would be arrested as her accomplice.

Autumn was long gone, its legacy of crisp, dead leaves swirled in deep piles across the pathways. They scrunched underfoot preventing soundless travel. As they left the city streets behind them a full moon rose in the clear night sky, bathing the landscape with a soft, silver sheen. Tonight it was far too bright for their purpose, yet so far they had been fortunate and had not encountered the feared patrols of the Schutzstaffel, the SS, Hitler's own elite police.

Karl had been working in Friedrichshafen, on the borders of Lake Constance in the south. The LZ129 airship was nearing completion and he was part of the team from Daimler-Benz working on the new diesel engines. He had come home for the Christmas and New Year holiday and gone straight to the beautiful house at Weissenhof where Elizabeth and her family lived. To outsiders, they were no longer engaged to be married but their betrothal had continued in total secret. Karl's mother had written to tell him of a big crackdown in Stuttgart against local professional Jews still remaining in the city. She feared for the safety of Elizabeth and her family.

He had reached the house to find it empty and ransacked. Desperate for news he'd gone to the only people he could trust, the small group of Stuttgart Quaker Friends. When he was eventually allowed into their Meeting House, he was overjoyed to find Elizabeth had taken refuge there.

"Thank God you are safe!" said Karl. As he wrapped her tightly in his arms, he was shocked to realise how painfully thin she had become. She was as beautiful as ever but her face had lost its youthful glow. Her complexion was pale, almost opaque, like a wax-faced doll. Her fabulous eyes appeared bigger and brighter, but they had a haunted look and the brightness was from moist tears.

He spoke to her gently. "You must tell me what happened at Weissenhof."

"Oh, Karl, it was terrible!" She began to cry as her story unfolded. "The Nazi soldiers came to the house many times. They took everything. New electric things Papa had bought; his radio, and Mama's new iron and cleaner. Then they took our silver and jewellery. They took Papa's paintings from the walls, and they rolled up the beautiful wool carpets and took them all away.

"The next day they brought a big truck for our furniture. When they carried away my piano they wrenched out my heart!" Elizabeth stopped to catch her breath and Karl stroked her hair to soothe her.

She continued her terrible tale. "Papa was forbidden to work as a lawyer. Only Mama's income from the University remained. I think it was Gestapo men who came and questioned her about her teaching of German history." Elizabeth was trembling and spoke haltingly. *"When she went to work the next day, she was sent away and told her post did not exist. Poor Mama was devastated!"*

"But where are they? What has happened to them?" said Karl, his anger mounting as he learned more of Elizabeth's terrible ordeal.

"I don't know!" her voice rose shrilly. *"I can't find out!"* She began to sob uncontrollably and Karl held her close to stop her shaking.

After a while, she continued her story. *"I went to visit my cousin Olga for two days to ask for help. When I returned Mama and Papa had gone! Neighbours said the Gestapo took them away and were looking for me."* Her beautiful eyes were wide and round with disbelief. *"I don't know if they are dead or alive. If I try to find them I will be arrested!"* She finally broke down completely in Karl's arms, filled with a despair which broke his heart.

He held her for a long time until she calmed and he knew the time had come for him to take full responsibility for Elizabeth, as if she were his wife.

"My friend, my friend, we must talk." It was the Quaker pastor, Herr Mueller. He sat beside them. His mouth smiled but his eyes were sad. *"Our group here in Stuttgart is under siege. Our meetings are constantly invaded by the Gestapo. They know we are helping Jewish families and are looking for proof. It is not safe for Elizabeth to remain here."*

He took a piece of paper from his pocket and gave it to Karl. *"This is the address of a safe house. It is a farm on the road to Frankfurt, about fifteen kilometres from here. They will look after Elizabeth, but it may not always be possible for you to know where she is."*

Karl looked desperate and Elizabeth clung to him. He searched his mind for an alternative, but there was none.

"You must leave tonight and get there as quickly as possible," said Herr Mueller.

Karl was in a dilemma, for in his heart he wanted to stay with Elizabeth and go into hiding with her. But his long-term plan for them to escape from Germany depended on his continued employment on the airship project. He had applied to join the crew as a mechanic when the airship was completed. She was due to join the LZ127, 'Graf Zeppelin' on the transatlantic routes.

They had covered about six kilometres, travelling deeper into the countryside. The moonlight reflected on the frost covered landscape; innocent white fields and tracks lighting their way. There had been no other sounds but their footsteps crackling on the frozen verges. Now they detected another noise, faint at first, it intensified, rumbling and whining. As it grew louder, it multiplied. Then Karl saw the lights on the road behind them.

"Quick!" he hissed. "We must hide! There's a convoy coming!"

"Oh! No! They are looking for us!" Elizabeth seemed too petrified to move. He put both arms around her and dragged her to the side of the road. They half fell and half rolled into a waist-high ditch, and lay like a bundle of rags in the spiteful brambles. As the lead truck reached the point where they had left the road Karl felt the cold, rank ditch water begin to seep into his shoes and clothes, and a hot, raw anger began to burn in his heart.

The lights from the procession of passing trucks raked across the ground, dipping down into the ditch and then up into the trees as they bounced over the deep ruts in the road, cut like the furrows in an old man's brow. Karl and Elizabeth hardly dared to breathe as they listened to the engines straining and whining in low gears.

The troop convoy drove slowly past their hiding place as the probing lights flashed by inches from their heads. Karl could see the white faces of the soldiers staring out from the back of the trucks. A discarded cigarette butt was tossed from one and landed at his feet. It was instantly extinguished in the sodden undergrowth.

A shout went up from the lead truck and was echoed down the line. One by one, the trucks juddered to a halt. Karl clasped Elizabeth closer to him, sure they were about to be discovered. An officer marched down the road from the head of the convoy. The drive crews jumped down from their vehicles and stood to attention along the roadside, giving the Nazi salute. Every member of the armed services had now to swear the Oath of Loyalty to the Führer and the National Socialists – the Nazis.

The officer was in a rage. He shouted and swore at the truck crews as he goose-stepped down the line. When he was opposite the ditch, Karl could see him silhouetted in the moonlight. As he turned his head the Nazi insignia on his peaked SS officer's cap glinted in the moon's light. He was furious at the convoy's slow progress and blamed the men for their badly maintained vehicles. They were, it seemed, bound for the Rhineland as part of the remilitarisation, and were now behind schedule.

Karl breathed a little easier; at least they did not appear to be looking for them. Then he caught a glimpse of the officer's features as he screamed obscenities at the truck crew nearest to them. Karl stared in horror at the sharply moving silhouette of the man as he punched then kicked one of the crewmen, leaving him in a crumpled heap on the ground. Karl knew he would never forget his terrifying voice or the cruel look on his face.

Eventually the Nazi marched back to the head of the convoy and the trucks resumed their journey at a faster pace. Karl realised with abhorrence that he could have been in one of them. So far he had escaped conscription, for his job was classified as work of national importance. He prayed that both he and Elizabeth would be gone from Germany before he was forced to fight for this detestable regime.

As the noise of the last truck faded into the distance, they waited for the silence to return. Elizabeth was shaking with fear and from the bitter cold. As Karl lifted his head above the ditch, a ghostly white shape swooped silently by inches from his head. The

183

movement was so close it ruffled his hair, filling him with momentary terror. The apparition swept past on a parallel course with the ditch: a night hunting barn owl seeking its prey.

"It's safe now, we must move on," he said gently, but Elizabeth was in no fit state to travel much further. Her recent traumas had left her very weak. He pulled her to him for warmth and rubbed her hands with his own. He swept her up in his arms and lifted her on to the bank, scrambling up beside her. Then he stood up, scanning the surrounding countryside in the pale, eerie moonlight. There was no sign of human habitation. "We must press on, my darling," he said, helping her to her feet.

"Yes, of course we must. My poor Karl," she said haltingly. "I have brought you so much trouble."

"Don't say that. It is the Nazis who have brought the trouble." His voice was full of contempt. "They are such evil men!"

They walked on for about an hour. Clouds were gathering, obscuring the moon, making it much more difficult to follow the road. Karl stopped; he could not tell how far they had come. On the left there was a gate in the hedge, and tracks on the ground indicated that a vehicle had turned in and out of the entrance.

"There must be a farm nearby," he said excitedly.

"It might not be the right one," Elizabeth said with less enthusiasm.

"Then we must find out, besides we can go no further tonight. Come on!" and he led the way as they climbed over the gate.

Now the night was all black shadows. Without the moonlight, they stumbled across the field which sloped down into a valley. Halfway, they stopped and saw the dark shapes of buildings clustered below. A farmhouse with smoke rising from the chimney stood at the centre surrounded by a yard, with outbuildings and barns within the perimeter of a dry stone wall. Further away on the other side of the farm stood a barn not connected to the house or yard.

"That's where we need to head." He pointed towards the lone building.

Elizabeth was too weary to care if it was safe or not and followed Karl as he changed direction to lead them round in a semicircle across the little valley. The air became damp and flakes of snow began to cloud their vision, clinging to their heads and clothes. In minutes the landscape turned from black to white, once more exposing them to view.

"We must hurry before it stops or our tracks will give us away." Karl tried to keep to the hedgerows but in the end they ran across the field to the big barn. They slipped and slithered the last few yards then stopped, their backs against the side of the barn, away from the house.

"Look, the dawn is breaking. We must hide before it is daylight," Karl said, trying to recover his breath. He was very aware of their vulnerability. "Then we can find out if we have come to the right farm."

"And if we haven't?" Elizabeth gripped his arm tightly. He knew the consequences should they fall into the hands of Nazi sympathisers; Karl did not want to think about that.

"If we haven't, we will move on when we are rested." He kissed her gently. "Do not worry my love; I will not leave you until you are in safe hands."

Any peace of mind or security they may have felt in that moment was quickly shattered. They heard the dogs only seconds before they saw them. Flight was useless and the door of the barn was locked fast against them. The barking grew louder from the direction of the farmhouse. As Elizabeth cowered in the doorway, Karl stood over her protectively.

The two dark German Shepherd dogs came snarling and barking around the corner of the barn. At first Karl was relieved to see they were pulling and straining against leashes. Then their handler came into view and Karl held his breath. The man had only to release his hold on the dogs and their fate would be sealed. In desperation he called out.

"Wait! Please, we are lost."

The man shouted to the animals. "Rudy! Oscar! Stay!"

He pulled the dogs back on their leads. Karl thought quickly; he had to gain time without revealing their true purpose. Although under control, the animals continued to growl and bare their teeth. The dog handler approached them warily, and stopped about six metres away from where Karl and Elizabeth were huddled against the barn door.

He challenged them. "Who are you? Why are you here?"

"We missed our road last night and have walked for hours." Karl laughed nervously as he spoke. "We thought if we cut across the fields we would find our way, but we are still lost." He held out his hands in a gesture meant to show they had nothing to hide.

The snow stopped falling, leaving a white carpet about three centimetres thick covering the frozen ground. Daylight was growing fast now and Karl could see the dog handler more clearly. He was big and strong but his fresh face showed he was just a youth. He still seemed uncertain what to do and the dogs began barking and pulling at their leads once more.

"Quiet boys, heel!" he shouted, and they immediately obeyed, turning within the length of their leads and sitting beside their master. "Where were you headed? Nobody travels at night these days, so why were you?"

He sounded more curious than accusing, so Karl decided to trust his instinct that the boy was not about to set the dogs on them. With careful movements he felt in his inside pocket for the scrap of paper Herr Mueller had given him.

"We were actually looking for Black Lodge Farm, and a farmer called Herr Bader." The boy did not react and Karl could not gauge if this information meant anything at all to him.

"What was your business with Herr Bader?"

"You know him!" Karl said, spontaneously.

"Your business?" repeated the boy. Now he sounded suspicious.

Still too cautious to tell the truth Karl said, "We were told Herr Bader was hiring, we are looking for work."

The boy began to laugh. "At Christmas time and in this weather? I don't think so! I don't believe you are looking for farm work. Look at you both, shivering in your city clothes."

He stood there shaking his head and Karl realised the odds were completely against them. He would have to take his chances with this boy.

"No, you are right." He turned and put his arm round Elizabeth. She could barely stand and if she did not have food and shelter soon, she could die. "Herr Mueller from Stuttgart sent us. Is this Herr Bader's farm?"

"Show me your paper," said the boy. Karl was beginning to think his trust had been misplaced. The boy did not move and Karl had to walk up to him, leaving Elizabeth alone. The boy read the note and put it in his pocket. Karl knew he could probably knock him out with one blow, but the dogs! No, he couldn't overpower them.

But then the boy was stretching out the hand of friendship. "I am Peter Bader," he said.

Karl's relief was overwhelming.

"My father is away but I can act on his behalf." Peter now spoke animatedly. "Herr Mueller and the Quakers of Stuttgart have been good friends to our family. We do not forget."

Karl shook Peter's hand vigorously. "I am so glad we have found you. We must help my fiancée, Elizabeth. This night has nearly killed her."

Peter took a set of keys from his pocket and unlocked the padlock holding the barn door shut. The dogs were almost docile now, as if they understood the human handshake had removed any threat previously posed. Karl lifted Elizabeth up in his arms and followed Peter into the barn.

Half the barn was taken up with bales of hay and the temperature inside was at least ten degrees higher than outside. At the far end was a wood-burning stove, the chimney of which rose about a metre before disappearing out through the stone wall. Peter threw open the stove door and began to light a fire in the grate. The kindling soon caught hold and he added some small logs to the flames and closed the door.

"We will soon have a good fire," said Peter, dusting his hands on his coat. "Bring the young lady closer to get warm. I am going back to the house and will bring you some food and blankets. Then you must tell me why you are here." He left, and the dogs silently followed him.

Karl carried Elizabeth over near the stove. He knelt down, letting her lie against him, facing the growing warmth. Her eyes were closed and she did not respond. He felt her pulse and checked her breathing. She was alive but totally exhausted. He said a silent prayer of thanks to God and the Quaker Friends.

It was not long before he heard Peter returning and he went to the door to meet him. Peter was towing a sledge laden with boxes and bundles.

"Santa Claus has come already!" Peter called out to him. "Look what he has brought."

Karl's heart went out to the young Peter. He did not even know them but was putting himself to a lot of trouble and some risk to help them. Peter stopped the sledge by the door and Karl helped him unload the supplies and bring them into the barn. There was a pile of thick blankets, utensils and food. There was also a small bottle of brandy.

"I hope your father will not be angry at your generosity to strangers," said Karl, liking the boy more and more.

"My Father is a true Christian and a good man. He will be pleased our family could help you."

They quickly brought the goods inside and Peter put a pan of soup on the stove to heat while Karl roused Elizabeth with a tiny *drop of the brandy. She opened her eyes and caught her breath as the strong liquid trickled into her mouth. Peter poured strong black coffee from a flask for both of them. It was sweet and hot, and to Karl it was pure nectar. Peter then tore wedges of bread to eat with the soup and soon both Karl and Elizabeth were eating ravenously. Peter waited patiently until they were satisfied.*

"Now you must tell me your story. I do not even know your names."

Karl then told Peter everything, for he knew instinctively they could trust him.

"Our problem now is that we cannot stay together." Karl was once again holding Elizabeth by the fire. She was drifting off to sleep and he squeezed her hand. "It is too late now for Elizabeth to leave the country legitimately. All her family's assets have been seized and we do not know where her parents have been taken. What she needs is a place to hide and new documents; a new identity as an Aryan."

Peter nodded his head. "I understand, my friend. This is not the first time we have helped displaced Jews, and it will probably not be the last. I know Father has contacts. It is possible to do what you ask, but it will not be easy."

"I have money saved," said Karl. "I am willing to pay."

Peter shook his head. "I don't know about that side of things. We will have to wait until my father returns. He and Mother have gone to my sister in Frankfurt. She is expecting her first child in a few days and I am in charge here until they return."

"Of course, Peter, I understand. I can stay three days only then I must return to Stuttgart and then back to my job in Friedrichshafen. But I am afraid to leave Elizabeth."

"You must not worry. I promise you I will look after her. When you go, I will bring her into the house. We have a room in the attic; it is hidden. If the patrols come they will not find her."

"How will I know what happens after that? How can I contact you? Letters are not safe."

Peter was thoughtful and silent. Then he got up and went over behind the hay bales. "Come over here," he called out. Karl followed Peter behind the stack of hay. There, propped against the wall, covered in grime and dust was an old motorcycle. "It's a BMW R32," said Peter. "It was my father's but it hasn't run for years. He had it from new in 1923."

Karl rubbed some of the grime off the tank revealing silver paint. "I know it," he said. "It was a special edition from the early model called the 'Silver Knight'."

"If you can make it run you can use it to go back and forth. You have a job and legitimate business; the patrols will let you through."

"Peter, my friend, you are too, too generous. I am sure I can make it run, but I will pay your father for it. I cannot just take it!"

Peter laughed. "Let us see it run first, then you can argue with him when he returns. Now I must go and see to the farm. You get some rest and I will return later with more food and tools for the bike."

They shook hands and Peter left, sliding back down the hill on the sledge. Karl put more logs on the wood-burning stove and it crackled with new warmth. He lay down next to Elizabeth and held her close. She was still sleeping, soundly now and her breathing was regular and peaceful.

Perhaps Elizabeth had been right all along. They had perfect love and there was nothing of which to be afraid. What was it she had said? – 'Perfect love casts out fear.' And so, thought Karl, do good friends.

CHAPTER TWENTY-ONE

SUNSET

London, England, February 2000

As Lisa drove them back to the Quays in her car, Jonno felt as though he had been away for days, not just a few hours. A sensation of being disconnected from his every day life pervaded his thoughts, as though he were part of a masquerade. His real life was taking place somewhere else and he needed to be there.

His mind was filled with thoughts and images of a dreadful night in Germany sixty-five years ago. Was it possible all that had happened to him in a past life? And the girl, his sweet, beautiful Elizabeth, he had loved her so much. He shuddered, remembering the evil Nazi officer. He had watched him drive away and yet he sensed the man's presence even now, as though he had been discovered, recognised. His skin crawled as he felt the Nazi's eyes were following him, watching his every move.

"It's only seven-thirty," said Lisa. "Can we go through the regression again? It's incredible the detail you recalled."

"Sorry," he murmured. "I don't think I can face that now. I feel as though I've just sat through a three hour long epic. I'm exhausted."

"Is that what it's like? Watching a film?" she asked, as they drove into the car park for the apartment.

He thought for a moment. "I suppose it's more like a vivid dream, but not just visual. It's more a true memory: smells, sounds and feelings."

"You seem more convinced now that it could be your own past life," she said, turning off the engine.

"Yes, I am." He looked at her and cupped his hands around her face. "Especially now you have become part of that life." He kissed her lips, deep and long, and looked again into her eyes. The memory of Elizabeth overlaid by the presence of Lisa, or was it the other way round?

"I still don't know how you can think she is me," she said.

"I just know," he said. "To think we could have been lovers for forty thousand years."

They laughed, for the idea sounded ridiculous. But as he looked into her eyes again, he saw Elizabeth and realised it could be true.

Entering the apartment, there sounded a cacophony of ring tones. They had deliberately not taken their mobile phones to Wembley, leaving them on the table. Lisa picked hers up first.

"Lots of texts, all from Sarah," she said, but before she could read them Jonno was answering the call on his phone.

Sarah's voice sounded loud and shrill. "Thank God you've answered at last. I've been ringing for hours!"

"What's up," he asked with mounting apprehension.

"Max has had a heart attack!" She was crying. "Please come now." Her voice was choking.

"Is he conscious? What do the doctors say?" Jonno's exhaustion fell away.

"He's slipping in and out. It's touch and go whether he will make it through the night. Please, just come, Jonno!"

"Where are you?"

"Kings Lynn, the Queen Elizabeth." Sarah sounded distraught.

"Sarah, stop panicking, I'll be with you in just over an hour." He spoke calmly and in control. "Is Mum all right?"

"She's coping... better than me." Her voice broke.

"Listen Sarah, you must stay strong for them. Give them our love and say I'm on my way. Max is a tough old stick so stay positive. I'll see you soon."

Lisa had heard all the conversation and was already re-packing Jonno's weekend bag, and one for herself.

"I'm coming with you," she said.

As he closed his phone, his hands were shaking and she took him in her arms. "Thank you, darling, thank you so much," he whispered softly.

Jonno had brought his own VW Golf into London and he took the wheel now for the familiar journey back to Norfolk. Once clear of the metropolis, he drove at high speed on the motorway, eating away the miles.

Lisa had drifted off to sleep but Jonno drew on an inner strength to keep alert and stay awake. Even so, memories of Max and his childhood days at Greengate flooded his thoughts. All the while, like a soundtrack, the haunting notes of the Moonlight Sonata were running through his head. It was as if now he had found Elizabeth she would not leave him.

As they entered the outskirts of Kings Lynn, he shook Lisa awake.

"Nearly there," he said, focusing his mind on the route.

She blinked and shivered, pulling her jacket round her and turning up the heater.

"You've done well on time," she said. "Hope you didn't trigger any speed cameras."

"Um, so do I," he mumbled.

When they arrived at the hospital, Sarah was waiting in the main entrance. She hugged them both and then led them through what seemed like miles of corridors. They came to the ward at last and entered a side room. Max was propped up on the bed's back rest and pillows, surrounded by drips and monitors, the umbilical cords of which were attached to him. Kathryn sat at his side, her cheek resting on the hand she held. She smiled at them, but her eyes were red and moist and she didn't speak. He went to the other side of the bed and gripped his hand round Max's fingers. The old man's eyes were closed.

"Hi, Max, it's me, Jonno," he said, raising his voice a little. Max did not react, "Give us a smile, Granddad." He felt a slight twitch under his hand and the ghost of a smile touched Max's face. His eyes seemed to move under the closed lids.

"Good chap," said Jonno softly, "You know I'm here then." Jonno smiled at his mother and sister, nodding his head. "Lisa is with me." He pulled Lisa close to the bed with his other arm.

"There, we are all here now Max," Jonno said, realising as he spoke that one family member was still missing. "You must hurry up and get better so we can take you home." He felt Max's hand move again and was reassured that his grandfather understood his words. He removed his hand and motioned to Sarah to follow him. They went out into the corridor.

"What about Paul? Have you been able to contact him?"

"He's on a weekend exercise in Wales," Sarah said, "and you know how they always end up."

"Plastered," said Jonno, "it's obligatory. Still, I'm surprised Paul is ever sober enough to drive, let alone fly."

"I've left texts on his phone and a message at his squad base," Sarah explained.

"You've done well," he said, putting his arm round his sister's shoulder, "There is nothing else you can do. I'm sorry we were out of touch for so long, I'll explain why later. Now I'm here, you have a break and take Mum for a cup of tea, she looks all in."

They walked back into the room together. Jonno went to his mother's side. He kissed her on the cheek. "Go with Sarah for a break, Lisa and I will stay with Max."

Reluctantly, Kathryn went with Sarah.

Jonno and Lisa sat either side of the bed and Jonno started chatting to Max as though they were having a two-way conversation. He talked about cricket and golf and memories from their lives together; everything he could think of, rather then let a silence fall. He squeezed Max's hand, anxious to elicit some reaction, some sign that he still clung to life and rational thought.

For a brief moment Max's eyelids flickered, and his mouth moved, but the effort required to form a word and speak was too much. However, Jonno felt reassured that his grandfather was still with them.

Kathryn and Sarah returned, changing places with Lisa and Jonno at the bedside. Jonno checked all the monitors and equipment and read the charts. He then went in search of the ward Sister. The prognosis was not good. If Max survived he would need bypass surgery, but his age was against that. The next twenty-four hours were critical. Jonno decided he could not leave the hospital for at least that period. He returned to the bedside. They all wanted to keep the night's vigil; they would deal with tomorrow when it arrived.

They took turns talking to Max and attempting to stimulate a response. Jonno seemed to have the most success, but he seemed more aware of the tiny movements in Max's face and hands. By three-thirty everyone was exhausted. Jonno had run out of words and was quietly thinking about the fishing trips they had all enjoyed with Max in years gone by.

He noticed the old man's eyelids flicker again and his mouth moved. Jonno put his face close to his grandfather's.

"What's that Granddad? Tell me again," he said.

Max opened his mouth, and in an almost inaudible whispering croak, he managed to say the words, "Lovely day." Then his head fell to one side and his hand went slack. Jonno felt the life drain away from his grandfather. The alarms sounded and the medical team rushed into the room. Jonno knew it was too late and they had lost him.

Kathryn stood wringing her hands. "What did he say?" she asked her son.

Jonno turned to his mother and took both her hands in his. He smiled through his own tears. "He said, 'Lovely day,' Mum. What day do you think he meant?"

Kathryn put her arms round Jonno's neck and clung to him. "Every day, son, he meant every day of his life."

CHAPTER TWENTY-TWO

OLD WOUNDS

Marham, Norfolk. February 2000

Max's funeral cortège set off at walking pace from Greengate Lodge. Frost had turned the ground white and freezing fog hung in the hollows. In the car following the hearse Paul sat with Kathryn, while Sarah was between Jonno and Lisa.

Nobody spoke. This was the third time the family had been united in grief. The passing of Sadie and now Max had reopened wounds, still raw and jagged, sustained by them when David had died. Their grandfather had been a surrogate father and they had all adored him. He had built a special relationship with each one of his grandchildren, trying to bring them all back together as a family. All except Paul. He had remained the outsider.

The funeral procession picked up speed, leading a long line of cars. Paul had not put in an appearance until yesterday. He had spoken with Kathryn on the telephone, but the others were annoyed that he had not seen fit to pay his respects during the intervening week. Bedford was not that far away and, like Jonno, he was entitled to take compassionate leave.

Now there were about fifty people all trying to cram into the tiny twelfth century church of Saint Mary's. As the coffin was taken from the hearse, Jonno looked back at the village green. He imagined Max walking out in his cricket whites, with his bat tucked under his arm; now that was all over. Not quite a century but a jolly good innings, as Max himself would have said.

Since his arrival Paul had been his usual cold and unresponsive self. Keeping his emotions deep inside, he was unreadable. After the service, the coffin was carried outside the church for the committal.

The overhanging trees dripped condensed, dank fog onto the mourners, and the rooks cawed ominously.

Following the brief, poignant graveside ritual, everyone made their way towards the cars. Jonno looked back. Paul had remained at the graveside, his head bowed. He was grieving in his own silent, insular way. Jonno knew his brother had loved and respected their grandfather above anyone else in his life.

The wake moved the few yards along the lane to the Cricket Club. Ian Walters, Kathryn's long time admirer, had insisted the club wanted to show their respects to Max by opening up the pavilion and providing the refreshments. Kathryn had agreed. It was a lot less harrowing for her than having to entertain so many people at Greengate Lodge.

Jonno and Sarah stood near the door to welcome and thank the many friends arriving, including the Station Commander, Group Captain Chris Bailey. Jonno proudly introduced Lisa as his fiancée and the atmosphere in the pavilion took on a lighter mood. Sarah looked a little happier now that the worst part of the day was behind them.

"There are so many people here," she said to Jonno and Lisa, quite overwhelmed by the turnout.

"Everyone, except Paul," said Lisa. The other two looked around. "He's not here," Lisa told them again, "I've checked."

"Why is it," said Sarah indignantly, "he has no sense of family responsibility? I despair of him."

"Well, don't say anything to Mum," Jonno advised as they began to mingle with the guests.

He was glad to see that Ian had taken his mother under his wing, supporting her as she talked with friends, many of whom had been at Max's eighty-fifth birthday celebrations the previous June. Max's life was the main topic of conversation, and the events leading up to his death were retold many times over. Eventually, Kathryn and Ian came back to the rest of the family. It was then Kathryn realised Paul was missing.

Jonno tried to spare his mother's feelings. "You know he is no good at this sort of thing, Mum," he said. Kathryn sighed visibly.

By mid afternoon, people were drifting away and it seemed a good time for the family to leave. Ian took them all back to Greengate in his car, and after extracting a promise from Kathryn to join him for dinner later in the week, he drove away as they entered the house.

Paul's car was still in the drive, so Jonno guessed his brother was somewhere around the house. He had not spoken with Paul in any depth since the Millennium and he knew he should make the opportunity now, however difficult it was. He found him in the sitting room: the room Max and Sadie had made their private retreat when the three boisterous children came to live with them. To Jonno the room was still sacrosanct. His brother was sitting at Max's desk, apparently going through the drawers.

Jonno stood in the doorway, and spoke quietly. "I don't think Mum wants us to touch anything yet."

Paul looked at his younger brother coldly. "Afraid I'll steal the family jewels?" he asked disdainfully.

Jonno didn't answer him but continued to watch from the doorway. His silent surveillance seemed to aggravate Paul more as he displayed all the menace of a ticking time bomb.

"I'm only looking at stuff. Did you want something?" He spoke as though Jonno was the interloper.

"Only to apologise in person for that smack in the mouth I dealt you at the Millennium party," said Jonno, trying to keep things low key.

"Oh, you mean this!" He pulled at the split lip still not fully healed. "Why apologise? I got heavy with your girlfriend, you slugged me, end of story."

"I didn't realise it was you, Paul, I thought it was a stranger. I wouldn't have deliberately hit you, even if you did deserve it."

Paul began to laugh, but not in any act of reconciliation. His laughter was contemptuous. "You poor sod," he said. "How did you get to be such a righteous bugger? Oh, yes, of course, I nearly forgot." He flapped his hand in a mock salute. "Flight Lieutenant J. Amis, DFC!" He laughed again. "What a joke you are? A DFC who can't fly because he's grounded!"

"Cut it out, Paul!" Jonno had tried to remain silent but could feel his temper rising as Paul baited him along.

"No!" shouted Paul. "You cut it out, Mr Headline Grabber!" His tone had changed and the jeering smile vanished replaced by a venomous sneer. "Always the attention seeker, you! – who are guilty of so much."

Jonno realised too late he had lit the mythical fuse.

Paul raised his voice again as a seething anger took possession of him. "Do you want me to lay the blame for all this family's troubles at your door?" he shouted. "I can you know!"

He slammed shut the drawer he had been looking into and stood up, confronting his younger brother. "You, with all your psycho-babble of fire nightmares from the day you were born!" He did not wait for Jonno to answer him but continued his raging. "The destruction of our home at Romney and dad's death; I lay all the guilt on your shoulders, my sanctimonious little brother!" Paul rambled on with a tirade of accusations, "Who was the one awake when we were all asleep? Who started that fire? You did! Johnathon Amis, you did!"

Jonno was speechless. How could Paul have harboured this weird scenario all these years? Twisted, bitter accusations which bore no resemblance to the truth.

Paul's shouting had alerted everyone else in the house and they rushed into the hallway outside the sitting room. Jonno remained in the doorway, keeping Paul at bay should he turn violent. But he had no intention of engaging in any verbal defence of his own character. Paul's claims were too outrageous and he was far too volatile.

Kathryn however, had no such qualms about tackling her eldest son. She pushed past Jonno, determined to defuse Paul's anger. Together they all presented a sombre scene, still dressed in their black mourning clothes.

She went towards him. "What are you saying? Have you gone crazy? You know that's not true."

"Do I?!" He turned his anger on his mother, spitting and snarling like an angry dog. "I only know what you chose to tell me, and you always were so protective of darling Jonno. How do you know he didn't start the fire?"

Kathryn stood her ground, but she spoke with a quiet control. "He didn't, because I know who did." Paul seemed not to hear her words.

Jonno felt compelled to intervene. "Paul, why have you brought this up today of all days? We have enough grief to deal with right now without this."

Paul started to rave again. "I was too young to question anything then, but this goes right back to that night." He shook his finger at them angrily. "Now Max has gone, I can speak out at last. He pointed at Jonno. "You started that fire. And you!" He suddenly turned, pointing at Kathryn. "You stopped me from rescuing my father!" Paul was beside himself with fury and there appeared to be a real threat to Kathryn's safety.

The two girls rushed into the room to protect Kathryn. Sarah shouted. "Stop this right now, Paul. You've gone too far!"

As she went to push Paul away from Kathryn, Jonno stepped between them, fearing for his sister and his mother. Paul lashed out wildly, but Jonno caught hold of the swinging arm and twisted him round in an arm lock, forcing him to his knees. They were the same height but Jonno's movements were quicker. He held Paul immobile.

"Listen to me!" Jonno spoke commandingly. "I don't know where you're coming from, but you are way out of order. You've no right to make all these wild allegations now, especially at Mum."

Paul would not be silenced and continued to struggle with Jonno. "Dad would be alive today if she had let me get back in the house!" Paul raged while Jonno held him fast in the arm lock. "You don't know what it's been like for me living with the knowledge I could have saved Dad's life and I didn't!"

Kathryn came close again. "Paul, Paul, you are not listening. I said I know what happened and you could not have saved Dad." She kept her voice low and did not shout.

Paul stopped struggling against Jonno and seemed ready to listen.

Kathryn went on. "None of you were told the contents of the official report on the fire. Max and I decided at the time, you were all too young and too distraught over David's death to handle the truth. It was difficult enough for me, and I swore never to tell any of you. Now I have to."

They all fell silent, waiting on Kathryn's every word. Her voice was shaking with emotion as she continued. "When David came home that night, we were all asleep upstairs. He locked up and went into what we called the middle room, between the dining room and the sitting room; the windows were fastened. The TV in there had apparently been on, and they said he had consumed around three bottles of beer. He had also smoked several cigarettes." Kathryn took a deep breath and continued speaking.

"The cause of the fire was given as him falling asleep with a lighted cigarette, which probably rolled under the armchair in which he sat. The chair had smouldered extensively in the unventilated room before it ignited, causing the fire. The report also said that David was in all probability dead from smoke and fumes inhalation, even before the fire actually took hold."

She turned to face her eldest son and addressed him directly. "So you see, Paul, you could not have rescued David after we left the house because he was already dead. And your little eight-year-old brother did not start the fire, because your father did."

Kathryn went to the window and stared out at the garden, her back to all of them. "My dear, darling David, whom I loved with all my heart, who took such great care of all of us, he made the fatal

201

mistake which took his life and our home." Kathryn stopped speaking, her head bowed.

Although his mother had absolved him from Paul's accusations, Jonno was devastated by her unexpected revelation. He let go of Paul and walked away from him.

There was a terrible silence in the room. Sarah broke down in tears and fled upstairs, followed by Lisa, leaving the suffocating emotions in the sitting room. Kathryn was shaking so violently Jonno went to her side and led her away. Paul was left alone.

In the kitchen, Jonno made tea and gave his mother one of the sedatives left by her doctor the previous week. About ten minutes later they heard the front door bang shut and the sound of Paul's car driving away at speed.

It was then Kathryn lost any vestige of control that remained in her. She sobbed as if her heart would break and Jonno could not console her. He ached for his mother, realising she had carried this terrible burden through the years, concealing the true manner of David's death. He knew she had done so out of pure love for them all, wanting to preserve the shining image of their beloved father, untainted by human fault or error. She had made such a good job of it that Paul had, over the years, wrongly concluded that the blame had to lie elsewhere.

Jonno did not think that Paul would easily accept their mother's explanation. Far from defusing his anger, it seemed Kathryn had fanned the flames of his fury.

CHAPTER TWENTY-THREE

GOOD NEWS

The day after the funeral the weather improved. The wind blew in gustily from the west, bringing a mixture of sudden showers and sunshine; cleansing spring weather. It was time to return their lives to some semblance of normality. So while Sarah stayed on at Greengate with Kathryn, Jonno drove Lisa back to the capital. Tomorrow they would both return to work.

As Jonno parked the car near the entrance for the Quays apartment block, black clouds gathered overhead, blotting out the afternoon sunshine. They ran, caught in a heavy downpour, racing each other into the lobby, drenched to the skin but laughing at their predicament. Distanced from the sombre, emotional constraints imposed on them by the events in Norfolk, they embraced with a sense of relief at being alone once more. As the lift ascended, their damp bodies and faces were pressed close together. Jonno did not want to waste a moment of the next few precious hours.

In the privacy of the apartment, wet clothes were peeled off like old skin. They didn't make it to the shower, at least, not then. As they stood naked, she trembled under his touch as his hands caressed her body. He felt the blood course through him as his need for her intensified. A physical need, but underscored by his deep emotional love for her – his Lisa, his Aphrodite, his Elizabeth. As they moved from the bathroom to the bedroom, it was this last thought which stayed with him through the urges and passion of the most intense lovemaking they had ever experienced together.

They must have slept for several hours, for when Jonno awoke it was dark. His watch showed seven-fifteen. Lisa slept on, but Jonno's thoughts were still of Elizabeth. The same woman but in a different body; the same love but in a different time. And what of himself? Karl was a different man in a different body and yet Jonno felt he knew him so well. He understood his thoughts and emotions; through the regression they had become his own.

"Penny for them," said Lisa.

He jumped, almost guiltily. Deep in thought, he had not realised she had woken up. "I was thinking about Karl and Elizabeth. Their love was very deep and strong, just like ours, but they were faced with a terrible situation. I must know what happened to them."

For a moment, Lisa looked as if she would question this statement, then she seemed to change her mind. "I'll see if Tony can see you again on Sunday. I'll phone him tomorrow."

Jonno felt he couldn't wait to resume the therapy. It had given a purpose back to his otherwise aimless existence.

Early the next morning he made the return trip to Marham. He arrived back at Greengate in time to join Sarah and Kathryn for a quick breakfast and to change into uniform for his return to duty.

"I'll be here for the rest of the week," he said to his sister. "Why don't you go back to London?" Sarah's grief over Max's death and the family quarrel which followed were still very apparent.

Kathryn added her voice. "That's what I've been saying. No good moping around here, darling. Granddad would not have wanted that."

"All right, I'll drive down after lunch, but I'll come back here next weekend," she said.

"That's great," said Jonno. "Then I can go to London and be with Lisa." He kissed them both and hurried out again.

On arrival, he reported back to the TIW to resume working in the photographic laboratory. He was dreading the tedium of his uncertain life at Marham airbase. Mid-morning, he received a message.

"The old man wants to see you at fourteen-hundred hours," said the messenger, a female clerk.

"Which 'old man' is that?" he asked, thinking there were more chiefs than Indians on the base.

"Top dog, Bailey. Who's a lucky boy then?" she chirped rather cheekily.

Jonno shook his head, "I'm never lucky," he said, as the girl scooted off again.

Chris Bailey was his usual affable self and repeated his condolences over Max's death. Jonno thanked him for attending the funeral. When he asked Jonno to sit down, he knew there was more to come.

"I have good news and bad news for you," said Chris. He looked over Jonno's head at some fixed spot on the wall. Then his eyes went down to his desk and he picked up a piece of correspondence.

"The bad news is that your referral to the Department of Community Mental Health will be delayed for at least six weeks. Your appointment with the Consultant psychiatrist will be notified nearer the time."

For Jonno, this was not bad news. It would, of course, delay a decision on his return to flying, but it would also allow time to complete more sessions with Tony and perhaps restore his sanity.

"The good news," Chris continued, "is that the MOD must have approved the job you did for them at Cardington. I have been requested to release you for three months, to go back and work with the airship people."

Jonno was quite taken aback. "Why me?"

Chris spread his palms with a puzzled smile. "Who knows what goes on in the heads of MOD men? But it does answer the question of what to do with you until the medics allow you back in the air. Which I'm sure they will in due course."

Although Jonno had been taken by surprise, he felt reassured by Chris Bailey's obvious confidence in him.

"Oh, and the other reason you're going," said Chris, "is that the airship chief specifically asked for you."

Jonno was even more surprised and wondered why Charlie had made the request. "When do I go?" he said.

Chris passed a letter across the desk. It was addressed to Jonno. "This is from their Director and gives you more details. You must have made a good impression on him. I wish you every success." Bailey's tone indicated the interview was at an end. Jonno stood and saluted him.

"Thank you, sir," he said. He picked up the letter, turned and left the office. Once he was outside in the corridor he ripped open the envelope. It contained a handwritten note from Charlie, along with the official MOD draft papers. He read the note:

Dear Jonno,

Good news! The MOD has awarded us a few more quid to get the Dolphin off the ground. They are also lending us a technical officer for three months. If you are reading this, you must have got the job! You should be with us the first week in March. Don't worry about accommodation, you can billet with me at my home for the duration. Everyone is looking forward to seeing you again. Also, the Dolphin is due with us that week.

Regards, Charlie.

Jonno read the letter twice and decided that, apart from its proximity to Paul, going to Bedford was good news.

That evening, after dinner, Jonno told Kathryn. "I have to go away again next week, Mum."

She looked surprised. "Are you rejoining the Squadron?"

"Unfortunately no, not yet. I'm going back to Cardington to work with the airship company. It's a three month secondment." Jonno poured their coffee into two bone china mugs.

"What will you do?" she said, as they carried the mugs over to the wicker settle by the window.

He laughed. "Good question, Mum. Apparently their chief asked for me. But I think the MOD chaps want me to guard the 'royal purse'. They are injecting a sizeable sum of money into the company. I'm familiar with their project, and some of the technology they're using is not a million miles away from that used in supersonic jets. I'm sure I won't be out of my depth." He sat down next to his mother.

"As long as you are able to do a good job, I suppose that's all that matters," she said quietly.

He knew she was concerned about his suspended career, so he tried to reassure her. "Chris Bailey thinks I will get back with the flyboys soon, so don't worry about me."

Kathryn relaxed a little, "I do hope so, son," she said.

As they sat by the window, the light from the room illuminated the patio against the darkness. Jonno could see the flowers of early spring bulbs clearly visible in Sadie's terracotta planters. "Will you be okay here when I go? Sarah said she will come back for the weekends." He was thinking about Paul, and the terrible things he had said.

"Oh, goodness," said Kathryn, "you two mustn't worry about me!" She stood up and started to clear the table. "I have lots of good friends here and Ian calls me most days."

"Do you like him, Mum?" He broached the subject cautiously.

"Ian is a very good friend." She stood still, staring off into the distance and Jonno could only guess at what she might be thinking.

"You know," he said, almost in a whisper, "I don't think Dad would have wanted you to stay single forever. He would have expected you to get on with your life and enjoy it."

Kathryn brushed crumbs from the table, as if to brush the subject aside. "I know," she said, "but the time has never been right."

"Well, we," said Jonno, "that is Sarah, Lisa and I, think this is your time. Take your chance for happiness now, Mum please, before it's too late."

She stopped and wiped her hands. To Jonno, she suddenly looked fragile and vulnerable.

"I'll think about it, son, I promise."

The next day Jonno received a further letter about the awards ceremony. It was to be held at the end of May. Her Majesty the Queen would make the presentations at Buckingham Palace. Jonno's stomach turned over. He had less than three months to turn his life around. He made a decision; if he couldn't meet that deadline, he would not collect the award.

Later in the week Jonno suggested to his mother that they should ask Ian round for drinks and dinner on the Friday night. To his surprise, she agreed and made the invitation herself.

"Can't let him think you're matchmaking," she joked.

Ian arrived promptly at seven-thirty. He was tall, with iron-grey hair. He could have been Max's brother, but years younger, for he was only in his fifties. Jonno insisted on being chef for the evening, leaving Kathryn free to be with their guest.

"I must return the compliment," said Ian, as they finished the meal. "You must dine with me sometime soon, and your young lady."

"Thanks for the invitation," said Jonno, "but I'm off again tomorrow and I don't know when I will be back home."

"Jonno is going to Cardington," said Kathryn. "It's for the MOD. A bit hush hush," she lowered her voice.

Ian cocked an eyebrow, "Mum's the word, eh?" They laughed at the pun.

Jonno didn't mind, even if the joke was on him. It was a joy to see his mother happy again.

When Jonno set out early on the Saturday morning for the drive down to London, he felt reassured that his mother had a reliable friend in Ian. It was good to feel he could shake off some of the burden of responsibility for the family which had fallen to him since Max's death. But he was also determined to try to heal the family unity. That much he owed to his grandfather's memory.

Paul's contemptuous outburst still mystified him. Over the years he had become accustomed to Paul's jibes and sarcasm. He was also aware of the cruel streak which had grown in his elder brother after their father's death. Now he knew why, and it disturbed him to realise the depth of Paul's hatred. Only their grandfather had kept Paul in check.

As he approached the capital, Jonno put the whole episode aside. His thoughts returned to his own life and problems. Although now these were more challenges than problems. In spite of all the setbacks, he sensed a new resilience within himself. Since his last visit to the clinic, and throughout the ordeal of Max's death, his nightmares had been a lot less severe.

Lisa was at the apartment when he arrived. Her first words were, "It's all on to see Tony tomorrow."

"That's terrific," said Jonno. "I just hope I can find Elizabeth again."

She stared at him frowning.

"What's the matter?" he said, realising the inference of what he had said. "You're not jealous of my past life lover, are you?" A smile spread across his face.

"Of course not!" she replied. There was a hint of irritation in her tone and she quickly changed the subject.

"Sarah is still giving me a lot of concern," she told him. Sarah had driven back to Norfolk as Jonno was on his way to London. "She hasn't been back to work," Lisa told him. "She said she couldn't face it; she is really depressed."

Jonno was surprised. "Oh! I thought she was pulling through."

"Well, she's not." she replied. "Let's hope she feels better after the weekend."

For now, Jonno and Lisa were alone again and they rearranged the day's normal timetable in the way that only lovers can. The day became bedtime and they stayed there until dark. When they rose, Jonno prepared and cooked supper.

"This is the second time in twenty-four hours I've been the chef," he complained, light-heartedly.

"Promise I'll cook tomorrow," giggled Lisa, digging him in the ribs as he juggled with the wok. He trod on her foot and she hopped away to the bathroom, laughing.

Later they dressed for a night on the town. It was ten o'clock when their cab dropped them off in the West End. After visiting a wine bar, they moved on to 'Salsa Havana' on the Tottenham Court Road. They drank and danced the night away to the sultry Latin rhythms. The first shafts of daylight were penetrating the night sky as they finally returned to the apartment.

It was as well Lisa had set an alarm for twelve noon, otherwise they might have slept all day. They just had time to wake themselves up in the shower and snatch a quick coffee before setting out for Wembley.

When Tony opened the door, he looked quite different. As he ushered them inside, Jonno realised it was the way he was dressed. Gone were the usual dark business suit, shirt and tie. Instead he was wearing designer cut jeans and a casual shirt.

"I hope we are not intruding into your day off, Tony," said Jonno.

"Of course not!" he replied, warmly. "You are my friends and I have been looking forward to your visit. To tell the truth, unless I am writing, Sundays here alone can be very boring. I've missed you these last two weeks. I was sorry to hear about your grandfather. How are things?" As Tony spoke to them, they moved into the lounge area and he served them coffee.

Jonno gave him a brief outline of the events in Norfolk and of his impending move back to Cardington to work on the airship project. "This surely must be the parallel connection I was looking for," he said.

"You maybe right," said Tony thoughtfully. "Only time will tell me if this is significant or just a strange coincidence." He turned his attention to Lisa. "And you, dear Lisa, how is your newspaper and the 'postbag'?"

"Everyone is fine, thank you, Tony," said Lisa, sipping her coffee. "I think there's another batch of letters for you to answer next week."

"I'll look forward to that," he answered, and then he turned back to Jonno. "So, how have things been otherwise since our last session? Are you still experiencing the nightmares?"

Jonno considered. "Yes, but they are not so intense; more like bad dreams and not so frequent."

Tony nodded, thoughtfully. "How are you in yourself? Do you feel any different?"

Jonno considered this. "I feel more in control of my feelings and emotions."

"Do you want to continue with our therapy sessions?" Tony asked him directly.

"Absolutely, we can't stop now," Jonno sounded a little desperate. "I must know what happened to Karl and Elizabeth. I feel I am drawing strength from their struggle, their lives. But it's almost like being haunted, and I need to lay their ghosts."

"That's a very interesting analogy," said Tony. "Your case is most unusual. I have never encountered any patient who could recall so much clear detail."

"What if Jonno's experiences are more than just regression?" said Lisa. Her question came completely out of the blue, taking Tony and Jonno by surprise.

"What do you mean?" said Tony.

"There's a lot being written about the work of mediums and spiritualists," she said. "I've read recently about 'possession'; when a spirit apparently enters a living person for its own purpose. Could that account for Jonno's detailed knowledge of Karl's life?"

Jonno looked at Lisa astonished. "You're not seriously suggesting that I'm possessed of an evil spirit, are you?"

"Not evil! No," said Lisa defensively. "And I'm not saying I believe anything, I'm just putting forward a theory."

Tony held up his hand and said, "I know nothing about spiritualism. That's straying into the realms of the supernatural: a place I try never to go. I prefer to remain within my own area of expertise.

"Past lives apparently occur under hypnosis, as you have witnessed. Whether there is any other influence at work is not something which even concerns me." Tony rubbed his hand over his mouth as if trying to find the right words. "My job is to find a solution for Jonno, not an explanation for what is occurring."

Tony turned to Jonno. "We will continue in the hope of giving you closure or to 'lay your ghosts', as you put it. You may discover other people you think you know from this life before the regression is complete, it is a natural part of the process. Your memories are all that matter."

Tony then turned back to Lisa. "I think you need to play a more active part in this therapy. Although, as I've said before, verification should not affect the value of the therapy, there are steps you could take if you want to look for more explanation."

"Such as?" said Lisa.

"Use your skills as a journalist to write a full account of Jonno's recall. I'll lend you the tapes if you like. It's up to you then if you want to prove if it is fact or fiction."

"Yes," agreed Lisa. "I could try."

"Let's see what happens today, shall we." He turned to Jonno once more. "Are you ready to try again?"

Jonno felt encouraged by Tony's words and with the way he had dealt with Lisa's concerns. Tony had realised she felt excluded and now he had given her a part to play.

They moved into the consulting room and the session began. This was his special time and the therapy was beginning to work, of that he felt sure.

When he heard Tony say the words, "Go back and find Karl," his subconscious took control and his spirits soared as he was buoyed up by a feeling of complete and utter amazement.

CHAPTER TWENTY-FOUR

HINDENBURG

Friedrichshafen, Germany, March 1936

Karl watched in total awe as the huge dark shape of the Zeppelin rose up gracefully and silently into the afternoon sky. This was the LZ129 and he felt a very personal connection to her. He had been with the development team for the last two years, shuttling between the engineering works at Stuttgart and the test-bed here at the construction site. Today the new airship was on her maiden test flight and she looked magnificent; more animal than machine, she had cast her leash and taken on a life of her own.

All around him faces were turned skyward in silent worship. The sheer size and scale of a giant airship in flight never ceased to amaze the people below, even those who had played a part in its creation. The ground crew, company workers and hundreds of onlookers had gathered to watch the largest airborne vessel the world had ever seen take to the skies. As the airship rose higher the silence was broken by a great clamour of cheering, shouting and applause erupting spontaneously from the watching crowd.

When the airship had reached an altitude of one hundred metres, Karl saw the giant propellers on the four massive diesel engines spin into motion, commencing their role to move the mammoth silver ship through the vast ocean of sky. He was filled with a mix of emotions. Joy and pride for the part he had played in the LZ129's creation, but also a nervous anticipation that his secret plan to escape from Nazi run Germany with Elizabeth was now one step closer. The airship was never out of sight and after a three hour flight over Lake Constance and the surrounding area, she returned to her birthplace, the giant shed at Friedrichshafen.

As the crew disembarked, Herr Franklein, their project engineer, came over to where Karl and the other men waited. They were all from Daimler-Benz and were very mindful of the importance of their role in the success of the new airship. There had been too many disasters in the past, but the LZ127, 'Graf Zeppelin' had proved the viability of the new breed of giant airships. She had already covered thousands of miles and made more than one hundred trans-Atlantic flights to North and South America, carrying passengers and mail safely through the skies. Now the new airship was set to double this capacity at faster speeds. Escape to America would be just a hop over the ocean, only two to three days away.

"Well, my men," said Herr Franklein, a smile of cautious satisfaction spreading across his face. "I think we are all to be congratulated. Dr. Eckener and Captain Lehmann were impressed with our diesel engines." The men were gathered round him. "You have all done extremely well. Tomorrow the trial flights continue to gain the Ministry's certificate of airworthiness. After that, the 'Graf Zeppelin' and the LZ129 are to embark on a publicity tour over the whole of the Fatherland. We will be away four days and three nights." Herr Franklein looked at the expectant faces around him. "Most of you will be on board for that flight, working in shifts to man our engines and train the permanent crew."

The men were ecstatic, clapping each other on the back, unable to contain their excitement in anticipation of the forthcoming flight. Karl hung back as the other men went off to make their preparations. He waited until the Project Engineer was alone before approaching him.

"Herr Franklein, sir," he said respectfully. "May I speak with you?"

"Yes, Stockhausen," he said, obviously still in buoyant mood. "What can I do for you?"

"I wondered if my application to join the airship crew permanently has been approved."

215

"I had hoped you would stay with the development team. We will be starting work on the next airship soon, the LZ130. You are part of an elite workforce. Your skills are exclusive to the airship project." Herr Franklein started to walk away.

"Thank you, sir," said Karl, following him. "But I want to fly with this ship."

Franklein stopped again, then he threw back his head and laughed. "Why not, why not young Stockhausen! Your engineering qualifications are first class. You will have to work very hard and learn everything about the airship, not just her engines."

"Oh, I will, sir! I will do whatever is needed to become a member of the crew, Herr Franklein, sir."

"I will put your transfer in hand," said Franklein. "Your employer will be Deutsche Zeppelin Reederei, who will operate the airship commercially. I will recommend you personally. The outcome will be in their hands, Stockhausen, and yours." He moved on again.

Karl ran alongside him, elated. "I will work very hard, sir, thank you, Herr Franklein."

The engineer turned back to Karl once more. "If you lavish the same attention on the airship as you do on your silver motorcycle, you will be sure to make the grade." Franklein moved away, still smiling to himself.

Whilst this was everything Karl wanted, he still had to work out how he could take Elizabeth out of the country with him. He had only been able to see her once since leaving her with Peter Bader at Black Lodge farm in December. The motorcycle was his lifeline to Elizabeth, but there was no time to travel to the farm before the airship flight.

The next two weeks were spent in feverish preparation and then on the appointed day in late March the LZ129, now proudly bearing the name 'Hindenburg', prepared to follow the 'Graf Zeppelin'.

Karl was now an official crew member. He had come on board the ship with the rest of the men two hours before the scheduled six a.m. lift-off. This was to be from Lowental, the Hindenburg's new operating base. Karl and his co-workers had been trained and drilled to perfection in their various job roles on six trial flights during the month of March. Now, with her airworthiness certificate assured, the ship was ready to commence passenger flights in April. But first DZR had been commissioned by the Air Ministry, or rather instructed by the Propaganda Minister, Dr Goebbels, to make their two airships available for this grand tour.

Karl was already at his post with the team of four mechanics who would man the operation of the forward starboard engine. They would each work a three hour shift, but now they were all crammed together in the engine nacelle for the start of the flight. The four engine nacelles were suspended laterally from the underside of the ship's hull; two each side, forty-eight metres apart and were accessed from the body of the ship across open walkways.

From his vantage point, Karl watched the airship take on supplies of election leaflets, swastika flags and government propaganda materials. As the passengers boarded, he could see many were government dignitaries and politicians. There were also uniformed members of the armed forces. Among them Karl noted a prominence of officers in the grey uniform of the SS. His thoughts returned to Elizabeth, hidden away on the Bader farm, and his cold hatred for the Nazis welled up inside him. He had managed to keep his anti-Nazi views hidden by avoiding political arguments at work, but his own situation was dangerous. If his visits to Elizabeth were discovered, the consequences were unthinkable.

The first shift of the flight was Karl's, making him responsible for the start-up process. The massive sixteen-cylinder, eighty-eight litre diesel engine took up most of the space in the nacelle, which was little more than a covered cage, open fore and aft. Karl operated the mechanism to preheat the engine oil. When the

217

temperature gauge reached 40 degrees celsius, he pumped the oil into the engine, ready for the flight. He monitored the range of gauges and instruments, anxiously checking the readings. The order for 'lift off' came at last and Karl was flushed with nervous excitement as he awaited his instructions from the bridge to 'start engines'.

At first, as the airship rose silently up, he looked out through the open rear hatch. To him, it seemed as though the ship remained stationary while the earth was falling away and all his breath was sucked from his body. Familiar landmarks filled his vision. Factory chimneys, gabled roof tops and church spires turned on their heads, then telescoped away as the airship gained altitude. The scene became a patchwork quilt of fields, houses and factories: Lake Constance, the shimmering centre piece in this landscape tapestry.

The cruising altitude was reached and at the given signal, Karl started the engine. Simultaneously, the other three engines were also brought to life. The huge propellers turned, slicing through thin air, as each engine developed 1,320 horse-power at 1,620 revolutions per minute. The voyage had begun. It was the first time the two great airships had appeared together in the German skies.

For the next three hours Karl remained at his post. Now he was thankful for the thick clothing issued to him, for it was bitterly cold. On his head he wore a fleece-lined leather flying helmet which helped to deaden the deafening roar from the engine. When his shift eventually ended Karl went thankfully to the mess room where a mug of steaming cocoa was thrust into his hand.

"Look, the iceman returns!" laughed Willi Schmitt. He was a junior officer – a humorous young man who had befriended Karl during training. Willi had fallen in love with Karl's 'Silver Knight' motorcycle and Karl had traded the loan of the bike to him for the promise of extra training on aspects of the airship outside his normal duties. Karl sipped the hot cocoa and felt the warmth return to his body, but there was no time to rest. Willi was going to introduce him to the gas-cell maintenance routines. They moved up

the ladders from the keel to the higher level axial corridor which traversed the centre of the ship like a spinal cord. As they walked its 280 metre length from stern to bow, Karl looked around at the gigantic honeycomb of lightweight duralumin rings and girders which formed the huge oval shape of the airship. It was called 'rigid', but he felt the whole structure was alive with movement, stretching and bracing against the elements.

Around them, the gas cells billowed and chaffed within the netted ramie cords and pulleys which distributed the lift from the hydrogen gas evenly along the length of the ship. He listened to the airship's voice as it sighed and sang, whistled and drummed. The entire interior was bathed in a diffused glow as daylight filtered through the ship's outer cover. Karl felt like Jonah inside the belly of the giant whale, for he was flying in a leviathan of the skies.

After his tour with Officer Schmitt, Karl returned to the mess. He enjoyed a welcome meal of beef and potatoes. Then, in spite of the cold, he returned to the doorway leading to the engine cage. From there he had a bird's eye view of the flight. The towns and cities below were festooned with flags. Crowds of people spilled on to the streets in carnival mood and climbed onto rooftops and vantage points to cheer and hail the airships. The thousands of sightseers were rewarded when the 'Graf' and the 'Hindenburg' hovered low over their heads. Then, to their surprise and delight, came the sound of martial music and electioneering messages, relayed from a loudspeaker installed in the 'Hindenburg's' control gondola. Karl felt a rush of emotional patriotism, even though he so strongly opposed the political messages being relayed to the crowds below. Swastika flags attached to small parachutes, and election leaflets were released from the airships over every village, town and city along the route.

They travelled north to the coast, east along the Polish Corridor, west over the regained Rhineland regions and south over the major cities of Köln, Frankfurt, and Stuttgart. Karl had tears in his eyes as he looked down on his home and realised his life would never be the same again.

On the second day of the flight, when he had completed his shift in the nacelle, he was ordered along the keel to the forward cargo hold. On the way he met up with two more off-duty mechanics following the same order.

"How are you doing, Stockhausen?" asked Dimmler. He had been with Karl during the construction phase.

Karl replied, "Apart from the cold out there, this is a great adventure!"

The third man, called Halder, was even more excited. "We are in a floating castle and I feel like the King!" he shouted, and they all laughed loudly as they entered the cargo area. But Karl's good humour turned to cold fear as the menacing dark shape of a Nazi officer loomed in front of them.

"Silence! You rabble!" he screamed at them. Then clipping his heels together, he raised his right arm and shouted the Nazi salute. "Heil Hitler!"

Instinctively, the three men responded likewise, but while the officer subjected them to a torrent of verbal abuse regarding their lowly position and lack of military bearing, Karl's memory was being jolted by a previous and equally terrifying encounter. The dark silhouette and flashing SS emblem were frighteningly familiar. This was the very same Nazi officer who had stopped the truck convoy on the road to Frankfurt on the night Karl had spirited Elizabeth out of Stuttgart. He remembered only too well the shrieking voice and his cruel face. He also vividly recalled the Nazi's unprovoked assault on the truck driver. The hair on the back of Karl's neck pricked as his fear of this particular man flooded his senses.

He tried to keep behind Dimmler and Halder and not make eye contact with their tormentor. He was afraid that somehow the Nazi would connect him with that night when he had hidden with Elizabeth in the filthy ditch. But the man was so full of his own *importance and had so little regard for the crewmen that he soon tired of their stoic compliance. He ordered them to do the job for which they had originally been sent, which was to release hundreds more leaflets from the cargo hatch while the airship hovered over the next town on their route.*

Eventually, he left them to their task and strutted off towards the passenger deck in the direction of the specially isolated 'smoking area' for passengers, where drinks were also served. The three mechanics continued dropping the wads of printed leaflets out of the hatch. They were all very chastened, but Karl sensed none of them had the courage to express their views on the incident. It was depressing to feel they were reluctant even to trust one another.

Later, Karl found Willi Schmitt in the crew's mess. He was detailing an electrician to a job in the control gondola. When the man had gone and they were alone, Karl told Willi about the SS officer.

"Ah! You have tangled with the 'Mad Major' my friend," laughed Willi.

Karl looked horror-struck.

"Major von Outen!" said Willi, and he clicked his heels together raising his right arm, mocking the Nazi's Hitler salute.

"Hush!" said Karl, looking round anxiously to ensure they were still alone.

Willi became serious and lowered his voice. "They say the Major is close to Field Marshall Goering."

Karl's eyes grew wide and fearful. "Do you think he will report us?" he asked the junior officer.

Willi shrugged his shoulders. "You did nothing wrong, but then..." his mocking smile returned and he wagged his finger in Karl's face. "You are not good little Nazi soldiers either." He lowered his voice again. "If the 'Mad Major' had his way we would all be in that uniform."

Karl sighed deeply and made up his mind to steer well clear of the terrible SS major and to concentrate on his duties. That would be his passport out of Nazi Germany and, God willing, Elizabeth's also.

After the four day flight over Germany, the two airships returned to Friedrichshafen. There the 'Hindenburg' was immediately made ready for her first transatlantic passenger trip. She set off for Rio de Janeiro less than two days later. Like most of the other new crew members, this was Karl's first trip abroad. He was both fearful and excited. As they crossed the great Atlantic Ocean he spied occasional steamers and sailing ships, like toy boats lost on a vast lake. Shoals of flying fish and schools of leaping dolphins appeared below in the constantly moving blue-grey mass of water. Karl agreed with Halder's sentiments; he was king of the castle looking out on a magical new world. The gloom of living in Nazi Germany now seemed a long way off.

The 'Hindenburg' arrived in Brazil on the fourth of April, landing at Santa Cruz. The air was hot and sultry, like a Turkish bath. The crew wore the least clothes possible, but Karl was still constantly bathed in perspiration. There was plenty of work to do on the airship, but on the second day the men were allowed a few hours off duty.

Karl, Dimmler and Halder were able to hitch a train ride on the newly built rail link to Rio where they made straight for the famous Copacabaña beach. They ran into the water in their undergarments. He would never have done such a thing back home. But in this flamboyant tropical paradise, where girls and men were parading their sun-kissed bodies and groups of musicians strummed guitars and played bongos and maracas filling the air with Latin rhythms, Karl felt uninhibited and anonymous. Five days later they were back in Germany and after a further two days of duty, Karl was allowed a whole week's leave. At last, he would see Elizabeth again.

In the evening after his last shift, he travelled to Stuttgart. The 'Silver Knight' motorcycle turned the journey from Friedrichshafen into a joy. When the road conditions allowed, he pushed the bike up to speeds over one hundred kilometres an hour, nearly as fast as the Hindenburg's cruising speed. That night Karl stayed with his mother and father and enjoyed a few home comforts. Early the next day he continued the journey to Black Lodge farm. His route lay on the old country road where he hoped to avoid any military traffic or checkpoints. Now his speed was much slower and at times he walked, pushing the bike over rutted cart tracks.

He recalled the freezing night journey with Elizabeth, back in December which had brought them to the farm. Today he was greeted with spring sunshine, green meadows and bird song. The hedgerows were bursting with sweet-scented hawthorn blossom, hazel catkins and wild garlic. The mix of perfumes overwhelmed his senses and raised his mood. He thought only of seeing Elizabeth again and the love in his heart was re-awakened.

Karl passed by the tractor gate entrance from where they had found their way into the valley. Today he wanted to approach the farmhouse from the front, to make a grand entrance on the silver motorcycle. Half a kilometre further on he took the turning, clearly marked with a sign, 'To Black Lodge Farm'. He freewheeled the bike along the track, intending to kick-start and rev the engine once the house came into view. That would let them know he was coming. Excitement mounting, he thought that perhaps Elizabeth would run out to meet him. As he rounded the last bend to his horror Karl immediately saw that Herr Bader already had visitors. Unwelcome visitors in the form of an army patrol.

As Karl put on the brakes the bike wobbled and he nearly fell, but he managed to turn it round, and swinging his legs to the ground he pushed the bike, quickly retracing his route back up the track. He forced his way into a clump of bushes, praying he had not been seen. He left the bike in deep cover then crawled through the undergrowth back towards the house, his heart pounding.

He could see Peter and his father with two soldiers near the single, open top patrol car; the driver sat at the wheel. They all wore army uniform bearing the Nazi insignia and armbands. Karl could see that thankfully, they did not wear the skull and cross-bones or the runes of the hated SS patrols. One of the soldiers was shouting at Peter and waving his arms about, but Karl was too far away to hear the words. There was no sign of Frau Bader or Elizabeth. Was she still safe, he wondered? Was she even there? His fear and hatred of the Nazi regime crept over him once more like a dense black fog, blocking out rational thought and filling him with a sense of total helplessness.

Eventually, the two soldiers boarded the patrol vehicle and the driver made a circular sweep of the farmyard, scattering protesting hens and ducks. Rudy and Oscar barked loudly, pulling on their chains as the patrol moved off up the track, passing a few feet from Karl's hiding place.

He waited until he could no longer see or hear the vehicle and he watched as Peter led his father by the arm and helped him into the house. Herr Bader looked on the verge of collapse. Karl went back to retrieve the motorcycle. He'd had a lucky escape, but he realised things were not right at the farm and he was frantic to know if Elizabeth was safe.

This time he approached on foot, pushing the 'Silver Knight'. He did not want to cause any more alarm to the family. The dogs began barking again and Peter's head appeared round the door. "Karl!" he shouted. "It's all right, Papa, it's Karl!" He ran over to where Karl waited at a respectful distance. Peter's command silenced the two dogs and he greeted Karl warmly, ushering him into the farmhouse kitchen.

But Karl was full of questions. "What has happened? Why were the soldiers here? Where is Elizabeth?"

Peter grasped his hand to reassure him, saying, "She is safe. We will go to her in a moment. The patrol did not come looking for her."

"Thank God" said Karl, with audible relief.

"True," replied Peter, "but I am afraid their visit will change everything." He glanced towards his father, sitting by the fire in a daze and taking Karl to one side, he spoke in a whisper. "They came for me. I am conscripted into the army. I have to report to the recruitment office in Frankfurt tomorrow. Papa cannot manage the farm without me, but they do not care!" His voice rose with anger.

"Oh, Peter my friend, what will you do?" said Karl in dismay. "How can I help you?"

"It is good you have come today," said Peter, apparently trying to stay in control of his own personal crisis. He looked at Karl gravely. "Elizabeth has been very ill. She is recovering, but now we will have to move her. It is too dangerous for her to stay if I am not here. Mama and Papa will need to hire help just to keep the farm going."

Karl was finding it difficult to take in what Peter was saying. "Where will she go?"

"Tomorrow, you must help move her to my sister Greta's house in Frankfurt," Peter said, anxiously. "She is the contact for Elizabeth's new identity papers. They are being prepared for her now."

"I have brought the money for them," said Karl. "But is she well enough to travel? Where is she? I must see her!"

Peter sighed at Karl's impatience. "Listen, I have to tell you this first. We have received bad news about Elizabeth's parents." Karl's eyes grew wide and his lips fell silent.

Peter continued speaking in a low whisper. "We discovered they were sent to the concentration camp at Dachau. Now we have learnt they are both dead: victims of Nazi persecution."

"Oh, dear God, no!" gasped Karl.

"We will tell her when she is well enough to bear such dreadful news," said Peter. "Come, I will take you to her now."

He led the way through to the dairy built on to the back of the house. At the far end he opened a cupboard door. Inside this he removed a panel revealing a hidden flight of wooden stairs, narrow and steep, leading up into the roof space. Peter took Karl up the dark stairway and called out, "It is I, Mama, the soldiers have gone, but we have another visitor."

The two young men entered a cramped room hidden above the dairy. There was no daylight, only the yellow flicker of a small oil lamp turned low. Elizabeth was lying on a little wooden bed in the corner of the room. As he approached this once beautiful woman who was the centre of his life, all he could see were two enormous eyes, wide with fright. Set in a face so pale and thin, it was only by her eyes that he could recognise her.

CHAPTER TWENTY-FIVE

FACT OR FICTION

London, England, March 2000

When the regression session ended after nearly five hours, Jonno was once again physically and emotionally drained. Nevertheless, when he and Lisa returned to the Dockland's apartment and went to bed, he found that he couldn't sleep. Around three o'clock he slipped quietly from the bedroom retreating to the lounge. There he sat in the dark, looking out over the marina, waiting for the dawn to break.

The night was clear, and he tracked a crescent moon until it disappeared behind the high-rise apartments to the right of his line of vision. Even this barely registered, for his head was still full of the wonderful and frightening images revealed to him while under the influence of Tony's hypnosis.

Now he was certain that he had once travelled in the giant German airship 'Hindenburg'. Even through recall, the experience had been exhilarating, yet completely different from the flying experiences of Johnathon Amis. As Karl, he had felt the pioneering spirit, conquering new horizons. Rather like the sixties astronauts might have felt going to the moon. That thought took him back into his dreams, which as a child he had interpreted as journeying in a giant spacecraft; now he could see the connection.

Although he had already known that the 'Hindenburg' had crashed to the ground in flames nearly seventy years ago, he still did not know what had happened to Karl and Elizabeth. He could speculate and half guess at the truth, but he needed to know for sure what had become of them and if the SS Nazi Officer, Major von Outen, had played a part in their lives and possibly their deaths.

Jonno was not sure how he would deal with that. And Elizabeth, his darling, beautiful Elizabeth; she had looked so pale and ill. He wondered how she had coped with her terrible ordeal and the death of her parents.

The journey from the farm to Greta's home in Frankfurt had been frightening. They'd travelled in Herr Bader's farm truck. Elizabeth had been wrapped in blankets and Karl had lain beside her in the back of the open truck, between the hay bales and covered with sacking. Peter and his father had travelled in the cab, for Peter had to report to the Army recruiting depot.

Jonno relived the moment they were stopped at a checkpoint. Peter produced his conscription papers and Herr Bader gave assurances that the hay was destined for market. Even so, an officious little soldier yelling Nazi slogans prodded the hay with his rifle, bayonet fixed. Jonno could still taste the fear in his mouth and feel Elizabeth clinging to him in sheer terror. Miraculously, they were not discovered and eventually reached Greta's house on the outskirts of the city and they slipped inside unnoticed.

Greta was a younger version of her mother. Her baby son, now three months old, was nestled into her ample bosom. Her long full skirt swished as she moved quickly to greet her guests and prepare hot food and drinks. As though in defiance of her ordeal, Elizabeth seemed brighter. She assured Karl and Greta she would soon be well again and able to help Greta with the baby.

Jonno was astounded by his recall of these events. They were as sharp and clear as recent events from this life – two distinct and different sets of memories. He heard the bedroom door click open. Lisa stood in the doorway in her towel robe.

"Are you okay?" she asked him.

"I'm fine, I just couldn't sleep," he answered, coming back to the present with a jolt.

Lisa went to the kitchen and returned carrying two mugs of tea. She sat with him on the sofa and as he put his arm around her shoulder, he sensed the same warm loving presence he had experienced when embracing Elizabeth. Daylight was beginning to filter into the room. As she turned her head she looked at him with Elizabeth's eyes and once again he felt the fear surrounding his past life. The memories continued to flood back and Jonno began to relate his memories to Lisa.

"Greta and her husband apparently collaborated with the Quaker Friends in Frankfurt. They had connections with a forger and Greta said the documents for Elizabeth could now be completed, including a passport."

Lisa picked up her pad and began writing notes.

"I gave them all the money I had saved from my wages," he continued. "They refused it, but I insisted they use it for medicine and to pay for Elizabeth's documents."

"How can you know all this detail?" she asked.

Jonno tapped his head with his fingers. "Don't ask me how," he said with equal incredulity. "It's just there, as though it happened yesterday."

"If you remember any more you must let me know," she said putting the notebook down. "It's time for us to get ready for our busy week ahead." She seemed tired and a little tetchy.

Jonno looked at his watch, it was six-thirty. "Yes, I'm afraid it is. I have to return to Cardington today. If you do as Tony suggested and write down everything like a sort of journal, perhaps then we can start to look for other evidence outside of the regression."

Lisa's mood brightened. "Now that is my forte. Research might prove what happened without you having to complete the regression."

Jonno nodded thoughtfully. "And you are the best one to do it. Where will you start?"

She picked up the notes she had been writing. "First I need to listen to all the tapes and write the account from the beginning." She moved into the bathroom and turned on the shower. "Then, if you agree, I think I will try to involve Sarah."

Jonno looked puzzled. "Sarah?"

229

Lisa smiled as she dropped her towel robe and entered the shower cubicle, raising her voice over the noise of the running water. "She's a bit like me; she needs some motivation and I know she wants to help you. But more to the point – she speaks German."

Jonno stepped into the shower behind Lisa, thinking that not only was she beautiful and very sexy, she was also pretty smart.

The following day Lisa was working at the apartment. She had taken time out to write the past life journal. Sarah was back from Norfolk but had still not returned to work in the busy law practice. When she emerged from her room mid-morning, she looked pale and drawn.

"You could do with some fresh air and a new purpose," said Lisa, hoping to bolster her friend's spirits.

"Doing what?" answered a despondent Sarah.

"Let's go out for a walk," said Lisa, putting on her coat and passing Sarah her sheepskin jacket. "I'll explain as we go," she said, leading the way to the lift.

Today was bright and sunny and although the wind was chilly there was a feel of spring in the air. As they started on a circular route round the dock area, Sarah walked with her hands thrust deep in her pockets. "I'm glad to see the back of February," she said. "The new millennium seems to have made a bad start."

Lisa agreed. "A lot of people seem to be having rough luck at the moment. However, I have an idea which will keep you and I busy, if you'll agree to help me."

They had stopped near a luxury yacht moored in one of the marinas. As the vessel rocked up and down on the water they watched a man on aboard sluicing the deck.

"I'm curious now," said Sarah. "Tell me more."

"Well," began Lisa, "do you remember I told you about Jonno's visit to Tony Reeve and the past life he revealed under hypnosis?" Lisa had explained some of the details when they were at Greengate, but Sarah's grief over Max had overshadowed everything else at the time.

"Yes," said Sarah, apparently recalling the conversation. "He worked at a car factory in Germany in the thirties, and his name was Karl."

The man on the yacht swished his broom down the length of the deck.

"He was engaged to a girl called Elizabeth," said Lisa.

"And she was a Jewess," remembered Sarah. "But how could you ever know if a past life was a real life?"

"You can't generally," explained Lisa. "Jonno has given such a lot of detail, as if it was a true experience. I have begun to write down his story of Karl and Elizabeth. Now I'd like to try to find if there's any evidence they were real people."

On the yacht, the man was leaning on the rail, smoking a cigarette.

They linked arms and moved on again.

The yachtsman waved, but they seemed not to notice.

"So what do you want me to do?" continued Sarah.

"You speak German," said Lisa. "I'm not sure where this will lead, but we may need a translator at some point."

"I'm going to visit one of our offices in Germany in a couple of weeks' time. It's all part of my training," said Sarah. "To learn more about their legal system and use the language."

"That's fantastic!" Lisa enthused. "Will you get to know your German colleagues?"

"Yes," Sarah answered. "I'll meet the people I deal with on the phone." She looked brighter already. "I know our firm has been involved in the restoration of Jewish property back to its rightful owners and their heirs, mainly through our Berlin and Vienna offices. It's been going on for years."

"Do you think your contacts might be able to help us check some of the detail?" asked Lisa.

231

"It will probably depend on what sort of information you have," said Sarah. They had reached the river and they crossed over the road to watch the boats moving up and down on the Thames.

"I'm making a full transcript from the tapes of everything Jonno said during the sessions so far," said Lisa. "But there is no guarantee he'll give any more details." She rested her hand on Sarah's shoulder affectionately. "Will you help me? I think it's important to Jonno to know if they really lived."

"Of course I will!" Sarah seemed full of enthusiasm. "If it's important to Jonno I want to be part of it. I'll make enquiries when I arrive and see who can help us."

Lisa was pleased to have involved Sarah. Having a plan had removed some of her own negative thoughts, particularly about Elizabeth. She knew exactly what she would do next. When they returned to the apartment Lisa scanned the internet on her laptop, and then she made a rather important phone call.

Jonno had returned to Cardington with a great deal of uncertainty in his mind. The prospect of working on the airship project for the next three months was quite daunting and he still didn't know why Charlie had asked for him. He did however, have a strong conviction that fate was pulling him in this particular direction for a reason. The regression had revealed the connection with the German airship LZ129, 'Hindenburg', and he was intrigued by this strange coincidence.

Hugh Charlton, or 'Charlie' as he was known to everyone at Cardington, was as good as his word insisting Jonno should lodge with him for the duration of his stay. His home was a comfortable fifties bungalow with a large secluded garden, situated on the edge of the village. The house was cluttered with piles of books and technical papers, but the guest bedroom was well furnished, with French doors opening on to the rear garden. On the bookcase Jonno found several volumes relating to the chequered history of airships from the past.

On his first evening with Charlie they discussed the part Jonno might play in the 'Sky Whale' project.

"I asked for you because I didn't need another airship techo," explained Charlie. "Your expertise lies in the systems used in supersonic flight. 'Fly by light', radar, GPS and satellite navigation. All the computer technology we want to use for 'Sky Whale' needs to be tried and tested in the 'Dolphin'. I'm hoping you can give us some input."

Jonno understood the technicalities but was not sure if he could fulfil the requirements. "Wouldn't a programmer have been more useful?" he asked.

Charlie laughed, "We've got one of those, Billy Watson is our computer boffin. No, it's your practical experience, handling these systems that we need. Besides," continued Charlie, "I have to like the people I work with. I know you will fit in with the team and Doc Hales agrees with me."

"Thank you both for the vote of confidence," Jonno smiled. "I hope you're not disappointed."

Charlie went on to outline more details relating to the project and his hopes for the success of 'Sky Dolphin'. Once again, his natural enthusiasm captured Jonno's imagination as they studied computer projection printouts and technical blueprints for the new airship which would arrive later in the week.

It was after ten o'clock when Jonno eventually retired to the guest bedroom where he immediately rang Lisa.

"Sorry it's so late, darling," he said. "How're you doing?"

"I'm fine, bar missing you," came her reply. "You'll be pleased to know Sarah is going back to work tomorrow, and she's going to Germany in a couple of weeks."

"Oh, that's great. What can she do to help our research?"

"Not sure yet, perhaps make some contacts out there."

"There's still so much in my head that didn't come out on the tapes."

"You must try and write it down, or tape it yourself before you forget the details," she urged him. "Then we can add it to the account."

"I will," he answered. "But it's like a series of video clips; snippets and scenes, all jumbled up." Lisa's suggestion was right. His recall was so vivid, the sights, sounds and smells so clear, that knowing what happened to Karl and Elizabeth had become just as important to him as resolving his own future.

"One other piece of news I hope will please you," said Lisa, breaking into his train of thought. "Biddy has given me the go-ahead to write about your airship project."

"Hey, that's great!" He could hardly contain his delight. "Do you think you could come up to Cardington later this week, when the 'Dolphin' arrives?"

"I'll find out tomorrow," she said. "Meanwhile ask Charlie if that's all right."

Jonno knew it would be, but ending their conversation took a long time, neither wanting to say the final goodbye. When eventually they did, Jonno lay back on the guest bed and flicked through one of Charlie's books.

There were lots of black and white photographs of the old dirigibles – the British R100 series and the German Zeppelins. Of the 'Hindenburg', there were several. Nothing looked familiar except one. Smartly dressed passengers in thirties' fashions were looking out from the airship through the slanting windows of the viewing gallery. They were pointing at features on the landscape below. Jonno closed his eyes and remembered the day of 'Sky Lark's' flight test. For a brief moment he had stood in a similar spot and viewed a strange landscape. He wondered if all his so-called hallucinations, all his nightmares, were also glimpses into his past life. Were his psychic senses working in reverse? Instead of predicting the future, were they retelling events from the past?

Jonno had never seriously thought about life after death or reincarnation. Nor had he consciously tried to develop his psychic feelings, they were just there. But now he was following a trail, and he knew he would not rest until it came to an end. Lisa also, was being swept along with him on this incredible journey, for she was part of his past life. Like passengers in a tiny boat, they were floundering in a fast flowing river. His hand was not on the tiller; their fate was already decided. His attention returned to the photographs in the book on the bed and he shuddered.

CHAPTER TWENTY-SIX

GOOD FRIENDS

On the following day in the heart of London, Lisa was looking for a space in a car park near Regent's Park; she found one and manoeuvred into it. It was ten minutes before her eleven o'clock appointment and she guessed she could walk there easily in that time. She locked the car and hurried out into the busy West End, not sure quite what she expected to achieve from this visit. But her experience to date as a journalist was that a good start usually led somewhere.

She walked briskly and soon located the address she had been given. She found herself looking up at a red brick Georgian property. With its glossy, black painted wooden door and brass knocker it could have been a private residence, but this was the famous Weiner Library, open to the public. It housed the world's oldest collection of documents and books connected with the persecution of Jewish citizens in Europe throughout the nineteen thirties and forties.

Lisa's appointment was with an archivist. She found her way up to the second floor, scanning the titles over the shelves and gazing at enlarged, spotlit photographs on the walls. The stick-like, skeletal figures in grainy shades of grey, with gaunt faces and huge eyes stared at her, crossing the time barrier, still begging the question – why?

Lisa had planned her questions carefully, for she felt she could not reveal the exact source of her information. The name plaque on the desk read 'Michael Jacob'. Behind the desk sat a small, wizened man in a dark suit. His face was brown and crumpled like a walnut, topped with thin wisps of mousey brown hair but he could have been any age, for his eyes shone with the brightness of youth.

He stood up as Lisa approached and shook her hand. "I am pleased to meet you, Miss Hartnell." He spoke very quietly with a hint of Yiddish in his voice. "Now, how can I assist you?"

Lisa sat down opposite him on a polished wooden chair. "As I explained on the telephone," she began. She lowered her tone aware of the library's hushed environment. "I am a journalist with the 'Sunday Voice'. I want to find out about tracing someone who lived in Germany before the war." She was deliberately vague.

"A Jew?" he said. "You want to trace a Jewish person?"

She avoided a direct answer. "I don't know if what I have is true or just a story."

He studied her face quizzically, his eyes were smiling. "It would be easier if we traced a real person," he said. "Do you have a name?"

Lisa realised Michael Jacob could not easily be fooled and she would have to be more forthcoming. She began again. "There were two people. They apparently lived in Germany before the war. I want to write about them, but there's a lot we don't know."

Michael was still smiling. "Perhaps we should start with what you do know. Then we can decide which agencies can best help you."

Lisa took out her notebook to write down the details she would give to him. "The man's name was Karl Stockhausen. He was not a Jew, but he was apparently engaged to a Jewess in 1933. Her name was Elizabeth. We think her last name was Ekhart. At that time they both lived with their parents in Stuttgart."

"Ah, a mixed relationship," he said gloomily. "How sad, most were doomed. Did they marry before September, 1935? That was when the Nuremberg Race Laws were passed. After that it became illegal for non-Jews and Jews to marry."

"They apparently did not marry before then," said Lisa. She was beginning to talk about Karl and Elizabeth with more assurance. "So I presume they never did."

"So what else do you know?" asked Michael.

"Elizabeth's parents were arrested by the Gestapo. She went into hiding, assisted by the Quaker movement, but she was moved from Stuttgart to Frankfurt. We think the relationship with Karl continued in secret, he did not desert her."

Michael nodded. It was a situation with which he seemed familiar. "Many did; even married couples denied their Jewish spouses, such was the fear at that time." He turned his attention back to Lisa. "Well, you have names, dates and places. It's not much, but it is enough to start a search. Proving their birth may not be too difficult, particularly the man, but finding out what happened to them, that is a different matter. Is this all the information you have?"

"At the moment, yes," said Lisa, tearing out the sheet and passing it to Michael. "My source has only a sketchy memory, but we are working on him to recall more details." She didn't want to tell him any more and decided this was a plausible explanation.

Michael Jacob looked at Lisa's notes. "The best lead you have is the Quaker connection. They helped many Jews throughout the thirties and forties and they kept some records. Where these survive, they are a valuable source of information. In fact, I would like to follow this up myself, if you agree."

Lisa realised that tracking down lost Jews had been Michael's life's work. He seemed to relish the thought of another quest. "I hope I'm not sending you on a wild goose chase, Mr Jacob," said Lisa. She felt uncomfortable that she could not tell him how the information had been obtained.

He smiled, unperturbed. "I will give you a list of agencies that you can contact for the registrations for births, deaths and marriages in Germany before the war. Many were destroyed by the Nazis, and later, in allied bombing raids. The Germans have made a remarkable job of putting many of the pieces back together since then. Some of these can now be found on your world-wide-web." Michael looked thoughtful. "Personally, I prefer to visit and speak with people, like today with you. Computers are so impersonal." He began making a list for Lisa, scribing the words in beautiful copperplate handwriting.

She watched him, fascinated, embarrassed by her own scribbled notes. Talking with people face to face was one of the reasons she loved journalism. Michael Jacob's personality reflected so much warmth, shrewdness and humility.

He passed his list to her. "I will telephone you when I have any news. Between us, we may yet find evidence of your German couple. I wish you luck, Miss Hartnell."

She carefully folded the paper and put it in her bag, then shook his outstretched hand. "Thank you for your time and trouble, Mr Jacob. I'll let you know how things progress."

When Lisa re-emerged into the busy West End it was raining hard. She hurried into a nearby sandwich bar and ordered a hot cappuccino. She took Michael's carefully written list from her bag. All the entries had addresses, phone numbers and contact names. She smiled to herself at the preciseness of the man and knew that she had made a good friend.

On Thursday, when Lisa joined the early morning meeting in Biddy's office, she was surprised to find the atmosphere quiet and subdued. Even Neal's usual cheerful greeting was reduced to a whisper as he handed her a coffee.

"Don't go, Neal," said Biddy, motioning him to sit down. "I've something to say to all of you." She stirred her coffee and stared at the brew circling in her cup. "I have decided to take early retirement," she said. "I will be leaving the paper at the end of May." There was a collective gasp of surprise. The announcement was as blunt as it was unexpected.

Neal spoke up first. "You can't retire, you're much too young!"

Biddy laughed. "Bless you, Neal, for that kind observation but I always promised myself retirement at fifty-five. See the world and perhaps do some freelance travel writing."

"But you're only fifty-two!" blurted Caroline, looking quite distressed. Then she turned her feelings round and joked. "I knew you'd never survive the office smoking ban!" Everyone laughed, smoothing the ruffled atmosphere.

"So why the early, early retirement?" asked Lisa, still not comprehending Biddy's revelation.

Her boss sighed. "My old Aunt Kate died last year and I've inherited her home in Dorset and a little nest-egg in the bank. So I've no need to wait for fifty-five."

Lisa realised there was no way they could entreat Biddy to change her mind. Her thoughts turned to the future for the rest of the team. So apparently did Biddy's.

"Now, I suggest you two girls should apply for my job. Then the 'powers upstairs' will know you are both looking for promotion."

"But surely Caroline will automatically be promoted," said Lisa.

"There's no such thing in this business," said Caroline, contemptuously.

"That's true," added Biddy. "You have to fight and claw your way to the top, like I did twenty years ago." She sighed heavily and for once nobody seemed to know what to say.

Biddy broke the silence. "Now you know what's happening in three months' time, we still have a paper to produce for next Sunday." Their attention was returned to the proofs for the next edition and the final editing of the features. Biddy asked Lisa about her work in progress.

"I need to go to Cardington to make a start on the airship story," she said, "tomorrow if possible."

"What's your angle?" asked Biddy.

"My theme is that this new airship project is like the phoenix, rising from the ashes of the old giant airships. Britain's R101 was built at Cardington, and like the 'Hindenburg', both were destroyed by fire. So I need to show what is different about the new giant airships and pose the question – do they have a long-term future?"

"That should stir up the debate, but don't get too technical," Biddy cautioned.

"No, I won't," said Lisa. "But they are a very safe form of transport now. I want to raise the profile of modern airships and generate public enthusiasm for them."

"Right," said Biddy. "Go tomorrow, but I'd like to see a draft sometime next week."

When the meeting eventually broke, somewhat later than usual, Biddy went off with Neal to see the Sport's Editor. Neal was angling after a move of his own to the sport's desk.

Caroline and Lisa looked at each other and both sighed.

"God, will I miss that lady," said Caroline, despondently. "She's like a big mother bear to me, full of growls and hugs. I'll never fill her shoes."

Lisa began to laugh. "There's plenty of room for you to grow," she giggled, patting the diminutive Caroline on the head.

"I'll tell you this," said Caroline, becoming serious once more, "I can't handle any more emotional upheaval in my life right now."

"What's up? Lisa asked. "Have you got man trouble?"

"I've always got man trouble," Caroline sighed. "This is a bad case of unrequited love."

"You mean you're in love with him but he's not in love with you?" Lisa asked, sympathetically.

"It's worse than that! I'm in love with him and he doesn't even know it!" said Caroline, characteristically waving her hands in the air.

"That's easy – just tell him," said Lisa.

"I can't tell him," she answered. "I just can't."

"Who is this apparently blind, deaf bloke?"

Caroline looked Lisa steadily in the eye and said miserably, "It's Tony, and he doesn't seem to know I exist."

Lisa's mouth dropped visibly. "I thought you were just flirting with him," she said. "Like you do with all the guys."

"So did I!" Caroline exclaimed. "Then one day I realised he was constantly in my head. Like a tape playing over and over again."

"Have you tried to tell him?" said Lisa, realising now that her friend was very lovesick.

Caroline looked more dejected than ever. "I've run out of excuses to phone him. He's always so utterly charming but so damned professional. I'd need Arthur's Excalibur to even make a dent in his armour plating – I swear that man is woman proof!"

Lisa smiled at the thought of Caroline wielding a giant sword. "If you like, you could deal with the postbag," she suggested.

"I'd like anything that will put us together in the same room, but it's not exactly a turn on, is it?" Caroline needed more inspiration.

Lisa felt like an agony aunt as she pondered over her friend's predicament. "You could add a fictitious letter of your own, asking for help over a love problem."

Caroline's face lit up. "Yes, I could, couldn't I…"

Lisa didn't need to say anymore.

CHAPTER TWENTY-SEVEN

THE 'DOLPHIN'

The 'Dolphin' lay on the floor at the dimly lit end of the shed like a giant chrysalis awaiting its transformation. The only way to unfurl the hull was to gradually inflate it with air. This process had already begun when Lisa arrived on the Friday morning.

Delighted at her unexpected visit, Jonno had met her train at Bedford station and driven straight to the number one shed at Cardington airfield. After he had introduced her as his fiancée to Charlie, Alison and Doc Hales, there was so much feverish activity in progress Lisa soon found herself isolated, as even Jonno became involved in the emerging shape of the 'Dolphin'.

Alison Lomax took her to one side. "Stick close to me, Lisa," she shouted over the general hubbub. "I've a folder of press releases for you, but meanwhile I'll give you a run down on the design concept as the airship inflates." Lisa watched the huge pile of laminated fabric grow as the compressors hissed and sighed and juddered, breathing life and shape into the airship.

After a while, Alison broke off from the technical explanation she had been giving and her face took on a big, wide smile. "This is so exciting for us," she confided. "There's been times when I though we'd never get this far."

"How long have you been with LTA?" Lisa asked her.

Alison's laughter rang out musically. "Forever, it seems. LTA was formed for the 'Sky Whale' project; that was three years ago. But this team have been together for over thirty years. I've been with Charlie for twelve and I'm still the new girl!"

Lisa smiled, thinking of her own position with the 'Sunday Voice'. Thoughts of the paper clicked her into 'newshound' mode and she began to write her notes. "If I can give your publicity a boost," she shouted to Alison over the din, "it may attract new sponsors and help your case with the MOD."

"We could certainly do with new sponsors," said Alison. "Our bank balance is turning pink."

Lisa spent most of the day quizzing members of the team and watching them work together. The atmosphere was electric as the hundred foot wide, double hull gradually filled the centre of the shed. 'Dolphin' was now at her full length of two hundred feet. The twin domes of the hull were still rising as the ballonets filled with pressurised air and mooring ropes were attached.

It was around seven that evening when they eventually left the site. The 'Dolphin' was now fully inflated and looked like a beached whale, filling the far end of the building. Leaving her overnight would detect any flaws in the hull.

They made a brief call at the pub for a celebratory drink. Jonno had told Lisa this was where he had seen Paul on his previous visit. They scanned the bar for any sign of his brother but they didn't stay long, deciding to go back to Charlie's home after their exhausting day. Charlie had driven them to the pub in his car – a resplendent, dark green Jaguar XJ6 of nineteen seventies' vintage. Lisa had also been invited to stay at Charlie's and she sat in the back of the car with Alison. They drove out of the car park and Lisa looked out of the front windscreen, over Jonno's shoulder. As the Jaguar's headlights raked across other parked vehicles, she spotted a familiar number plate.

"That's Paul's car!" she said to Jonno, leaning forward. "Did you see it?"

"I saw it," he replied. "But Paul wasn't in it and I didn't see him in the bar."

"Are you talking about your brother, Paul?" said Charlie, unexpectedly.

"That's right," said Jonno. "I introduced him when you brought me here in January. If you remember, he was rather rude."

"I've seen him since," said Charlie, "at the shed."

"Really!" Jonno's voice rose in surprise. "What did he want with LTA?"

Charlie was driving along the dark lanes towards his home. "I don't really know why he came. We had a visit from an RAF security officer about the closure of their station. We have to provide our own security from first of April, although there will still be RAF police on the perimeter. Paul came with this guy, but I had the impression he had just tagged along."

"That's a bit odd," said Jonno. "But then everything my brother does is odd. Did he say anything?"

"Not to me, he didn't," Charlie parked up outside the bungalow. "But he did to Alison."

Yes," said Alison, "I didn't think anything of it at the time, but afterwards Charlie thought he had spoken without authority and out of the other man's hearing."

"What did he say?" asked Lisa.

"He asked when we would have our own security in place."

"Did you tell him?" Lisa questioned.

"I just said it was in hand and we should be ready by April first," replied Alison.

"But Paul doesn't work in security. He's a pilot, not a policeman," said Jonno perplexed. "I wonder what he's up to?"

Lisa's brain was also working on the reason for Paul's interest in LTA. "When was this, Alison?"

"Couple of weeks ago," Alison replied. "Before Jonno came back."

They left the car and followed Charlie into the bungalow.

"I'll put the kettle on," said Alison, making for the kitchen.

Lisa followed her. "And will you be ready by first of April?" she asked, continuing the conversation.

"I hope so; we'll have closed circuit television and beams in the working area. It's impossible to alarm the hangar itself," Alison replied. She made four mugs of steaming hot coffee. "Why, do you think we are at risk?"

Lisa considered carefully. "You certainly need to address security before I publish any details about your project in a Sunday newspaper," she said to Alison, but inwardly she was thinking about Paul and what possible reason was behind his visit to the company's project site. Was it just curiosity?

Later, the girls made a supper of toasted cheese sandwiches and more coffee. Hunger satisfied, they sat and talked airships for hours. Lisa asked Charlie for his input to the feature. Her ideas seemed to fire Charlie's passionate enthusiasm all over again. Out came the books from the guest room as he gave them a potted history on lighter than air technology, stretching back over a hundred years. In spite of the disasters of the past, Charlie put forward some very convincing arguments why modern airships should be given another chance to become part of accepted modern air travel.

"Imagine a massive flood or an earthquake situation," said Charlie to Lisa. "'Sky Whale' could transport a thousand tons of aid in a matter of hours, with the ability to land anywhere. It could become a floating hospital or lift hundreds of refugees out of a disaster area."

"Perhaps you should sell your airships to the United Nations," Lisa suggested.

"Unfortunately, neither they nor anyone else will buy a paper plan," said Jonno, "Charlie has to complete development first."

"And that," said Charlie, "costs lots of money. If we can't get sufficient funding here, as I told you before, we may have to take the project abroad."

"That would be a tragedy!" Lisa protested. "I hope my feature can stop that happening."

"If airship funding was measured by the enthusiasm of its fans, I could build a dozen 'Sky Whales'!" said Charlie. The statement was upbeat but the tone reflected his despondency. Lisa began to realise that one feature in a Sunday paper could not, on its own, save the 'Sky Whale' project.

It had been a long, busy day and it was nearly one a.m. when they at last turned in for the night. Jonno and Lisa lay in the guest-room bed in a lazy embrace.

Lisa closed her eyes, ready to drop to sleep but Jonno seemed wide awake, his head still full of helium lift. "Are we seeing Tony on Sunday?" he asked.

"I'll find out tomorrow," murmured a sleepy Lisa.

"Good!" said Jonno, with renewed enthusiasm. "I need to find Elizabeth again."

Lisa was too tired to answer, but she felt a stir of apprehension and wondered if Elizabeth was supplanting her in Jonno's affections.

When Jonno awoke it was still dark but he knew he had been dreaming again. His arms were locked around Lisa and he marvelled she was still asleep, for he knew he had held her very tightly, at least he had in his dream.

It was another sign that Tony's therapy was working. His dreams had never manifested clear images like the regression. They were just fleeting glimpses, shadowy and indistinct, but they had always unleashed overwhelming emotions within him, which remained after he woke; deep love, fear, terror and utter horror. In turn these had taken over his body and erupted into the traumatic physical reactions which, when witnessed by others, had given rise to so much speculation over the condition of his mind. He sighed with relief. The dreams might still haunt his nights, but the intense physical reactions were moderating. He was gradually gaining control over the images from his painful past.

In tonight's dream he had held Lisa, no – he had held Elizabeth, very tightly. He had been protecting or supporting her. His arm muscles had developed cramp and his fear of dropping her had been the overriding emotion. But why? What lay under that fear? There was another shadowy image in his head, one he had tried not to acknowledge, but like his other demons he knew he

247

must; the dark image of the SS Nazi officer encountered on the road to the farm. He had featured in his dream this night – once more the source of his fear.

He was now convinced Lisa had been Elizabeth in his past life as Karl Stockhausen. But the Nazi officer, his tormentor in that same life, had also resurfaced in his present life to torment him again. It gave him no satisfaction to realise that this man could now be his own brother.

As dawn broke and daylight melted the shadows in the room, Lisa stirred. He would not discuss his conclusions about Paul with her. She was having enough difficulty over Elizabeth's part in his past. Lisa had been his rock and supported him through all these months, but he could not expect her to understand everything. Now he could see light at the end of his long dark tunnel, he would have to be content with that, or risk losing her forever.

They had arranged with Charlie and Alison to go back to the shed this morning. They would then drive down to London after lunch. It was Saturday and everyone took their time getting up and organised. Alison cooked a full English breakfast and they were all eating in the dining room when Charlie received a call on his mobile phone. It was Doc Hales.

"What's up, Doc?" Charlie grinned, with his usual opening gambit to Geoff. As he listened in silence his features tightened into a worried frown. "Oh Christ, bloody hell!" he blurted out. His profanities caused everyone at the table to stop eating. "Okay, Doc. Will you alert the duty security officer at the station? Good man; I'll be with you in ten minutes." Charlie dropped his phone back into his pocket and stood up, abandoning his breakfast. "Sorry, folks, we appear to have had a break-in. I've got to go."

"Dolphin?" said Alison alarmed.

"She appears to be undamaged, but we'll have to inspect every inch of her," called Charlie, grabbing his coat and checking for his car keys.

"You go, Charlie. We'll follow in a few minutes," said Jonno. His mind was racing. "I want to check this out too."

As Charlie left the bungalow, Jonno and Lisa looked at one another; they didn't have to say anything. They both knew that the law of probability was that the intruder was well known to them both.

Twenty minutes later Jonno arrived at the shed with Lisa and Alison. They found Charlie and the Doc examining the main door and talking to the duty RAF security officer.

"Any damage to 'Dolphin'?" said Alison apprehensively, looking past the door to where the new airship lay at the far end of the working area.

"None we can find so far," replied Doc.

"And this door is untouched," added Charlie.

"So what alerted you, Doc?" said Jonno.

"This," said Doc, and he unfurled a large black flag on a metal flagpole. It bore a white painted effigy of the skull and cross blades. "It was attached to the 'Dolphin'."

"How?" Jonno stared at the piratical emblem with unease.

"They'd tried to pierce the hull fabric with the pole but the laminate is strong as steel. In the end it was just pushed into the ground," Doc explained, as they all walked towards the 'Dolphin'.

"And is that it?" said Lisa. They were all baffled by this peculiar scenario.

"Bloody pranksters!" said Charlie with distain.

Jonno was beginning to revise his own line of thought. Maybe it had been local kids playing pirates. "Mind if I have a look round?" he said to Charlie. "Pranksters or not, the crucial point is that someone gained access to the airship."

"You're right," said Charlie. "Doc and I will go over the 'Dolphin' while you start on the shed."

"I'm going to do an inventory check of the work area and check the components," said Alison. "I know every item that was there."

249

Jonno fetched the torch from his car and he and Lisa began to look around the huge shed. The lighting was confined to the front and working spaces. 'Sky Dolphin' lay at the end of this front section. Beyond her, the only illumination was from the rows of windows set in the high sides. Age and grime had reduced their ability to cast much light on the vast area.

Jonno swung his torch along the bottom of the side walls. It was obvious that the old steel structure was falling into disrepair. There were numerous weak points where an intruder could have entered, but he was looking for signs of a recent disturbance.

They found the place eventually, about five hundred feet from the main door on the side adjacent to the second shed. What alerted them was quite bizarre, but was apparently meant to be found. A household size matchbox left open and empty. From that they followed a trail of spent matches which led right up to the 'Dolphin'. Tracking back to the matchbox, they found the place in the wall where a corroded section of steel had been prised apart and then pushed back roughly into place from the outside.

"Do you think it was just pranksters?" said Lisa, looking at Jonno.

"No, I think it was Paul." Jonno felt gutted. In his book the matches had weighed the odds of probability and hardened them into a certainty. "All this," he said gesturing towards the trail of matches, "is a statement of intent directed straight at me."

"But why would he?" She voiced her disbelief. "Surely he wouldn't really torch the airship; what's to gain from that?"

"Oh, yes, I think he would." Jonno sighed heavily, burdened by his inevitable conclusion. "But his true motive is to put me in the frame."

CHAPTER TWENTY-EIGHT

TIME OUT

They left for the drive back to London later than planned. Whatever the intruder's intention had been, he had succeeded in disrupting LTA's work schedule and putting a damper on Lisa's visit. Their journey was made in near silence, each engrossed in their own thoughts.

Lisa had remembered to make the call to Tony and the therapy session for tomorrow had been confirmed. Jonno had so many questions buzzing round in his head. He wondered if tomorrow would give him the answers he so desperately sought. What had happened to Karl and Elizabeth? And had the dark Nazi resurfaced again in their lives to terrify and torment them?

They had nearly reached the City when Lisa's phone rang. It was Caroline and Jonno listened to Lisa's side of the conversation.

"Yes, I'm good." She glanced over at him. "So is he. What's up?"

"You mean tonight?"

"Nothing planned. Hold on, I'll ask." She held the phone away from her ear and spoke to Jonno.

"Caroline wants me to cover the London Eye press briefing. It's tonight and she can't be there."

"Okay by me. Is there room for two?" he asked.

"Can I take Jonno?" She laughed at Caroline's reply.

"He's good at that. No worries, we should be there around eight o'clock."

"Bye, Caroline." Lisa put the phone away in her bag.

"What am I good at?" he asked.

"Taking pictures," she said. "You can be my official press photographer."

The huge modern Ferris wheel called the London Eye had been erected for the Millennium, but had not been ready to open to the public until now. Tonight members of the press were invited for a night-time preview and Lisa and Jonno arrived as dusk fell and the lights came on.

They watched as the enormous wheel made its almost invisible revolutions, bathed in luminous blue light. A complete turn took thirty minutes. As the individual space-age capsules reached ground level, passengers were shepherded off and they boarded while the wheel continued turning. As Jonno and Lisa's capsule began climbing up into the night sky, they could see a vast area of the City and the river as London's night-time illuminations came to life. Lisa took the camera from him and busied herself taking shots for the paper.

He looked down. He was used to this view of the world but it wasn't the same as from an aircraft. This was like the ascent of the 'Hindenburg' before the engines were started; that silent moment when the earth had telescoped away and turned on its head. Now London too slipped away and he saw the chimneys and spires of Germany and the glittering jewel of the Bodensee. The only thought in his mind was his undying love for Elizabeth.

He felt her touch his arm and clasp his hand.

"Are you all right?" she said.

He was startled as he looked into her beautiful eyes.

"Elizabeth!" he said, gripping her hand tightly.

She stared at him, a look of incredulity spreading across her face. She shook his arm. "Wake up, Jonno!" she whispered sharply into his ear.

He rubbed his eyes and looked again. The last few moments were a blur of confused thoughts. "Lisa?" he said.

She sighed audibly. "Don't sound so disappointed."

He didn't answer her, but he realised his momentary hallucination had caused him to blunder yet again. Her reaction had been frosty to say the least, and she seemed to freeze him out for the remainder of the event, preferring to chat to other members of the press enjoying the ride. He waited until they were back on the ground and walking through Jubilee Gardens towards the car.

"Lisa, I'm sorry about what happened up there, but I don't have any control over these things."

She continued walking briskly. "I thought we were over all that, but you seem worse than ever."

He couldn't understand why she was apparently so angry. "I don't think I will be free of these happenings until I know what happened to Karl and Elizabeth." He cast around for something positive to say to her. "Perhaps we'll find out tomorrow."

They returned to the apartment but the tension of the incident stayed between them. Jonno found it impossible to bridge the gap; he could not even get close to her. That night they went to sleep without making love.

When he awoke the following morning, Lisa was already up. He found her in the kitchen making tea.

"I didn't dream last night," he said, hoping this might soften her mood. She walked past him into the lounge with the tea and gestured towards the table. Her notes for the regression journal were spread across it.

"I've been writing up the notes in the hope of making some sense of your thoughts," she said curtly, ignoring his comment. "You said they moved Elizabeth to Greta's house at Frankfurt and the forged documents were being prepared. Was there anything else you haven't told me?" Her tone was clipped and unemotional.

Jonno was thoughtful for a while and then he said, "Apparently, years before, Greta and Peter's aunt had a baby girl who died. She was also called Elizabeth. Her identity was being used for the false documents. My Elizabeth would be given the identity of their cousin, Elizabeth Bader."

Lisa shifted uncomfortably. "Your Elizabeth?" she said with emphasis.

Jonno heard the mild rebuke in her words. "Karl's Elizabeth," he corrected himself. "I think the plan was that with papers identifying her as part of the family, she wouldn't need to hide anymore."

"Anything else?" she asked again.

"I remember saying goodbye to Elizabeth and promising we would go to America on the airship as soon as she was well and the documents were completed. That's it; I don't know what happened after that and I'm not sure that I want to."

Lisa shuddered. "You could stop now. You don't need to put yourself through something potentially so traumatic, do you?"

He looked into Lisa's eyes and realised she didn't want him to find out more. Then he saw Elizabeth again, pleading with him, her life totally in his hands, utterly dependent on his judgement.

"I can't abandon her now," he said softly. "I need to continue."

Lisa stood abruptly. "This is all getting very weird," she said brusquely. "It's scary too, and I'm not sure I know you any more. Are you Jonno or are you Karl?"

He had the same problem. Was she Lisa or was she Elizabeth? But now he could see she was becoming very agitated again.

"I think," Lisa said with controlled determination, "that we both need a breathing space. There is too much going on for either of us to make proper judgements. Plus all this business with Paul, I'm having difficulty making sense of anything." She remained standing, a little aloof.

Jonno felt disadvantaged. "What do you suggest? I'm due back at Cardington tomorrow."

"And I've got masses of work on this week, as well as finishing the airship feature." She picked up the mugs and moved into the kitchen.

Jonno followed, very aware of her continuing hostility. "What's bugging you?" he asked, tired of playing guessing games.

She turned to face him. "Elizabeth," she said, accusingly. "You seem utterly obsessed with her. It's almost as if you were having an affair!"

Jonno was taken aback. "But you are her!" he protested, and then he lowered his voice, "you have her spirit."

She put out her hand defensively. "Look, Jonno, the regression was meant to be a cure for you. I don't feature in that and I don't want to." She moved past him, back into the lounge without making contact and avoiding his eyes.

He followed her. "I have to complete the regression. Remember you pressurised me into this in the first place."

She turned to face him. "There are times, like now, I wish I hadn't. It's changed everything." An invisible barrier was growing between them.

"I don't think you mean that," he said, surprised at her outburst. "I did this for you."

"Oh, no, that's not how it was!" Her eyes were blazing. "You know that's not true." She was almost shouting. Her emotions seemed to be overriding her normal logic. "I can't take any more. You'll have to go to Tony on your own today. I need to step back from the actual regression."

He was totally confused by this sudden change in her attitude. "Is that's what you really want?"

She wouldn't look at him and went over to the big window; she was nervous and jumpy. "You may be Karl reborn, that is part of your therapy." Her voice was highly charged and emotional. "But I am not Elizabeth. I am Lisa Hartnell, born 1976." She waved her hands in a circle and turned to face him. "I am not part of your past life, Jonno, and if you want me to be part of your life now – you must let go of the past."

He felt hurt and confused. "I can't do that until the regression reveals what happened to Karl, how his life and Elizabeth's life ended."

She turned away again, her arms folded defensively as she stared though the window. The barrier had become an electric fence.

"What will you do about the journal?" he asked, looking for a way back into her mind.

"I'll write it from the tapes when I feel I can deal with it," she replied without turning round.

He decided to try and play it cool. He wasn't going to beg. "Okay, I'll go straight back to Cardington tonight and I won't phone you until you are ready."

He walked away, back into the bedroom to dress and leave. He wanted to howl in protest and tell her she was being unreasonable and illogical. But it was beginning to dawn on him that Lisa, the professional journalist, understood the whole hypnosis, past life regression concept. She could deal with that, even write about it, with calm, intelligent detachment. But Lisa, his fiancée, the girl who loved him, could not deal with the situation. On an emotional level she felt threatened and confused. He had recognised the warning signs that this could finish their relationship.

When he was ready to leave, she followed him to the door. He spoke calmly, making no attempt at physical contact. "I'll wait to hear from you then," he said. The words came out hollow and detached, as though someone else had said them.

She still didn't seem able to look at him, scuffing the carpet with her foot. "Yes, all right," she answered. "Tell Alison, I'll phone her tomorrow, I've some questions on the feature."

"Oh, so you're still going to do that?" he asked.

"Yes, of course," she said impatiently. "That's different, that's work. Goodbye, Jonno." She turned and ran into the bedroom and shut the door. The barrier was now firmly in place. Reluctantly, he left the apartment, quietly closing the door behind him.

Tony stood at his front door, looking confused. "You're early," he said looking past Jonno. "And you are all alone today."

Jonno guessed his face told a sorry tale.

"Come in, come in, Jonno." He closed the door. "Something's wrong, isn't it?"

Jonno shrugged his shoulders. "Sorry I'm early. I didn't know where else to go."

"Don't apologise. I'm glad you did. Come through." He took Jonno into the reception lounge and heated the coffee. "You'd better tell me all about it."

Jonno did. Relating all the occasions that Lisa had become upset over his insistence she was Elizabeth. Tony listened in thoughtful silence until Jonno ran out of words.

"I'm not surprised," he said. "That's why I suggested she write the journal. Did that not help?"

"She is writing it and I thought she understood better because of that." Jonno's voice dropped despondently. "Now I'm not so sure. In fact I don't know if the regression is bringing me any closer to a cure. Things seem to be getting worse for me."

"Nothing will improve until you find the source of the original problem, probably the end of Karl's life."

"And Elizabeth?" he asked.

"Elizabeth's also, especially if Karl witnessed her death." Tony spoke frankly. "For these two people were linked by their love, just as you and Lisa are joined together by love."

"Were," said Jonno, barely disguising his misery.

Tony smiled kindly and poured the coffee. "I must do everything I can to change that." He handed Jonno the cup. "Are you ready to go through another therapy session?"

"If I could, I would like to stay under until we find a resolution." He shook his head in despair. "I must find out what happened to them."

"Let's continue as we have been and see where it takes us." They moved into the consulting room and Tony set up his tape player. It seemed to take a long time for Jonno to relax and succumb to Tony's hypnotic suggestions.

When eventually he heard Tony say the words, "Go back and find Karl," his subconscious took control. He was instantly aware of the exhilarating sensation of riding a motorcycle. The engine roared and he recognised the road on which he travelled. He was on his way to the airport at Frankfurt am Main.

CHAPTER TWENTY-NINE

THE VOYAGE BEGINS

Frankfurt am Main, Germany, May 1937

"Hey, Karl!" called Willi. "Come over here and see the new duty roster." Airship Officer Willi Schmitt stood in the doorway of the staff entrance to the Deutsche Zeppelin Reederei building at Frankfurt am Main's airport.

Karl had just arrived for his shift. He secured his motorcycle to the stand and hurried over to his friend, calling out to him. "I hope we are both on the first sailing, Willi!"

He felt a nervous excitement rising from the pit of his stomach. It had been a long winter but now the airship was due to begin the 1937 North Atlantic sailings. If all his planning came to fruition, the 'Hindenburg's' first flight to Lakehurst of the new season would be his last.

"I don't like to tell you," said Willi, shaking his head. "But your name is not on the crew list for 3rd May."

Karl ran his finger down the list with growing agitation. "There must be some mistake," he said. "I have to be there! Look, there are dozens of names. Why am I not on the list?"

Willi shrugged his shoulders. "Some of the crew from the new LZ130 will be on board for training. Perhaps there are just too many men for the accommodation," He put his hand on Karl's shoulder. "I will see what I can find out."

Karl was mystified by his omission from the crew list. "Willi, I have to be on this first trip."

His friend's normal jocular manner was for once deadly serious. "I know this, and I do understand."

By involving Willi in his secret plan, Karl had made him party to the conspiracy. Karl did not know which was worse, actually carrying out the plan or having to abort it.

"Look," said Willi, moving Karl's attention to another notice. "You are on the list for the following week, 11th May. Perhaps we could change the arrangements. It is only one more week."

Karl shook his head. "Everything is ready for Elizabeth to leave this week. Any further delay could put the Bader family in grave danger."

Karl and Willi had become close friends during the 1936 season of sailings. Although Willi Schmitt was a junior officer and Karl was only a mechanic, away from their duties the two had a common bond; in fact two bonds. They were both secret 'anti-Nazis', and they shared a passion for motorcycles. The former had secured Willi's agreement to help Karl and his Jewish fiancée Elizabeth, to leave Germany permanently on the airship. The latter had prompted Karl to bequeath his beloved 'Silver Knight' motorcycle into Willi's care after his departure.

Willi's part in the conspiracy was to obtain a passenger ticket for Elizabeth and watch over her during the voyage, which as an officer he was able to do. The greatest risk lay in her forged documents, so they had decided that a last minute request for a ticket would give the authorities little time or the opportunity to make checks which might reveal flaws in her new identity.

Willi looked at Karl's anxious expression. "You will have to leave this to me. Once I have purchased Elizabeth's ticket, just be ready and I will get you on board somehow."

"You are my true, true friend, Willi," said Karl, breathing an enormous sigh of relief.

"We will speak later," said Willi. "But now we must both continue with our work." They hurried away to attend to their separate duties on the airship. There was still much to do before the first sailing, now only sixty hours away.

Willi's instructions were simple and straightforward. The airship was due to leave on the evening of the 3rd May. At the end of Karl's shift before the sailing, he would stay on board the airship, hiding in one of the cargo holds. When the sailing crew embarked he would mix with them and appear to be working as normal. That way he would avoid the crew's pre-flight check in. After that, no one would bother about his presence. There would be so many extra hands on board, the crew would outnumber the passengers.

"Just steer clear of the other officers and say as little as possible," said Willi. "Your familiar face will not arouse suspicion."

Karl was not so sure, this was a complication he had not anticipated. "I will be like a stowaway," he said.

Willi laughed, "Only when you sleep; three nights and then freedom for you and the beautiful Elizabeth. I am so looking forward to meeting your lucky lady!"

Karl lifted his head proudly and spoke with hushed reverence. "Make no mistake, Willi, I am the lucky one." In spite of all the difficulties of his continued association with Elizabeth, Karl did indeed still consider himself the luckiest man alive.

During 1936 there had been a slight improvement in their situation. The operational base for the 'Hindenburg' had moved from Friedrichshafen to Frankfurt. Karl no longer had to make the long journey to visit Elizabeth, for Greta and her husband lived just outside the city. Now that Elizabeth had recovered from her illness and the death of her parents, she had bloomed once more into the beautiful girl with whom Karl had fallen in love. 1936 had also seen a lessening of the Nazi controls and persecution within Germany. The Fatherland had been the host country for the international Olympic Games and had shown its benevolent side to the rest of the world.

It had proved but a brief interlude. Once more the authorities were clamping down on the so-called 'enemies of the state'. Under

261

the Nazi flag, Germany's military power grew stronger, as did Hitler's hated SS and Gestapo. Seeking out and eliminating Jews was once again the Nazis' deadly priority. It would be only a matter of time before Elizabeth was tracked down and arrested. It was imperative she leave the country now.

That evening, once darkness fell, Karl took Willi to Greta's home to meet Elizabeth and finalise the arrangements for her departure. The plan had to be executed smoothly and not arouse the suspicions of any watching officials.

"I'm afraid you may not see me at all during the journey," Karl explained to her. "Willi will be your contact on board and can give me messages. You must always be very careful what you say and stay in your cabin as much as you can."

Elizabeth looked disappointed, "Will I not mix with the other passengers?" she asked innocently.

"Yes, when you board and for meals," said Willi. "Be polite, and act very shy. Conversation will lead to questions. Most of the passengers are seasoned travellers and they love to gossip about their travelling companions. We must try and keep you out of the limelight."

"That will not be easy," said Karl, smiling at Elizabeth with pride. He had to pinch himself and look deep into her eyes to be reminded that this was truly his Elizabeth and they were, in fact, about to elope.

Her appearance was greatly changed. Her body was rounder and more curvaceous, her face had filled out and her beautiful eyes were shining once more. But it was her hair which was most changed. Her dark copper tresses were gone, replaced by lighter, almost blonde locks, waved in the modern fashionable style. Karl touched the curls. "Is it real?" he asked.

"Of course it is real!" She laughed at his comical expression. "Do you like it?"

"Oh yes, it is beautiful, but you look so different," he answered.

"The man who supplied my documents said it would give me a more Aryan appearance. See, I am like it in the passport." She showed Karl the passport photograph and she twirled with pure excitement, "I cannot wait to go with you, Karl, to America!"

Karl and Willi exchanged worried glances. The journey would be fraught with danger for all of them. Protecting Elizabeth might prove a lot more difficult than they had imagined.

On Monday the 3rd May, Karl's shift had begun at six a.m. He should have left the airship at two o'clock when the sailing crew arrived. Instead he waited until there was no one around and disappeared into the bolthole he had selected the previous day.

Either side of the keel walk, which ran from nose to stern along the bottom of the airship, was a labyrinth of storage tanks and cargo areas. Karl had found a place to hide in the spare parts store. Crammed into his kitbag was a blanket roll, for he would have to sleep here, clean clothes and a few treasured possessions from home.

He had visited his parents in Stuttgart two weeks ago and hinted to them he might go to America for good. They had not questioned him; it was best they knew nothing of his plans. His Mother gave him some family photographs and a silver crucifix. They hugged him very close when he said goodbye and he prayed they understood his mind and his motives. He also prayed they would not be penalised by his actions.

He was very apprehensive about the subterfuge surrounding his presence on the airship; he would much rather have been a listed crew member. Willi, however, had persuaded him that this way there would be no record that he was ever on board. When he and Elizabeth disappeared on the other side of the Atlantic, they would have plenty of time to cover their tracks before he was missed. Even so, he waited until the new crew were all on board and the pre-flight preparations were well started before emerging *from his hideaway and mixing with the men. As Willi had predicted, no one seemed to notice the extra hand.*

Karl was like a cat, moving silently from one area to another. He wanted to see the passenger bus arrive from the Frankfurter Hof Hotel, where Elizabeth had gone for her document and baggage check in. If she was on the bus it would mean she had passed this first important test, both of her papers, and her ability to play her part as 'Elizabeth Bader, teacher of pianoforte'. Karl waited inside the forward starboard engine nacelle, under the pretext of checking the airflow shutters. The passenger bus arrived, driving right up to the giant airship. From his vantage point Karl could see the passenger stairway, which had been lowered to the ground immediately behind the control gondola. Now he could see the first passengers leave the bus, escorted by the SIPO security men, and walk towards the stairway.

Gentlemen in tailored suits, children, some dressed like little sailors, and ladies, young and old in fashionable attire. There was no sign of Elizabeth and he felt his chest tighten. Suddenly, there she was, stepping down from the bus and walking across to the passenger stairway. She looked incredible; he could hardly believe this elegant young lady was his fiancée. She could have stepped straight from the pages of a glossy magazine or a picture palace screen, like the ones Karl had seen on his trips to America the previous year. He had no doubt now that Elizabeth could play her part but how would he cope? Would he be able to abscond from the airship and find a new life for them together? He had thought of little else for the past four years, but now he was full of fear for their future.

He watched as Elizabeth reached the stairway and was relieved to see Willi Schmitt greet her and escort her up into the airship. Willi had secured her late ticket by saying she was his cousin, thus giving him the opportunity to converse freely with her during the trip without arousing suspicion. The last of the passengers had come on board and the bus drove away. Just as

Karl began to move another vehicle screeched to a halt at the bottom of the stairway. Karl clenched his jaw as he recognised the familiar shape of an open-top military car. The driver jumped out and opened the passenger door. Karl felt as though his heart had stopped and his blood had ceased to circulate. He watched in horror as a uniformed officer of the SS mounted the stairway, shouting commands to the driver regarding his luggage. His boots thudded ominously on the stairs like a beating drum. Major von Outen was boarding the 'Hindenburg'.

Karl retreated to the isolation of his bolthole to await the airship's departure. As the ship began its silent ascent, he counted the seconds. He knew what the men in the gondolas could see as they rose above the Frankfurt am Main airport. It was dusk, and the lights of the city would be coming to life, like distant stars piercing the grey twilight. He knew the exact moment for start up and he felt the familiar shudder transmit through the ship as the four great diesel engines kicked into life.

The arrival of von Outen was a bitter blow and a further reason for him to remain hidden. He thought of Elizabeth, all alone on this huge vessel and wished he could be with her and protect her. Instead, he must stay here, shut away. Eventually inactivity drove him into a restless sleep.

CHAPTER THIRTY

REVELATIONS

London, England, April 2000

On Monday morning Lisa arrived at the office late and flustered with an apology on her lips. As she opened her mouth to speak, Biddy forestalled her.

"Don't apologise, please," she said, barely looking up from the paperwork strewn over the desk. "I'm only too pleased to see you at all."

It was then Lisa realised that apart from Biddy's own enormous presence, the office was empty. "Where is everyone?" she said, pouring coffee from the percolator for both of them.

Biddy looked up. "Neal has finally got his transfer to the sports' desk and Ms Trump has taken it upon herself to visit our friend Tony Reeve with the 'postbag'." She did not seem best pleased about the latter.

Lisa smiled to herself, remembering her last conversation with Caroline. "Well, she does have an ulterior motive, you know."

"Um, yes, I do know. She's been swooning over the poor guy for weeks." Biddy looked despairingly, and then she stood up from her desk, turning her attention to Lisa, "Well, how did the airship visit go?"

"Sky Dolphin," said Lisa, "that's its name. It looks great, but it's not ready to fly yet."

"What about your feature?" Biddy asked. "How is that coming along?"

"I've masses of notes," she said, taking her pad from her bag. "I was hoping to knock them into shape today."

"All right," said Biddy. "You can have 'til lunch time. Caroline should be back by then, so we'll run the preview meeting for next Sunday's edition this afternoon." She went off to the photographic department, leaving Lisa alone.

She moved to her own desk and emptied her bag of the weekend's debris. It was difficult for her to concentrate. Rewriting her notes into a readable feature brought the whole weekend back into sharp focus. She was already beginning to feel guilty about her stance with Jonno the previous day. It was true to say she felt stressed and under pressure, but that was not just to do with their relationship or his obsession with Elizabeth.

When Biddy had announced her retirement plans, she had made it clear she expected great things of her two feature writers, also that she hoped one of them would be appointed to her post. Yet Caroline had not shown any real interest in promotion. Now Lisa knew the reason, she felt under pressure herself to play a more active role in the running of the department. Ensuring they met the deadlines and produced the quantity and quality of work necessary. She loved her job but she was no longer sure quite what was expected of her. The last thing she wanted to do was usurp Caroline's place on the promotion ladder.

Her morning was interrupted by several phone calls and queries, but her thoughts constantly returned to Jonno and the emotional gap now between them. Her hand fell on her other notebook, the larger one containing her account of his past life. She flicked through it, realising the enormity of detail it contained. She had highlighted passages where the memories touched real events, the parts of the story she had considered possible to verify; a quest she had already set in motion. Now there would be another set of tapes from yesterday's session to add. She wondered what had happened when Jonno visited Tony the previous day.

Lisa felt mortified that she had allowed what amounted to jealousy of a memory to come between them. If she were to continue helping Jonno, she would have to put her emotional involvement to one side. Jonno had said he could not abandon Elizabeth and must continue to the end. Lisa came to a decision, she also would continue with writing the account, but she would not contact Jonno, not yet. He had to find an end to his past life before they could resume their relationship.

For her own part, the question of finding evidence was still to be addressed and she felt her dilemma over her own feelings rested on this very point. The phone rang again and she was startled back to reality. She answered crisply. "Features; Lisa Hartnell speaking."

"Ah! Miss Hartnell, Michael Jacob here."

She had immediately recognised his distinctive voice. "Oh, hello, Mr Jacob, how are you?"

"Very well, thank you," he replied. "I have some information which may interest you."

"You have," she said, barely disguising her surprise.

"I have had a response from my contact in the Quaker movement. I don't know if the information is relevant to your search or not. If you would do me the honour of joining me for lunch today I can explain to you what they have said."

Lisa did not hesitate. In spite of the pressure she was under at work, a meeting with Michael Jacob immediately rose to the top of her list of priorities. She would square it with Biddy later.

By the time she put the phone down she already felt much better. Uncertainty was fading away and she returned with renewed vigour to the task of completing her airship feature. The one o'clock appointment with Michael could not come soon enough.

Jonno was very aware of the irony in his situation. As he returned to Cardington, and the 'Lighter Than Air' project, his heart and his spirits were heavier than lead. He could not blame Lisa for wanting some space, and deep down he was sure she still loved him. The problem was he was in love with two people – the past and the present Lisa. She had unwittingly been instrumental in bringing Elizabeth back from the dead. She wasn't a ghost, but in Lisa's eyes she was like a rival; a former lover now demanding all his attention, and she was right – he was obsessed with Elizabeth. For in his past life as Karl Stockhausen she had been his one true love. Jonno was now reliving that life and it was eclipsing his own.

By the time he caught up with Charlie in shed number one, the place was once more a hive of activity. Charlie beckoned Jonno to follow him and he had almost to run to keep up with the project manager. For an instant his head reeled with the now familiar sensation of déjà vu.

Charlie stopped in front of 'Sky Dolphin'. "At the team briefing this morning, we agreed to pull out all the stops and compress the pre-flight preparation schedule from six weeks to three."

Jonno whistled. "What's the plan?"

"We're going to work in two shifts round the clock." Charlie was looking around as he spoke, apparently even now multitasking. "Officially, I'm the day boss and Doc is covering the night shift, but I doubt either of us will get much rest."

"Well, at least that should take care of night security." Jonno was remembering Friday night's incident. "Any leads on the break-in?"

Charlie shook his head. "The RAF security guys said nobody got past them that night."

Jonno didn't voice his own thoughts. If Paul had been seen he wouldn't have aroused suspicion. "What's my role now, Charlie?"

Charlie beamed at him. "Well, as you're not on my payroll, you can work twenty-four-seven!" He laughed. "Seriously, you'll stick with me. The engines are due here this morning. I want you to supervise the unpacking and testing. They'll go alongside the proto on the test bed." Charlie pointed to the area where they had been running the new diesel engine on test for several weeks. Today's delivery would be of the further two diesel injection engines which would power 'Sky Dolphin'. The third engine would provide all the onboard power.

Modern airships were usually powered by aero-petrol engines, but Charlie was following the thinking of the 'Hindenburg' development team all those years ago. Diesel fuel was less combustible and although it was a heavier oil, the lower fuel consumption would extend the airship's flying range. This would be crucial for the giant 'Sky Whale' when she was eventually ready.

As Jonno went off to check the delivery arrangements with Alison, his thoughts returned to the 'Hindenburg' and the strange quirk of fate that now found him working with the new engines.

It was seven p.m. when Jonno and Charlie called it a day and returned to the bungalow. Alison had gone ahead and dinner was ready and waiting.

"You are an angel," Charlie said in reply to her 'sit down and eat now' command. They had not stopped all day, surviving on endless cups of coffee.

The tempting smell of Alison's home cooked pork chops and assorted roast vegetables reminded Jonno that he was famished. "I think 'angel' should be promoted to 'goddess', Charlie."

Charlie and Alison exchanged amused looks.

"I do have plans for her," he said.

Alison blushed. "Eat your dinners and hush your talk," she scolded in her delightful lilting intonation. After that, the only sounds to be heard were of clicking cutlery and contented sighs.

At five minutes after one p.m., Lisa's cab had stopped in The Strand outside the Italian restaurant suggested by Michael Jacob for their lunch date. By evening the area would be thronged and the restaurant filled with theatregoers, but now foot weary shoppers and tourists took refuge in the intimate friendly eating house. Cool blue tablecloths and vases of fresh flowers adorned the tables and the perfect pitch of Italian opera music played softly in the background.

She could see Michael sitting at a table by the window. He stood as she approached. "My dear Miss Hartnell, how good to see you again." He shook her outstretched hand and courteously pulled out a chair for her to sit down. They each ordered a pasta dish and began exchanging pleasantries, agreeing to call each other by their Christian names. Anxious as she was to hear Michael's news, she waited patiently until they had finished their lunch before broaching the subject of their meeting.

"I am very curious to know what you have found out, Michael," she asked as their plates were removed by the patron, who enquired if their meal was to their liking. He left them, promising complimentary coffees to follow. Michael put his hand into his inside jacket pocket and pulled out an envelope. From this he withdrew a sheet of paper and passed it to Lisa. She could see from the printed heading it was a letter from The Quaker Society of Friends, with a Stuttgart address, but the text was in German.

"I'm afraid I need a translation," she confessed.

He smiled and nodded his head. "I have it here also." He pulled out a second sheet. "What do you know about the Quaker movement, Lisa?" he asked, still holding the folded paper.

She thought for a moment. "Not a lot, I'm afraid. I think it began around the sixteenth century from one man's religious experiences and spread into a worldwide network of societies of friends. They don't have churches or chapels, just meeting houses. They support one another and do welfare work. That's about all I know, I'm afraid."

"And basically, you are right," said Michael, smiling and nodding again. "Quakers believe that God is within all of us; places of worship are irrelevant. They respect the existence of other religions and work in a quiet way, leading only by example. During the twelve years of Nazi rule in Germany, Quakers were among the only true and trusted friends of many who were persecuted."

The coffee arrived but Lisa was intrigued, listening to Michael. "Weren't they persecuted along with other religious groups?" she asked him.

"No, not at first, for when Germany was defeated at the end of the First World War, many people faced starvation. The Quaker

271

movement played a very big part in organising feeding programmes and getting the country back on its feet. They were very well respected by the people and the government, even after 1933 by the Nazi government."

When Michael paused to drink his coffee, Lisa realised this diligent man thought it important for her to understand the background to the Quaker philosophy before revealing the information he had obtained.

He continued speaking. "Their strength is in communication. A small 'meeting', as they call their groups, say in Stuttgart, could have a need to help people in their area. Assistance would arrive from other 'meetings' in Germany or even from abroad. Quakers from Britain, America or other countries would travel whenever and wherever there was a need. They were especially concerned to help those being persecuted by the Nazis."

"But surely," said Lisa, "such actions must have put Quakers at risk?"

"Oh, yes, of course," he agreed. "As time went on and more people were helped to escape the country or go into hiding, many Quakers were themselves then imprisoned, tortured, sent to the concentration camps, even killed."

Lisa felt angry and disturbed. These events had happened before she was born but looking at Michael, she could see the hurt and despair carved into his features – his emotions raw.

"Every part of Germany was ruled by the local Nazi Council," Michael spat out the name as if it were poisonous. "They had replaced the Town and City councils, but were often the same people wearing a Nazi badge of office. Old neighbours, including Quakers, rubbed along together as they always had in the past. The difference was that under the Nazi badge, local officials had draconian powers to seize and arrest suspected dissidents. So on a local level, a lot depended on past friendships. Also, Quakers worked according to their own consciences. The movement did not expect individuals to oppose the Nazis if this put them and their families in danger."

"So how might this have affected the Jewish girl, Elizabeth Ekhart?" Lisa still felt awkward asking Michael for information about a person who may not even have existed.

Michael drank the rest of his coffee, and then he unfolded the second sheet of paper and began to read.

"Regarding your enquiry into Jewish persons with the surname 'Ekhart' living in Stuttgart in 1933, most official records of Jewish families were destroyed by the Nazi government. However, since that time, as you are aware, much work has been done to restore these. Several families of this name now appear in official records. None entirely match the criteria you gave. Details of Jewish persons helped by the Stuttgart Quaker Meeting for this period do not exist. Records were not kept for obvious reasons. We therefore had no trace of a female named, Elizabeth Ekhart.

"As you mentioned that this person may have been moved to the Frankfurt area during 1936 or 1937, I contacted Friends at the Quaker Centre in Frankfurt am Main. Many displaced persons passed through there before leaving the country as exiles or refugees. Forged documents were sometimes procured for those evading arrest warrants or to establish a non-Jewish name. A few records of these were recovered from a private source and given to the Society during the nineteen fifties. From these I have compiled a list of the female names used on forged documents around that time, which may be of assistance to your search. On passports, the status and profession were also given:

Fraulein Mary Hess-Nurse
Frau Elsa Grover-Nurse
Frau Helga Brant-Teacher of Languages
Fraulein Elizabeth Bader -Teacher of Pianoforte
Fraulein Martha Kline -Doctor of Medicine

"These names were apparently used but no actual documents have been found. There were no records of the original names of the recipients of these documents and no record of how, or if, any of these persons eventually left Germany.

"I hope this information may assist you with your enquiries."

As Michael stopped speaking, Lisa was overwhelmed by a sense of total incredulity. He passed her the translation and her eyes immediately homed in on the list of names at the bottom of the letter. The words jumped off the page. 'Fraulein Elizabeth Bader – Teacher of Pianoforte.' She opened her mouth to speak but no words came. She could not begin to express her profound feelings at this amazing revelation.

Her reaction had registered with Michael. "There is something significant?" he asked, studying her face.

It was with difficulty Lisa controlled the urge to jump up and kiss him, but instead she replied, "Oh yes, very significant." She pointed to the name in the list. "This is so incredible. It was only yesterday that the name 'Bader' was given as a possible link to forged documents made for the girl 'Ekhart'." She lapsed into silence, her mind racing back through the notes she'd made on Jonno's last regression memories.

Michael broke into her thoughts. "And this lady's profession. Was she a piano teacher?"

"Did I not explain that connection before?" Lisa remembered how cagey she had been over giving Michael too much detail.

"No, Lisa, you only gave me names, dates and places. You said your source only had a sketchy memory."

Lisa tried to assemble her thoughts. All along she had wondered if Jonno's recall of Karl and Elizabeth might be just another of his mind tricks: a product from the tortured memory of his own family tragedy. She felt guilty now about her lack of faith in him and in Tony Reeve's therapy. Even though she had asked Michael about looking for evidence, she had not really expected

274

him to find any. She had been totally wrong, and it was time to put things right. She would start by telling Michael everything she knew.

"The girl Elizabeth Ekhart was apparently training to be a concert pianist until Hitler's boycotts of the Jewish people put an end to her career and then destroyed her family." Lisa was beginning to see Elizabeth as a real person and to empathise with her plight.

"Now I know this," said Michael. "I can make more enquiries for you. Good, this information is very good."

Lisa felt everything was more than good – it was wonderful!

The work in shed number one progressed at a fast pace. Once the engines were set up, Jonno moved on to join the team preparing the electronic systems for installation. More helium arrived in vast gas cylinders and closed circuit television was installed inside and outside the shed. The possible threat posed by intruders, be they pranksters, malicious vandals, or persons engaged in industrial espionage, was now taken very seriously. The pirate flag had served as a timely warning.

For the first time since leaving the Gulf, Jonno felt connected to the real world again. He immersed himself in the project and tried not to think about anything else. Trained to develop a high level of concentration, he drew on all his technical knowledge and ability to assist the objective. Namely, to have 'Sky Dolphin' in the air in record time, with all her projected components installed before the first test flight. They could then be enabled and tested over a shorter time span. Charlie had been determined that 'Sky Dolphin' would be a record breaker from the word go.

Nevertheless, when Jonno was away from the site, the loneliness of his personal situation returned. Lisa had not contacted him. It had been two weeks now since they had spoken and in spite of his outward calm, his inner-self was in turmoil. His fingers had hovered over her number on his mobile phone a hundred times. The ball however, was in her court and until she served it back into play, the game was apparently over. He thought about contacting Sarah, but she had been away in Germany and he didn't know if she had returned. A call to Kathryn however, was long overdue, and she would be able to answer that question.

"Hi, Mum," he began when she answered his call. "It's your prodigal son."

"I was wondering when I'd hear from you, I thought you'd left the country. You sound a bit down, are you all right?"

Trust Kathryn to immediately pick up on his mood, he thought. "Just a bit tired," he said, evading the question. "I'm still at Cardington and we're working round the clock to launch the new airship. Is Sarah back from… Berlin, wasn't it?"

"Yes, she flew back Friday and was here all weekend. But it wasn't Berlin, she went to Frankfurt."

Jonno was surprised at this. "Oh, I didn't know that. How is she?" As he spoke, he realised Kathryn would wonder why he didn't know all this from Lisa.

"She's blooming. Full of her trip and demonstrating her renewed fluency in German, and guess what? She seems to have fallen for one of the chaps she met out there. She didn't stop talking about him all weekend. They kept phoning each other. Goodness knows what her phone bill will come to."

"That's great news. She's always been too fussy about boyfriends. I thought she'd never find anyone good enough."

He heard Kathryn laugh and then she asked him the inevitable question. "How's Lisa? I haven't heard from her."

That in itself was significant; Kathryn was Lisa's surrogate mum. Again he avoided a direct answer. "We're both working flat out. I haven't been to London the last two weekends, but she's okay." Jonno knew his mother would see right through his explanation.

"Everything all right between you two?" she said cautiously.

"I hope so, Mum. We're both very busy; Lisa wanted a bit of time and space." Not wanting to elaborate, he changed the subject. "How's Ian?"

"Ian's very well and so are we together."

Jonno could hear a new sparkle in his mother's voice.

"What you youngsters call 'an item', I think."

"I'm very pleased for both of you, that's wonderful."

"Yes, it is," she said with a little giggle. "I feel twenty-one again. He spoils me with flowers every few days and little notes in the post, even though I see him most days. When are we going to see you again?"

Jonno hesitated. "Not for a while, I'm afraid. The project will keep me here for a few weeks, but I'll let you know soon."

"I'll look forward to that, son," said Kathryn. "Give my love to Lisa. Oh, and send her some flowers. It does a girl's ego a power of good."

He smiled at her wisdom. "I will, Mum, I will."

That night, when he was at last able to retreat to Charlie's guest room, Jonno looked forward to a good night's sleep. He felt relaxed and certainly more cheerful than he had since returning to the project. Today they had started on the programme to install the new diesel engines and so far the work was going well. Prompted by his mother, he had also phoned the florists and ordered a bouquet of red roses to be delivered to Lisa tomorrow. On the card he had requested the words, 'I love you, Lisa, please phone, Jonno.'

As he drifted off to sleep he wondered if she would. Then his thoughts returned to his previous life. Karl and Elizabeth had remained true to each other throughout terrible circumstances. Nothing had broken the spirit of their perfect love. Jonno was at the very edge of sleep. Almost without realising where it came from, he heard his own voice say, "Go back and find Karl."

He felt himself drifting into a deep slumber. Time was indeterminable. He was stiff, cramped and cold, as though waking from a very uncomfortable sleep.

CHAPTER THIRTY-ONE

ATLANTIC CROSSING

Airship 'Hindenburg', North Atlantic Ocean, May 1937

"Are you awake?" whispered a cautious but familiar voice.

Karl hadn't been, but his eyes opened wide and his skin pricked with a moment of fear as he gathered his wits. He was relieved to see it was Willi crouching down into the narrow space beside him.

"Tell me what is happening. Is Elizabeth all right?" said Karl, "and why is von Outen on board?"

"Patience, my friend," said Willi. "Elizabeth is settled in her cabin now and I trust she is sleeping, but we could have done without the 'Mad Major'."

"Why is he here?"

"I heard Captain Lehmann say to Captain Pruss that DZR had received threats to sabotage the airship. There are some anti-Nazis in America that do not want the airship to land there. Our 'Hindenburg' wears the swastika on her tail fins. Major von Outen is on the look out for a saboteur."

"If I am discovered they will think it is me!" Karl exclaimed.

"Your best cover is to blend in with the crew. It is more dangerous for you to hide than to be seen." Willi's reasoning was sound and Karl trusted his friend.

"Tell me about Elizabeth," said Karl. "Was everything all right when she boarded?" He could not disguise his anxiety.

"She is fine now, but at first there was a problem," Willi told him. "I wanted to show her to her cabin, but none had been allocated for her. Herr Kubis, the chief steward, said her name was not on the passenger list. He became quite surly with me. We had to produce her papers and her ticket all over again."

"What happened?" said Karl.

Willi went on to explain that because her ticket was purchased on the last day, someone at the ticket office had not added her name to the passenger list. He continued. "Luckily, Captain Lehmann was in the public rooms to greet some important passengers. He heard Kubis remonstrating with me and he intervened," said Willi, quite gleefully. "I wish you could have heard Lehmann put him in his place.

"He said to Kubis, 'Does the young lady have a valid ticket?'

"He replied, 'Yes, Captain Lehmann.'

"Then the Captain said, 'Are her papers in order?'

"Kubis again said, 'Yes, Captain Lehmann.'

"Lehmann then said to him, 'Good God, man, what are you fussing about. There are seventy berths on this ship and less than half are taken. Give Fraulein Bader a cabin immediately and make sure she has every facility made available to her.'"

Willi laughed again at the memory. "Then Captain Lehmann gave Elizabeth a little bow and he said to her, 'I hope you enjoy your trip to America, Fraulein.' You were right to say we would not be able to keep Elizabeth out of the limelight," said Willi, and he stood up ready to leave.

"I cannot thank you enough for taking care of her, Willi," said Karl. He took out his pocket watch. "I will go back to the engine cage when the crews change."

Willi checked his own watch. "That will be in fifteen minutes time, at midnight. We are approaching the English Channel now and will fly along England's south coast. I will try and speak with you again tomorrow, but now I need to get some sleep." He patted Karl on the back and wished him luck, and then he was gone.

Throughout the next twenty-four hours Karl mingled more freely with the crew, even going to the mess for meals. The new faces of trainees and the familiar faces of regular crewmen acknowledged him without question and he began to relax. Below the airship, the blue-grey mass of the North Atlantic Ocean shifted endlessly from horizon to horizon.

During the afternoon, an urgent message whispered round the ship's company. This was soon followed by the sharp barking voice of Major von Outen. He was making an inspection of the 'Hindenburg' and her crew. Karl's instinct was to hide, but he remembered Willi's words and stayed at his self-appointed post within the forward starboard engine nacelle, with two other duty mechanics.

Major von Outen, accompanied by a senior Luftwaffe pilot who was a passenger on the voyage, eventually reached their section of the airship. He stood in the opening to the walkway which led from the airship to the engine cage. Karl could see von Outen looking down on the watery abyss hundreds of metres below. After a few moments hesitation, the Nazi moved on. Karl inwardly sighed with relief and smiled to himself. He could be mistaken, but did the apparently invulnerable Major von Outen have a fear of heights?

Karl waited anxiously that night for a visit from Willi. It was after ten o'clock when the young officer slipped into the hiding place.

"What a day this has been," he whispered to Karl. "We have been run off our feet! Five captains who all think they are in charge, and the 'Mad Major' with his pig-dog Nazi salutes." Willi collapsed in a heap next to Karl groaning. "Enough, enough!"

Karl chuckled at his friend's play acting. "Tell me about Elizabeth," he said. "It is agony not being able to see her."

"Oh, Elizabeth, yes, it seems she has struck a chord with our Captain Lehmann." Willi sat up next to Karl. "Today, Lehmann wanted to know all about my 'cousin'. I had to answer his questions carefully not to arouse suspicions, but he was genuinely concerned about her. When I said she was a piano teacher he was very interested. As you know, Lehmann himself is very musical and also

281

plays the piano. Then he asked me if she would play for him after dinner."

"And did she?" asked Karl, pleased but anxious.

"Yes, she did," said Willi. "I listened from the viewing gallery and she played beautifully; I think it was Chopin. Lehmann was entranced and so were the other passengers. Then the Captain played some Brahms. We had quite a concert"

"I wish I could have been there and seen Elizabeth," said Karl.

"I just hope all this attention does not make problems for you both," said Willi. "Captain Lehmann has invited Elizabeth to dine at his table tomorrow evening, and he has asked her to play the piano again."

The following day, Wednesday the 5th of May, was the last full day of the voyage. The 'Hindenburg' was due to arrive at Lakehurst Naval Air Station around noon the day after. Strong headwinds, and route detours to avoid stormy weather conditions, had already slowed the airship's westerly progress and she was now running behind schedule.

Karl had spent the night in a frenzy of anxiety. He was desperately concerned that Elizabeth would find the prospect of spending the forthcoming evening, in the company of the airship's most senior officers, completely overwhelming. A dangerous but, he felt, essential plan was forming in his head. He must try and see her before tonight. Willi had told him the number of her cabin, which was on 'A' deck. In theory it would be easy to go up there, but the risk of being challenged by one of the stewards or an officer, could put their entire escape plan in jeopardy. By mid-afternoon Karl had convinced himself it was a risk he had to take.

He decided to make his move in the hour before the passengers were due to be served evening dinner. From his hiding place he had to go about fifty metres along the walkway towards the bow. He was wearing his work overall and he made his way cautiously along the keel. When he reached the first stairway he went up, two at a time, to 'B' deck. This was not a restricted area for crew. In fact on this floor there was a crew mess and an officer's mess either side of the kitchens where the passenger's food was also prepared.

Karl went to the 'B' deck washroom where he removed his overall. There was a spanner in one of the pockets which he now transferred to his trousers. He was wearing the clothes he had brought for leaving the airship: his best suit and shirt. They were a little crumpled but they would have to do, so he stashed the overalls under the washstand knowing he could collect them later. He opened the door and listened for movement outside. When he was sure the corridor was empty, he slipped out of the washroom and hurried back to the stairway, this time going up to 'A' deck, knowing it was out of bounds to all crew except stewards and officers.

'A' deck was not like any other part of the 'Hindenburg'. Modelled on the great ocean-going passenger liners, here was the luxury hotel that floated in the clouds, constantly leaving the occupants speechless. As Karl reached the landing from the stairway, the warmth and the opulence of the surroundings seemed to take him into another world. The floor was carpeted and the fabric covered walls were unadorned and very modern, with concealed lighting behind the ceiling panels. Maps and murals had been painted on to the larger walls. The lightweight seating and chairs were clad in rich leather and the tables were covered with pure white damask cotton. The perfume of real flowers used for decoration filled the air. It was also considerably warmer than in the rest of the ship, with warm air ventilation shafts circulating heat generated through the airship's onboard power supply.

If he had planned it, Karl's timing could not have been better. When he reached the top of the stairs, the landing was empty. From there, the landing divided into four passageways. Two led to the day rooms situated to port and starboard. The other two gave access to the passenger cabins arranged in four blocks down the centre of the airship. Karl could hear a buzz of excited voices coming from the day rooms. He slipped quietly to the end of the passage on the port side and observed that everyone there had moved into the viewing gallery where windows, set at a forty-five degree angle, allowed passengers a commanding view of the outside world. A state of high exuberance, pointing fingers and the words, 'Land ahoy', alerted him to the fact that the 'Hindenburg' had successfully crossed the North Atlantic Ocean. He took the opportunity provided by the distraction and hurried back to the cabin area.

Elizabeth's cabin was number seventeen. He moved quickly up and down the passages, constantly fearing discovery. Number seventeen was located in the second passageway, two cabins from the end on the inner side of the double line. Karl's nerves were as taut as a newly strung violin as adrenaline fuelled his movements. His hand was almost on the door handle when he heard one of the other doors opening behind him. There was nowhere else to go. Before him were the last four cabins, either side of the passage, and then a dead end. Behind him someone was emerging from one of the other cabins. He did not dare to turn round but he reached out for the door, not stopping to knock and praying it was unlocked. The handle gave under the pressure of his shaking hand and he slipped inside the cabin. As it closed behind him, he leaned against the door, visible trembling, still expecting to be challenged by someone outside.

The cabin was very small. Elizabeth was standing right before him, dressed only in her petticoat and under-garments, like a heavenly body all in white. Her features were frozen with the startled look of an animal in panic, caused by the abruptness of his entry. She opened her mouth as if to cry out in alarm, but as Karl lifted a finger to his lips, begging her to be silent, her expression changed from fear to incomprehension and then to joy as she moved towards him and fell into his arms.

"Oh, my darling!" she exclaimed, clinging to him and kissing his lips and face.

"Hush, hush, dearest Elizabeth," he entreated her. "I think someone is out there!" Whoever had been outside had moved away, further up the passage. They both kept perfectly still and listened and as they did so, they looked into each other's eyes. There had been little time or opportunity for romance in their lives. Only the memory of the carefree days when they first fell in love, before the hated Nazis came to power, had sustained their belief that they were destined to love one another forever. Karl's fears began to subside as he became more physically aware of Elizabeth in his arms. He ran his hands over her bare arms and shoulders, feeling the soft warmth of her skin. The deep love, which he had carried for her all this time since he was little more than a boy, was rekindled now with the passions of a man.

They remained locked in the security of their embrace for a long time. It was a beautiful moment which neither wanted to end. Given other circumstances, it would have gone much further, for that was what they both desired, but time and the vulnerability of their situation dictated otherwise.

Elizabeth stood back from him at last. Still speaking in a hushed whisper she said, "You have taken a terrible risk coming here."

Karl nodded his head. "I know, but not seeing you when you were so close to me was agony. Willi has been wonderful, but I had to see you for myself, to know if you really are all right."

"The airship is truly wonderful," she said. "But I shall be very glad when we can leave it and be together, just as we planned." She clasped her arms around him once more.

Karl responded to her caresses, kissing her gently. "Then we shall be together for always, my dearest, sweet Elizabeth."

"But now," she said, standing back from him. "I must be ready to dine with the airship Captain and play the piano for him!"

"I know, Willi told me all about it," said Karl. "It is why I came to see you. Are you worried? Will you be all right?"

A nervous smile passed across her face. "Captain Lehmann is a very fine gentleman and very musical. I am sure I shall be well looked after by him. Just so long as the terrible Major von Outen is not there, I will be fine."

"I also have a plan to stay near you this evening," said Karl.

"Oh! But you should not do that," said Elizabeth, quite alarmed.

"No one will see me," said Karl, anxious to reassure her. "But I will be there for you should anything go wrong."

Elizabeth suddenly seemed to become flustered. "It will go wrong if I am not ready soon." She moved away from him, took down her gown from its hanger and stepped into the simple long dress made from pale blue taffeta.

"You look lovely," said Karl.

"It is thanks to Greta I have any clothes at all," said Elizabeth. "We have spent the last few months trawling the markets for remnants, and sewing them into these dresses for me." She moved to the washstand and splashed cold water on her face and combed her hair.

"I must go to the dining room now, my Karl. What will you do?" she asked him.

"I will wait until all the passengers have gone to dine and then I will move," he said. "Perhaps you will see me later."

A worried frown crossed her face. "Please don't do anything dangerous," she said. "I am sure I will be perfectly safe with the grand Captain Lehmann."

"I am sure you will be," he said, and he kissed her lightly on the forehead. "Good luck, my darling and play well for our Captain." He opened the door, the passageway was deserted.

"I will," she whispered, and then she went down the passage and disappeared around the corner.

What Karl most desired was to witness her playing the piano. That would take place later in the lounge on the opposite side of 'A' deck. There would be too many officers and stewards around for him to risk showing his face there during the evening.

He knew the accommodation was only half full and that a number of cabins would be empty. It was possible these might be at this far end of the passage. All the passengers were now at dinner so he slipped outside and crossed to the cabin opposite. He put his ear to the door and listened. Assured it was empty, he tried the handle; it was unlocked. At a glance he could see it was also unoccupied, so he went inside and closed the door.

On this side of the passage, the cabins backed directly on to the lounge. Because of the need to keep the airship as light as possible the dividing walls in the passenger section were very flimsy. He guessed he could easily put his fist through the wall with one punch. Well, perhaps not his fist, he thought, but with his pocket penknife he might to be able to make an opening sufficient for him to become like a fly on the wall. He decided to come back here later and make his spy hole. Right now he needed to find out what was happening in the 'Hindenburg's' dining room.

CHAPTER THIRTY-TWO

MILES APART

London, England, April 2000

When Jonno had woken up the following morning, it had taken him a while to work out exactly what he had experienced.

During his first consultation, Tony Reeve had been at pains to explain to him that all hypnosis was self-hypnosis, and that in time, he should be able to access his subconscious mind on his own. Jonno had not realised he had absorbed the ability to do this.

But he was still not sure if last night's experience had just been another dream. One thing was clear, the details were very precise and he had apparently moved forward in learning more about the lives of Karl and Elizabeth. He also now felt he knew with certainty that they had travelled on the 'Hindenburg' when the airship had made its final voyage.

When Sarah arrived back at the apartment from her visit to Germany, she was immediately drawn by the distinctive perfume of the roses. Lisa had arranged them carefully in a new vase.

"How beautiful," said Sarah, stroking the deep red velvet petals. She picked up the card and looked pointedly at Lisa. "Have you phoned him?"

"Not yet," Lisa looked unsettled. "I'm not sure I can give him the answer he wants. We haven't exactly broken up, but I still need time."

Sarah sighed. "Why is love so complicated?"

Lisa didn't have an answer to that, so she changed the subject. "Tell me about your trip to Germany and this mysterious new man in your life."

Sarah turned away from the roses. "Oh, Lisa, I've so much to tell you." She picked up her suitcase, carrying it into her bedroom. Her eyes were shining and her cheeks glowed.

Lisa followed her, very aware of the change in her friend. "Don't tell me, let me guess." She leaned against the door jam. "You've fallen in love."

The colour rose in Sarah's cheeks. "How did you know?"

Lisa laughed. "It's written all over your face," she said. "What's his name?"

"Philip, Philip Deeg," Sarah pronounced the name with a guttural German accent. "But that wasn't what I was going to tell you," she said as she opened the case and began unpacking.

"What then?" Lisa moved into the room, perching on the bed.

Sarah stopped sorting her clothes and sat next to her. "It must have been fate," she said.

"Tell me." Lisa was both intrigued and impatient.

"I stayed at the home of Petra Gruben; she's my counterpart at our office in Frankfurt. It felt a bit awkward to ask her about tracing Karl and Elizabeth. That period of German history can still be a touchy subject, but I need not have worried. She took me to a party and introduced me to her friends. That was where I met Philip." Sarah stopped speaking and seemed to lose her concentration.

"And?" prompted Lisa.

"Oh, and," Sarah returned to planet Earth, "Philip works for the 'Fritz Bauer Institute'," she paused, apparently waiting for Lisa's reaction.

"Hang on a minute," said Lisa, looking puzzled. She knew the name but couldn't make the connection. "Aren't they like the Simon Wiesenthal people, still looking for Nazis?"

"I didn't have a clue what they did," said Sarah. "Philip told me that now the Institute is more an educational resource, helping Germans to understand and confront their recent history, to make sense of what happened."

"Yes, of course." Lisa had remembered the name from Michael Jacob's list of agencies which she had given to Sarah, and from internet searches she had made herself more recently. "Fritz Bauer was a Nazi hunter and he initiated some of the war crimes trials during the sixties."

"Right," said Sarah. "The Institute operates in his memory, but Philip explained that today their role is education. Their fact finding research, however, is very extensive and it is still going on."

Lisa cut in. "So did you find out anything about Karl or Elizabeth?"

"Philip is following it up for us," Sarah explained. "I wanted to tell him about the regression, but I didn't."

"You were right not to," said Lisa. She knew how difficult it had been for her with Michael Jacob. "Now, I've got news for you," she said triumphantly, and she told Sarah about the forged document information she'd had from Michael.

"If you're not with Jonno now, why do you still want to do this?" asked Sarah.

"I suppose it's the journalist in me, a story I have to finish." She caught hold of Sarah's hand, "He has to resolve his problems alone now; I can't help him any more."

Sarah leaned over and hugged her. "Do you think it will help if we can establish Elizabeth's real identity from the past?"

"It might," answered Lisa. "Tony says Jonno will not move on until he can recall Karl's end." A hush fell between them, "That means his death. It's another reason why I have stepped back; he has to confront this on his own."

"But we can still look for evidence," said Sarah. "Knowing it is all true will surely help, won't it?"

"Tony says it doesn't matter, but like you, I think it does," said Lisa.

"Thank goodness next weekend is the Easter holiday. I'm going back to see Philip again," said Sarah. "Why don't you come with me?"

"What, and play gooseberry?" joshed Lisa.

Sarah smiled at that. "He's taking me to Stuttgart to check the records there. Do come, please."

Lisa fell silent, thinking.

Sarah persisted. "If I can book you on to my Wednesday evening flight, you must come."

Lisa didn't really need much persuading. "If I can arrange the time off work, you're on!"

"There's a letter here for you, Jonno." Alison called out to him across the shed as she reached the work space. Her arms were laden with files and papers.

Jonno was working half in and half out of the 'Dolphin's' cargo door. The opening was large enough to load a jeep. On a rough rule of thumb if the 'Dolphin' could successfully carry eight jeeps then 'Sky Whale' would handle the twelve battle tanks, which was her projected payload. The reinforced ramps were designed to work like a roll-on roll-off ferry. That was the theory but at the moment they didn't.

He walked over to Alison. "For me?" he said, taking the envelope. Any thoughts he had that Lisa might have written to him were dispelled when he saw the official envelope forwarded from the Marham Station Commander's office. It was the long overdue appointment with the consultant psychiatrist, the Wing Commander, arranged for the middle of May. He knew he must see Tony again before his appointment with this military shrink, but there was still no word from Lisa.

"Is everything all right?" Alison's words broke into his sinking spirits. Something about her enquiry confirmed his suspicion that Alison knew more than she let on.

"You know Lisa and I are..." he hesitated, "let's say estranged." He scanned through the letter again and sighed.

"I know," said Alison, in a motherly tone. "I don't know the details, but she has said things to me that I think you should know."

Jonno looked up, surprised.

"She still loves you," said Alison. "But if you want her back… you have to change." She smiled and briefly touched his arm, and then she walked away.

Jonno knew exactly what Lisa had meant. He walked out of the shed, pulling his mobile phone from his pocket. He brought up the number for Tony's Wembley clinic and rang through. He was lucky; Tony could see him on Friday, even though it was the Easter weekend. He would go alone.

He had only just put his phone back in his pocket when it bleeped, announcing the arrival of a text message. He looked at the screen and almost dropped the unit, it was from Lisa. 'Thanks for the lovely roses. I am going to Germany with Sarah for Easter to meet Philip. I will contact you on my return, Lisa.' He replied immediately, 'Thanks for the text, have a good trip, love you always, Jonno xx.' Although this meant they would be even more miles apart, he began to feel his prayers might yet be answered.

The pre-flight preparations had been going smoothly until the problem with the cargo door, now they were falling behind. On Tuesday the entire computer system went down and could not be coaxed back into life. Jonno sat in the navigator's seat and stared at the display screen. Billy Watson, the computer boffin, lay on the deck, his head inside the main processor. Jonno read out the on-screen information and Billy fiddled with the components; but nothing was working.

The onboard computer controlled everything. The engines and fuel system; the navigation system's fibre optic flight control, the aircushion landing system, the payload distribution which linked into the helium gas cells, and the cargo doors. Without the computer, the airship became a useless gas bag.

He sensed the frustration around him as Charlie and Doc Hales worked out their options. Jonno remembered his experiences with supersonic jets. Onboard computer systems were notorious. Even during active service after dozens of test runs and hours of pre-flight preparations, at the point of takeoff the whole darn thing could fail. He recalled several instances when his and other crews had to abort their planned flights or scramble to a reserve aircraft to carry out a sortie. But at LTA there was only one 'Dolphin'. For this mission – there was only one airship.

Wednesday was spent trying to locate help. While Charlie and Doc worked out the addition of manual override controls for the doors, Jonno and Billy made dozens of phone calls.

Jonno had many contacts within the RAF; people he could lean on for expertise or suggestions when the software wouldn't run and engineers with boxes of tricks for when the hardware failed; the 'Dolphin' needed both. He eventually located the right guy at the right place. He would have to drive to Kent to collect the components which would hopefully fix the glitch in the main processor.

The German Autobahn was wide, straight and fast and Philip was a very good driver. By coincidence, he drove the same car as Jonno: a Volkswagen Golf, except it was left-hand drive. In the front Philip and Sarah were playing a little game. He would speak in English and she would reply in German; then they would change over. In between, Sarah translated the conversation for Lisa's benefit, but Lisa was absorbed with thoughts of her own.

Her lack of contact with Jonno was beginning to rub like a sore, open wound. All her reasons surrounding the self-inflicted trial of separation counted for nothing against the fact that she missed him and she loved him. Coming back to Germany had made her think about what was really important to her. She wanted to mend her broken promises and be with him. But first she had some unfinished business, for she was not going to return empty-handed.

She could see why Sarah had fallen for Philip. He was very good-looking; blond and blue-eyed; more Nordic than Germanic. He was also a good communicator, with near perfect English.

Sarah's impish humour and Philip's stoicism seemed to make a good pairing.

The previous day they had travelled from Frankfurt to Stuttgart and visited several local civil registration offices. Philip was used to following up research in these places and he did not demur from using his work credentials to obtain the information they sought. Lisa had given him 1909 or 1910 as possible years for Karl's birth and Jonno had referred to Karl's father by the name 'Manfred'.

The third district office they visited was in Unterturkheim, the home of the original Mercedes-Benz plant. As both father and son had worked there, it followed that they probably also had lived there at the time. This deduction was proved right and, by flashing his "Fritz Bauer' identity card, Philip had been able to obtain a copy of a very interesting birth certificate. Now, sitting in the back of the car Lisa studied the facsimile for the hundredth time.

'Karl Hermann Stockhausen, born 13th February 1909. – Father, Manfred Hermann Stockhausen, Engineer. – Mother, Anna Marie Stockhausen.' So now she had proof of a sort, that Karl and Elizabeth had been real people and that Jonno had not dreamt them up in his torrid imagination. But what had eventually happened to them? Finding the answer to that might save Jonno from the trauma of reliving Karl's death through the regression. Lisa wanted to spare him that if she could. It was Philip who had suggested today's excursion. They were now continuing their drive south to visit the Zeppelin Museum at Friedrichshafen.

Jonno set off on Thursday, promising Charlie he would be back by Saturday morning so work could continue over Easter. He spent the day at the giant avionics computer centre at Rochester. Honeywell computer systems were adapted and produced by them for flight and flight-testing systems used in aircraft throughout the world. 'Dolphin's' computer had been modified from one of their products.

The IT expert was baffled by the fault which had developed. "There's only one explanation," he said to Jonno. "The hard drive was damaged through a virus in the software."

Jonno stared at him, at first not comprehending his meaning; then it dawned. "You mean the system was got at?"

"Looks that way to me," he replied. "I would suggest you tighten your security and check everyone with access. This should fix it, but it won't stop it happening again."

The thought that the main computer had been accessed and deliberately spiked came as a bombshell to Jonno. He couldn't work out how Paul could have been responsible but, as his brother was his chief suspect for the break-in, nothing could be ruled out.

When he left the site late in the afternoon with his box of components, discs and reams of technical information, he put them in the boot of his car and mentally closed the lid on the problem until his return to Cardington. Now he had problems of his own to solve.

Lisa climbed the open stairway leading up into the LZ129, 'Hindenburg'. It was like entering a time capsule and she was overawed by the scale of the construction. She tried to imagine how it must have felt to fly in the great airship all those years ago, even before passenger airplane travel was a reality. How courageous the travellers were, putting their trust implicitly in the new technology and flying across the world in a giant hotel floating in the sky.

Lisa, Sarah and Philip had joined the other visitors to the Zeppelin Museum's star attraction; a thirty-three metre long reconstruction of part of the 'Hindenburg' airship. Even this small replica section gave Lisa a very real impression of the huge impact such a vessel made on all who came into contact with the giant Zeppelin.

The museum was housed in the old Harbour Railway Station, right on the edge of Lake Constance. Later, Philip took the girls to the first floor restaurant. While they enjoyed an excellent lunch and a bottle of German Moselle, they also drank in the stunning views of the Bodensee and the Swiss Alps beyond.

"So, my beautiful English ladies," said Philip, addressing both of them. "What do you think of my country now?"

"The view here is magnificent," said Sarah, her gaze alternating between the window and Philip's face.

"This trip has been a revelation for me," said Lisa. "I can't thank you enough for your help. Today has put what we call 'the icing on the cake'."

"Today is good," Philip replied, "but it is not yet finished."

Sarah squeezed his hand. "You're quite the magician, Philip. What other tricks are you hiding up your sleeve?"

Philip looked up his jacket sleeve and shook his arm. The girls laughed at his puzzled expression, and then he smiled at them saying, "Why do the English always talk in rhymes?"

Lisa and Sarah laughed again. "You mean riddles!" giggled Sarah.

"Well, for my next trick," said Philip, "I have arranged for us to visit the archive and library here this afternoon. I am hoping Lisa will find some more useful information."

"What are we looking for?" asked Lisa, becoming serious once more.

"Your young couple, Karl and Elizabeth," said Philip, resting his elbows on the table and pressing his fingers to his temples in a thoughtful pose. "You said they had possibly travelled to America on the 'Hindenburg', and that they could have been on the final flight."

"That's right," answered Lisa. "But we don't know for sure."

Philip shared out the last of the wine between them. "Well," he said, "here at the museum, there are detailed records with the names of all the crew and passengers: the survivors and those who perished."

Lisa caught her breath.

"So," continued Philip, "we may be about to find out."

Jonno arrived at Tony's clinic on Good Friday morning, early and slightly dishevelled. He had eventually found a room at a motel out of town but had slept badly: fitful and with disconnected thoughts. It made him frustrated and angry to realise there was apparently no end to his problems. He was also acutely aware that the common denominator running through them all was Johnathon Amis.

Tony ushered him into the lounge and gave him a coffee. "All alone again today?" he asked, as he sat down opposite Jonno.

"Lisa's gone to Germany with my sister," he offered by way of explanation, "but we're still not reconciled." Tony gave him a sympathetic smile.

"How have you been otherwise?" he asked. "It's three weeks since your last visit."

"I've been kept very busy at Cardington, working on the new airship project."

Tony nodded his head, "Yes, amazing connection. But in yourself, how have you been?"

Jonno considered, "I had a very strange experience the other night. It might have been a dream but the images were very clear, more like the regression memories."

"It could have been self-hypnosis," said Tony, leading him through to the consultation room, "That's good! And a big step forward," he said, as they settled in their respective places. "You must tell me what you remember before we continue." As he spoke, Tony started the tape running.

Jonno lay on the couch and began to relate the events, now vivid in his conscious memory. He recalled finding Elizabeth in her cabin and wanting to follow her as she left him to dine with the elite officers on board the airship.

"Do you think we will learn their fate today?" Jonno was desperately seeking an end to his traumas.

"I don't know when closure on your past life will come, Jonno, maybe today – maybe not, but when it does you will know it is finished and you will be able to lay it aside and get on with your life again."

As Jonno settled himself on the couch, he was very aware of Lisa's absence. He tried to relax, but knew he was too tense. Tony talked him through the breathing exercises and gradually he calmed.

"You love Lisa very much," said Tony, in his deep resonant voice.

Jonno was not yet hypnotised, but deeply relaxed and able to speak his innermost thoughts aloud. "She is everything to me," he replied.

"I think that you are everything to her, and that she loves you very deeply," said Tony.

Jonno breathed deep and long. If he could just hold on to that thought he would be able to endure anything. As he heard Tony's voice say the words, "Go back and find Karl," he had a vision of Elizabeth in a blue taffeta dress. He must watch over her and keep her safe from harm.

CHAPTER THIRTY-THREE

CENTRE STAGE

Airship 'Hindenburg', North America, May 1937

Karl wanted to see Elizabeth at the Captain's table and emboldened by his success at reaching the passengers' quarters, he left the unoccupied cabin and went to the end of the passageway nearest to the dining room.

There was a lot of activity here, with a number of stewards clustering round the dumb waiter which was set in the wall. Plates of food were being hauled up on a rope pulley from the kitchens on 'B' deck. He watched as they were collected by junior stewards, many of whom were the extra trainees, and ferried into the dining room.

He caught the attention of a young trainee steward he had seen earlier in the mess room. The boy, known as Curly, was red in the face. Beads of sweat glistened on his forehead as he hurried back from a trip into the dining room. Karl seized on this opportunity and spoke to him.

"What's the matter, Curly? You don't look very well." The boy was startled by Karl speaking to him while on duty and he looked round nervously.

He whispered. "I have a bad headache and a temperature. I think I have a fever." He wiped his brow with a handkerchief. Karl pulled Curly to one side.

"You should not be serving food if you are unwell. Come with me." The boy didn't seem to realise Karl had no authority over him and followed him down the stairs to 'B' deck and into the washroom. Karl told Curly to remove his steward's uniform and

299

bathe his face at the washbasin. Karl dressed himself in Curly's shirt and waistcoat.

"You stay here and rest," he said sympathetically. "I will complete your shift for you." The sick boy didn't question Karl. He seemed only too grateful he had been relieved of his duties.

Karl left him and ran back up the stairs, joining other stewards carrying the plates from the dumb waiter. He was not trained to wait at the tables but he knew enough to look the part, taking his cue from the other stewards and keeping well away from the watchful eye of Herr Kubis.

His eyes quickly took in the layout of the room. Separate octagonal tables, set for eight people filled the carpeted area. The Captain's table was at the far end, nearest the bow and the viewing gallery. He could see Elizabeth seated between Captain Lehmann and Captain Pruss, with Captain Witteman sitting opposite. They looked resplendent in their DZR uniforms: she a picture of innocence in her blue gown. His heart melted to see her in such exalted company and he edged nearer to that end of the room, carrying a jug of iced water to cover his movement. As he approached them, he heard Lehmann speak to Elizabeth.

"I hope you will not find three old airship men too dull company this evening, Fraulein?"

"I am sure I shall not, Captain Lehmann," Elizabeth replied demurely. "It is very kind of you to invite me." Two senior stewards were waiting at their table and attending to their needs. Karl kept out of their way, holding his jug of water.

It was at this moment Major von Outen entered the room. He was with General Erdmann and two other officer pilots of the Luftwaffe. The room was soon full with passengers come to take the evening meal together in one sitting. Karl was horrified to see von Outen and his party occupy the table next to Elizabeth. He saw a change in the airship Captains' relaxed mood. In their furtive glances to one another he thought he detected a closing of ranks between them to exclude the overloud Nazi from their conversation.

If Major von Outen was aware that his presence was not welcomed by the occupants at the next table, he apparently chose to ignore it. His seat was closest to Captain Lehmann and he leaned back towards him, discourteously addressing him from behind.

"You will be pleased to know, Captain Lehmann," he said in an overbearing loud tone, "that I have inspected your 'flying sausage' again today and everything appears to be in order!" He laughed raucously, and the Luftwaffe officers joined in. "When Field-Marshall Goering spoke to your Dr Eckner, he called your airships 'flying sausages!'" Major von Outen's tone was insulting, but he and the pilots continued to laugh.

Karl had to keep moving and appear busy, but he was careful to keep out of Elizabeth's sight. If she showed alarm it could give him away. A passenger at another table clicked his fingers at Karl and called for water. As he moved away to fill the man's glass, he saw von Outen turn round and look towards Elizabeth. Her eyes were downcast looking at her plate.

"And who is this little Fraulein sitting at the great airship's Captains' table?" von Outen's voice boomed, brimming with sarcasm and obvious contempt for the Merchant Officers of the skies.

Captain Lehmann however, answered him with dignity.

"Fraulein Bader is the cousin of one of my officers," he said. "She is also a very accomplished pianist."

Major von Outen threw his head back laughing. "Well, we already have an acrobat clown on board," he said, referring to the mime artist, Ben Dova, who was a passenger on the ship. "And now we have a pianist!" he exclaimed loudly. "Quite the flying circus, Captain Lehmann, I shall look forward to being entertained."

Karl's jug was empty and it was time for him to leave the dining room. Herr Kubis did not notice one steward slip away and Karl hurried back down to the washroom and found Curly snoring on the floor. He quickly changed back into his own clothes and left Curly's uniform on top of the sleeping youth. No doubt he would get

301

into trouble but Curly didn't know who Karl was. Now Karl had to carry out the second part of his plan to watch over Elizabeth in the lounge during the piano concert.

He carefully retraced his steps back to her cabin and re-entered the empty cabin opposite. The high level bunk-bed had been pushed up against the wall. Karl lowered it into position, climbed up and lay on it full length. He set to work with his pocket penknife. The fabric wall covering had been stretched over the metal support struts and coated to give a stiff, dirt proof surface which had then been painted. On the cabin side Karl cut a flap, wide enough to put his face through to the second surface. In this he cut a much smaller flap about two centimetres across. Both flaps of fabric would easily drop back into place and he hoped they would not be discovered until after he had left the airship.

When he gently put his eye to the second hole, he was pleased to find that he had an excellent view of the lounge. He could see across to the viewing gallery and when he looked down, the special lightweight baby grand piano was directly beneath him in the corner of the room. Karl had seen it many times during the construction, for it had been put on board even before the walls had been added to the passenger accommodation. When dinner was over people would come into the lounge for the evening, particularly if they knew there was to be a piano concert. He would have to wait awhile, but he felt much safer here than he had in the dining room. Laying still on the soft mattress of the top bunk, his eyelids felt very heavy and soon he drifted off to sleep.

Karl was dreaming. It was the Stuttgart Summer Music Festival and he was listening to Elizabeth play her solo repertoire. She began with a waltz by Brahms.

He awoke with a start and stared with momentary confusion at a ceiling just a few inches above his head. Reality dawned, and he quickly pushed his face into the aperture in the wall and located his eye to the spy hole. He instantly withdrew his head, afraid he had been seen. The room was full of people, sitting and standing, but they all seemed to be looking in his direction. Cautiously, he looked again and listened. Elizabeth was directly below him, sitting at the piano. It was her playing which had triggered his dream and which now also attracted the eyes of everyone in the lounge.

The Brahms finished and Elizabeth played a second waltz and then a polka. Karl was entranced, as he always had been by her perfect command of the pianoforte, and it was evident she had captured the collective admiration of everyone there. He studied her audience. Captain Lehmann sat quite close, avidly following the performance. People were seated all around, but the usual level of conversation from such a group was absent. Behind Lehmann in the centre of the room, Major von Outen was seated, wearing his Nazi officer uniform. Karl could see his face quite clearly and he looked even more sinister. He too, had his eyes fixed on Elizabeth but he also appeared to be drinking heavily. When the applause broke out for her, von Outen was unmoved, his face remained cold and calculating. Karl was filled with dread as he pondered the Major's motivation.

When the polka ended, Elizabeth stood up to allow Captain Lehmann to take her place, but the audience continued clapping and calling for more, "Encore, encore!" "More, more!" they shouted.

The Captain walked towards her clapping his hands. Karl could hear everything very clearly.

"Bravo, bravo," said the Captain. "Our passengers obviously know true talent when they hear it, my dear. You are a very fine pianist."

Elizabeth stood up. "You are too kind, Captain. Please will you play now?"

"Oh, no, it is you they want to hear and so do I," he replied. "Now tell me, what is your favourite piano composition?"

Karl heard Elizabeth say, "Oh, Debussy's 'Clair de lune', I know it by heart and it is very popular."

Captain Lehmann gestured for her to sit down again and said, "I am afraid I have been summoned back to the control car; we have a little problem with the weather. Please continue your wonderful playing, my dear Fraulein Bader." He briefly touched her hand and then he turned and left the room.

For a moment Karl thought she would run after him. The other two Captains were nowhere to be seen, but von Outen and the pilots were still seated nearby, drinking heavily. She was looking around frantically for a familiar face and Karl desperately wanted to go to her.

Once more, she seemed to take refuge in the music. As she began to play the Debussy there was a collective sigh in the room and a brief ripple of applause. For the whole ensuing four minutes, no other sound was heard but the haunting melody as it rippled from Elizabeth's agile fingers and filled the room. When it was finished the reaction was tremendous, with clapping and calling for even more. She stood and took a little bow and then she tried to leave, but she was forced to retreat back to the piano as a group of Americans surrounded her, bombarding her with questions. Karl could hear snippets of their comments to her.

"You must be a professional concert pianist, surely?"

"Where did you study?"

Elizabeth just stood there, as if struck dumb.

"Why have we not heard of you before?"

"What concerts have you played?"

She spoke eventually. "I know not what you ask," she said, "I am just a piano teacher."

Karl could see she was trying to walk away, but an immaculately dressed man barred her way. He thrust out his hand, "My name is Philip Mangone, Fashion Designer of New York City." He shook Elizabeth's hand vigorously. "I know I could get you a concert date at Carnegie Hall. You would be a sensation, Miss Bader, and I would design you a complete new wardrobe of

304

clothes!" The group surrounding Elizabeth became very excited at Mr Mangone's proposition to the young German piano teacher.

"She will be a star in New York!" said another gentleman.

"Yes, but we heard her first, dear," said the lady with him.

Philip Mangone spoke again. "Where are you staying in New York, Miss Bader?"

Karl held his breath waiting for her reply. Elizabeth stuttered and stammered, "I... don't understand... I don't know..."

Mr Mangone thrust his visiting card into Elizabeth's hand, "You must telephone me in a couple of days, I will arrange everything. Forget the teaching – you are going to be a star, Miss Bader, a star!"

Karl despaired that she would be able to get away from these people. She was being besieged by them with questions about her background she could not answer. He had hoped Willi might have been in the lounge, but his non-appearance pointed to his being on duty elsewhere and Elizabeth was alone.

At last the American admirers moved back, but then Karl watched with mounting dread as Major von Outen stepped directly in front of her, blocking her exit. Elizabeth appeared rooted to the spot. The Nazi caught hold of her hand and his lips brushed her skin. Simultaneously he clicked his heels together, as if mocking her American admirers.

"A moment of your time, Fraulein," he said, almost as if she had a choice. Karl's face was so close to the Major's head, he could see the steel grey glint in his eyes as he held Elizabeth's frightened gaze in a ring of barbed wire. "Like these Americans," he continued addressing Elizabeth with mock courtesy, "I am curious to know why such an accomplished, true Aryan pianist, should have remained undiscovered by the German concert circuit. Have you never played in public before?"

Karl knew she had of course, but before the Jewish boycotts and under the name 'Ekhart', with her Jewish background undisguised.

She looked at the floor. "No, sir, I have not." It was the only answer she could give.

"I am sure you know, Fraulein, that the Nazi Minister of Education and Culture is very keen to nurture Aryan musicians and artists. It would be a pity if your talent was lost to the Americans." He tapped his thigh with the flat of his hand. It was a small but ominous gesture.

Elizabeth kept her eyes fixed on the floor. Karl could see her lean against the piano for support. "I am only going to teach," she said meekly.

"I think you should return to Germany with me!" He had raised his voice in a commanding tone. "Senior Nazi officers enjoy good music. The Führer himself loves to hear the piano played well. I would arrange it myself."

Karl felt helpless. Everything depended on Elizabeth remembering what they had rehearsed if she was questioned about her future.

"I am afraid my nerves would fail me under such a distinguished audience. I have been very ill recently and am travelling for reasons of health. An aunt at Long Island has agreed to take care of me." She had remembered.

Major von Outen's eyes narrowed to fine slits and his sallow complexion became red and blotchy. Karl did not know if von Outen believed her, but neither did he seem ready to let her go.

"Something tells me I should investigate you and your story a little more, Fraulein. I want to see your papers, now!"

Karl had watched von Outen with growing despair. The Nazi's final demand was loud and clear. If the 'Mad Major' got his hands on Elizabeth's documents, all their plans would be in ruins. It flashed into his head that he might just have time to remove them from her cabin. He slipped from the top bunk and carefully opened the door to the passage, but it was already too late. He closed the door again as he sensed, as much as heard them, coming down the passage and stopping outside. He risked a furtive peep through the *crack in the opening. Elizabeth looked cowed, like a frightened mouse, while von Outen towered behind her, the vulture in waiting. She hesitated at the door as if making a last attempt to fend off the inevitable.*

"My papers have been inspected twice, Herr Major, at Frankfurt and here on the airship, they are in order." She was trying to speak calmly, but her voice trembled.

He leaned over her and pushed open the door. "I will be the judge of what is in order," he replied. His voice was thick with cynicism, but his words were slurred.

She still did not move. "I would like to request the lady stewardess be in attendance, sir. This is my private cabin." She spoke with quiet dignity, though her voice was shaking.

Karl was frantic, but full of admiration that she had found the courage to challenge von Outen's unethical conduct.

Power and an excess of alcohol were fuelling the man's actions and he would not be thwarted from his course. There was an angry noise in his throat, like a venomous snake preparing to strike. "I am a Nazi officer of the Schutzstaffel – I make the rules!"

Karl watched in horror as the 'Mad Major' pushed Elizabeth through the doorway, then he followed her inside, shutting the door. Karl moved across the passage and put his ear against the door of Elizabeth's cabin. He was afraid, but angry and very desperate.

He felt the Nazi's weight against the other side of the door and heard the clipped tone of his voice. "Your documents, Fraulein." He could hear shuffling but no reply and guessed Elizabeth was removing the documents from her bag. There was no sound from the cabin and he became anxious again, realising the Nazi must be examining Elizabeth's passport. He heard the Major's voice again. It seemed that the large quantity of alcohol he had consumed during the evening was beginning to have an effect. His words were slow to come and his tone less sharp, "I think," he paused, "that your passport – is a forgery."

Karl's heart lurched and he heard Elizabeth gasp, "No, no!" she stammered. "You are mistaken, sir!"

"I think not!" His voice quickened again, "which means you are not who you say you are." Karl felt the door move and realised the Nazi had moved away, towards Elizabeth. He opened the door a crack and saw she had her back against the opposite wall. Von Outen was very close to her and apparently relishing her discomfort.

"So, little Fraulein," he said. "You will now return with me to Germany, where you and your documents will be re-checked by the proper authorities!"

Karl wanted to burst into the cabin. He heard Elizabeth's voice, very weak, saying, "No, no! This cannot be... this cannot be..." She was speaking more to herself than to him.

"If your documents are forgeries, you will be arrested and imprisoned, or perhaps – worse – poor little Fraulein." His tone had changed to one of mock concern, and he put his hand on her shoulder.

Elizabeth seemed to recoil in fear, as though it was a branding iron, but he was so close their clothes brushed.

"I could, of course, make things much easier for you if you will comply with my wishes."

She just looked at him dumbly, not understanding his evil intent but Karl did and his hand gripped the spanner in his pocket.

Von Outen's hand grasped at the neck of Elizabeth's dress and pulled it from her shoulder. His other hand slid round her back and tore at the fastenings, which came away.

She struggled and began to shout in protest.

"If you cry out I will strangle you with my bare hands!" he hissed through clenched teeth as he dragged her on to the single low bunk bed. He was breathing hard, excited by his sexual urges and his power over a helpless girl. "If you are a Jew, as I suspect, I will keep you as my whore. You will do exactly as I tell you, and you will play the piano for me, when and where I say." His eyes were *wild and staring like a mad, crazed animal as he unfastened his trousers and held Elizabeth's trembling body in his vice-like grip.*

Major von Outen was apparently so exulted by the wicked act he was about to inflict on the girl he had been lusting over all the evening, he could not have heard the faint footfalls cross the cabin floor or seen the shadow that fell over him.

Karl held the spanner in his hand, but his fury was so intense that the single blow he dealt to the back of von Outen's head would have been just as powerful had he used his bare fist. The full weight of the mad Major's body slumped unconscious over Elizabeth. Karl lifted the spread-eagled form of von Outen from her and dragged the near lifeless body on to the floor.

Elizabeth gasped for air as she sobbed and shook uncontrollably. Karl wrapped her near naked body in the bed cover and held her tightly like a little child.

"Hush, hush, my dearest, you must be quiet. These walls have ears and we must not draw attention." Elizabeth was in shock but she understood his meaning and buried her head into his shoulder to muffle her cries. Gradually, she became quiet and still. All they could hear was the deep rasping sound of von Outen's breathing.

Elizabeth raised her head and said, "We can never get away now, Karl. It is finished." Tears rolled down her cheeks, her expression one of utter despair.

Karl held her close and said, "No, it is not finished, it is only just beginning. We will land in a few hours time. You and I can both hide in this vast ship and we will slip out with the freight. I know the routine at Lakehurst, it will be easy. This evil Nazi will not have you or me. We can still escape, but we must hurry before he wakes up."

Karl's words gave Elizabeth new hope. "What must we do?" she asked him.

"First, you must dress in your warmest clothes, for it is much colder out there than in this passenger section." While she did as he said, Karl packed all her belongings into her travel bag. Her

documents went into the inside pocket of his jacket with his own. All the time, he kept a wary eye on the still unconscious Nazi Major.

Karl suddenly held up his hand to alert Elizabeth. "Listen!" he whispered. They could hear movement in the passage. His stomach turned over, for someone was outside the cabin.

There was a gentle rap on the door and then a voice said, "Elizabeth, it is I, Willi. Please open the door." It was Karl who opened the door. He grabbed Willi's arm and without explanation pulled him inside.

Willi opened his mouth to speak and then looked in horror at the scene before him. "What has happened here?" he began. He stopped and stared in wide-eyed disbelief at the man on the floor. "Is he dead?" he said, bending down to examine him.

"No," said Karl, "but he deserves to be. He attacked poor Elizabeth and would have dishonoured her had I not knocked him unconscious when I did."

Willi looked grim and shook his head. "I am sure your action was very necessary, but now you are in deep trouble. Did he see you?"

"No, he did not. I am sorry you have become involved, Willi. You must go and disassociate from my troubles. Elizabeth will come with me now to hide until the airship lands. We will take our chances on getting away at Lakehurst."

Willi looked at his pocket-watch. "It is after midnight and we have still not reached Boston. The weather is putting us further behind schedule and we may not land for a further twelve hours." His concern for both of them was very evident. "That is a long time to stay hidden."

Karl tried to display a confidence he did not really feel. "I know the ship well. We can stay out of sight. Just so long as 'he'," he pointed to von Outen on the floor, "does not come looking for us."

Willi touched Karl's shoulder. "I will perform one more act of friendship to help you both," he said. They looked at him expectantly. "I will take our friend here back to his own cabin on the pretext he had too much to drink. Perhaps when he wakes he will not remember. In any event, I will watch him like a hawk."

"I owe you so much, Willi. I hope I can repay you some day. I will help you move him and then Elizabeth and I will disappear into the body of the airship, where nobody will find us."

CHAPTER THIRTY-FOUR

LOOSE ENDS

Cardington, Bedfordshire, April 2000

Jonno had returned to LTA as promised, on Easter Saturday morning. He went straight to the giant shed where the project team were anticipating his arrival with the expectation of children awaiting Santa Claus.

Billy Watson, more anxious than the others, came over to the car and helped Jonno unload the boot. They carried the processor and box of components over to where 'Sky Dolphin' was waiting to be brought back to life. Billy set to work reattaching the plugs and leads while Doc Hales started up the generator to provide power while they worked on her in the shed.

Charlie was looking apprehensive; so much rested on the computer being up and running again. "Did they give you any indication what went wrong?" he asked Jonno.

Jonno was careful to ensure he was not overheard by the others before he told Charlie the conclusions of the IT man at Rochester Avionics.

Charlie looked aghast. "You mean it could have been deliberately corrupted?"

Jonno held up his hands. "That's what the man said; believe it or ignore it at your peril."

Charlie sighed. "What do you think?"

"Firstly, I think we should keep quiet about it, or the team will feel everyone is under suspicion and morale will suffer. Secondly, it could relate to the break in. Maybe the pirate did wreak havoc after all."

Charlie was thoughtful. "Well, one thing is certain; he won't catch us out again. Security is my top priority from now on."

Two hours later, Billy gave Charlie the thumbs up sign. It was all systems go and the team soon picked up on the various tasks assigned to them and work began again in earnest.

Jonno had been overseeing the installation of the diesel engines. Two would drive the airship and the third was to provide all the onboard power requirements. In spite of the modern technology and computer operated systems, certain aspects of this airship were remarkably similar to the 'Hindenburg', albeit scaled down. He found it difficult to comprehend that his knowledge of the giant German airship was so comprehensive. It was as if he had worked on board her yesterday. In a sense he had, and he tried not to think about all that had happened during that final flight, and what was still to come.

That was the problem. He still did not know if Karl and Elizabeth had escaped. Until he had that closure, he knew that his own life would not return to normal.

Sunday morning saw the whole team back at work once more. In contrast to yesterday, Charlie was very upbeat. He called everyone together to make a special announcement.

"I want to thank you all for your hard work over the last three weeks. It has all been worthwhile and due to your supreme efforts our 'Sky Dolphin' should be ready for her maiden test flight later this week." There was big cheer and spontaneous applause from the team of seventeen men and women who made up the project team. Charlie continued speaking. "I can't thank you enough for all the long hours you have worked and for giving up your bank holiday this weekend."

As the group dispersed, Charlie's mobile phone sounded. Jonno heard him say, "Yes... she has clearance... you can let her through. Thanks for the call." He put the phone back in his pocket and walked towards Jonno, grinning from ear to ear. "Seems we have a visitor from the press. Miss Lisa Hartnell of the 'Sunday Voice' has come to see 'Sky Dolphin'!"

Jonno watched Lisa's car approach from the direction of the perimeter gate and he felt his heart rate start to rise. As he walked over to meet her, he said a silent prayer of thanks and hoped that the 'Dolphin' was not all she had come to see.

He opened the driver's door and she smiled at him, almost shyly, as she climbed out.

"I thought you were away in Germany," he said. He eyed the new jade green sweater she was wearing over figure hugging jeans. The familiar aroma of her perfume caught him off guard and he had to resist the urge to fold her into his arms. He did not want to make assumptions about her visit.

"I was," she said. "I flew back last night, earlier than planned." She leant back into the car, reappearing with a pile of pristine copies of the 'Sunday Voice'. "Today's edition," she said, "page twenty-six." She thrust the wad of papers into his hands, opened the top copy and folded it back, replacing it on the top of the pile. Her face was beaming with pride. Jonno scanned the page as they walked over to Charlie. He would have to wait to find out why she had returned from her trip early.

The feature was headed, 'British Airship seeks Flying Partners.' There were several photographs of 'Sky Lark' and 'Sky Dolphin' and an artist's impression of the 'Sky Whale'. Charlie and Doc enthused with Lisa over her coverage of their project and the hope that it might catch the eye of private investors. Alison appeared from inside the shed with a tray of coffees and biscuits. As Lisa supped the hot drink and basked in the tributes of everyone reading the feature, her eyes locked on Jonno.

He had barely read his copy. His eyes were already following her, waiting for a sign or signal. He moved closer to her.

"Why did you come back early?" he asked.

"I thought Sarah and Philip should be alone," she answered. They walked away from the others. "Besides, thanks to Philip, I had achieved what I wanted from my visit."

"Which was?" said Jonno, curious about her reason for going to Germany.

"I think we need to talk," she said, looking a little serious. "Can we go somewhere later?"

Jonno's spirits inwardly soared. "I'm sure there must be a restaurant somewhere in Bedford where we can find a table this evening," he said, "Chinese or Indian?"

"Either would be fine," she answered with an encouraging look, "as long as it's just you and me."

Bedford's premier Chinese eating house, 'The Bamboo Garden', was busy with Easter trade but had promised Jonno a table for six p.m. As they took their seats and sipped their drinks, an awkward silence fell between them; the expanse of empty white tablecloth emphasised the void. They started to speak at the same time, then stopped, and laughed together instead.

"You first," said Jonno.

Lisa began again. "The reason I went to Germany was to do with Karl and Elizabeth."

"Oh," said Jonno, surprised and curious.

"We talked about it, you must remember, the evidence gathering to support your regression."

"And did you find any?" said Jonno, with growing interest.

She stretched out her hand and touched his. "Yes, I do believe I have."

Between the arrival of the prawn crackers and the end of their meal, Lisa told him what she had discovered. From her bag she produced the facsimile birth certificate for Karl and the letter from the Quaker movement about the forged passports. Jonno studied both documents. His face reflected a mix of emotions from amazement to joy and then relief.

"It's incredible," he said. "You've found real proof of both Karl and Elizabeth. He had stopped eating and leaned back in his chair. "So now do you believe I wasn't making it all up?"

"I never thought that, Jonno," she answered, looking straight into his eyes. "What I did feel was that you needed to know it was the truth, to prove to yourself that you are perfectly sane and normal. Am I right?"

Jonno looked at the documents again and knew that Lisa was exactly right. It was his own self-doubt that had followed him since the Gulf incident, dogging his footsteps. "You're in the wrong profession," he said with a smile. "You should have been the psychologist."

"There was something else I discovered only yesterday," she said, "and I hope this will please you most of all."

They were holding hands across the table. Jonno felt certain that Lisa now wanted to resume their relationship and he was once again mesmerised, watching the light reflecting in her beautiful green eyes. Whatever else she had to say, it couldn't be better than this.

"Philip took us to the Zeppelin Museum at Friedrichshafen. It's an incredible place, we must go back there sometime, together." She paused to sip her drink. Jonno's mind trawled back through his regression memory of the airship's construction site at Friedrichshafen.

She continued telling him about the visit. "In the library we saw details of everyone who was on the final 'Hindenburg' flight. It was all there, those who died and those who survived: the crew and the passengers. All the names were listed, but there was no mention of Karl Stockhausen or Elizabeth, as Bader or Ekhart." Lisa looked almost triumphant, but Jonno did not react. "Don't you see," she said. "They didn't die in the airship disaster because they weren't there!"

Jonno gave a big sigh, and wished he could accept Lisa's findings as she obviously did. "I went to see Tony on Friday," he said.

She waited for him to continue.

"He has another set of tapes for you, if you want them."

"Of course I do," she said. "Finishing the journal is very important, for both of us."

Jonno shook his head despondently. "I'm afraid it isn't finished yet. Neither do my latest regression memories tally with your evidence gathering."

Lisa seemed confused. "But these records are official, based on evidence from the time," she insisted.

"Oh, I don't doubt their origin or authenticity," he said, anxious to reassure her, "and in a way your evidence is correct. Neither of their names appeared in the official records. Karl was not listed as crew and Elizabeth was not listed as a passenger, but they were on board the 'Hindenburg's' final flight, as you will learn in due course."

"But what happened to them?" she asked. Her concern was tinged with a touch of frustration.

"I still don't know," he said, remembering all the frightening events that took place on the 'Hindenburg'. "The end is close, and yet it remains as elusive as ever. I sometimes wonder if I will ever find out what really happened."

It was after eight o'clock when they left the restaurant and walked, hand in hand, back to where Lisa had parked her car. Jonno pulled her towards him, raising her left hand up to his lips and kissing it. She was wearing his engagement ring.

"Dare I ask if we are still engaged?" he said.

"I never considered we weren't," she answered. "It was breathing space I needed, and so, I think, did you."

Jonno wrapped his arms round her and sighed. "I really am trying to change you know." He searched her eyes, looking for a favourable response.

She nodded in agreement. "I thought I had found a way out for you, but apparently I was wrong." She broke from his embrace and rummaged in her bag for the car keys. "I have to return to London tonight," she said, taking him by surprise.

"Oh, I hoped you would stay over," he said, not easily concealing his disappointment.

Lisa avoided his eyes, saying, "I think that part of our relationship should stay on hold until you are able to find the closure you seek," she hesitated, "… to your past."

He was silent, thinking about her pronouncement. This meant he would have to go on alone. There could be no future with Lisa until he could finally let go of the past. "I don't know when I can see Tony again," he said, "I have to be here every day at the moment. Test flights begin later this week."

"I'll speak to him," she said, "and see what can be arranged. "Please don't be discouraged, darling." They embraced and kissed again. "This time we will stay in touch and, like you said, the end is very close now."

Lisa drove him back to Charlie's home and they said their goodbyes. He didn't try to persuade her to stay, but as he watched her drive away he knew that the strong bond which had once held them together was now just a fine thread. If it broke, he could lose her forever.

When Lisa entered Biddy's office on the Tuesday after Easter, she knew instinctively something was amiss. Her two senior colleagues were engrossed in conversation and they looked up as she entered the room.

"Come and see this," said Caroline. "Your airship feature has produced fan mail."

"Hardly that!" said Biddy. "This is hate mail."

Lisa quickly crossed the room to the desk. Biddy handed her a single sheet of paper and she read the typed text out loud.

"The Cardington airship is doomed. It will end like all airships, in a ball of fire. Further publicity by your newspaper will hasten its demise and yours! This is not a prophecy – it is a promise!"

Lisa's spirits sank to an all-time low. Hate mail by the lunatic fringe was common in the newspaper business, but it always left a nasty taste and, of course, the paper had to react responsibly.

"It's not from any group seeking publicity, because it's not signed," said Biddy.

"No," agreed Lisa. "This is a one man headcase."

"Or woman?" offered Caroline.

Lisa shook her head. "Definitely one man," she repeated.

Later that morning she spoke to Alison at LTA. She read the anonymous letter to her over the phone. "I expect you'll have a visit from the police soon," she told Alison. "It's editorial policy to inform them when a threat has been made."

Alison's derisive laughter came over the phone line. "Whoever it is, they've grossly underestimated our technical advancements. Helium is inert and the hull fabric is bullet and fire proof." She sounded quite indignant. "She won't explode either, unless they use a bomb. Do you think it's connected with the break-in?" Alison asked her.

"There's nothing else to go on, so I suppose the answer has to be yes," said Lisa. But in her heart she didn't want either incident to point to Paul because it would look so bad for Jonno.

"I can't understand any of this," said Alison. "Everyone in this area is all for airships continuing at Cardington. It's traditional and it keeps other, less welcome development away."

Lisa didn't want to be drawn about the motives of a possible suspect. "Can I leave it to you to explain to Charlie? I didn't want the police to contact you first."

"That's all right, Lisa. You mustn't worry. Our security is tight as a drum now." Alison sounded reassuring. "By the way it was lovely to see you on Sunday. When are you coming back?"

"Soon, I hope, Alison," she said, and signed off. Lisa realised that with an arsonist on the loose, it could be sooner than she planned.

By Friday morning the 'Sky Dolphin' was ready for her maiden test flight. Even the weather was good, with few clouds and only a light wind. The advanced diesel injection engines were in and running, and had been fine-tuned by Ted Baines, who was an ex-RAF flight maintenance engineer now on the project team. Jonno was working on the navigation system, where he felt much more at home. Dolphin had been fitted with the fibre optic flight control system, or 'fly-by-wire' as he knew it from his Tornado days.

They were following the same procedure used for all the 'Sky Lark' tests. This time, however, the flight would be manned. Charlie, Doc Hales, Jonno and Ted Baines would be the 'Sky Dolphin's' first crew. Jonno was acutely aware how important this initial test was to the project. When he'd heard about the hate mail received by Lisa's newspaper, he had contemplated once again about his brother Paul being the culprit. Whether or not this was the case, Jonno considered it was his duty to ensure nothing happened to mar the airship project's progress.

The control section was not a separate gondola but an integral part of the airship. It was situated in the centre of the lower section of the hull, between the two hover cushions; Charlie called it 'the bridge'. The entrance was via the roll-on cargo door. A roll-off door was located towards the rear end of the ship. The special flooring to hold the cargo had not yet been installed.

The crew had to establish the critical start-up regime for takeoff. The time-honoured tradition of 'exiting the shed' would have to be followed. Although it was feasible, 'Sky Dolphin' had not yet been tested to manoeuvre at ground level. A tow truck was used to hold the nose and the two blue tractors brought up the rear while the airship was brought out of the shed and taken to the bottom field.

Charlie immediately swung into action. Like an orchestral conductor, he called out for each part of the operation in precise order. As with 'Sky Lark', they would test the aircushion landing system first. The engines were started and the bow-thrusters employed to control the nose. Then the aircushions were deployed and the reverse air suction commenced to enable the hover skirts to hold the airship to the ground. The tow truck and tractors were moved away. Now the hull, two hundred feet long by one hundred feet wide and fifty feet high, was independently held under its own power, defying the buoyancy of the helium gas to lift the 'Dolphin' off the ground.

The test moved on and the ascent began. Jonno's dark eyes scanned the instrument panel. He watched the altimeter go up to two hundred feet and stop. The twin diesel engines took over and 'Dolphin' began to carry out a series of planned manoeuvres. Charlie called out his instructions and Doc, in the pilot's seat, carried them out. Jonno read the instruments and relayed the readings back to them.

Everything was proceeding according to plan and Charlie's face lit up with a big broad grin. "What do you think of airship travel now?" he asked Jonno. "Bit different from your Tornado, eh?"

"It's different all right," answered Jonno, but in his mind he wasn't making comparisons with a supersonic jet, he was thinking about the 'Hindenburg', and in particular that last flight. His mind clicked into a different time zone, a different world. The windows of the control section looked out over the English countryside, but the sensation of airship flight was the same. They were floating so smoothly that they appeared not to be moving at all. It was only when Jonno looked down on the scene passing below that the act of moving became a reality. The green Bedfordshire countryside dissolved into the blue-grey mass of the Atlantic Ocean. The sound of the engines was just a distant hum, and yet it was so familiar.

Experiencing Karl's fear and trauma during that final voyage had been a terrifying experience. He had watched helplessly as their sworn enemy had boarded the airship and, like a predatory beast, hunted down his poor, darling Elizabeth. Only his timely intervention had saved her from a fate worse then death. But now they had both become fugitives. He had assaulted a Nazi officer and their chances of escape would have been almost zero.

The hum of the engines was driving him on. What had happened after he and Elizabeth had disappeared into the body of the airship? It was a vast area, but had they been able to remain hidden until they reached Lakehurst? Had they somehow escaped from the inferno? Many people had. They had not been listed among the dead, so maybe they had escaped through the cargo hatch and run away to freedom.

Good or bad, he must know what had happened, how it had ended. The answer seemed always just beyond his reach. He must go back and find Karl again.

CHAPTER THIRTY-FIVE

FULL CIRCLE

Airship 'Hindenburg', North America, Thursday 6th May 1937

Like a silent shadow, Karl slipped back through the empty corridors of the passenger accommodation towards Elizabeth's cabin.

He stopped briefly under the lamp illuminating the bust of the old President, after whom the airship was named, and checked his pocket watch; it was nearly one a.m. The 'Hindenburg' was due at Lakehurst Naval Airport about twelve noon. That meant they must hide for at least eleven hours. Karl felt the blood rush to his head and heard his heart beating in his ears. The prospect was daunting.

He cursed the hand of fate which had brought them on this particular voyage and yet in reality he knew he had only himself to blame. Why had he been so impatient to embark on his carefully laid plans? Why had he not listened to Willi and waited just one more week until the next sailing? Then he would have been on the crew list and the wretched, evil von Outen would not have been on board. The entire journey had been like a very bad dream. A sailor would say it was jinxed.

He had just left Willi in the Major's accommodation where they had laid the man, still unconscious, in his bed. Karl prayed he would never wake up again. When he returned to Elizabeth, waiting for him in her cabin, she was making a brave attempt to stay calm and strong. She had dressed in a grey woollen suit. The skirt swung below her knees and a wide belt nipped in at her tiny waist. Black boots covered her slim ankles and a thick cape rested on her delicate shoulders.

"Everything else is in here now," she said, lifting up the travel bag. Her face looked pale and tense, though she tried to smile at

him encouragingly. "See," she said. "It is lighter now that I am wearing the warmest clothes."

Karl kissed her lightly on the forehead. "I will carry it," he said, taking the bag from her. "We are over Canada now, and we must move to the keel while the ship is quiet." He sensed her fear as he felt his own.

She clasped her hands over his. "Whatever happens now, Karl, we are together at last. From this moment on, we must never be parted again."

Karl closed his eyes, trying not to give in to despair; they needed to draw strength from each other.

"Remember, my darling," she said in a soft whisper. "As long as we love each other nothing can harm us, for perfect love casts out fear."

Karl shivered. She had said these beautiful words once before. Their future then had seemed frightening, but now it was terrifying. He must remain calm and follow the only course of action they could take. He carried the bag and took Elizabeth by the hand. "Follow me," he said. "We must stay silent. Stop if I stop. Run if I run."

She nodded her head in silent understanding and they stepped out into the passageway.

They had negotiated the two stairways down to the keel without being observed. Karl had even remembered to retrieve his overalls from the washroom on 'B' deck. If they were to hide, it was important to leave no trail. He led Elizabeth to his 'bolthole' at the back of the spare parts store.

"You can rest here," he said, settling her on his makeshift bed. "I must work out our next move."

"How can we manage with our luggage?" Elizabeth asked.

"Do not worry," he replied. "I have already arranged with Willi that he will take care of your trunk and bag. When we have an address he will bring them to us, perhaps on his next sailing."

"An address?" said Elizabeth, as though the thought had not occurred to her.

"Of course, my darling, we will have to find lodgings and arrange for our wedding as soon as possible."

Elizabeth's eyes lit up. "Oh, yes, our wedding! How wonderful," she said, in an excited whisper. "These present troubles will be as nothing once we are married." She threw her arms around his neck and cried. "We will be so happy, Karl!" Her words were joyful but her tears flowed.

Karl gently removed her arms and began re-packing her travel bag, adding his own meagre belongings. He then put the nine hundred Reichsmarks he had managed to save into his jacket pocket. The rest of their essential items went into his kitbag; this he would carry on his back. "I will take your travel bag to the cargo hold now, as I arranged with Willi," he said, brushing his lips against her outstretched hand.

Elizabeth sighed. "He is such a good friend to us. How can we ever repay him?"

Karl kissed her cheek as he knelt beside her. "Willi is our true friend. I have given him the 'Silver Knight'. Perhaps we should call our first son after him."

Elizabeth gasped with surprise, and then she began to laugh.

"Hush, dearest!" entreated Karl. His anxiety broke their happy exchange. As they looked into each other's eyes, their expressions turned from joy to dismay. He stood up, not wanting her to see his fear. "You must sleep now," he said. "I will return soon, and then we will have to move."

He waited until he was sure the keel walkway was deserted before going to the baggage room and storing the luggage. Karl then began to scout for a new hiding place.

The keel was a rabbit warren. Oil, fuel and water were the lifeblood of the airship: the tanks and pipes forming the arteries and veins. As these moved within the ship's undulation, the linkage strained to maintain its rigidity and there was a constant smell of

325

diesel fumes from escaping oil vapours. Myriad storage places ensured the load she carried was spread throughout the length and breadth of the ship.

Overhead, running right through the airship's central void, like the arrow from Eros's bow, was the axial walkway, piercing the heart of the ship. Rising up from the keel at intervals, were ventilation shafts – long tubes encased in square towers made from the same lightweight duralumin struts used in the airship's frame. These towers continued up, through the axial walkway, right to the top, exiting the airship as huge vents on top of the hull. Through these, excess gas or stale air could be vented out and fresh air drawn in.

Cloaking both walkways was the silken fabric of the sixteen massive gas cells. Inflated with the hydrogen gas, they filled the top of the ship, swelling out against the ramie cord netting, buffering them from the skeletal rings. They fell against the walkways in the fashion of giant ladies' circular fans. From the axial way, one could just catch a tantalising glimpse of the ship's skeletal structure and the keel walkway below, before the constantly moving silken folds would once more obscure the view.

When Karl returned to Elizabeth, she was sleeping like a little child. His watch showed it was after three a.m. Exhausted, he squeezed in beside her on the makeshift bed. She stirred as he wrapped his arms around her, and soon he too dozed off into a shallow sleep.

A harsh shout, like a pistol crack, further up the keel walkway, brought both Karl and Elizabeth wide awake. They stared at each other with wide, frightened eyes. They had both recognised the voice of von Outen. Karl's pocket watch now told him it was after five a.m.

A second voice spoke. "Can I assist you, Herr Major? You seem unsteady, sir." It was Willi's voice.

Karl crawled to the edge of the keel walkway and with his head at floor level, he stole a look in the direction of the voices. The Major looked dishevelled, still in his uniform from last evening. He was staggering and Willi moved to support him.

The Nazi began to rant. "I've been attacked! I am injured." He put his hand to the back of his head and Karl saw him wince in pain. He raved on. "I want the man responsible. He must be arrested and shot!"

Willi played along. "Where did this happen, Major?"

Major von Outen seemed confused, or else he realised the implication of his own guilt. "In... in...? don't remember where... I was hit over the head!"

"Who would dare do such a thing, and for no reason?" Willi was a born actor. "Perhaps you just banged your head on one of the bulwarks or ladders."

"No, no! I was hit! Look at this lump." He bent forward and allowed Willi to examine his head, but he was very unsteady, as though concussed.

Willi placed his arm around the Major, supporting him again. "Well, they would not be here in the keel, sir. It must have been another passenger. Come with me and I will get a doctor to look at your head. Then we will go to the smoking room, so you can rest." He went with Willi like a compliant child; he had lost his bark and bite.

Karl smiled to himself, thinking, he may not have killed the evil bastard, but he had certainly curbed the man's physical and mental powers. He crept back to Elizabeth and told her what had taken place. "One way or another, I think Willi intends to make von Outen forget his accusation."

"The man is too evil to let it go," she shivered. "When he remembers me, he will pursue us both."

"He will not take us! Come," Karl caught hold of her hands. "We must move now." He stood upright and pulled her to her feet.

"We are going just a little way along the keel to a cargo store on the starboard side."

"Why there?" she asked, as they gathered the bedding.

Karl hoisted his kitbag on to his back. "You will see soon enough. We must hurry before the six o'clock shift change." When he was sure the walkway was empty, they moved out and Karl took her by the hand, leading her down the keel to the cargo area he had selected earlier.

The bottom of the airship's hull was punctuated with viewing windows which looked straight down. Some were below the passenger accommodation, but there were others set at intervals. One of them was in this cargo store, in the floor-opening hatchway. This area was in the centre of the ship's belly, and would be at the lowest point when the 'Hindenburg' landed.

The airship was travelling light, with overseas mail and only a few boxes of freight. All the freight appeared to be in this store. The boxes were marked with the familiar stamp of Mercedes Benz, and Karl guessed they contained car parts, urgently required for luxury limousines, by an American dealer prepared to pay a higher price for speedy delivery. Karl pushed the boxes near the door to guard the entrance and they sat on the floor.

"See, Elizabeth," said Karl. "We have a grandstand view and a means to make our escape when the airship lands." Karl wiped the window clean and they looked down on the world below. The ship was passing over open sea once more. There was a morning mist rising from the surface. "Look! See that light flashing," he said, drawing Elizabeth's eyes to a pulsing beacon far to their right. "That will be the White Island light. It marks the Isle of Shoals, off the coast of New Hampshire." Karl had learned his geography well from his previous transatlantic trips. "That is America, but we still have a long way to go before we land."

Just before six a.m. they heard sounds of the impending shift change and moved into a corner, away from the light of the window and the entrance. Sleepy voices attached to muffled footsteps shuffled up and down the keel as men moved around the airship. Karl and Elizabeth could hear snatches of their conversation.

"This flight has taken so long!"

"We have been fighting a headwind all the way."

"There'll be no 'time off' when we land."

"No, it will be all hands to the pump to turn her round, double-quick." There were grumbles and moans at this.

"We have to leave on schedule or the passengers will be too late for the Coronation."

"That will make the new King and Queen of England very cross!"

"Perhaps we will fly over London and drop in on the procession!" Peals of laughter echoed down the keel.

Karl and Elizabeth were huddled in the corner, listening. She looked to him to confirm what they had heard. He nodded his head. "We probably won't land before late afternoon now," he said, looking glum.

She became despondent again. "Willi cannot watch the Major all that time; he has to be on duty." She pressed her body close to Karl for warmth and reassurance.

It was very cold in the cargo room and Karl wrapped his arms around her under the cape. He lifted her chin and tilted her head towards him, kissing her gently on the lips. They kissed again, deeper, longer. The fire of suppressed passion and deep longing smouldered between them and the cold surroundings ceased to exist. Together they began to caress each other, their fingers seeking bare flesh to touch and fondle. Karl opened his coat and shirt and she slipped her ice cold fingers inside, running her hands across his bare chest and round his back. His own self-control snapped, and he kissed her neck. She opened her jacket and blouse with trembling fingers.

He tried to stop himself. "I don't want to hurt you, my darling, after what he did to you."

"Oh, Karl, you could never hurt me. We love each other, so that makes it right. If we are caught today by that evil Nazi, I may never see you again."

Karl realised she was as aware of their perilous situation as he was himself. "I love you, my Elizabeth, with all my heart and soul. I could not live without you."

"Nor I without you, dear Karl, and I want you to love me with your body also. Then our love will be truly perfect."

As they became locked once more in a deep, loving kiss, they sank down on the floor, hidden from the world and all its perils, lost in the arms of their love. The airship 'Hindenburg' flew on, through the wind and rain of a deepening depression, and in their eyes Karl and Elizabeth became man and wife. The ship continued the journey relentlessly, towards Boston and New York, and the innocent fugitives fell asleep in the honeymoon of their love.

When Karl awoke, he could again hear the murmur of voices along the keel. He looked at his watch; it was five minutes before twelve noon. Elizabeth opened her eyes and smiled up at him. He kissed her gently on the lips. "We have slept through the morning," he said. "Are you hungry?"

"I am starving!" she replied.

"I will follow the men to the mess room and bring back food for us." He stood up, adjusting his clothing and pulling on his work overalls. "See, now I am just another mechanic."

Elizabeth stood, shaking out her crumpled clothes. She turned away from him, coyly fastening her buttons. "Be careful, my darling," she said, turning back to face him. "Please do not leave me here alone too long."

"Take this," said Karl, and he gave her his pocket watch to hold. "It is noon now and we should soon be over New York City; that will be a fine sight."

Karl waited near the entrance until a group of men coming off shift passed the doorway. He slipped out behind them as they all made their way towards the mess room.

One of them dropped back beside him, it was Halder. "Hello, Stockhausen, where have you been?"

Karl normally worked with him on the forward starboard engine. "I was sent to the forward port to train new crewmen." Karl's lie sounded plausible, even to him.

"I missed you yesterday too," Halder said.

"Officer Schmitt has been sending me all over the ship," said Karl. "He thinks I am the odd job man." That was a second lie, and he mentally crossed himself.

Halder laughed. "Well, it beats freezing your ass off out there on the arms. This rain is relentless."

"Not like Brazil, eh?" Karl joked.

Halder growled his approval. "Oh, yes! Stuff New York, give me Copocabaña and Brazilian girls any day!"

They reached the mess and joined the queue. Halder was served first and he drifted off with his lunch, talking to other men in front of him.

The smell of cooked food reminded Karl he was famished, but he asked for bread and cheese, saying he was going back on duty. The grumbling kitchen hand gave him a paper bag with bread, cheese and a meat pie. He also took a glass bottle of lemonade; the only drink he could carry away.

After visiting the washroom, he went back down to the keel. As he reached the bottom of the stairs, he heard voices and footsteps behind him. The crew all wore rope-soled shoes on the ship to prevent sparks creating a fire hazard. The voices seemed in disagreement with each other. One stomped on the treads with heavy steel-tipped boots. Karl dodged into the nearest side store, out of view.

Within seconds the 'Mad Major' reached the keel. Karl could see him, just outside his hiding place, wearing a fresh uniform. The

331

SS runes were clearly visible at the collar. In place of his cap, a bandage was wrapped around his crown and forehead. He turned to confront Willi, who was running after him down the stairway. The major visibly seethed with anger, and Karl watched in horror as the man drew his pistol out from the shoulder holster.

"Herr Major, no!" exclaimed Willi, recoiling. "You cannot enter this area with a firearm, it is forbidden. Even your boots are a risk, you could cause a fire and the airship would explode!"

Major von Outen became more enraged. "How dare you tell me what I cannot do?" He waved the pistol under Willi's nose. "I am Major von Outen of the Schutzstaffel! I am taking command of this… this… airship!" he stuttered, "in the name of the Führer! You will assist me to search for the attacker."

Willi dodged round him to escape the Major's indiscriminate arm waving and to block his passage down the keel. "Now, sir, you must not excite yourself. The doctor said you must rest."

"Rest!" he exploded at Willi. "How can I rest when someone is trying to kill me? It is the saboteur! We must find him or he will explode your bloody airship."

The Nazi's behaviour was irrational and dangerous, and Willi continued in his attempts to placate him. "Captain Lehmann has instructed me to stay with you and ensure your safety, sir."

"I am perfectly able to look after myself," said von Outen, becoming even wilder. "Lehmann is a fool! He would not listen to me. When we return to Germany, I will have him sacked!" He pushed passed Willi. "I will have you all sacked and ground your damned airships!"

He began poking in the store next to where Karl was hiding; they were both food stores. The Major came back out, waving the gun around in an alarming manner. "Field Marshall Goering will make a squadron of airplanes from all this steel!" he shouted at Willi and banged the butt of his pistol on the nearest strut support. It clanked, echoing through the metalwork.

Willi changed his tactics. "We will be over New York soon, Major. Captain Lehmann has promised you the ship will be searched when we land. Let us go to the smoking room and you can drink a toast to the glorious Fatherland." Willi drew himself up to attention and raised his right arm. "Heil Hitler!" he shouted, with all the panache of a true Nazi supporter.

The Major's response was predictable, given his devotion to the cause. He holstered the pistol and returned Willi's salute. "Heil Hitler!" he repeated, sharply clicking his boot heels together.

"Come with me, sir," said Willi. "The 'Hindenburg's' best schnapps awaits you. We will toast each and every minister in our glorious leader's government." The promise of more free alcohol was a strong motivator and confirmed Karl's previous suspicion that the man was addicted to alcohol. Willi was using this to advantage and Karl waited anxiously for the major's response.

"Very well, Officer Schultz, but I will return here when the ship lands. No one will leave this damned 'flying sausage' without my authority!"

"Of course, Herr Major, and I will assist you, sir." Willi seemed to be enjoying playing the Nazi at his own game, and ignored his erroneous naming. He turned him around and led him back up the stairs.

Karl breathed again; that had been a very close encounter. Willi had once again proved himself to be more like a brother than just a friend. When Karl was sure the walkway and stairs were empty, he hurried down the keel, back to Elizabeth.

When he entered the cargo space at first he could not see her. "Elizabeth!" he whispered urgently. "I am here. Where are you?" He heard a stifled sob, from the far corner of the area. He hurried over and found her, wrapped in a cocoon of blanket, quite hidden, she was crying. He huddled beside her. "Oh, my darling, it's all right, I am here." He took the watch from her shaking hand. It showed half an hour after two o'clock.

"I thought you would be taken," she sobbed. "I thought he would shoot you!"

Karl held her close and didn't answer. He had thought the same when he was trapped in the food store.

He opened the paper bag he was still clutching. "Come, we must eat," he said, giving her some of the bread and cheese. Then he broke open the glass stopper wired to the lemonade bottle and passed it to her.

She drank, and the bubbles took her breath away, making her cough. They laughed together and ate the food, while Karl pondered on what they should do next.

CHAPTER THIRTY-SIX

IN LIMBO

Cardington, Bedfordshire, England. May 2000

"Wake up, Jonno!"

Charlie was standing right in front of him, waving a hand in his face. Startled, Jonno blinked, and realised he had lapsed into a hypnotic daydream. He felt acutely embarrassed. He was supposed to be a highly trained RAF navigator, seconded to this company for special duties. Only Charlie's apt choice of words had brought him out of his trance.

He shifted uneasily in his seat and avoided Charlie's scrutiny by looking at the screen. "I wasn't asleep, Charlie," he said. "I was concentrating. What did you say?"

"I was talking about the lift ratios, when we carry cargo." Charlie looked at him, slightly nonplussed. "The importance of the payload distribution."

Jonno had not heard any of this, but he covered with a suitable reply. "Of course, but it's all built into the computer programme."

"Yes, but what I said was," said Charlie, emphasising each phrase, "since the computer went down, I can't wait to test it." He continued looking critically at Jonno. "I hope fitting the cargo floor goes ahead next week as planned."

"It will, Charlie," said Jonno, for he had organised this next important stage. "No problems there, or with the computer programme, you'll see."

"I'd like to have a half page in the Business Section in next Sunday's edition?" said Lisa. She raised her request to Biddy during their morning meeting.

Biddy looked surprised. "Whatever for?"

Lisa opened her folder and laid her work on the desk. "I'm working on a follow up to the airship feature. We've had a lot of interest from individuals and bodies like the Airship Heritage Trust, and we've published letters which support keeping airship development in this country, but no joy so far on finding a financial backer. The MOD have put their 'penneth' in, but LTA needs more private funding to continue work at Cardington."

Caroline chipped in. "Yes, but what's new since your last piece?"

"I've photos and a review from Alison of the 'Sky Dolphin's' first test flight," Lisa spread the prints out on the desk. "She looks very impressive."

Biddy studied the colour prints and was thoughtful. "Do a mock-up and I'll get you a meeting with Dave Preston in Business News. If you can sell it to him, you'll get your space."

Lisa was pleased to have crossed this hurdle. She left the office determined to push the boundaries of her journalistic skills to the limit to help the airship project.

Caroline had followed her, and she handed Lisa a package. "From Tony," she said, "it's the tapes from Jonno's last session at the clinic."

"Oh, thanks, Caroline," said Lisa. "I'd been meaning to pick them up all week."

Caroline looked relieved. "I didn't like to ask how things are between you two."

"Better. Not quite back to normal, but definitely better." She didn't want to elaborate. "How about you and Tony, is everything okay with you two?"

Caroline crossed the fingers on both her hands before she answered. "Pretty perfect is how I would describe things at the moment."

Lisa had guessed as much. These days Caroline seemed to be walking on air. "I'm really pleased for both of you," she said. "Oh, and tell Tony thanks for the tapes."

Lisa returned to her desk. She was impatient to continue with her feature, but something else was nagging at her which she knew she must resolve. Alison had emailed the photographs attached to the test flight review and a personal message which Lisa had only scanned through. Now she printed a copy and re-read the final paragraph with a growing feeling of disquiet. Alison had said:

'I thought I'd better tell you about something concerning Jonno. Charlie was rather worried by an incident during the test flight. Jonno apparently seemed to lose concentration for several minutes. Charlie told me his eyes glazed over and it was as if he was hypnotised. Charlie said he had almost to shout at him before he came out of it. After that he was fine, but Charlie was baffled by his odd behaviour. I know you said Jonno has had a few problems and I witnessed a similar incident during the 'Sky Lark' test, but I'm not sure Charlie wants to risk taking him up again. It would be a shame if he had to leave the project now. Let me know what you think.

Love, Alison.'

Lisa's disquiet turned to fear for Jonno. If he had to leave the airship project now, it would probably spell the end of his career in the RAF.

Jonno spent the next few days ensuring that the cargo floor was assembled to Charlie's exacting specifications. This included a cage-like structure of side and overhead struts, rather like Meccano pieces, to which the cargo could be secured.

He had sensed a slight cooling in Charlie's demeanour towards him since the first test flight and he had been disappointed not to be included on a second test two days later. Charlie had said he wanted other team members to experience 'Dolphin' flight, but Jonno was sure Charlie's confidence in him had taken a knock.

Jonno was concerned about the consequences of his unfortunate lapse in concentration. The regression memories he had experienced were amazing, and he now felt he was one step nearer to discovering the mystery of his past life. But it shouldn't have happened during the test flight, not in the presence of the LTA team. His career was once more in jeopardy. The incident might have been minor but in the aftermath, its echo grew louder.

He drew comfort from the restoration of regular contact with Lisa. During their daily telephone calls he deliberately didn't talk about his past life or the state of his present mind. He was totally convinced that closure was close. What he really wanted was to see Tony again, but he could not leave Cardington to visit him at this critical time. For one thing, he was keeping a very close eye on night security, even getting up in the night and making his own checks when the night-shift work pattern had stopped. He was in a 'Catch-22'.

By Friday the work on the cargo bay was almost complete and both doors had been fitted with the reinforced ramps for the roll-on roll-off facility. Charlie looked approvingly at Jonno.

"It's a first class job; shall we test it?" said the Project Manager.

Jonno jumped at the chance to make amends. He rounded up four drivers, directing them to bring suitable vehicles into the shed. 'Dolphin's' engines were started and the roll-on cargo door opened. The vehicles were driven in and spread along the hull. The actual cargo area was less than twenty-six meters long by four meters wide and three meters high. More than ample for Jeep size vehicles. The extraction fans worked well and quickly dispelled the exhaust fumes. Even if the projected eight vehicles were loaded there was still plenty of space for other cargo. Charlie was satisfied that all the computer readouts were within the calculations for weight and distribution.

"Okay!" he shouted to Jonno. "Wheel them out."

The roll-off door was opened and Jonno marshalled the vehicles out, one by one.

Charlie looked pleased. "Tomorrow, could you have eight suitable vehicles ready when we take her out of the shed?" he asked Jonno. "We need to test loading and unloading with the aircushion in operation."

"I think I will pay our neighbours at RAF Wyton a visit and see if we can requisition any Jeeps," answered Jonno. "Then we will really know if the weight calculations are correct. It will also give us a good photo opportunity."

"Good man, good thinking," said Charlie, and Jonno felt he had regained some of Charlie's confidence. "By the way," Charlie said, "your Lisa tells me she is running another feature for us this Sunday, on the Business pages. She is still trying to conjure up a financial backer for us."

Jonno smiled. "When she sets her mind to do something, there's no stopping her," he said.

"Oh, and apparently she is coming up here on Sunday and bringing a prospective member of an American business consortium."

Jonno looked surprised; he didn't know anything about this.

Charlie thumped the base of his hand to his forehead. "Oh, dear," he said, "not sure if I was meant to tell you about that, but I think you know the guy."

Jonno looked at him questioningly. "Who is he?"

"Dr Tony Reeve; I think that's his name," said Charlie, and he walked off, leaving Jonno momentarily speechless.

By Saturday he was beginning to think he had regained his lost 'Brownie points' with Charlie. The second test of the cargo area had been a complete success with eight jeep-size military vehicles from Wyton. Not only had they tested the aircushion landing system but Charlie had taken the 'Dolphin' up with the load on board. Jonno had however, remained earthbound.

He didn't let it get him down, for tomorrow he would see Lisa again. He rang her almost immediately to confirm the arrangements and she put him in the picture regarding Tony Reeve's apparent interest in the project.

"I was talking to Tony about your regression tapes when I happened to mention my features on the airships." He heard amusement in her voice. "Tony's attention meter shot up one hundred percent. Then he told me he was part of an American business group that was keen to invest in new British technology. So he wants to see your airships. Now how strange is that?" Lisa sounded delighted by this turn of events.

"Just goes to show," Jonno said, feeling equally pleased, "solutions are sometimes closer than you think."

"My second feature in the Business supplement comes out tomorrow, and I'm bringing Tony to Cardington with me." Her enthusiasm bubbled down the phone line. "Charlie has promised to take us up in the 'Dolphin'. I can't wait."

"I may not be able to go with you," said Jonno, and a note of regret crept into his voice.

"Oh, I expect you will," said Lisa breezily. "I'll speak to Charlie."

He smiled at this. If Lisa had found a potential backer for the project, he couldn't imagine that Charlie would refuse her anything.

Much later that evening, Jonno was jolted out of his euphoria by another telephone call. He had returned to the bungalow and retired to his room. As he drifted off to sleep, his mobile phone rang. He reached out for the handset and saw on the display that the caller was his sister, Sarah.

"Hi, Sarah, you're a late caller." He was surprised, and roused quickly from semi-sleep. "Is everything okay?"

"Yes," she said. "I'm with Mum for the weekend. Is everything all right there?"

"Fine," he answered. "I'm looking forward to seeing Lisa tomorrow." He was going to say more about the planned visit but she cut across him.

"I know all about it," she said, almost dismissively. "Jonno, I'm calling to warn you; to alert you to something."

"What's up, sis?" Her concerned tone banished all thoughts of sleep.

"It's Paul," she said. "He's making threats again."

"What, to you and Mum?" he said, with mounting alarm.

"No, not to us," she said. "To you and to the airship." She sounded really worried.

Jonno's mind flipped back to the break-in and the hate letter. "What has he said, Sarah?" There was a pause and he sensed Sarah's hesitance to bring accusations against Paul.

"He was ranting again really, like he did before." She tried to explain. "I rang him about something else and he started going on about you and the airship. He'd heard about you taking some RAF jeeps up on a test flight."

Jonno cut in. "Yes, I arranged it with the transport people at Wyton. I though it would get back to him."

"Well, he knew all about it. He wasn't making any sense, Jonno. He said that you didn't deserve the DFC because you'd been grounded and he'd make sure you never collected it."

"What else did he say, Sarah?"

"He started on about airships again, saying they were a threat and a menace. Then he said he'd blow it up!" Sarah sounded really worried.

"Did he actually threaten to?" Jonno asked her.

"It was probably just talk," she said. "I'm sure he had been drinking, but his exact words were, 'I'll torch that bloody gas bag and blow it to bits and hope that stupid little sod is inside!'" Sarah's own liberalism surfaced. "I can't believe he means to do it, Jonno, but I had to warn you."

341

"No, I expect it was all talk again," he said, wanting to allay her fears. "You did right, but don't worry, sis, the 'Dolphin' is practically fireproof and we've good security, but thanks for the warning."

"There's something else," Sarah continued, a note of apology in her voice. "I rang Lisa first, to ask her if I should warn you."

He cut in. "She obviously said, yes."

Sarah's voice came back sounding even more anxious. "Jonno, she was really upset. She's never trusted Paul, and I think she may be on her way tonight."

"Way, where?" he said, bemused.

"To you, to the airship; I'm sorry, Jonno. I should have known she would react like that. She was spitting fire by the end of our call." Sarah seemed distraught.

"It's all right, sis," he said, trying to reassure her. "I'll ring her straight away and turn her round. She won't be in any danger and neither will I." He sounded more positive than he felt.

When the call ended, he immediately rang Lisa's mobile. There was no reply. He left a message on her voice mail. "Don't come to Cardington until tomorrow, as planned. Charlie and I can handle Paul via the surveillance if he shows. He is all talk. Ring me soon as, please. Love you lots, bye for now."

Her non-reply reassured him that Lisa had gone to bed and that Sarah was over reacting. He sat back down on the bed and worked out his options. He didn't want to alarm Charlie, not yet. He, however, would have to return to the shed. If necessary he would stay there all night.

CHAPTER THIRTY-SEVEN

NIGHT VISITORS

A ground mist hung around the airfield, damp and cold. As he approached shed number one on foot, the security light protecting the main doors triggered with an audible clunk. Jonno shivered, startled by its sudden intrusion into the dark, eerie silence. It thrust its beam across the forecourt, illuminating the lower half of the structure through curls of white drifting mist.

Around one a.m. he had left his car parked near the perimeter fence, away from the open car park and taken a powerful flashlight from the boot. As he surveyed the car's tool kit for anything else that might proof useful, his hand had moved instinctively to the kit's largest spanner, which he then dropped into the pocket of his dark parka coat. It rattled against the large bunch of keys which opened all the locks. He had then quietly closed the boot lid.

He moved away from the blinding light facing the doors and began a recce of the outside of the shed. Covering the side adjacent to number two first, he stopped at the point where the break-in had occurred, examining the corrugated steel walls in the beam from the flashlight. He had personally supervised the welding in of a new section, making this area considerably more robust than the rest of the building. As he had performed this routine several times in daylight, he now knew most of the weak points. Repairing them all would have been beyond the project's resources. Ten minutes later he had circumnavigated the vast shed and was satisfied no new disturbances had occurred in the dilapidated outer walls.

The front facing security light had switched off and Jonno did not want it to reactivate. Should Paul, or any other intruder, be intent on penetrating LTA's security to gain access to the airship, he wanted it to be tonight while he was ready and waiting; the time had come for a showdown with the enemy.

Right now his best option was to use the newly installed CCTV monitoring system. He hurried away from the shed, thankful that his rubber soled trainers made little sound on the old concrete roadway. He stopped at the single storey hut block and unlocked the door to Charlie's office. Inside he remained in the dark and switched on the surveillance monitor. There were three cameras at the shed. One outside on the front pole opposite the main doors below the security light; one inside the main doors, facing the moored airships in the central area; and one further down on the left inside wall, trained directly on to the 'Sky Dolphin'. At night the images were only visible if the adjacent security lights were triggered.

Jonno peered at the screen which was split into four quarters, but could see only misty grey outlines. He went over to the window and opened it. Apart from the RAF guard stationed at the main gate to the airfield half a mile away, the whole area was deserted. This office was about thirty yards from the sheds, but any sounds would travel well through the silent night air. He made himself a cup of steaming hot coffee in Alison's makeshift kitchen and settled down to wait in front of the monitor screen. He rang Lisa's mobile again; it was now switched off.

As he sipped his coffee, Jonno examined his motives for coming here alone tonight. What would he do if Paul did turn up, spoiling for trouble? And why was his brother apparently so intent on wrecking his future? He recalled the moment when his subconscious memories of events from seventy years ago had prompted him to believe that Paul and the SS Nazi, Major von Outen, both possessed the same vengeful spirit, hell-bent on destroying him.

If only he knew what had eventually happened on the 'Hindenburg', he might be better prepared to deal with Paul. The Nazi's vengeance had been directed at Karl and Elizabeth. Was Lisa part of Paul's plan? He had already tried to seduce her and had been rejected. The Major had attempted to rape Elizabeth and been thwarted by Karl. The parallels were frighteningly similar. But in this life, Paul was part of his family and Jonno did not know how he would react should his brother attempt to carry through the threats he had made. Perhaps he should make a final attempt to reason with Paul to avoid trouble; Jonno felt he owed that much to his mother and sister.

By three a.m. he was overcome with tiredness. Tomorrow promised to be a busy day with the planned visit from Lisa and Tony Reeve. A few hours' sleep seemed very desirable right now, if not essential. After two hours keeping watch nothing had happened, so perhaps it was all just a hoax, aimed at nothing more than causing him disruption. He decided to make a further recce of the shed and then go back to the bungalow and catch some sleep.

He closed the window and went over to the monitor. As he reached out to switch it off the screen suddenly burst into life as camera three was triggered by the security light. Jonno stood immobile, staring at the side-on image of 'Sky Dolphin'. The light reached out towards the front end of the shed, and camera two showed a less intense view of the airship's bow end. As he continued to stare at the screen, Jonno was sure he detected a slight movement at the bottom of the picture, indicating something or someone had moved their position, ducking out of the camera's range.

He instantly upgraded the night's operation from medium risk to full-scale alert and his thoughts transferred into actions. Now he needed back up and as he made for the door, he called Charlie up on his mobile, the call tone repeated in his ear as he ran. He had covered about twenty yards before he heard the voice mail message kick in.

He cursed, but knew Charlie would check his phone regularly, even at night. He slowed his pace, keeping his voice low to leave a message, "Intruder in our shed, Charlie. Picked him up on CCTV,

I'm going in." He knew he should wait for back up, but his decision on that score would depend on who was in the shed. If it was a stranger he would keep watch and wait, but if it was Paul – he would prefer to deal with Paul himself.

To stand any chance of getting the upper hand, the element of surprise needed to be in his favour. Avoiding the front and main doors, which were still firmly shut, he sprinted down the long side of shed number one to the point of the previous intrusion. Now he was running on grass and he held the flashlight low down, so that the moving light would not reflect up to the shed's high windows, alerting the intruder to his presence. His adrenaline was pumping fast, but his thoughts were perfectly clear and focused. He must identify the enemy and apprehend him. If possible, before the back up arrived. What happened after that was very much in the hands of fate.

The corrugated walls appeared undisturbed and he moved quickly, further down the side of the massive old building. He homed in on the next weak point fifteen yards further on and found the new entry. It had not been there earlier and, as he stepped towards the opening, his foot twisted awkwardly on a piece of hardware hidden in the tufted grass. He slumped to the ground, groaning with pain, but quickly recovered, and sat up, massaging his ankle and cursing under his breath. Reaching out for the offending object, he picked up a pair of scissor cutters. He recognised them as aviation tin snips for cutting hardened steel. They had been used to cut and peel back the new opening, probably left in situ to invisibly curl the steel back in place when the intruder left. They would have made little or no noise.

He flexed his foot – no bones broken. There was a rustling sound of footfalls in the grass from the direction he had come. His flashlight had gone out when he fell; now he was almost invisible. He froze for a second and watched the beam of a torch coming towards him, flicking along the bottom of the shed as he had done himself. Jonno rolled silently on to his knees, ready to leap forward, praying his ankle would not give way. His hand went to his coat pocket and he clutched hold of the car spanner. A dark silhouette followed the torch beam, moving closer to him, apparently oblivious to his presence. When the figure was within striking distance, he sucked in a deep breath to boost his muscle power and leapt forward in a classic rugby tackle, clasping at the legs and knocking his opponent to the ground.

There was a muffled scream as he fell on top of someone, but Jonno was taken aback by the unexpected lightweight of the body he had felled. The scream was high pitched and female. He knew instantly – it was Lisa!

Relief, concern and fear that he had injured her flooded his head. Initially stunned, she began to struggle under the weight of his body and to scream in earnest. Jonno realised he still held the spanner in his hand, thankfully not used, and he flung it aside, clapping his hand over her mouth.

"It's me!" he hissed, somewhat angrily. "What the blazes are you doing here? I nearly killed you!" Her tensed up body relaxed and she emitted a sob as he sat back, releasing his hold on her.

"You bloody nearly succeeded!" she hissed back with equal venom, holding the back of her head.

"Didn't you get my voice mail telling you not to come?" He was still annoyed and concerned that he had attacked her.

She mumbled almost incoherently. "My battery's flat."

They couldn't see each other clearly, but he lent forward again, cradling her head against his chest, gently rubbing the back of her crown.

"Are you hurt badly? Oh, Lisa, I'm sorry!" He was full of relief and self-recrimination. He should have known she would come to his aid. Now was not the time for an inquisition.

His mind was returned sharply to the night's true purpose as the hairs on the back of his neck began to rise. He had detected the sound of movement in the vicinity of the hole in the shed wall. He was kneeling on the ground, holding Lisa with his back to the opening. Totally exposed, he was a sitting target. If he leapt up, Lisa would be left unprotected. He had lost the advantage of surprise and knew the odds were now stacked against him.

He guessed at his true assailant's next move. "Don't do anything stupid!" he shouted, hoping also to alert Lisa to the imminent danger. There was no reply, except a quickening of footfall behind him. He saw a black-gloved hand reach down and pick up his spanner, glinting silver in the grass. Remembering his vow to the family, he began to say, "We can talk this through...."

The blow struck the back of his skull and, as he slipped into unconsciousness, he was aware of Lisa writhing in his arms; she was screaming and struggling under him. Everything was the wrong way round. Surely, she was struggling under von Outen's body and he, Karl, held the spanner? He had delivered the blow, surely?

The airship was due to land and he had attacked the Nazi officer. They must run! They must hide! Elizabeth was calling to him. He must find Karl and go to her, for they were in terrible danger.

CHAPTER THIRTY-EIGHT

JOURNEY'S END

Airship 'Hindenburg', New York, Thursday 6th May 1937

They heard the sounds of the crew changing shifts again for what would be the last time on this flight. Karl's pocket watch showed the time was three p.m. He felt the change in air pressure as the 'Hindenburg' dropped to a lower altitude. Suddenly, they were startled by the airship's horn as it blasted out three times on a loud note.

Elizabeth became excited. "Are we there?"

"Not quite, but we are over New York. Let's go and have a look."

They moved to the window in the centre of the floor and Karl pushed the boxes to once more shield them from the doorway. The Manhattan skyscrapers towered up towards the airship. People stood on the roofs of some buildings and they seemed almost within touching distance. In between the towering blocks, the criss-cross grids of the roadways were just thin lines, as if at the bottom of deep straight canyons. The returning horns of the cars in the streets rose up towards the airship, barely heard, the cars seen only as tiny dots below the giant buildings.

The airship continued the tour of New York, encircling the city and harbour, acknowledging the louder hoots and whistles of the ships and boats with the 'Hindenburg's' horn. They circled the Isle of Manhattan and passed over the famous Statue of Liberty. There were lots of sightseers crowded on the high balustrade around the statue's head.

"I can almost see the colour of their eyes!" gasped Elizabeth in amazement.

Karl smiled at her. "We have come to a wonderful country, my darling, where we can be free and happy."

Elizabeth threw her arms around his neck. "I cannot believe we have come to America at last, Karl." She pressed her tearful face next to his. "But I would be happy anywhere on earth so long as I am with you."

Karl sighed with pleasure, but also with concern. He had to think practically, they were still in terrible danger. "It will be about another hour before we land at Lakehurst Air Station and we must be ready to make our escape." He began to think about how they could leave from this hatchway without raising the suspicions of officials.

A familiar and ominous sound reached his ears and broke his train of thought. Heavy boots once more on the walkway! He went to the entrance, peering into the passage. Major von Outen was back on the keel walkway, staggering in a drunken stupor. He was searching everywhere, and he was alone!

Karl's adrenaline began to race. Elizabeth had crept up beside him, her face full of alarm. He clasped her hand. "We must move from here until he has gone."

"Move ... where?" She began to tremble and looked petrified.

Karl held her firmly by the shoulders. "You must be brave a little longer and trust me." He scanned the passageway once more. At that moment, the Nazi was out of sight. "Come now, quickly!" He grasped her hand and began to run, down towards the stern end of the ship, pulling her behind him. The gas cell fabric provided some cover as it billowed between the metal strut supports and side rooms.

"Where are we going?" whispered Elizabeth in panic when they stopped.

"Up!" said Karl pointing to the ladder. "You must go first."

She looked up in alarm.

"I will catch you if you slip. Don't look down. Hurry now!" he urged her.

Elizabeth closed her eyes and took a deep breath. She began to climb the ladder to the axial walkway overhead. Karl followed close behind, shielding her as she went unsteadily upwards. They reached the top of the ladder and moved along the narrow platform. He motioned for them to lie down. They clung together and tried not to make a sound. From up here, they could see only part of the keel below and they waited for the Nazi's expected challenge.

It did not come; they had not been seen. Every now and then Karl heard the sound of boots on metal. The Major was apparently still searching further up the keel-way. They were now lying head to head on the upper platform and the strong smell of diesel fumes reached them from below.

"Where is Willi?" Elizabeth whispered, close to his ear.

"He will be on duty for the landing," Karl answered softly.

They heard von Outen shout out, in anger and triumph.

"He has found our belongings!" Elizabeth began breathing erratically.

He attempted to soothe her. "Please be calm, Elizabeth, I have all our papers on me and the money," he said, although he did not feel calm himself.

Her eyes were full of tears. "He will keep looking now until he finds us, we are trapped."

"Hush, dearest," he touched her face with his fingers. "Remember – perfect love…"

"…casts out fear." She'd completed their mantra and her voice steadied.

They looked down and saw the Nazi reach this end of the ship. He swayed as he walked, apparently very intoxicated, and in his hands he carried Elizabeth's cape. They almost stopped breathing. The man could barely stand and had completed his search of the lower keel. In his drunken state, there was no question he could scale the ladder, but it did not seem to occur to him; he didn't even look up.

He began to rant. "Now Lehmann will have to listen to me, damn him! The Jew woman has vanished with an accomplice. They are both saboteurs!" He started to retrace his route back up the keel, staggering and falling against the side supports as he went away.

They remained motionless until the Nazi had gone. Karl breathed a sigh of relief. "We will have to stay where we are now," he said.

"We cannot escape from up here, surely?" said Elizabeth in despair as they sat close together.

"No," he answered. Karl knew the 'Hindenburg' had reached Lakehurst. It was four o'clock and she should now be preparing to land. "We will have to stay hidden on aboard after we have landed, and wait until von Outen has left the ship. We can then slip out under cover of darkness during the night."

Elizabeth nodded her head, in agreement. "That sounds a good plan!" she said, and they settled down on the high axial way again and waited and waited.

Karl checked his watch in dismay; it was long after four o'clock. The ship had not landed and it was flying again, high in the sky.

They had moved further along the axial walkway, away from the open ladder. This delay seemed interminable and he had no idea what was happening. Karl was used to being out in the engine nacelle, where he could plot every minute of the journey. Being shut away made him feel very claustrophobic. Elizabeth sat with her head pressed into her skirt in an attempt to filter the air; the fumes were making her feel sick.

The only explanation for the delayed landing was the weather conditions. Westerly gales had dogged the entire trip, slowing their speed and testing the Captain's expertise to read the weather charts and divert the airship's forward course to avoid potentially hazardous winds. Karl knew the charts would be constantly updated

352

by the navigation officers. If conditions were stormy at Lakehurst, neither the Captain nor the American ground commander, would risk the 'Hindenburg's' safety in a dangerous landing.

Karl leaned against the base of the ventilation shaft which was between gas cells four and five. Elizabeth was propped up beside him, half asleep. The conditions were very turbulent and from here he could hear the wind howling and the rain lashing as the storm vented its force against the ship's outer cover. Lightning flashed like the defused blink of a giant's eye through the semi-translucent fabric of the hull and thunder rumbled in the distance; they were flying ahead of the storm. Karl watched the minutes tick away on his watch and consoled himself that the airship would eventually have to land whatever the hazards.

At fifteen minutes after five o'clock, the 'Hindenburg' began to turn. As she changed direction in a wide circular sweep, he felt the metal structure strike up howls of protest. The whale-like distress calls of wires and struts and girders reached his ears in a cacophony of discord. This had to be the signal that 'permission to land' had been granted.

There was a sudden flurry of activity on the keel walkway beneath them. Elizabeth's eyes opened wide with fright and they drew close together, tucking themselves into a tight ball so they would not be spotted. He knew the landing routine precisely. Those men not on designated duty would congregate in the centre of the keel, and await the captain's instructions to go fore or aft to trim the ship, and maintain the equilibrium. It was possible someone on gas cell maintenance would come up to the axial way to check the valves, but the actual venting-off of the gasses would be controlled from the gondola by the captain. Voices echoed up from down below; the men were following procedures and instructions were being given and repeated up and down the keel walkway.

Among these, Karl picked out Willi's voice giving orders to the men. Then he heard a great deal of shouting and arguing; he knew this was not from the crew. He could not make out the words being said, but the most raised voice was well known to him – it was Major von Outen again.

The 'Hindenburg' was well into the landing process, but she seemed to be constantly changing direction. Karl presumed they had approached from the east, but now the airship seemed to be making another tight u-turn to approach the landing mast from the opposite direction. The airship was once again under enormous stress to put the eight hundred foot long, rigid structure into so tight a turn. The metal girders screeched and howled in protest once again. All the while the ship was reducing speed and dropping in altitude.

They were in the stern end of the airship and Karl felt it was now lower than the forward section. The men on the keel had moved away; they would have been sent up into the bow to correct the heaviness in the stern.

It was then they caught a glimpse of von Outen directly below them. He was strutting down the keel-way in a cavalier manner, oblivious to the intricacies of the landing procedure. In his hand he clutched a bottle of schnapps, stopping to drink straight from the bottle.

He muttered expletives and shouted out. "Lehmann is a fool! He will not believe the girl is a Jew or a saboteur!" He took another mouthful of the schnapps. "... I will find her... and her accomplice, the murderer!" He emptied the bottle and threw it to the side where it smashed against a metal support. They saw him draw his pistol from the shoulder holster and start down the passageway again towards the stern. This time nobody was around to stop him.

"Come, Elizabeth," urged Karl in desperation. "We must get completely out of sight. If he fires the pistol the whole ship could blow up!"

"Where... how...?" Elizabeth muttered feebly, once more in a state of panic.

Karl stood behind her and put her arms onto the ventilation shaft. "We will climb up here between the gas cells."

354

The metal work was cold and wet with condensation and Elizabeth began to waver, shaking her head in sheer fright. "No, please, no!"

He pressed his body close to hers. "Trust me, darling, or we will be caught!"

She began to find the footholds, and with Karl close behind her, they climbed slowly up the open framework of the shaft cover, disappearing between the billowing silken fabric of gas cells four and five.

There was a loud hissing noise. "What's that!" she said in alarm.

"It's all right, they are venting off the gas to reduce the lift," he reassured her. The noise continued for about fifteen seconds. As Karl's hand sought for grip, he touched a rough surface that moved and he was momentarily startled. A length of rope hung down the outside of the shaft. He looked up and saw it came from the roof of the ship. It looked like one of the pulley ropes used during construction and should have been removed. This one had concealed itself against the shaft and been overlooked. It hung all the way down to the axial walkway, now about four metres below them.

More gas was released from the adjacent cells, hissing up through the ventilation shaft. The ship lurched once more, changing direction yet again. Suddenly, there was a loud bang overhead as a metal tensioning wire cracked and sheared away from its mooring, piercing straight through the gas cell immediately above them. It sounded exactly like a pistol shot and in fright, Elizabeth gave an involuntary scream as she lost her grip on the frame. Her body swung to the left and her right foot slipped from its hold, dangling in midair. Karl made a grab for her right hand taking her weight and swinging her body back towards the shaft.

He had been startled by the noise himself, but Elizabeth seemed to have gone into shock and fainted. He was holding her dead weight with one arm; her right leg still hung away from the

355

strut supports. To his horror, her boot slipped from her foot and tumbled downwards. It hit the axial way, bouncing off and falling to the keel below. He heard von Outen cry out in a victory yell, and he knew their last chance to escape was fading away.

The airship was moving very slowly now. Karl briefly thought the landing lines would soon be thrown from the airship's nose for the American landing crew to catch and pull the airship down to the mast. His nose detected a different smell, but one he recognised – hydrogen gas, laced with bitter odours was leaking into the hull.

The great 'Hindenburg' was filled with a deathly silence, as if all life had stopped. Then he could hear the awful tap and scuff of the Nazi's boots as he scaled the ladder and traversed the axial-way towards them. Karl wrapped his arm tightly round Elizabeth, holding their combined weight against the ventilation shaft. Her head had dropped back at an alarming angle, for she was still unconscious.

He could hear the Nazi's heavy breathing below him. The man was exhausted from his climb and seemed quite disoriented, as though he had forgotten why he was there, and he did not seem aware that those he sought were above him. He slumped down on the platform at the base of the shaft. The pistol was back in the holster and he began searching all his pockets.

Karl's whole body ached with the strain of maintaining his position and holding Elizabeth's weight without moving. He watched the enemy below him in utter despair as the 'Mad Major' took a silver cigarette case out from his pocket and put a cigarette in his mouth. He then produced a lighter from another pocket and lit the cigarette. He drew on the lit tobacco, making it glow brightly in the half-light, oblivious to the terrible risk he was taking by smoking in this forbidden area.

The odours from both diesel fumes and scented hydrogen gas were overpowering. If Karl had been alone, he could easily have dropped down on top of the dazed Nazi and knocked him over the side, to fall to the keel and certain death. But he held Elizabeth in his arms and she was more precious than life itself. He looked down again. The Major seemed still in a drunken stupor of half-consciousness. He had dropped the cigarette and it had rolled towards the ventilation shaft, still alight.

The airship was moving once more in the final manoeuvre to reach the mooring mast. More gas hissed out through the shaft and Karl worried about the gas, now also escaping from the tear in the cell into the hull. He heard the engines running full astern to stop all forward movement, and then they went back to idling.

His muscles cramped and he tried to flex them. Another smell reached his nostrils – smoke! He looked down and saw that the grimy pulley rope was smouldering; its splayed end fibres had fused with the burning cigarette. Months of accumulated dirt and diesel fumes had provided the perfect fuel for a hot, hungry spark. His eyes were smarting and would not focus; he was seeing double vision. The rope smouldered and glowed and he watched in fascinated horror as the spectre of burning lights travelled towards them. He could feel the heat as two flaming images moved into parallax, fusing together, growing in intensity. All escape options had now vanished.

He yelled out to von Outen. "Major! We are on fire! I am coming down!" Elizabeth stirred in his arms, brought round by the smoke and heat from the burning rope, which was choking both of them. Karl knocked it with his foot and it began to break away: hot fragments dropping down towards the keel and the fuel lines.

The crazy Nazi was suddenly on his feet, alive and alert. Between the drifting smoke, Karl could see him dodging the burning embers and pointing his pistol up towards them. Elizabeth began to clutch at Karl and she screamed in terror.

"You are under arrest!" shouted the Nazi.

"We are coming down!" Karl shouted as he tried to find footholds and stop Elizabeth's weight from swinging them round.

The Major seemed beyond reason. "You have fired the ship! You are the saboteurs! You will die now!"

357

He fired the pistol directly towards them. Karl froze in abject terror and was only vaguely aware of an unearthly scream from below him as the 'Mad Major' lost his balance and fell from the axial-way. Elizabeth had ceased to struggle and he stared at her lifeless form, swinging in his arms.

The bullet had passed right through her head, exiting within an inch of his face. It had disappeared, piercing through the folds of the gas cell which hung around them. The fire, begun by the crazed Nazi's smouldering cigarette, continued leaping up the rope, dropping hot burning fragments down onto the fuel lines. In that moment Karl welcomed his imminent death as a blessed release.

The gas in the air around him began to glow. The burning rope sucked hungrily towards the escaping gas. Their two bodies, suspended from the ventilation shaft, were illuminated by a brilliant aura of light. The entire shaft glowed around them, as if they were encased like shadow puppets in a magician's magic lantern.

Karl stared at the trickle of blood oozing from the small hole in Elizabeth's forehead. It ran down her pale cheek, dripping on to his jacket. Her body was still wrapped in his arms and she also began to glow, as if she were lit from within, as she swayed gently against him.

He cried out, "Elizabeth, my Elizabeth! Don't leave me, wait for me!" He felt the intense heat around him, but also emanating from her. She seemed to spring back to life as electrical impulses gripped her body, transmitting to his. She burst into flames and his body fused with hers; the flames consumed him, eating him alive!

As the last vestiges of consciousness left him, he heard and felt the intense force of the gas cell as it exploded, leading to catastrophe. Darkness, solitude, and a great sad silence then ensued. Elizabeth had gone. She was lost forever and he was utterly alone.

CHAPTER THIRTY-NINE

SABOTAGE!

Cardington Sheds, Bedfordshire, England, May 2000

Jonno opened his eyes and blinked. Everything was black and his head throbbed painfully, as if he were under the anvil's hammer. His vision was blurred, but he forced his eyes to stay open and tried to remember what had happened to him.

He was lying out in the open, on grass damp with dew; his body was stiff and cold. As he turned his head, it hurt like hell. His eyes gradually began to refocus and he could see a starlit sky above him and make out the dark shape of the Cardington Shed. There was a torn section in the steel corrugation – a gash in the shed's defences.

Snippets of information filtered through the fuzz in his brain and slowly he recalled the night's events. Sarah's phone call; an image on a TV screen; running in the dark, then finding the opening. He had tackled someone, and then he had been attacked; hit over the head. He put his hand up to the back of his head, blood oozed from a painful lump. After that he remembered, even more clearly, he had been in another place and undergone a separate more terrible ordeal.

The memories of the 'Hindenburg's' final moments flooded back and the horror of his death gripped him once more. Elizabeth had died in his arms, shot through the head by the crazed Nazi Major. The feelings of sheer terror and disbelief he had felt in that moment filled his mind once more. The overwhelming grief he had experienced, mourning for his lover, lost forever.

These were Karl's emotions but he, Jonno, felt them now. He had held Elizabeth's limp and lifeless form for just a few bitter seconds. All that sweet joy of life, all her love and devotion to him and their planned expectation of a new life together – wiped out with a single bullet. Her beautiful sparkling eyes, green like summer meadows rippling with golden celandine, were closed to him forever. And then, to his terrifying agony and exquisite ecstasy, the flames had consumed them both. They had vanished without trace, cremated to dust in the intense heat of the 'Hindenburg' disaster.

Jonno lay still, staring at the opening in the base of the shed wall. He could hear screaming and shouting coming from within the shed itself: female then male. His mind made the quantum leap back to the present. That was Lisa's voice he could hear! She was yelling out his name, calling for help. Was the other voice the Nazi, Major von Outen? No, not him, he was dead!

Jonno struggled to his feet and a searing pain shot through his ankle. He began to recall earlier events in more detail. Lisa had been with him, but now she was apparently inside the shed; it would not have been from choice. He looked at his watch in disbelief. The illuminated display panel showed three twenty-seven a.m. Only twenty-seven minutes since he first saw the figure on the CCTV monitor. So he could only have been unconscious for a few minutes.

He scrambled towards the opening and crawled through the gap, pulling his coat hood over his head for protection. Once inside, he rolled to the right to avoid triggering the security light and then he stood upright, listening. He heard Lisa scream and yell out again. The sound was muffled, but it was easy to locate her position – she was inside the 'Sky Dolphin'.

The hole in the wall had brought him into the shed opposite the stern end of the airship. The 'Dolphin' was moored in the centre of the vast eight hundred foot long building. In front of her, nearer to the big doors, were the 'Sky Lark' and the current edition of the CR15 blimp. The lights and security cameras in the working area were not currently activated and the remaining length of the shed was dark and empty.

The 'Dolphin's' hull emitted a phosphorescent glow, casting a ghostly silver light on the surrounding dark area. She seemed to throb with life, like an alien flying saucer. Jonno could hear movement now, coming from the other side of the 'Dolphin'. He moved silently across the dark open area to the other side of the shed, keeping his hands and face covered and well back from the airship, out of the range of the lights. It was however, movement by the intruder which now triggered both the security lights simultaneously, flooding the shed with brilliant illumination.

Jonno had assumed all along that the person who had attacked him, and now held Lisa as a hostage, had to be Paul. Prepared as he was, when his eyes focused at last on his enemy, he felt the jarring surge of shock reaction as he stared with incredulity at the black-clad figure that came into view. The man appeared to be nearly seven feet tall, wearing a full-face welding head-shield, which totally ruled out visual identification. This was not Paul as Jonno had envisaged; the jolly pirate out for a bit of mischief-making. This weird, ominous figure seemed to have a much darker purpose.

He was also wearing a backpack, like a diver's oxygen tank. Attached to this was a long barrelled gun, which he held. Jonno was not equipped for a close encounter with a 'Darth Vader' look-alike. If it was Paul, any hope of a resolution within the family had just run out. Jonno recognised the weapon his enemy carried, not as a firearm, but as something much more sinister. What he faced was a man-portable incendiary device – a flamethrower!

The figure had not yet spotted him and, ignoring the pain in his ankle, Jonno began to sprint straight towards his assailant. He knew the weapon's range was about eighty metres and that his best chance was to get up close fast, and disarm him – to run right into the arms of the tiger. But the figure had picked up the movement and wheeled round to face the threat, pointing the weapon forwards. Jonno darted diagonally to the right, still closing in, reducing the distance between them. As he changed direction again, a stream of liquid was propelled from the gun and instantly ignited, as if by a giant gas lighter. The fireball flew along the ground like a serpent's tongue, devouring the dirt floor and billowing upwards, growing in volume and intensity as it hit the air. The blast knocked Jonno to the ground, but he somersaulted away, out of its range. Not finding a target, the flames died as quickly as they had begun, but the effect was terrifying.

He now knew for sure that he, not the airship, was the real target. Only Paul could have schemed this fearsome and evil form of execution. The bile of fear rose in his throat; death might be seconds away. Speed and his wits were all that could keep him alive.

He could still hear Lisa's cries and he desperately wanted to go to her. That, he knew, was exactly what his assailant wanted him to do. The fact she was shouting so loudly allayed any thoughts that she might be badly injured.

It was time to move again. Right and back, zigzagging all the while, but keeping the enemy in full view. The figure in black stood watching Jonno as he continued his random zigzag pattern. The man began to laugh: an unearthly cackle distorted by the head mask, but Jonno still recognised the voice – it was Paul.

"Fitting end for you, brother!" he shouted, moving his stance to keep track of Jonno's position. But Paul was hampered by the cumbersome equipment and his lack of peripheral vision. Another tongue of flame leapt from the gun, travelling about twenty yards in the direction Jonno had stood a split second before. The fireball hit the shed wall and the blast blew a hole right through the steel shell. The flames clawed upwards and black smoke billowed out, combining with the smoke palls from the first blast. Again Jonno was blasted off his feet and he felt the shockwaves jar his bones like a blow from a sledgehammer, the acrid choking fumes heightening the fear that his mad sibling was following a predetermined path towards total destruction.

He forced himself on to his feet again to keep moving, but he was unbalanced and his vision was distorted. He moved in towards the airship for protection, out of the direct range of the flamethrower. The focus now had to be to decoy Paul away from 'Sky Dolphin'. If not, both he and Lisa would be barbecue meat. He leant against the airship's hull for support and continued moving round its outer edge, away from Paul's view. How long could he hold out? Where was Charlie he thought fleetingly?

The little 'Sky Lark' was moored about twenty feet away. Jonno sprinted towards her with all the speed he could muster, ignoring the pain in every part of his body. Paul's reactions were slowed down by the head-shield and backpack, and Jonno darted behind the test craft before his brother could track him to aim the gun.

Paul began shouting again, this time loud and clear, even thought he was out of sight. "I've got you now, you little sod. You and your airship can fry together in hell!"

Jonno thought that Paul must have removed the head-shield to make this electrifying speech, and that he was quite close, on the other side of the 'Sky Lark'. In that instant, he heard the terrifying whooshing sound of the flame-thrower in action once more. This time apparently aimed directly at the 'Sky Lark'. But the heatproof shielding of the test craft's hull produced an unexpected reaction. Instead of blowing straight though the fabric and torching the interior, the flames flew right round the outside of the hull, momentarily engulfing the entire surface, then bouncing back outwards on impact.

Jonno was already lying face down on the ground. He felt the force of the blast and the searing temperature of the flames licking round him. Now his clothes were on fire, burning through to his skin. With his little remaining strength, he rolled himself along the ground to extinguish the flames, tearing at his scorched clothing with his fingers. He heard an agonising scream and realised it was his own. Pain blotted out the last vestiges of consciousness and reality drifted away.

He sensed he was floating upwards, out of his body, up into the top of the high shed. The scene below was shrouded in billowing smoke and flames. He could not see clearly and he did not know the fate of the 'Sky Lark', or the 'Dolphin' and Lisa, or Paul – or even himself.

He was drifting through the air, drawn up towards one of the high windows. There, a brilliant light shone with such intensity that the glass appeared to disintegrate. He passed right through and was then enveloped in a tunnel of pure white light. It felt as though he was being pulled by a magnetic force towards a pulsing source of energy. He was not alone. Ahead of him was another figure, in silhouette. The figure turned towards him and as he came closer he could make out the shape and features of a woman; it was Elizabeth.

She was surrounded by a wonderful aura of bright light. Glowing with youth and perfection, she was exquisitely beautiful, just as she had been on the day they first met. She smiled and stretched out her arms towards him, willing him to come into her loving embrace. Her fabulous, deep green eyes were beguiling, and they shone with the joy and expectation of their reunion.

The distance between them was only a few paces, but a voice in the distance was also calling to him.

"Jonno! Where are you?" The voice echoed up the tunnel. He stopped still, listening, "Please don't leave me now. I need you, I love you!"

Elizabeth was waiting, her arms still outstretched, her face beseeching him to come closer. He felt himself moving towards her, but then he experienced a strange feeling of disconnection, as though part of him was peeling away.

He stood motionless in the tunnel, illuminated by the brilliant aura that surrounded Elizabeth, and he saw an apparition of himself walking forward. As he watched his own form walk away, it too was surrounded by an aura of light. He was being torn apart, and momentarily, he became an empty shell; all his emotions were leaving him going towards Elizabeth in a replica of his own body.

The two spirits came together as one in a loving embrace. Jonno could see that although the man resembled him, it was not him. Yet he knew him well. The spirit had dwelled in him for a very long time – it was Karl.

The two figures seemed oblivious to his presence, lost in their own world. Reunited at last in their perfect love, they were surrounded by a single aura of glorious light. They turned away from him and continued their journey through the tunnel, moving towards the pulsing energy and the even greater source of light. Still locked together, they became smaller and smaller, until all Jonno could see was one tiny image, like a dove flying towards the sun. It fused with the greater light and disappeared. The orb of brilliance then receded into the distance and the tunnel was closed to his view.

He fell back to earth with a jolt. He was lying on his back on the floor of the shed, looking up to the high east-facing windows. Dawn had broken and the early morning sun was visible. A watery circle of light, it was almost white in a cloudless sky of gathering light, giving its promise of life to the new day.

He heard the voice calling again, much louder now.

"Please, Jonno, can you hear me!" The frantic shouting continued. "It's me, Lisa! I'm in the 'Dolphin'. Help me, please, Jonno! Jonno!"

His eyes grew wide open in shock and disbelief. He was alive! Pain filled his mind and body, but he was alive! He began to crawl from his position and saw a scene of devastation through a dim reddish, smoky haze. The all too familiar smell of burning assailed his nose and eyes, and smoke choked his throat and lungs. As he crawled out from behind the heat-scorched shell of the 'Sky Lark' and towards the 'Sky Dolphin', he saw Paul lying face down, the gas tank still on his back. He was amazed Paul had not blown himself up in the blast-back from the flamethrower. He couldn't see the gun attachment. It was probably under his body.

He began to crawl towards his brother, but Lisa's cries diverted his attention. He changed direction towards 'Dolphin's' bow doors, which were open. His mind began to work better as his brain clicked into gear, computing the facts and options needed for survival. Help could not be far away; smoke and flames had billowed out of the shed when Paul blasted through the wall.

Jonno didn't know how long ago that was. He also did not know if Paul was dead or alive, but he didn't have the strength for another confrontation with his brother. He and Lisa had to get out of the shed. The 'Sky Lark's' damaged hull was smouldering, and fires were burning everywhere, but the 'Dolphin' was still in one piece and so apparently was Lisa.

One of the blue tractors was parked nearby and Jonno pulled himself up into the driving seat and started the engine. All the time he was watching Paul's prostrate body, lying where he had fallen. He did not appear to have moved. Jonno drove the tractor towards the big shed doors, up to the lever which worked the opening mechanism and prayed the power was still intact. He climbed from the tractor and reached up, barely able to bear his weight on one leg. He pulled the lever down and the huge shed doors began to open.

Elated by his success, Jonno drove the tractor back down the shed towards the 'Dolphin'. Scorch marks were visible on the hull, but otherwise she appeared undamaged. Paul had failed to lure him into the larger airship and fulfil his evil intention to blow them all up together. So far Jonno had outwitted him, but he knew better than to be complacent where his brother was concerned.

He abandoned the tractor and found he could stand on both feet, although his legs were painfully burned. By rolling away from 'Sky Lark' and tearing off his burning clothes, Jonno had saved himself from severe burns. He hobbled through the 'Dolphin's' open bow door, and operated the manual closing mechanism, so recently installed. Lisa began screaming again, this time in fear and terror, anticipating a further attack from Paul.

Jonno called out, "It's me, Lisa! I'm coming!" His voice became a croak and he began to cough. It was dark inside and he crawled towards the control section, following Lisa's voice to find his way.

"Jonno, Jonno, you're alive! Thank God! I'm tied up in here, please hurry!"

He was totally disoriented. "Where are you? I can't see anything."

"I think it's 'the bridge'. The controls and computers are in here." She was gasping for breath and sounded frantic.

Jonno shuffled painfully on his knees. His adrenaline was pumping fast, keeping his spirits up above his pain threshold. He found his way into the control room. Here, a little light entered through the all-round windows. Lisa was lying on the floor, half hidden under the pilot's control panel. He located her and grasped at her arms. Her hands were tied behind her back with a thin corded rope; this was looped round her feet, drawing them up behind her and her knees were bent in an unnatural and painful position. She had been trussed up like a chicken ready for roasting.

He seethed with anger as he tried to pick at the knots. He had lost his coat and everything he had carried, but he delved into his trouser pockets and found his tiny pocket penknife which he always carried, more for luck than for its usefulness. But it was sharp and the two inch blade was exactly what he needed to prise and cut away Lisa's bonds. She groaned softly as her body uncurled.

He gently rubbed her wrists and ankles to restore the circulation, "Are you hurt?"

"Sore and bruised," she answered, flexing her arms and legs, "Oh, and I hit my head when he pushed me under here. I think it's bled."

He bent over her in the half-light. Pulling her to him, he kissed her forehead and tasted blood trickling from the wound. He sensed he had been here before; it was a very familiar scenario but this time he must rescue her and save the airship.

"Lisa, I need your help. Can you stand?"

"I can try," she said, and they helped one another on to their feet, leaning against the control panel.

"We need to get the 'Dolphin' out of the shed." He moved into the pilot's seat and started up the computer. The interior lights came on automatically.

"But doesn't she have to be towed?" she asked, taking the adjacent navigator's seat.

"She has been up to now. But dire circumstances call for desperate remedies." He threw the switches for the airship's landing lights, angling them in the forward position. "Can you see Paul lying over to our right, behind 'Sky Lark'?"

She craned her neck to look out of the control viewing windows. "Yes, I can. Is he dead?"

"I don't know. He's been out a long time, but I survived the same blast, so we can't be sure." Jonno started the engines, warming them up to running temperature.

"What are you going to do?" Lisa said, wiping away a trickle of blood on her nose with her sleeve.

"We've got to get out of here, and salvage the airship. This is the quickest way," he said, and he diverted the engine power to inflate the aircushions. "I want you to keep your eye on 'Darth Vader' out there, and pray very hard that my strategy will work."

"I love you, Jonno," she said, but she kept her face pressed to the window, watching for any sign that Paul might be alive.

Jonno also maintained visual contact with the instruments and the invisible navigation line, vertical and horizontal, which he must follow to steer the airship out of the shed. But he still felt elated to hear those words and to know that she had returned to him. He was in a great deal of pain, but he managed a smile. "And I love you, my darling Lisa."

The aircushion landing system was modelled on the great British hovercraft. 'Sky Dolphin' had so far only used the reverse air suction inside the two skirted shoes, designed to hold her to the ground. Jonno was about to test the theoretical ability of the airship to lift off the ground, and travel like a hovercraft. The problem was that the helium lift would overtake the ground effect of the lifting body causing the airship to rise too quickly. He needed to keep the airship low down, but reduce the aircushion suction, or even reverse it. The physics of this method of moving the airship at ground level, had been the subject of much debate at project meetings, but so far it was untried and untested.

"Jonno, look!" Lisa thumped her fist against the glass and pointed towards Paul, "He's moving!"

Jonno looked through the window and saw Paul on his knees, groping on the ground. The gas tank was still strapped to his back and he was attempting to stand up. Jonno returned his attention to the airship's controls. There was no option now but to test all the theories.

The aircushion's landing mode was at full revs, sucking the airship to the ground. Jonno threw the switch to reverse the vacuum, whilst bringing the bow thrusters into play to control the airship's nominal nose. The helium lift began taking the airship up and he started the forward thrust, much sooner than normal.

"He's up on his feet," Lisa said, in alarm. "Oh, my God! He's putting on the helmet!"

"Keep calm, Lisa, we'll be out of here quicker than he can fire!"

The airship began to rise too fast and the nose dipped forward, nearly tipping them out of their seats. Lisa gave a little scream and Jonno felt the sweat tickle down his face. He stabilised the trim, expelling some of the gas through the top ventilators and cut off the air flowing out through the cushion vents, then he reduced the forward speed. They were over the top of the other two airships, the altimeter now showed thirty-feet and they were still climbing; the shed roof loomed fast. He must not allow the ship to gain any more height.

"Oh, no!" Lisa covered her face with her hands and dropped down below the window. "He's aiming that gun at us; we've had it!"

Jonno glanced down to where Paul was running after the moving airship. He could see him pointing the gun attachment at them and he appeared to trigger it, but nothing happened. Paul stopped and banged the barrel on the ground.

"It okay, Lisa, the gun doesn't appear to be working." Jonno returned his attention to the controls. They were almost at the shed doors, but the ship was too high and swaying from side to side; he did not seem able to control the forward thrust of this giant machine and he expelled more gas through the top ventilators. He remembered the feeling of being in his Tornado, flying at twice the speed of sound, fifty feet from the ground. The adrenaline of the 'fear factor' came back into play once more as he made split-second decisions in this new hostile situation.

The airship's path had been up and down like a scenic railway and now it was dropping again; the altimeter showed twenty-two feet. He took a quick look for Paul, but couldn't see him. "Where's he gone?" he shouted to Lisa.

She scanned the ground. "He's behind us, he's fiddling with the tubes from the gas tank, reattaching them, but he's taken off the helmet."

Jonno was attempting the impossible. He threw the aircushion into reverse. Although now only fifteen feet from the ground and still dropping, the airship's air vents sucked in air and pushed it out under the two giant cushions, either side of the control car. They were now almost in hovercraft mode.

Jonno could do no more and concentrated on steering through the shed doors. The 'Dolphin' lurched side-ways to the left and he countered the swing, pulling the wheel hard right. She tipped and lurched in the opposite direction.

Lisa yelled. "We're going to crash!"

Jonno didn't answer, concentrating his efforts on the four solid hazards surrounding the ship. Then he saw Paul sprint ahead of them, out of the shed. The airship was only just above Paul's head as they came out through the doors into the open.

"I can see blue flashing lights on the road! There's dozens, all coming this way!" Lisa's voice was ecstatic.

"Keep watching Paul! I can't get any lift!" he yelled. The altimeter was still at fifteen feet.

"He's aiming at us again!" screamed Lisa. "For god's sake, get us up!"

Jonno threw the switch controlling the air vents to maximum blow and engaged full speed. The downward blast under the airship was twice the force of a landing helicopter. The airship was right over Paul's head just as he successfully ignited a huge fireball aimed up at the 'Dolphin'. The air blast from the vents met the fireball from the flame thrower, pushing the roaring heat and flames back down towards the ground. They splayed outwards, like an inverted mushroom, igniting everything in their path. As the airship rose up and sped away, Jonno and Lisa looked down. The spot where they had last seen Paul exploded as his gas tank blew up. A secondary fireball rose up in the centre of the inferno. Everything within a thirty yard radius was burning with a fierce intensity.

Sweat poured from every gland of Jonno's body, but they had climbed to an altitude of over eighty feet. Still climbing, he circled the 'Dolphin' around the airfield, watching the emergency services arrive on the scene. He could see Charlie's Jaguar and Doc's car in amongst the police vehicles, fire engines and ambulances. The airfield pulsed with patterns of blue flashing dots in the swirling smoke. Bright orange flames still licked up into the sky, but they could not reach him now.

Lisa threw her arms around the back of his neck, and she sobbed in utter relief. Jonno thought of Paul and how it had ended for him, and he said a silent prayer for his brother.

371

As they continued their circular flight in the 'Dolphin', Jonno was in no hurry to land. It was serene and silent up here. In spite of all that had happened in the last few hours, he was at peace with himself at last.

In the east, the morning sun was gaining height, pushing life into the shadows. A line of dots moved across the sky. Each dot had wings, and they followed, one behind the other in a silhouette of flight across the sun, towards the new day.

Lisa clasped her hand over his. She leaned towards him and kissed his cheek. His love had returned to him, and he knew they would stay together forever now. For they too had a perfect love and it had travelled with them, lighter than air.

THE END